Praise for *The Unraveling of Wentwater*

"Lakin (*The Wolf of Tebron*) mixes classic fairy tale elements (witches, spinning thread from nettles, water spirits) with wisdom elements from the Bible in a highly imaginative amalgam that examines the making of meaning and the making of mercy. Lakin's clever revival of the power of fairy tales as she continues The Gates of Heaven fantasy series makes one miss them as a vehicle for instructing the young."

—*Publisher's Weekly*

"Once I picked it up, I couldn't put it down. For one thing, I'm a sucker for good writing, and wow, can C. S. Lakin write! I'm in awe of people who can take us to imaginary worlds that don't exist and make them feel real. She does this in this book and brings a very creepy but magical fable to life. It's a story of superstitions and the reality within. If you're looking for a little escapism in your busy world, I highly recommend this one!"

—**Kristin Billerbeck**, author of *A Billion Reasons Why*

"Take the fable of Snow White, disguised almost beyond recognition, add a huge portion of love for language and the power of words, throw in a collection of sometimes haunting tie-ins to previous books in the series, and you have the components that make up this very unusual story . . . The writing is gorgeous as always, a true pleasure to read. Her best tale yet."

—**Grace Bridges**, publisher, Splashdown Books

"The Gates of Heaven is the series that introduced and converted me to the fantasy genre. And this book is every bit as good as its predecessors. Lakin moves the story beyond the traditional fairy tale and explores the contrast between knowledge and superstition, pitting village against town—and ultimately finding that both come up short. It is also a love story, and the story of what one is willing to sacrifice to save loved ones. It's a ripping good story."

—**Glynn Young**, Faith, Fiction, Friends

"*The Unraveling of Wentwater* is a first-class fairy tale that deals with the power of words, and the never-ending struggle to find balance between justice and mercy and knowledge and faith. Combined with romance, betrayal, revenge, and redemption, it is sure to please all fans of this series."

—**Jonathon Svendsen**, NarniaFans.com

"C. S. Lakin has written another wonderful book. Focusing this tale on words and their importance, she unravels the two extremes of Wentwater. Then, revealing the necessity of both logic and superstition, intellect and emotions, she weaves together two communities that need each other with the greatest word of all. . . . I can't wait to read this book again. I highly recommend *The Unraveling of Wentwater* to anyone who enjoys an extremely well-written fantasy.

—**La Tawnia Kintz Reviews**

"Ready for another entrancing story from The Gates of Heaven series by C. S. Lakin? *The Unraveling of Wentwater* doesn't disappoint. Enter into a world where superstition, miscommunication, prophecy, love, envy, hope and truth all clash their voices into a cacophony striking the heart of their land. . . . Set aside a whole afternoon or evening, because once you start reading you may not be able to stop."

—**Marcy Weydemuller**, Mythic Impact

Praise for *The Land of Darkness*

"Sprung from apocalyptic vision, this adult fairy tale, which is the third in the Gates of Heaven series, brings freshness and vibrancy, based on strong ethical principles, to the realm of the imaginary. . . ."

—**Lois Henderson**, Bookpleasures.com

"Another incredible book in The Gates of Heaven Series. C. S. Lakin has done it again—written a masterful tale that is a page turner from start to finish. . . . The suspense and intrigue is enough to keep the reader on the edge of their seat."

—**Beverly Frisby**, Beverly's Bookshelf

"C. S. Lakin's deftly written book *The Land of Darkness* yet again unfailingly impresses me with its colorful language and subtle, yet effective allegorical language. . . . . This tale is still very fresh, and it has its own beating heart of deep meaning underlying its fairy-tale skin. . . . She is one of my favorite writers at the moment, whose books evoke some of the same charm as many of Madeleine L'Engle's books."

—**A Bibliophile's Reverie**

Praise for *The Map Across Time*

"The novel is fast-paced and tightly plotted, which means that the reader will quickly be drawn into the complex twists and turns of the story and, in fairy tale tradition, led toward a surprising yet satisfying conclusion."

—*Publisher's Weekly*

"*The Map across Time* is a fairy tale in the classic sense of the term. As J. R. R. Tolkien pointed out, fairy stories serve to draw the reader into a mythical world that conveys the joy of the gospel. Lakin's tale meets this noble task head-on. Not many Christian novels manage to blend great storytelling and scriptural truth—but here is a book that does!"

—**Bryan Litfin**, author of *The Sword and The Gift*

Praise for *The Wolf of Tebron*

"Much richer and deeper than traditional tales from fairy-land . . . what Lakin does so well with her fairy tale is to provide images which remind us of what God has done for us."

—**Mark Sommer,** Examiner.com

". . . Lakin's work is stylistically beautiful. The exotic locales are vivid, from dark north to burning desert to misty jungle. I found myself looking forward to each leg of Joran's journey just so I could experience another part of her story world."

—**Rachel Starr Thomson**, Little Dozen Press

"This book is filled with beautiful literary allegory and symbolism. I enjoyed the fairy tale world C. S. Lakin created for her characters to navigate. I love how the story unfolded in the end and look forward to more in The Gates of Heaven series."

—**Jill Williamson**, author of *To Darkness Fled*

"Lakin has masterful control of the writing craft, developing her characters and drawing the reader to see the world through their eyes."

—**Phyllis Wheeler**, The Christian Fantasy Review

THE CRYSTAL SCEPTER

**Other Books in
The Gates of Heaven Series**

The Wolf of Tebron

The Map Across Time

The Land of Darkness

The Unraveling of Wentwater

THE CRYSTAL SCEPTER

A FAIRY TALE BY
C. S. LAKIN

LIVING
INK

The Crystal Scepter
Volume 5 in The Gates of Heaven® series

Copyright © 2013 by C. S. Lakin
Published by Living Ink Books, an imprint of
AMG Publishers, Inc.
6815 Shallowford Rd.
Chattanooga, Tennessee 37421

Print Edition   ISBN 13: 978-0-89957-893-4
EPUB Edition   ISBN 13: 978-1-61715-322-8
Mobi Edition   ISBN 13: 978-1-61715-323-5
E-PDF Edition   ISBN 13: 978-1-61715-324-2

First Printing—January 2013

THE GATES OF HEAVEN is a registered trademark of AMG Publishers.

Cover designed by Chris Garborg at Garborg Design, Savage,
Minnesota, and Megan Erin Miller.

Cover Illustration by Gary Lippincott
(http://www.garylippincott.com/).

Interior design and typesetting by Reider Publishing Services,
West Hollywood, California.

Edited and proofread by Christy Graeber and Rick Steele.

C. S. Lakin welcomes comments, ideas, and impressions at her websites:
www.cslakin.com and **www.gatesofheavenseries.com**.

Scripture marked NLT is taken from the Holy Bible, New Living Translation, copyright © 1996, 2004, 2007 by Tyndale House Foundation. Used by permission of
Tyndale House Publishers, Inc., Carol Stream, Illinois 60188. All rights reserved.

Scripture marked NKJV is taken from the New King James Version. Copyright ©
1982 by Thomas Nelson, Inc. Used by permission. All rights reserved.

Please note that Scripture verses quoted by characters in the novel are paraphrased
as the author deemed appropriate for the story.

Printed in the United States of America
18 17 16 15 14 13 –V– 7 6 5 4 3 2 1

To Leebears, who insists the trolls
are not evil, just misunderstood

• PART ONE •

"The lion has come up from his thicket, and the destroyer of nations is on his way. He has gone forth from his place to make your land desolate. . . . For this, clothe yourself with sackcloth, lament, and wail. . . . And it shall come to pass in that day that the heart of the king shall perish." (Jer. 4: 7–9 NKJV)

ONE

I N THE CHILL morning half light, King Cakrin knelt beside his fallen nephew. He ducked his head as an arrow whizzed past, grazing his cheek with a caress of fletching. More arrows sliced the cold—whispers of further invasion—but Cakrin barely heard them. He lay the scepter down on the frosty tundra of the northern Wastes, its heart beating bright and strong in the crystal chamber of the faceted handle, although Cakrin wondered how that should be so. How could his heart still beat when Carthin lay here, pierced through, not much past childhood yet every bit a man, having fought in more skirmishes against the *Tse'pha* than Cakrin could count?

Cakrin set his nephew's face to memory, wishing not to remember him like this—wan, lifeless, a visage glazed with pain. He lifted his head and looked about. Where was Carthin's twin brother? Cakrin dreaded that answer as he surveyed the mist-drenched fields strewn with the dead; the call of carrion birds was now the only sound piercing the heavy drench of death, except for the pitiful moans of those soon to join the fallen.

He let his attention linger on the boy's empty stare, eyes gray and stark as the ice-encrusted land there on the northern border of Elysiel. Cakrin silently cursed Vitra and her evil brood, ever relentless in their attempt to reclaim the land he had sworn to protect from her kind—the barely sentient creatures spawned in evil under the steaming fissures, knowing little else than killing and devouring, more ancient than the sacred site itself. Would they never stop? What would it take to end this, and why was heaven silent?

Cakrin wiped his sweat-soaked hair from his forehead and leaned closer to Carthin's still-warm face. With a pained cry he shut the boy's eyes, and shut his as well. Clenched them against the new day dawning that promised only a faint sun would emerge on the far horizon instead of the victory he'd hoped for. But the calls of his men across the expanse forced them open again. He rose, wiped blood off his sword and sheathed it, then picked up the scepter, its shimmering light enwrapping him in a ghostly cocoon and tinting the air a translucent blue. The crystal staff lay cold in his grip as he held it aloft and let the pulsing heartbeat carve a path through the fallen men and beasts; Cakrin noted with bitterness that there were few of the enemy among the slain. He would come back later and retrieve his nephew and entomb him—if heaven would grant him breath to do so.

He hardly heard the spit of the next volley of arrows flanking him as he trudged to the outcropping of rock materializing out of the mist to the east, ice crunching under his boots and the acrid smell of the Wastes searing his nostrils. The dawn's haze, seeping around the shapes of his men huddled in the cold, swept them with golden light, giving them the appearance of those who had but glimpsed at the *Tse'pha* and had been turned to stone, the silent sentinels now littering the Wastes in vast numbers and mired in a grave of mud. Cakrin studied each face, but Clarin was not among them. Nor was his own brother, Crispin. He counted ten, maybe twelve, standing against stone. They tipped weary heads in respect.

"Is this all that's left of the front?" Cakrin asked Rolan, his oldest commander and the one who had led the charge that night.

Rolan gave a solemn nod. "Sire, your brother's been hurt. I sent him back with the wounded."

Cakrin searched Rolan's face as he swallowed hard. "How bad?" Rolan's expression told him.

The king loosed the scabbard about his waist and considered the speed of the wagon and the distance it had to travel. He would need to ride hard. "Any word of Clarin?"

Rolan shook his head, then cleared his throat. "Sire, we should retreat. We can do no more here. A runner brought word the northern pass is secure. For now." He added when Cakrin said nothing, "Your horse is saddled and ready."

Cakrin looked at the men's expectant faces—grimy, hardened with exhaustion and hunger, ever patient. He blew out a breath. The true sign of Elysiel men was their patient endurance, honed from war crouched on their doorstep these endless centuries without letup. Now the attacks were growing more fierce and lasting longer than ever seen in times past. And Cakrin knew why. It was his fault, all his fault.

As he signaled his men to follow, leading them along the crags south toward their makeshift encampment, he stared blankly at the scepter. *The matter of the heart is the heart of the matter.* How many years had Vitra been trying to kill off the Keepers and all the potential heirs to the throne? No doubt since the first king, Lantas, gave his heart to save the land and protect the Keeper—and heaven had placed that heart in the scepter, appointing his heirs to be the *ra'wah ten'uah*—the Keepers of the Promise—from that day forward. Thirty kings after him had wielded it, their own hearts merged with the scepter's heart, under vow to protect and keep the site—and Elysiel—sacred and safe. Now, there remained only three heirs. If his brother succumbed to his injuries, that left Clarin, his only nephew, as his second. And since none of his own three daughters had as of yet married and birthed a son, Clarin would be Vitra's next target. Without an heir in place for even one moment, she and her hordes would no longer be restrained; the site would lose its protective power. She would overrun his kingdom and reclaim all for herself. He wondered if the words of the prophecy would see fulfillment during his reign: *"And it shall come to pass in that day that the heart of the king shall perish . . ."*

More men met them at the clearing. Smoldering fires tainted the air with stale smoke as the men rubbed cold fingers and reapplied bandages. Despite the lingering danger, Cakrin noted they moved deliberately, unhurried, as they broke camp and gathered weapons and stores. Rolan brought him his horse and handed over the reins. The destrier spurted hot breath through its nostrils as it stomped its hooves impatiently. Cakrin strapped his sword and scepter behind the saddle.

"Crispin will be at the healer's," Rolan told him as Cakrin put a foot in the stirrup. "God speed and carry you safely home."

"You as well," Cakrin replied. His eyes conveyed the thanks he knew his words would fail miserably to express. Rolan nodded in understanding and commiseration, and Cakrin looked upon his men, one by one, as they watched his departure.

"Go home," he told them, "to your wives and little ones." He wanted to add: *"And hold them tightly in your arms and tell them you love them. You may not get another chance."*

Instead, he said, "Eat, get some sleep. We will ride out again on the morrow."

He spun his horse about and kicked at its sides, but the beast needed little urging to flee this place saturated with death, a vast empty land void of trees and forage. Within his borders, his enemy could not lay hand on him or his family. So to draw his army out beyond the boundary, they ravaged and terrorized the outlying farming villages, people ill-equipped to defend themselves. In the last few years those villages had become their battlefields and graveyards—what was left of them.

His thoughts raced along the dusty roads of the past while ◆ his horse kicked up ice and mud as it galloped along the rutted lane. He passed no one as the sun broke through the gloom of the Wastes behind him and the first glimpses of Elysiel greeted him, hints of welcoming green peeking through the shredding mist, a lovely fall day materializing but giving him little comfort. The days of peaceful rides over the moors with his wife lay long behind him, and even now her face was hard to conjure, reminding him again of the blessing and curse of his calling.

He knew when the scepter passed on to him this would be his lot—burying wives and children and friends. Many would consider longevity a gift, but it was a gift with a price. *The heart costs your heart*, the saying went. Nonetheless, it was his charge, his sacred duty. He'd made a vow as his father had before him, and his father's father. He held no regrets. His father had outlived three wives, eleven children, twenty-eight grandchildren—and innumerable great-grandchildren. There'd been plenty of heirs for the ghosts to pick from in days past within the required three generations. But the *Tse'pha* had taken care of that once his father died and he'd been designated the next Keeper. His father had urged him to marry in haste and sire sons, but he'd hesitated. He let the years drift by, determined not to watch those he loved age and die while his own bright eyes sparked with life, the crystal heart beating one with his, stretching his days into uncountable decades.

And then he had met Angella and could resist no longer. But she had only given him daughters before she grew old. Angella was the first love he'd buried and Cakrin swore she'd be his last. He couldn't bear to go through such sorrow again. For now, he had his daughters' comfort and laughter to buoy him. And one day they would marry and bear sons. But would that day come soon enough? He feared not.

A horn sounded his approach to the gate with a bright flurry of notes, and the portcullis rose. His guards pressed against the walls as he barreled under the stone archway into Elysiel. The land awoke as it always did the moment he crossed the boundary, speaking its stories of farmers beginning their day, rigging their plows to furrow the rich loam that produced crops in abundance year-round under Elysiel's balmy climate. It told of every plant and tree, of fruit quickening on branches and vines, of hens laying and insects burrowing deep underground. Whatever stupor lingered in his head from the sleepless night of fighting flitted away with this prickling awareness. Even so, thoughts of his brother crowded out all others clamoring in his head, and worry spurred him to hasten to the healer's cottage nestled in the copse of alders he now made out across the ridge steaming with mist.

With the sun warm on his shoulders and sweat easing down his neck, he shucked off his leather jerkin and stuffed it behind him, wishing he could do the same with the clinging images of his men slain and rotting on their beds of lichen and muck with no one to bury them. But those visions would never leave him, only join with the myriad others already burned into his memory.

At the cottage door, he slid off his lathered horse before it could steady its feet, then threw the reins over its head and loosened the cinch. He left it to graze the knoll and seek water from the nearby creek, since no one came out to attend him—another disturbing sign.

He paused and closed his eyes—now that he had no choice but to face the truth—and let the land tell him his brother's fate. Out of all the thousands of heartbeats and breaths taken in and released within the borders of his kingdom, of both men and beasts, he singled out Crispin's. His face tightened and he bit his lip. It was as he feared. Worse still, he searched across the whole expanse of

Elysiel and could find no trace of the twin, Clarin. Dread washed over him and despair followed in its wake. With those two unwelcome companions in tow, he entered the cottage.

The healer stood in the threshold of a far room and bowed low at his approach. Cakrin knew him well. When the old man lifted his head, their eyes met, each knowing words offered no balm.

"I've made him as comfortable as possible, Sire."

Cakrin laid his hand in gratitude on the healer's shoulder. "Thank you."

"I'll bring you something hot to drink."

Cakrin nodded, and the healer left him to spend these last few moments with his brother alone.

Candles sputtered as Cakrin stepped into the small room. A cloying scent of eucalyptus and myrrh hung in the congested air. His brother lay on the cloth-covered table, eyes closed, his chest rising and falling in jerky motion. Cakrin came beside him and studied Crispin's sallow face in the dim candlelight, the lines of age etched deeply into his skin, making him appear so old at the end of his too-short life. He let his gaze travel down the blood-saturated sheet draped over his brother, aware that the gash across his stomach was deep and irreparable. Crispin had lost too much blood in transport, despite careful efforts to bind him.

Cakrin laid a gentle hand on his brother's cheek. Crispin's eyes fluttered, then opened and found him.

"You . . . you're here," Crispin wheezed, then shut his eyes and sucked in an elusive breath. "Thank the heavens . . ."

Cakrin had to ask. "Clarin?"

Tears squeezed out Crispin's eyes. "Fell . . . beside me."

Cakrin's throat clenched in pain. He didn't have the heart to tell of Carthin. He hoped his brother would run out of breath before he could form the question. But Cakrin had a sense Crispin already knew.

"Get word . . . to Calli . . ."

Cakrin stroked his brother's cheek and thought about young Calli. All Crispin had left in the world—his daughter. She'd been living in the faraway kingdom of Paladya, carrying for her Aunt Carryn, their only sister, who was widowed and childless. How her heart would break when she learned of her father's death. And Carryn—would the news kill her as well? It would do no one good to send word, not now. Perhaps in time he could ride south and deliver the grim tidings himself. If Vitra withdrew for a season. He snorted at the likelihood of that happening anytime soon.

He had not heard from either his sister or niece in months, and that fact only added to his distress. He'd been assured Carryn was being treated with kindness, although it was well known the new king felt only contempt for House Ardea and all those associated with it. Being the deposed wife of the murdered King Declan afforded her only the least of courtesies, banished as she was to the poor, squalor-ridden section of town. How often he had urged her to return home! But she had grown attached to the seaside city, and when her health started failing, Calli offered to go tend to her. Now Cakrin was glad of their distance, for it mercifully spared them this pain. At least for now.

The healer slipped into the room and set a steaming cup on the side table. "I've summoned the women, Sire. To prepare him . . ."

Cakrin watched Crispin's chest heave with one last rattle, and was not surprised when it failed to lift again. Now his brother would join their father in the marble crypt, alongside the tombs of the kings of Elysiel that had served as Keepers to the sacred site for thousands of years.

He leaned over and kissed his brother's clammy forehead, then, dismissing both the healer and his hot tonic, strode out of the cottage and into the bright day. A rush of sights and smells and sounds assaulted his mind, tingling his awareness with the prodigious proliferation of life and the bustle of activity in his kingdom. He let the sensation of peace and safety lull him, although it failed to offer any real comfort.

After locating his horse down by the creek, he splashed water on his face, the cold shock of it a welcome—and a reminder of a much-needed bath.

Ignoring the ache in his bones and the deeper one in his heart, he tightened the horse's girth and swung up in the saddle, sensing the scepter behind the cantle, its power and influence pulsing in synchronous rhythm with the blood flowing in his veins.

The ghosts of Elysiel's kings encircled him as he walked the destrier at a steady pace toward home under a serene and undisturbed blue sky, but they gave him little solace. All he wanted was to hold his daughters and soak in a tub until every last bit of grime and blood leached away. But he knew he would be met with attendants and questions and advisors and reports that would steal the rest of the day from him. And then the morrow would come, and he would ride north yet again to face Elysiel's foes.

With a heavy sigh he reined his horse from the dirt lane onto the cobbled road that would lead him to the steps of the castle.

As he stared straight ahead, the awareness of every living thing in his kingdom thrumming in his mind, one thought kept pummeling him. He was now the only one left to stand in the gap between Vitra and his kingdom. He would do well to stay alive.

All of Elysiel depended upon it.

TWO

TELL ME AGAIN why I must attend this insipid . . . garden party I'm hosting for my father's enemies?" Pythius scowled at his reflection in the massive ornate mirror, its gold-leafed molding framing his impressive figure. A fine enough figure, he thought, without having to dress in this overwrought finery that pinched his waist and choked his throat.

He slapped at the tailor fussing with the waistcoat buttons. "Leave, moron." He turned to Urstus once the servant had pattered across the expansive bedroom and eased the door closed behind him. "Well?"

His father's aged advisor made no attempt to mask his irritation. "Sire," Urstus said with a severe look, "the crown sits precariously on your head. If you do not want to lose both, you do well to stop complaining and start pandering to those who plot in secret to cut short your reign."

Pythius blew out a breath and fiddled with his cuffs. "Do I really have to wear all this ridiculous clothing?"

"You're not taking my warning seriously—"

Pythius spun to face Urstus. "Do you think I am a fool? I know I have enemies. But who would dare rise up against me with the forces I now command? I've conscripted every able-bodied man in this kingdom into my service. And you of all people know I have guards in every corner, eyes in every street. Nothing escapes my notice."

"Overconfidence and arrogance have brought down many—"

"Enough!" Pythius turned and studied his face in the mirror and his anger loosened. "Just tell me who I must impress and what words to say. I will put on my best smile and give them a show. Tell them how much I value their loyalty and support." He snorted and smoothed back his hair to fall lightly over his shoulders. "Happy?"

Urstus handed Pythius a broadcloth coat trimmed with gold filigree. "Sire, your father murdered their beloved ruler in his ruthless invasion. You are only nineteen. You think five years is a long time, long enough to erase people's memories. But one does not forget such atrocities so quickly, young king. And it takes more than posturing and empty promises to make amends."

"So we ply the dissenters with food and drink to help their amnesia along? Come now, surely you see this is a waste of my time. Only a heavy hand and the instilling of fear will stay an attempt to usurp my rule. Let the socialites and brown-nosers dally with the remnants of House Ardea in my stead; they have little else to do but consume the delicacies of my table and benefit from my largesse."

Urstus smirked and Pythius scowled again. Was that a look of masked cynicism in his advisor's expression? He was weary of Urstus's continual admonitions, and of being treated by the remnants of his father's coalition as if he were still a child. The time was coming, and, yes, it would be soon, when Urstus would meet with a tragic accident. The thought sent a rush of excitement through his limbs.

He fastened his scabbard around his waist and laid a hand on the pommel of his sword. "Go. I will join you shortly in the garden."

Urstus smiled with a gracious nod of his head and exited, but Pythius sensed the cold reprimand left in his wake. The old man kept a reserved demeanor and cautious distance. Just what were his ambitions? Surely more than coddling a "naïve" young ruler.

He reached for the bejeweled crown and positioned it on his head. Did his father's advisor suspect him? Pythius still wondered after all these years. He chuckled, thinking back to that night, only weeks after his father had seized the throne from Declan. How easy it had been for Pythius to accuse House Ardea of treachery the morning after he himself—yes, single-handedly—sliced his father's throat open while he slept. That was the first time he had drawn blood by his own hand, and how delicious the experience! And in the mayhem that followed—the "scourge of the lion"—Pythius had remained calm and authoritative, watching from the battlements as his soldiers flushed out the remnants of King Declan's faithful, the blood-red banners of his roaring lion sigil wavering in the brisk ocean air in victory. And they thought him a mere child!

By murdering his father he had conveniently accomplished two things—eliminating the one who barricaded his access to total power, and fomenting an upheaval that gave him leave to slaughter all who might oppose his ascension to kingship. During the past five years his Eyes and Ears had dragged a few traitors out from the shadows to suffer his merciless judgment, but he knew Urstus was right. No doubt his hard-handed rule angered many. But such was the lot of all powerful kings, was it not?

He thought of his brother, Andrius, who had been slain the night of the invasion. He had been the same age Pythius was now. Pythius had found him facedown in the tiled hallway with a spear thrust in his back. The image of Andrius's lifeless body haunted his sleep for weeks—not due to grief, for surely he held no affection for his garrulous, empty-brained brother. No, it was the certain finality of death that had disturbed him. And that recurring nightmare that strangled his heart in a chilling grip. In it, he had built huge storehouses for his treasures, and as he proudly gazed upon his earthly wealth, a man came up to him, laughing at his folly! Each time, in his nightmare, the man ridiculed him, making Pythius feel like a worm. "You fool! Thinking you have stored enough to last for years and can now sit back and enjoy the fruits of your labors. Tonight your life is forfeit—and all you have will be given to another to enjoy!"

As he poured himself a drink from the decanter on his dressing table with a shaky hand, he pondered the fragility of life. This bag of bones, blood, and flesh—so easily killed, as if the life within each person were only a tiny spark of candle flame that took just a pinch to snuff out. And if misfortune or illness didn't claim one's life unexpectedly, the full length of years still passed like a watch in the night.

He had schemed and murdered to attain all this power and wealth—his to enjoy, to revel in. Yet . . . so fleeting.

It wasn't fair. No matter how hard one worked, how much wealth one amassed, all had to be left behind for some stranger to enjoy. Years of toil—only to watch the rewards of his hard work slip through his fingers. No doubt God meant to play this cruel trick on his creatures—giving them a longing for life and snatching it away before they could truly enjoy it. A meaningless and sickening tragedy!

He upended the chalice and let the liquid burn his throat as he swallowed. What did he care about diplomacy and mollifying his enemies? Urstus had been nagging him to form an alliance in marriage—his perfect solution to quell what he referred to as the "current unrest." Why should he marry—and especially into the House Ardea? That would open the door to more treachery and risk. How could he lie in bed with a woman who might slice *his* throat open as he slept soundly? Urstus was a fool. Diplomacy solved nothing.

What he needed was a magical amulet or something that would ensure a long life, some charm that would insulate him from attack and make him invincible. If only such an object existed! What he would pay for that. Why, he'd sell his very soul if he could live without fear of death. Without always having to watch his back, suspicion hounding his every waking minute. Was there a place, anywhere in the world, where death had been vanquished?

He recalled the former king had employed a soothsayer, but was the seer still alive, or had he been a victim of the scourge? Pythius couldn't recall his name, but surely Urstus would know. One who dealt with the dark arts might have insight into such things. Surely someone would!

He slammed the chalice down and strode out the bedroom doors. Servants stopped abruptly in their duties to drop to the floor as Pythius marched past them on his way to the garden at the rear of the palace. There, he was met at the beveled glass doors of the library by his tutor, Artus, who had taught him his letters and history back in their former kingdom on Hardscrabble Isle, that pile of rock where little ever grew and the winters froze a man's blood if he stayed motionless too long. No wonder his father had been so keen all those years to invade Paladya—with its mild sea breezes, tranquil harbor, fertile farmland. Pythius grunted. But had his father been able to enjoy the spoils of war? No. All he had schemed and yearned for came to naught at the edge of a sharp knife. Futility—the portion given to men.

"Good day, Your Majesty," Artus said in his usual overly cheery voice. The tutor's smile revealed his large yellowed teeth and fat lips. Pythius toyed with the idea of ordering his tutor to grow a moustache—a bushy one—to hide his ugly mouth. And maybe a long beard to drape over that protruding belly. His tutor was just another leech, fattened on the bounties of Pythius's kingship.

Pythius grunted a reply as Artus went on in his chattery manner about how elegant the king looked and what a fine day it was to entertain guests and how circumspect and prudent it was for the king to present a hand of friendship to those allied with House Ardea.

"Yes, yes, it's so gracious of me. Tell me," Pythius demanded in a tone that caused Artus to clamp shut his runaway mouth, "do you know of any land in the entire world where death does not exist?"

"No death? Why, of course not, Sire. Death is the ultimate king. He rules over all without exception, without mercy. There is no escaping his reach."

Pythius snorted at his tutor's poetic description. Couldn't the man ever give a sensible answer without lapsing into metaphor? "A simple yes or no would suffice, Artus."

Artus chortled, and Pythius felt his face flush with anger. The fool still treated him as if he were a lad under his tutelage, someone he could dismiss out of hand whenever he chose. He was another who needed to be taught a lesson to respect his king, oh indeed. But what lesson?

The glass doors swung open, and the warm fall breeze blew into the library and swirled Pythius's musings in the air. With an overbearing smile, Urstus gestured Pythius to enter the garden. Trumpets rang out in loud, clear tones, a staccato of fanfare announcing the king's entrance. Pythius sighed and fussed with his constricting waistcoat. He made a vow he would send his tailor to the stocks for contriving such torture. Maybe then the fool would take more careful measurements!

Pythius turned suddenly to face Artus, who had stepped aside to allow him to descend the marble steps to the rose garden. He paid little heed to the crowds lining the cobbled garden path as a memory wriggled to the surface of his mind. The trumpets repeated their bursts of sound, and Pythius cursed the noise under his breath as he fought to grab hold of the glimmer of memory.

"Didn't you used to tell us tales when we were boys—of a hidden land? One in which the kings never died?"

Artus frowned and looked out at the waiting crowd. "Sire, shouldn't you be—"

"They can wait one more minute, can't they? The food isn't going anywhere."

Pythius noticed Urstus stop at the bottom of the staircase and give him a pleading glare. Oh, how he wished everyone would stop telling him what to do all the time! He was king—didn't that give him the right to make his own decisions?

He pursed his lips at Artus, who cleared his throat. "Well, yes, let me see. Um, perhaps you are thinking of the tale of *Shambhala*, the mythical land in the northern Wastes that enjoys such heavenly favor the sun always shines and the crops grow in abundance year-round—"

"Yes, yes! But what of the kings? Didn't you tell us that . . . they had some magical power . . . or something . . .?"

Artus nodded in the midst of his agitation. The trumpets sounded again, their notes lingering on the air in expectation. "A scepter, Sire. Of crystal."

Pythius laughed. "Yes, that's what it was!"

"But it did not grant the kings victory over death, only a mere . . . delay, one could say. But it is a fairy tale, and although rumor has it this land truly exists, no one has ever been able to find the entrance—"

"It is hidden?"

"Not so much hidden as under enchantment. Only those granted permission may enter. But, Sire, this is mere childhood fantasy. Why concern—"

"Do you have writings that tell of this land?"

Artus apologized with his eyes. "I . . . will have to check. Perhaps."

"See that you do." Pythius pointed into the library. "Now."

Artus's eyebrows rose, but then he bowed and excused himself, the gaiety drained from his face. Pythius frowned as he watched his tutor waddle away. Mythical land. Fairy tales. Surely there must be some truth to the story. If only he could remember more . . .

As he marched down the steps, to the clear relief of all his guests and even greater relief of his attendants, Urstus slipped in alongside him. Together they strode the length of the path until they came to the giant terrace, the flooring of which depicted the lion insignia with its fierce teeth and proud expression, in shimmering tiles. He stood on the lion's open mouth. His father had hired the finest masons to construct the stately terrace, intending to give stirring speeches as he looked out on the beautiful Paladyan gardens with the tranquil harbor as a backdrop. But his father had never lived to see its completion. And now, as Pythius uttered his vacuous words of welcome and appreciation, he wondered just how long he would live to enjoy his reign. The faces in the crowd stared back, duplicitous in their smiles and in their polite applause. Annoyed, Pythius brought his speech to a hasty end and looked for an attendant to bring him something strong to drink.

He made his rounds, greeting his guests and making small talk, with Urstus never far from his side. Pythius scanned the spacious grounds. His guards were posted at close intervals, and their presence could not go unheeded. They each wore not just the blood-red vestment with the lion sigil but also an impressively large sword strapped to one side. No one would dare attempt an uprising here, today. But there were no guarantees regarding tomorrow, he reminded himself with bitterness.

Eager to be done with this nonsense, he welcomed another group of guests, then left them all to turn their attention to the long tables of food. He pictured them as pigs grunting and snorting as they stuffed their faces into a trough of smelly table scraps. That was how he saw them beneath their expensive garb and pasted-on smiles—naught but greedy swine. He nodded at Urstus, who stayed behind talking to some old woman who looked as if she might keel over at any moment in the heat of the afternoon.

Artus's face lit up upon seeing Pythius come into the library. "I've found something that might interest you, Sire." His big yellow teeth showed in a grin that lifted his bulging cheeks.

Pythius shut and locked the doors behind him, the cool of the room drying the sweat on his neck and forehead. He fumbled unbuttoning his waistcoat, and once free of its binding, let out a big breath and tossed the coat over the stuffed armchair beside him.

"Show me," Pythius demanded as he undid his cuff ties and rolled up his sleeves.

A thick book lay open on the table, its pages stained and edges tattered. "This is one of the tomes of history from Declan's library. It tells of the various regions surrounding the kingdom, their geography and resources, alliances and trade routes—"

"Must I have another of your tedious history lessons? Get to the point."

"The legendary Shamhala does exist—although in present day it is called Elysiel." Pythius waited while Artus continued to grin. He wanted to pinch the man's lips closed and hide those ugly teeth. "You've not heard of Elysiel, Sire?"

"No."

"I'm certain I spoke of it during your studies of the House Ardea."

Pythius figured he'd probably slept through those lessons. As if boring genealogies of a defeated king's family held any import now.

When Pythius said nothing in reply, Artus walked to the glass doors and looked through to the gardens.

"So, is this Elysiel the hidden land spoken of in the tale—with its magic scepter and immortal life—"

"Not immortal, only lengthened days—"

"Well, is it?" Pythius snapped the book shut and came to Artus's side.

His tutor's grin wilted. "I . . . I don't know, Sire."

Pythius shook his head and clenched his teeth. He was about to tell his tutor to go join the other pigs feasting at the trough, when Artus pointed through the glass.

"But there is someone here who would know."

Pythius's breath caught. "Who? Tell me."

"Lady Carryn."

"Who is that?"

Artus turned, about to say something, but held his tongue. He cleared his throat and said evenly, "The woman standing with Urstus. She is Declan's widow."

Pythius strained to get a look at the former queen, who stood hunched over talking to his advisor.

"Why would she know anything about this land, this . . . Elysiel?"

"Why, that is where she hails from. If you remember from your history lessons—"

"I *don't* remember, so just tell me!"

Artus loosed a tight breath. "The king of Elysiel had formed an alliance years ago with Declan, needing his aid to fight wars in the north. Declan sent his army and got a queen in the bargain. After

your father took the throne, he spared her life—at Urstus's urging—but relegated her to an impoverished, seedy part of the city
in which to live, perhaps hoping she would come to harm. I hear
she has been suffering from a long and debilitating illness. This is
the first I've seen of her in years."

"Why, she's old."

"Yes, as was King Declan, when he died."

Pythius grunted. So much for a magical land where everyone
lived under heaven's favor and enjoyed long life. Still . . . the image
of a crystal scepter burned in his mind. If this land truly existed,
perhaps at least some of the tale might be true. It certainly was
worth his time to find out.

He watched through the glass in silent thought, his eye upon
Lady Carryn all the while. A young woman in a pale-blue gown
with long hair the color of eggshell came to her and took her arm,
then led her out the back entrance to the garden. Pythius did not
recognize the woman escorting the former queen to her carriage,
but even at this distance he was struck by her beauty. She moved
with elegance and grace, and her countenance seemed composed
and peaceful. He could read none of the phoniness or deceit in her
manner so evident in his other guests.

"Who is that?" His breath came out little more than a whisper.

"Who, Sire?"

"That woman, there. Helping the queen into her coach."

Artus craned to see, then opened wide the library doors for
a better look. A balmy draft brushed against Pythius's face and
blew his hair off his shoulders. Artus stood quietly beside him as
the carriage driver shook the reins and the pair of horses began to
transport their passengers down the lane.

"I believe, Sire, that is the Lady Calli. The queen's niece. She
arrived last spring to care for her aunt. I believe she is staying with
her. She must have just arrived to fetch the queen."

Pythius thought a moment, staring out into the ornate gardens but seeing nothing but the gentle features of Lady Calli's face. Artus left his side and returned the hefty book to its place on a high shelf.

"Will that be all, Sire?"

"What? Oh, yes. Wait. Summon my messenger."

Artus nodded.

"I think I will pay Queen Carryn a visit. Ask her about Elysiel."

"And perhaps get to know her striking niece . . ." Artus smiled, once more exposing his hideous teeth and fat lips. Pythius balled his fist, wondering how much it might hurt his fingers to smash his hand into his tutor's mouth.

"Go. And tell no one my intention."

"Oh, certainly not, Sire. We wouldn't want your enemies to know you planned to venture into such a dangerous part of the city. Perhaps it would be best if you went in disguise."

Pythius scowled. "Disguise? I will not cower; I am king of Paladya!" He waved his hand in dismissal. "Go. Fetch my messenger. Then scour this library for anything else you can uncover of Elysiel. Bring what you find to my chambers when you've finished. Is that understood?"

Artus bowed his head, no doubt trying to hide the gruesome grin he sported. Why did it seem everyone was laughing at him? What fools his subjects were, thinking his youth meant he was ignorant and inept. He was tired of their condescension. No matter. He would show them. If they felt he ruled with a hard hand now, wait until he formed that hand into an iron fist. He would rip out any seeds of dissension or talk of rebellion before they could sprout into a wild garden he could not control.

There had to be a way to protect his life and ensure his rule. Oh, to have such power—to be immortal, invincible. Impervious to the devices of his foes, to the ravages of time!

As he stood on the threshold of the library and watched the milling crowds eat his food and drink his wine, the tale of the magic scepter knit together in his mind. Pieces came to him, telling of a line of kings, a scepter containing a beating heart, a strange and magnificent circle of crystal slabs hidden in a cavern of ice. Surely, Artus could find writings of this tale in Declan's prodigious library. Among the thousands of books, there had to be at least one that could shed light on this mysterious land.

And if not, there was the Lady Carryn. She could tell him all he needed to know. And if she resisted . . . well, he had his ways of extracting information.

What if the tales were true? What if a magic scepter did indeed reside in Elysiel, and one could only enter by special invitation? Why had he never heard of this land back on Hardscrabble Isle? What would cause a king to want to drape his land in secrecy? As the questions battered him, he regretted he hadn't paid more attention to all those history lessons. But no matter. It wasn't too late to learn. And learn he would—all he could about this strange land, and the power it hid.

A vision of that exquisite young woman drifted into his thoughts, and his heart pounded hard in his chest. He'd never given any woman much thought. They were brought to him to satisfy his pleasures, and then discarded. But there was something about this woman he couldn't dismiss. Well, no doubt she would be at her aunt's residence, and his visit would allow him to examine her more closely. Just out of curiosity, of course. He would never let any woman get too close—regardless of Urstus's constant urging that he form a marital alliance. He was the lion of Hardscrabble Isle, now the king of all Paladya. He had smashed all the eggs in the heron's nest—all that posed a threat. The heron sigil of House Ardea no longer flew over a single rooftop in Paladya. He needed no one, trusted no one.

When his messenger came running in, breathing hard, Pythius told him, "Deliver a missive to Lady Carryn of House Ardea. Inform her I will be visiting tomorrow at noon. No need for any special preparations; I am calling out of . . . concern for her health and welfare. If she tries to decline, let her know the matter is settled."

The messenger bowed and ran back down the stairs. Pythius smiled. He would get his questions answered and also get Urstus off his back. Hopefully, his advisor would be impressed by his king's deep concern over the aging, frail former queen. A sign of wise diplomacy and maturity.

Pythius laughed. At some point he would rid himself of all his father's "leftovers," once they'd outlived their usefulness. Then, all of Paladya would come to learn that the lion's claws were still sharp and could rip flesh to shreds. "The scourge of the lion" had sent terror into the hearts of all in the city, but soon his subjects would learn their lion had not gone to sleep. He would be roused once more, and this time the scourge would leave a bloody trail in its wake so vicious his legacy would become the stuff of nightmares.

THREE

CALLI PLUMPED the pillow behind her aunt's head, then smoothed out her covers. Aunt Carryn always wanted the window open to allow the ocean air to luff the lacy curtains in a soothing rustle. She'd told Calli the soughing sound reminded her of the way the breeze back in Elysiel tumbled down the icy mountains and swept through her home with the fragrance of snow and alpine meadows drenched in summer sun.

She stepped back and studied her aunt, pleased with the color that had returned to her cheeks of late. "Can I not convince you, sweet aunt, to return home with me? So many miss you and would welcome you back."

Carryn let her head fall against feathers and sighed. "I've often yearned to see Elysiel one last time ... but Paladya has been my home for so long—"

"Yet what is a home without family?" Calli shook her head as her aunt closed her eyes with a dismissive smile. She wished she understood this foolishness. "Now that you have mostly recovered from your long illness, surely you could make the journey."

"Child, enough. The years have taken a hard toll on my heart and my bones. Even a comfortable carriage cannot smooth out the ruts and rocks of the Great Northern Road. You know the months of travel required. And besides . . ."

Calli waited next to the bed and breathed in the moist sea air that swirled in the small chamber. There was something intoxicating about the ocean's scent that made her lightheaded and sleepy herself. A flit of sadness crossed her aunt's face, but Calli knew better than to make mention of it. She poured three drops of tincture into her aunt's water glass.

"Besides what?" She gently touched Carryn's shoulder, and the old woman's eyes opened with effort. Upon seeing Calli's proffering hand holding the glass, she frowned.

"It will make me sleep too long. I must be alert for the king's visit."

Calli made a small noise of disapproval. "You should not miss a dose. The healer was adamant—remember?"

"The healer did not have to worry about offending his king. I cannot afford to do so."

"Pythius will understand an old woman requiring rest, recovering from an illness."

Carryn frowned once more. "Will he? You have been here long enough to have heard of his temper. He makes demands; he does not take no for an answer. He will expect me to entertain him."

"Oh, please, Aunt. What concern must he have with you? Your husband is dead now these five years. You have no ties to the palace, have nothing that would interest him. I will see him in, serve him tea and cakes, and if he insists, I will let him peek his head in and give his regards."

Calli set down the glass and pulled the covers around her aunt's neck. Carryn coughed with weak effort. She replied, her voice gruff, "Why did he not, then, seek me out at the party—if all he wants is to give his regards?"

"We left early. Or maybe he plans . . . to privately apologize."

This time her aunt's eyes opened wide in amusement. "Since when does the lion of Paladya go around the city apologizing to

House Ardea? No, he has something else on his mind. And I must know what it is. I do not trust him."

Their words fell into silence, spreading thick in the space between them. Seagulls squawked in the distance, circling the harbor, their cries wreathing the small cottage. "You said *besides*," Calli said in a soft tone, wondering if her aunt had already fallen asleep. "Why you refuse to go home."

Without stirring, Carryn answered in a tone that matched Calli's. "I have grown so old. And Cakrin . . ." A sigh rattled her chest. "I couldn't bear to have him see me like this. I want him to remember me young, the way he will always be to me—youthful, strong, with years of life stretched out ahead . . ."

Calli cupped her hands over her aunt's. The skin felt dry and slippery to her touch, and the bones brittle underneath. She thought of her uncle, King Cakrin, with his bright smile and sparkling gray eyes. How his youthful arms had embraced her when she left last year. He was six years older than Carryn but looked no older than a man in his middling years. It never failed to astonish her how the wisdom of the land fed his soul and the scepter renewed his blood, kept his heart stalwart. He grew in vigor while all those around him slowly wasted away. Calli sighed in understanding. She knew how close her aunt and uncle were. All three siblings were, with her father the youngest. The last living children of the former king, who had lived nearly eight hundred years before he handed the scepter to her Uncle Cakrin.

A sudden sweep of nostalgia brushed against her heart, but she pushed it aside. She had vowed to remain in Paladya and tend to her aunt until Carryn was either completely well or dead. And even though Carryn kept urging her to return home, reassuring her she was fine and able to take care of herself, Calli saw through the ruse—well-meaning though it might be. But she would not bow to her aunt's urgings. King Cakrin had asked her to care for Carryn, and she would keep the vow that she made before heaven and her king. Honoring a vow was an indisputable matter of principle in Elysiel. *"Better to not vow than to vow and not pay,"* was a saying she'd heard her whole life, and one she followed with all her heart.

The loud jingling of breeching made her turn and go to the window. She pushed aside the fluttering curtains and spotted a simple carriage pulled by two horses. Despite a lack of adornment and rich detailing, there was nothing ordinary about this finely stitched carriage with the leather and brass oiled and shining, untouched by the ocean's salt and abrasive winds. This was a carriage that rarely ventured through the rough cobbled streets of the docks and fishing district. A bit disconcerted, Calli knew just who had pulled up to her aunt's door—and more than an hour before the scheduled time.

She stole a quiet glance at Carryn, who despite her refusal to take her medicine had fallen deep into slumber, her chest rising and falling in a relaxed rhythm. Calli had no intention of waking her—lion or no. She shut the bedroom door with a quiet click, then hurried to open the front door before her guest could ring the brass bell mounted at the entry, whose loud sonorous clang would no doubt rouse her aunt.

She was surprised to find a simply dressed young man with an eager, bright face standing on the step, hand raised about to knock. When he tipped his head and said hello, Calli cast a glance at the carriage, wondering if this man with such striking features and polite manner might be the driver. But when the man gave a brisk nod to the driver up on the buckboard and the carriage drove off, Calli sucked in a breath and dropped to her knees.

"Your Majesty, forgive me . . . we weren't expecting you so soon . . ."

She felt a light touch on her shoulder encouraging her to rise. She straightened and found herself staring into dark inviting eyes.

Her heart pounded at his proximity, but there was no place to retreat to on the small porch. His unrelenting gaze flustered her, although she was no stranger to royalty. Rather, she felt a bit like cornered prey. Yet she sensed no condescension or lechery in his look, only the kindest of concern.

"Please," he said in a gentle voice, "we're not at court. Frankly, I would be honored and relieved if we could drop formalities. Call me Pythius."

Calli fumbled to find the edge of the door and managed to step back into the cottage. She gestured to welcome him inside. "I'm honored by your visit . . . Pythius. My name is Calli. I'm Carryn's niece. Please, do come in."

To her surprise, the young king took her hand and kissed it, all the while keeping his eyes on hers. Her mind numbed, wondering at the conflicting accounts she had heard of this lion's cruelty and brash manner, her heart wanting to quell the resounding suspicions and distrust. She had not expected the king to be so utterly charming, and although she knew he was her age, she had somehow expected him to seem older, hardened, stern.

As she showed him into the foyer and settled him into her aunt's favorite stuffed chair, he looked around with a pleasant smile. He sat with the posture of royalty in clothes of a peasant—although upon closer examination Calli noticed the dark breeches were spun of silk and not flax linen or wool, and his pale tunic was of the softest and finest cotton she had seen outside Elysiel. And a peasant would no doubt have to spend close to a year's wages on the supple deerskin boots adorning the king's feet.

"I've come to pay a visit to your aunt. Is she not here? I know I am early, and for that I apologize—if it has caused any inconvenience. I thought it best to alter my schedule, and dress . . . a little less conspicuously than usual."

"Oh, no, Sire. You have not inconvenienced us at all. We have been . . . eagerly looking forward to your visit." She felt a flush of heat rise to her cheeks, and she turned toward the small kitchen. "I'll bring you some tea. My aunt is in bed, resting—"

"Then let her rest. Perhaps after we've chatted awhile she'll be up to a brief conversation."

Calli busied herself preparing a tea service. She set the cakes Carryn had purchased from the baker yesterday on the delicate scalloped plates alongside the teapot and cups. "How do you like your tea?" she called from the kitchen.

"With milk, please. But do not trouble yourself with anything elaborate."

Calli returned to the foyer carrying the silver tray. As she set it down on the table and poured milk into the cups, she allowed herself a glance at the king of Paladya. She tried to imagine how traumatic it must have been for him, just a boy really, witnessing the deaths of both his father and brother within a fortnight, having lost his mother as well years earlier. He was surrounded at court by his father's former advisors, who were grooming him to rule a foreign country far from the land of his birth, and he had inherited a contingent of enemies that intended nothing but his demise. What great restraint and diplomacy Pythius must have to mete out each day, under terrific pressure. So unlike the kings of Elysiel, who ruled in harmony with all the land and its people, cherished and honored. And all this burden on the shoulders of one so young, with so little experience. She did not envy her guest's position, but seeing him now—away from the pomp and expectations thrust upon him— she felt a stir of compassion for the heavy burden he carried.

When they had sipped their tea in silence for a minute or two, Calli said, "I imagine this might be a refreshing break for you— getting away from the palace and all your many duties."

He looked at her over his teacup. "Yes, yes it is. So many demands are laid upon a king—from the moment I rise until I retire for the night. Although, important concerns regularly deprive me of sleep. I've often nodded off at inappropriate times"—with this he gave a slight chuckle colored with light self-reproach—"and felt a kick under the table from Urstus, my advisor . . ."

He laughed in such a lighthearted, warm manner that Calli felt her cheeks flush again. His charm and handsome face unsettled her, and no doubt he noticed.

"While we wait," he said, setting down his cup and giving her a look that made her heart race, "perhaps you might tell me about yourself. How long you have been here in Paladya, what your kingdom is like? I have only heard bits of tales of your fascinating land, and I suspect that much was an exaggeration. Would you indulge me?"

"Of course, Sire—"

Pythius laid his hand so suddenly upon hers that her voice snagged in her throat. "Please, I hear 'sire' and 'your majesty' and 'your highness' all day, until I wonder if I've misplaced my name and only exist as a title. I would be gratified if you would call me Pythius."

"All right . . . Pythius." The name rolled off her tongue awkwardly. Even though her own king was her dear Uncle Cakrin, once she had come of age, she ceased referring to him by the affectionate names she used during her childhood. From her name day onward she called him sire, as was expected. The title was not just a formality or used out of respect but reflected the deep regard for his position and the responsibility he bore for all her people.

"There," he said, his hand still remaining on hers and shooting warmth up her arm. "That wasn't so hard, was it?"

He urged her with his eyes to continue speaking and released her hand to sit back in his chair. She did her best to give him an engaging description of her land and people, the geography and customs and pastimes, and told a little of her father and twin brothers. As she spoke, though, she sensed the king growing restless with the telling. Afraid she was boring him, she said, "Perhaps I should go check on my aunt—"

His firm tone prevented her from rising. "Tell me—I was told tales of Elysiel as a boy. And although what I'd heard matches your description somewhat, there are a few puzzling details I wonder if you might clear up for me."

"Such as?" Calli swallowed, knowing the stories of the first Keeper and of the scepter had seeped over the centuries into the outlying lands. Those in Elysiel were not under compulsion to keep their history a secret, yet her people were a private lot, and the years of war had made them wary of confidences outside the borders of her land.

He leaned forward, eagerness shining in his eyes. "Is it true the king wields a magic scepter—one that gives him immortality?"

Calli laughed before she could restrain herself. She threw a hand over her mouth and composed her thoughts. Pythius tipped his head and pursed his lips. She caught a glimpse of the lion behind his polite expression.

"Did I say something humorous?" he asked.

"No. Forgive me. It's just when . . . you word it that way, it does sound a bit like a fantastic tale."

"But there is truth to it, yes?"

Calli nodded. "The scepter of which you speak is made of a solid spire of crystal. It was given to the first king of Elysiel thousands of years ago for his willingness to sacrifice his life to protect the sacred site—"

"What site is that?"

Pythius leaned over the table, so close she could hear him breathe. She placed her hands in her lap for fear he might take them again and fluster her even more.

"Long ago heaven set up a circle of protection in Elysiel—one of seven sites heaven ordained to prevent evil from gaining a stronghold over humanity. The northern Wastes are home to great evil, an abomination our kings have been battling since the first recordings of history. The site protects our land, favors it with the mild clime and bountiful year-round harvests. The evil cannot penetrate our borders."

"And the scepter—what is its role?"

"The Keeper, who suffered a mortal wound in defense of the site, pleaded heaven to allow the kings of Elysiel to take on the role of Keeper from that time onward. As a seal of the covenant, heaven placed King Lantas's heart into the handle of the scepter, and there it beats to this day, in union with the heart of the current king. As a result, each king that has wielded this scepter enjoys . . . a longer life than most—"

"How long?"

Calli caught a curious look in Pythius's face. She suddenly sensed this was the true reason for his visit—to learn of the scepter. "Quite long, but . . . only a king of Elysiel may wield the scepter. It is said that if one who has not been ordained attempts to possess it, in that day he will surely die. And its powers do not extend outside Elysiel's borders. Many have tried to steal the scepter, but you see—the effort would be for naught. And one cannot become king by mere choice. He must be a blood heir of Lantas's lineage, a male of the first three generations, and must be chosen by heaven itself."

Calli let out a tense breath. For a moment she felt a strange discomfort, but then, as she saw Pythius's face soften into a smile, she relaxed. She could understand the temptation and desire to attain such a treasure as the scepter, and no doubt a man like Pythius, with his power and influence, would desire such a boon, but she hoped she had quelled any thoughts he might possibly entertain of taking the scepter for his own. She added, "And there is also a prophecy that tells of the time when the scepter will fail."

"Fail? How?"

"When the last king dies, at the hand of a violent invader who will turn the land to ice. The heart will break and the power will diminish. Or something like that. It is a tale that has been told and passed down through the centuries, but is not written in any of our histories, and so no one quite remembers how it goes. Perhaps it's only a fancy someone invented. No one seems to give the prophecy much credence."

Despite Pythius's smile, a veneer of disbelief lay across his face. "I see. And what about the tale that Elysiel is invisible or . . . hidden? I have been told many have tried to gain entry into your land, but none—to my knowledge—have ever found a way in. What of that?"

"There is truth to the tale, Sire—"

"Pythius," he instructed evenly.

"Pythius," she corrected, earning herself a glowing smile from the king. "Our land lies under enchantment, and so no one may enter without . . . invitation. Those who attempt to gain entry unannounced or unwelcomed find themselves turned around or confused. They often end up wandering lost until they recover sense or become weary and hungry enough to head home."

Pythius laughed and shook his head. "That's a pretty trick. If only I had the power to seal off my private chambers in such manner so as to get a few hours of undisturbed rest!"

Calli smiled and felt the tension in her limbs ease. Pythius bit into one of the cakes with a thoughtful expression on his face, which afforded her the opportunity to rise and go check on her aunt. "I'll see if my aunt can be woken."

Pythius stood and held out a hand to stop her. Calli hesitated, just inches from him. He tipped his head to meet her eyes, as he stood nearly a head taller than she. When he laid his hands on her shoulders, she shuddered.

"I did not realize your aunt was still recovering from a difficult illness. It would be terribly rude for me to disturb her rest." He gave her a sweet crooked smile. "And you have been so kind to care for her—giving up your beautiful land and family—living so far from your father and brothers to tend to a sick aunt. Such a noble sacrifice of your time."

His words flustered her; she could only stand there and stare at him.

"See, now I've embarrassed you. Sometimes I am a loss how to speak with women. I haven't been around all that many in my life. Funny—I have been taught rules of diplomacy and educated in oration and law, but in none of my lessons was I ever told how to speak properly to a woman."

"You do just fine, Sire—excuse me . . . Pythius."

He lifted a hand from her shoulder and brushed away a strand of hair that had fallen into her face. His touch sent a tremor through her body. She could not move or breathe or even blink.

"It is so refreshing to hear my name spoken. Without harshness or malice, or from the chastising lips of my tutor. You make my name sound almost . . . lyrical." He paused, then said, "Calli." He let her name settle between them. "What an unusual name. Does it mean anything?"

"My full name is Callandra—after a small white flower that grows out of the cracks in the ice upon the mountains in northern Elysiel."

"Ah, a perfect name for you. No doubt you are as delicate and yet as strong as your namesake."

When Calli's face flushed once more with heat, he said, "See, I've embarrassed you again. Forgive me."

Calli managed to mumble, "No, it's quite all right. I'm just not used to men uttering such . . ." How could she be standing here speaking to the king like this? Surely she was overstepping the bounds of propriety and becoming too personal with him.

She wiggled free from the hands still resting on her shoulders, not allowing herself to look into Pythius's face. Even so, she sensed his piercing gaze, his strong presence that washed over her and threatened to engulf her. She had never felt so drawn to someone as she did in that moment, and a yearning grew in her heart that became an entangling vine, squeezing her lungs and cutting off her breath. She reached for a chair as her head swooned.

He fell to his knees beside her and searched her face. "Are you unwell? Shall I get you some cold water to drink?"

She waved her hand, hoping to assure him she was fine, as words stuck in her throat. A quiet knock at the door startled them both. Calli made to rise, but Pythius strode to the door before she could gather the strength.

"It's only my driver. I'm afraid our short visit must come to an end. If I stay away too long, a small army will be sent out to look for me."

Calli nodded as Pythius went to greet his driver and instruct him to wait with the carriage. She stood and smoothed out her dress, woozy and confused by scattered emotions that flitted in her stomach like tiny butterflies.

Before she could thank him for his visit and offer to pass his kind regards on to her aunt, he met her halfway to the door, where she had intended on seeing him out. He took her in his arms and drew her close to him, then put a finger to her lips. She trembled all over as he whispered warmly into her ear.

"Oh, Calli, what a sweet treasure you are. I am so glad heaven saw to it that we met today. Ever since I became king, I have been hated and feared. But with you, I feel neither. Perhaps . . . just as your Aunt Carryn brought alliance and unity to Paladya and Elysiel through her joining with King Declan, there might be hope we can bring about peace and restoration to this troubled kingdom through a similar union. In exchange, I would gladly lend support with my armies to help protect your borders, as King Declan had done so faithfully."

Calli's jaw dropped, and a tiny sound was all she could make in response. His words swirled in a muddle in her head.

Pythius lifted her chin and made her look at him. "There, I've gone and done it again. Your face has gone pale with shock. There must be something I can do to set your heart at ease." His deep, penetrating gaze caused blood to pound her ears. She felt intoxicated as if with the sweetest wine, and could do nothing but drink him in, her heart parched with a terrible thirst.

"Maybe," he said in sudden inspiration, "this will help."

In an instant, his lips were on hers, and he kissed her with a tender passion that set her trembling even more. Her arms seemed to find their own way around his waist, and he pulled her close, the kiss drawing all breath from her body and igniting a fire that burned hot to her core.

"Yes," he said, pulling back and smiling sweetly. "That did the trick. You now look . . . the very picture of health and radiance."

Calli felt her skin glowing like a thousand stars, then a shiver went up her spine. Surely he was toying with her. Who was she to him? A foreigner in his kingdom, no one of any rank or royalty that could matter. Perhaps he was much more "familiar" with women than he let on. She couldn't bear the thought that he might be playing with her, just to amuse himself. What was she thinking to let him touch her like this?

She realized he was standing at the door staring at her. "Calli," he said in a tone that pushed its way past her objections into her heart, "will you let me summon you to court?"

She pushed words out her mouth. "Whatever for, Sire?"

He frowned at her formality, but his expression was playful and acquiescing. "To show you my sentiments are serious. Will you at least allow me the chance to prove to you the sincerity of my words?"

Even if she wanted to say no, her aunt's words rang in her head. *"He makes demands; he does not take no for an answer."* She nodded, and Pythius smiled with a look of relief and sheer joy. Maybe her suspicions were unfounded; she did not think any man could pretend such feelings as the king of Paladya now expressed.

He took her hand in the opened doorway and gave it a light kiss. She tipped her head in acknowledgement as the driver stood patiently by the carriage door and the horses pawed the cobbles in the warm morning breeze. Out of the corner of her eye, she looked furtively around to see if her neighbors might be watching this exchange.

"Until our next meeting, Callandra."

He gave a brisk bow and walked down the steps to the lane. The sight of him leaving sent a sharp pain to her heart. She let out a long-held breath as he stepped into the dark compartment and was driven away. She watched the carriage wend down the narrow lane and turn at the corner, staring long after it had vanished from sight. The memory of the kiss he had given her stayed fast on her lips, even after she plodded back into the drab little cottage, where the walls felt oddly constricting. As she set the cups and plates on the tray and started for the kitchen, she heard her aunt call out from the bedroom.

"Calli, is that the king? I've overslept; come help me dress."

Calli walked to her door and opened it. Her aunt was sitting up in bed, fussing with her tangled covers.

"No need, sweet aunt. The king has already come and gone."

A flash of concern lit up Carryn's face. "Why didn't you wake me?"

"He insisted I let you sleep. He had a cup of tea and one of your cakes and told me to tell you he hoped you were recovering fully."

"That's all? All he said?"

Calli turned from her aunt, not wanting to let her see her face, which, no doubt, told much more than Calli was willing to disclose. As she made for the kitchen, she answered, "He had to get back to his palace. Duties and responsibilities and all that. You would know."

"Well, I still think he must have had something else up his royal sleeve. Did he do or say anything unexpected? How did he seem to you?"

Calli turned to see her aunt standing in her nightdress in the doorway, her hair matted as if a seagull had tried to make a nest in it while she slept. How did he seem? "Thoughtful. Considerate. Polite." She wanted to blurt out other words like *handsome, intoxicating, with the warmest arms and lips* . . . Instead, she pushed aside the memory of his affections and heated the kettle.

"Well, I don't trust him—and you mustn't either. He may seem as gentle as a cat, but the lion is there, under the surface, waiting to attack. Mark my words."

"Yes, Aunt," Calli answered dutifully. "I will." But rather than frightening her, her aunt's words sent a rush of excitement through her heart. If Pythius was a vicious lion in disguise, that was something she would have to discover for herself by heeding his invitation to court. Maybe her aunt was right that the king had ulterior motives for calling. Perhaps Pythius had only suggested an alliance in marriage due to pressure from his advisors. Maybe his personal advances were only motivated by politics.

Her aunt hobbled over to her padded chair and sank into the cushion. Calli smiled as the kettle whistled, putting a finger to the lips Pythius had kissed, in remembrance. Maybe all that was true—so what of it? It was his duty to form alliances to ensure peace. He was only suggesting what any wise, responsible king might consider. And surely her own father would approve—a new, stronger alliance with Paladya.

As she brought her aunt a cup of nettle tea, she made a decision. If Pythius proposed to her, she would accept. It would be the right thing to do, a mature, wise choice benefitting everyone involved. How could she refuse him?

She closed her eyes and relived the way his warm arms had encircled her, with his sweet words caressing her ears. No, the matter was settled; she would brook no argument from her aunt. And, truth be told, she knew that she would not be able to resist the king of Paladya, even if she wanted to.

Pythius stared blankly out the carriage window as the horses' hooves clattered on the filthy, trash-strewn streets of the ramshackle neighborhood. Rows of small fishing dinghies bobbed in the swells and thumped against wooden docks, and sweaty, undernourished men fished from the piers and hauled crates up ramps to the fishing vessels. What an ugly blight; he breathed relief in leaving this squalor behind. He was pleased—more than pleased—at the girl's response to his amorous play. He had thought he would have to work much harder to gain her interest, knowing that a woman of her nobility would not be impressed with the usual tricks. But her words troubled him. She was hiding something—of that he was certain. Maybe even lying to him. But, no matter. If anyone could detect treachery and dissembling, it was he. He was the master of deceit and knew its faces. And hers was surely a face that harbored a secret.

But he had his ways of drawing secrets out. Some responded to threats and torture, others to bribery and diverse methods of subtle persuasion. Drawing secrets from a woman was his favorite challenge. It was a fine art he had honed over the last few years, and one he greatly enjoyed engaging in, as the pleasures were innumerable and created little mess. The fact that Calli was beautiful and graceful would only make his job that much easier.

He would take his time, earn her trust. Uncover those secrets. And through her he would gain passage into Elysiel—perhaps under the guise of paying the king a visit? He would have to push for a quick marriage. That way her relatives would have no time to attend the wedding. He and his new bride could then journey to the fabled Shamhala—as his tutor referred to it. A magical land flowing with heaven's favor.

Pythius laughed in a burst of excitement. No doubt the tale Calli had told of the scepter was a lie. He didn't blame her for wanting to protect her king and her land. He understood her loyalty and respected it. But he suspected the scepter was there for the taking—should anyone find a way into Elysiel. Surely that was the reason for the enchantment barring entrance to her land—to prevent someone from stealing the scepter! How obvious!

While the carriage rolled through the harborside streets, making for the great stone palace up on the hill, he mulled over the things he would say to Calli when he summoned her to court. In the quiet confines of the coach he practiced his sappy compliments and enacted his great love and need to have her rule by his side. He would convince her of his gratitude and spill out his admiration for her desire to help bring peace to Paladya. And of course he would repeatedly tell her how beautiful she was, since that was all women really wanted to hear.

Once he set his phrases to memory, he scowled, pushing his impatience and frustration down as if they were molten lava seeking to spew from his gut. He did not like being patient. He did not want to wait even one more day to set his plans in motion. But wait he must. He could only rush things to a point, and wooing a woman as cautious and intelligent as Calli would take careful deliberation. He could not afford to show his hand and frighten her off.

No, that would be unwise and unpleasant. For then, should she refuse him, he would have to resort to his more . . . undignified ways of coercing information from her. And he would hate to have to destroy such a pretty like bird. Better to have her perch willingly on his arm than be crushed in his fist.

The massive iron gates swung open to admit him into the palace grounds. His many guards stood at attention as the carriage rolled by, reminding Pythius that his residence was more like a comfortable prison, protecting him from his enemies. He would never feel truly free or safe until he had that scepter in his hand.

He chuckled as he pictured Urstus's gleeful face upon learning of his king's plans to wed. And whom he planned to wed. Why, Urstus would be absolutely stunned by Pythius's brilliant diplomacy in uniting with Elysiel. Finally, Pythius would get the old nag off his back. Yes, his plan was perfect. The scepter was as good as stolen, and surely would give him immortal life and make him invincible. He would allow nothing to stand in the way of his heart's desire, and when he returned victorious, he would eliminate the remnants of his father's contingency—the meddlesome, irritating older men who treated him like a child.

And his enemies? Why, those dissenters would soften once they witnessed his smiling bride. Declan's queen had been beloved of the people. No doubt they would be enamored with Calli as well. Why, he could even encourage her to give a speech rallying the support of all his subjects, ushering them into a new era of peace, prosperity, and healing. Now there was a grand idea! Who could distrust words coming from such a noble and sweet mouth, from a member of the royal family of Elysiel? And Urstus called him naïve and undiplomatic! What a stupid old fool. *Yes, what great pleasure it will give me on the day my sharp blade severs that swine's head.*

The carriage rolled to a stop before the marble steps to the palace entrance. His driver opened the door and Pythius stepped out. He let his gaze travel from one end of the impressive edifice to the other, admiring how ornate and architecturally exquisite his residence was. All his—by way of intrigue, murder, and cunning. And he intended it to stay his for a very long time. All he had to do was move the first piece into place to begin his checkmate—sending a messenger to summon Calli to court.

He thought of the way she had trembled in his arms—so innocent and impressionable. And naïve. No, he would not have to use force with her. He saw the way she had looked at him—with longing and need. She would come at his call. He laughed thinking of the lie he'd told her. How he didn't understand women. But he knew them—knew them all too well. And Calli was no different from any of the dozens of women he used and then discarded. She would not refuse him—although a small part of him hoped she would.

He had to admit it would be so much fun to see her scream in pain.

FOUR

CALLI PATTED her forehead and eased herself into the cushioned settee, hoping the brisk winter breeze blowing up from the harbor would lessen her nausea. Would this horrid morning sickness never pass? Looking out at the docks rocking and tussling on the swelling tide, appearing so tiny from her purview high upon the rocky promontory, only added to her discomfort. She closed her eyes instead, and dreaded Pythius's return. His harsh words still rang in her head. As if it was her fault she was too sick to travel north.

Ever since their marriage at winter festival, Pythius could not stop speaking of their planned journey to Elysiel. At first she thought his desire was born of kindness and consideration for her worry. She had sent numerous letters to her father and brothers, and although she knew it often took weeks for a missive to arrive in Elysiel—having to first be sent to one who had leave to cross the border and then journey to the heart of the kingdom to deliver it— she ought to have received a reply by now. Her father wasn't one to write much, but surely he would have been quick to respond to her news! These last months of silence troubled her deeply.

She had been so taken by Pythius's urgent pleadings to marry in haste. He could not wait another moment to wed her, to have her by his side, to dispel his aching loneliness. He stifled her desire to postpone the wedding, to allow for her family to attend and share in her joy, by assuring her he would accompany her to Elysiel without delay to pay a visit to her father and a tribute to her king. His gentle, impassioned words had swayed her; she had been helpless to resist. And so, they had married—in a glorious ceremony before the entire city, it seemed.

Her heart ached in sadness and remorse. Such happiness she had felt! His arm around her and his face beaming with joy. She had never envisioned herself in such a blessed situation—married to the king of Paladya, who claimed he loved her more than life itself.

But only days after their union, Pythius's affection had cooled. She understood the court's demands and his need to attend to kingly matters. But his tone turned harsh, and he spoke curtly to her during their few intimate times together. And the tender advances he had shown her disappeared and were replaced by distraction and dismissal. Had she done or said something to offend him? Was she somehow a disappointment to him?

Tears slipped down her cheeks as she put her hand over her stomach. She had hoped the news of her pregnancy would shake him out of his foul mood, thinking perhaps the prospect of being a father might soften his hard disposition. At first he was joyous, but when the sickness assailed her and had not let up, he grew even more embittered. And only this morning, he argued with her attendant, Agatha, who adamantly insisted the queen must not travel in her condition—and certainly not on so difficult a journey as the one to Elysiel. To her horror, he pushed the sweet young woman and knocked her to the floor in his rage. And rather than apologize, he had stormed out the chamber mumbling to himself.

She had not wanted to admit it, but the truth stared her down and she could not ignore it. Pythius had only married her to gain entrance into Elysiel. It was all he talked of. And although he couched his desires in pleasant phrases—of the honor of meeting

King Cakrin and wanting to offer his assistance and armies in fighting the Borderland wars—Calli sensed obsession and urgency driving him. Only once he had brought up the subject of the scepter and the sacred site, politely asking questions but pinning her with a stern look. And when she'd laughed again at his idea that the scepter granted immortality and a magic cloak of protection, he had slammed his fist on the table, his face burning red with rage. "You lie!" he had screamed at her.

That had been two weeks ago, and since that confrontation, he had not returned to her bed chambers except to inquire impatiently if her sickness had ebbed. Her loyal attendant, who kindly brushed away the king's cruel outburst as of no account, prepared her tinctures and teas in hopes of alleviating the nausea, but nothing seemed to help. Only time, she was told. In time, it would pass. Yet nearly four months had passed and she still woke each morning racked with nausea.

The door to her chamber blew open and slammed against the wall. She startled and turned to see her husband, who stood at the threshold dressed in his warm coat and riding boots. The strange look on his face set her stomach fluttering. He studied her as she lay on the settee, with an expression of disgust evident on his features.

"I have the carriage readied for you. Tell your attendant to pack your things. We are leaving midday for Elysiel."

"But, M'lord, how can I travel? I fear—"

"You do well to fear, M'lady, if you refuse to cooperate. If you intend to be ill, what matter is it *where* you are ill—in your bed chamber or in a carriage?"

Calli's skin grew clammy. "But, you heard the healer. The journey might endanger the child. We cannot take that risk—"

He strode up to her and she cringed, curling back protectively, her hands wrapped around her waist. His eyes widened at her obvious fear.

He sneered and spoke in a whisper that seethed. "What a fool I was—to think you would make a fine queen. You belittle me, disrespect me! I am sick of your defiance and excuses." He lifted his hand to strike, and Calli squeezed her eyes shut in expectation of the blow to come. When it didn't, she risked a glance and found Pythius had dropped his hand and was staring vacantly out the window. His voice was now calm and subdued.

"You are right. You mustn't risk the child's safety. I have waited for this interminable winter to pass, and spring is now stirring. But I cannot tarry longer. I must meet with your King Cakrin and pay my respects, and discuss how my army might serve his in these wars he is fighting. Don't you see I am trying to forge an alliance with your king? Yet you oppose me, and laugh at me!"

Calli kept quiet, watching the lion stalk behind his eyes and hearing the roar rising in his throat, something she had been seeing more and more frequently. Just as her aunt had warned—but she had not listened. She replied with quiet sincerity, "I meant no disrespect, M'lord."

He tipped his head and scrutinized her, a scowl planted on his face. "Tell me how to enter Elysiel."

Her mouth dropped open. "I . . . I am not sure. I have never journeyed back and forth across the boundary, and should I return, the . . . land would recognize me and allow me admittance—"

"Have you never welcomed anyone in? How can you not be privy to this knowledge?"

Calli shrugged in apology. "I knew no one outside Elysiel. I had no cause to—"

"Enough!" Pythius stomped and shook his head. "You are useless to me." He blew out a hard breath. "I will find my own way in. Perhaps your king will hear of my approach and send someone to meet me."

He drew close and placed his hand on her cheek. Calli trembled, but not from the warmth of his touch. Fear stabbed her heart as an ominous sense of danger nudged her. She thought he meant to kiss her, but instead, as he gazed into her eyes, unblinking, an unremitting darkness lay beneath his gaze.

"I will pass on your regards to your father and brothers. And will return as quickly as I can. Urstus will manage the kingdom in my stead, so until I return, it is your duty to present yourself at all the required affairs and submit to his authority. If you do not, believe me, I will hear of it . . . and there will be consequences."

Before Calli could think of a kind response to assure him she would do his bidding, he marched out the door without so much as a good-bye. Moments later she heard his voice below her window, speaking to his page.

She ignored the upwelling of bile in the back of her throat as she stood in a dizzy rush and looked down into the courtyard. She watched with dread as her husband swung up onto his horse, partnered with a packhorse loaded down with supplies and attached by a lead rope to his own mount's saddle. As he rode off in haste, she wondered at his decision to travel alone, unattended. The sight unsettled her, and her presentiment of doom grew unbearable.

Yet he was but one man, and even if King Cakrin invited him in, what threat could he pose? Maybe her pregnancy was dislodging her reason. No doubt once Pythius met with her uncle, he would understand. Understand how the king ruled by the grace of heaven, and how the scepter was linked to the land, and to the heart of the king. Perhaps Pythius would return then, satisfied that she had been telling the truth. And maybe her uncle's gracious, kind manner would win Pythius's allegiance.

She sat at her desk and began a new letter to her father, alerting him to Pythius's approach and expressing once more her concern that she had still not heard from him since her wedding. Her heart welled up with misery, overflowing onto her paper in drops of water that smudged the ink.

At that instant the tiny baby in her womb jerked, and she placed her hands on her belly in wonder. Her baby! Despite the flood of worries seeking to drown her, the prospect of holding her baby in her arms buoyed her in hope. Pythius would be gone for months; he might not even return until after their child had been born. Already this tiny life inside her warmed her heart. The thought comforted her, that even in the midst of her loneliness and worry, she had a child to look forward to.

She concluded that she would be a dutiful, cooperative queen, and stay out of Urstus's way. The old man, despite his authoritative, brusque manner, was at least polite to her, even though he hardly acknowledged her presence. Well, it would suit her to be invisible these months of Pythius's absence. And if her aunt was unable to visit her at the palace, Calli would call on her each week to give her some company. She had hardly seen her aunt since becoming queen—between Pythius's demands for her presence at court and her morning sickness.

With these thoughts comforting her aching heart, she finished her letter and slipped it into the envelope. As she heated the wax and pressed her seal onto the paper, she prayed her baby would grow and thrive and bring joy to her marriage. Maybe once her husband held his baby in his arms, he would find the peace he was seeking. She had to hope for the best. She hated to think of any other outcome.

King Pythius rode north, pushing the horses hard and fast while daylight still held. His anger was slowly subsiding, allowing the thrill of his quest to invigorate him. Finally, he was on his way! For half a year he had been planning this moment, and although his search to find more writings on the magic scepter had come up dry, Artus had uncovered an ancient tome that delved deeply into the history of Elysiel. In its pages, Pythius studied the lives and deeds of each of the thirty-odd kings that had wielded the scepter, and although they had certainly died, some had lived nearly a millennium! To think of living such a long life—it sent a shiver through his bones and made him wish he had wings. The legend of this sacred site fascinated him—giant slabs of crystal erected in a circle within an ice cavern. The circle of crystal was said to have tremendous power, preventing evil from seeping into the kingdom. Could its secret be unlocked and the power harnessed?

And even more fascinating were the strange tales of the evil that ravaged the northern Wastes. Some texts told of an ancient creature called the *Tse'pha*, a snakelike abomination that spawned broods of dark beasts in the thermal region of the far north and had tremendous magical powers. There the creatures lived and bred, in bubbling pools of hot noxious-smelling mud among vents of steaming geysers that scorched the land and killed the vegetation with sulfur-laden minerals. Why those beasts had fomented war against Elysiel for centuries now, he could not discover. Maybe this *Tse'pha* wanted access to the site. If these slabs of crystal indeed protected the boundaries of the kingdom, allowing no one unwelcome in, then they surely contained great power—a power a creature like the *Tse'pha* might battle long and hard for, even across centuries, without relenting.

He knew he had a long, difficult journey ahead, one that would take many months. Once he crossed the Paladin Mountains and trekked north on the Great Northern Road, he would encounter few inhabited regions. From what Artus had outlined, the weather north of the Paladin range was harsh and unpredictable. The Barrenlands were inhospitable, and game would be hard to find. Interminable stretches of icy tundra posed danger to his horses with its thin sheeting of ice masking the miring mud beneath. Both Artus and Urstus had opposed his departure, but who were they to stop him? He had spent his childhood hunting from the back of a horse in a land just as hostile and unyielding. His journey worried him not a bit. Except for the little matter of finding Elysiel and the entrance to that kingdom. Surely, someone in the vicinity would know a way in—or at least some method of announcing his arrival. And no doubt once the king received word of just who his visitor was, Pythius would be welcomed and escorted across the border.

Calli had been vague in her description when he asked for geographical landmarks indicating his proximity to Elysiel. Was she stupid or being deliberately elusive? He couldn't tell. Her continual off-putting drove him mad. No matter, he would find his way. Although the Northern Road ended more than a hundred leagues south of Elysiel, turning into a rutted cart road that led off in numerous unmarked directions, she noted he should start to see small outlying hamlets and signs of trade. Apparently Elysiel traded many goods with neighboring lands to the south and east, although, from the way she told it, her kingdom needed nothing they couldn't produce themselves. If he kept at good speed and his horses lasted, he should arrive in Elysiel midsummer at the latest.

As he started his ascent up the winding trail through the King's Pass in the Paladin Mountains, he slowed and stopped to survey his kingdom. Tranquil Harbor shimmered in the evening light, the small whitecaps glistening like gems scattered across the water. Small boats tied at mooring rocked in the swells, and off in the distance, beyond the harbor, the Regent Sea shone like a pink mirror reflecting the painted dusk. The panoramic sight of his kingdom spread out before him stirred a sense of pride in his accomplishments. This—all his to rule, armies at his command, subjects to tax. The wealth and richness of the entire kingdom— all his. And yet, a spirit of restlessness and dissatisfaction stirred in his soul. It still wasn't enough. There were other lands to conquer, other subjects to subdue and bring into submission. Untold riches and treasures to seize and stockpile.

A wisp of his nightmare then returned, of the cynical man pointing at his storehouses. His words scraped against Pythius's ears, and he wished he could shut him up. *You fool! Thinking you have stored enough to last for years and can now sit back and enjoy the fruits of your labors. Tonight your life is forfeit—and all you have will be given to another to enjoy!"*

Pythius slid off his horse and turned his back to the sea. He forced the haunting words out of his head and gazed at the peaks towering to the north and west that blocked his view of lands he knew nothing about. Seven sacred sites, Calli had told him. Where were the other six? Were they also at the heart of chosen lands that experienced heaven's favor? Lands where those living near the site prospered beyond imagining?

When he returned with the scepter, he would speak to the head of his great army—Ka'zab. Perhaps he knew something of these sacred sites and where they might be. Ka'zab was not a man Pythius felt comfortable around—not one bit. Pythius did not know when and under what circumstances his father had conscripted the secretive, foul-mouthed mercenary, but Ka'zab was efficient, and so long as he was paid well, he did his job. Any job asked of him, regardless of how messy. Pythius knew the man held no feelings of loyalty to his throne—or to any monarch, for that matter— and that made Pythius more than uneasy. However, he was wise enough to know he needed a man like Ka'zab at his side, and he would pay whatever was required to keep him, if not loyal, at least free from treachery.

He turned and set his face north, kicked his horse's flanks, and in little time crested the pass. Through the twilight, he made out only a few tiny lights in the far distance below him—either campfires or an isolated cottage or inn. Beyond lay the thousands of leagues he had yet to travel. Heaven help anyone who tried to hinder him in reaching his destination; they would taste the sharp edge of his sword and not live to regret it.

FIVE

THE MIDSUMMER sun did little to melt the imbedded chill in Pythius's joints. Despite his efforts to persuade his horse to hasten, the old nag plodded along unresponsive. Not even a beating with a stick would inspire this poor excuse for a horse to move faster than a snail's pace. But it was either that or walk the rest of the way carrying his belongings.

He had run through more horses than he could count. Two had died of exhaustion, another had fallen—tripped over a gnarled half-buried root, and Pythius had had to skewer it with his sword to end its misery. Another had misstepped and cracked through the tundra and into a mudsink. Pythius had been forced to scramble to detach the saddle and bedroll before the beast succumbed to the mud and disappeared from sight in a wail of terror. He had looked on, helpless to aid the floundering beast or drown out its death cries. Fortunately, he had been able to acquire replacement mounts, although at one lonely place in the middle of nowhere he'd had to leave the dead beast for the carrion crows and jackals to feed upon, then set up camp along the road and wait many days until a driver in a cart gave him a lift to the next village, which was a week's journey to the north.

The Barrenlands were truly unbearable, and he was tired of the empty, inhospitable terrain and the biting wind that, had it but teeth, would have stripped the skin from his bones. After so many months of his interminable journey, his skin felt rough and calloused, his hands were chafed, his lips ached and bled, and he had lost much weight due to his continual inability to sight game of any kind larger than a packrat. A long, scratchy beard wrapped around his neck; he grew it to stave off the chill assaulting his skin. And it was summer! He hated to think what conditions awaited him should he tarry too long in Elysiel and have to travel back to Paladya during winter.

But he had finally come to the place Calli had described: the branching cart road and the small hamlets. Finally he'd been able to have a real bed to sleep in at an inn, and hot stew and bread, although the fare had been meager and bland. No matter. He imagined once he was welcomed into Elysiel, the king would throw a feast in his honor and shower him with comfort. No doubt King Cakrin would welcome news from Calli and the girl's aunt, and his offered hand of alliance. Pythius would then spend a few days at court, playing the role of the honored dignitary, all the while plotting how to steal away with the scepter.

He chuckled as he directed the horse over a rise and down toward a wide prairie of stubbled grass. He could just imagine the ire and panic that would set in when the king discovered his precious scepter gone. Pythius's many months of trekking over the Barrenlands had afforded him much time to devise an infallible plan. He would be sure to abscond with a fast horse, after touring the royal stables and determining how to manage that. With his saddlebags laden with stores for the trip home, stolen from the kitchen, he would be ready to escape in the quiet hours of night without any notice. He would then ride off the main roads and traverse the wide swaths of small trees he had seen stretching for leagues to the south. Once he was certain no one pursued him, he would shave off his beard, shear his hair short, switch into peasant's clothes—clothes he had already stolen off a drying line at a humble cottage in the dark hours before dawn—and he would be unrecognizable. He would "borrow" some old draft horse from a nearby farm and plod down the road as the king's soldiers raced past him in pursuit of their thief.

He reined in his horse and scanned the outlying land before him. The two farmers he had spoken with in the last hamlet had given him directions to the border of Elysiel, not at all distressed by his questioning once he implied he had welcome business with the kingdom. Calli had spoken truth when she said the neighboring hamlets traded with Elysiel. Of course, he didn't dare ask them how to get in, knowing it might rouse their suspicions. He learned from their talk—after his plying them with drink had loosened their tongues a bit—that the blessed weather and prosperity of Elysiel apparently seeped across the borders and into the string of hamlets to the south. No wonder so many small villages had sprung up close to the boundary, hugging the cherished land in order to flourish beneath its benevolent shadow. Pythius had indeed noticed an evident change as he neared his destination. Almost instantly the bitter wind and stark wasteland had given way to sun-drenched sweeping fields of grass, with babbling creeks meandering through them—something that had perked up his horse and set it eagerly grazing. The sudden change in scenery and weather was truly remarkable—and a welcome relief.

Now well-fed and rested, he sat his horse and eyed the strange-looking brook that bisected the far edge of the grassland. Perhaps it was a trick of light, but it shimmered like glass or ice, the surface a bright, unmoving sheen. Odd, Pythius thought. He surveyed the area and found it quiet and empty. Not a soul traveled this particular road, and now that he thought about it, he hadn't seen anyone on it since he'd taken the left fork, as the villagers had instructed.

Beyond the brook, more grassland spread to the northern horizon—a veritable sea of vibrant green. But there was something odd about that grass as well. It looked as if it were a painting, almost too picturesque and sublime, with the sunlight glinting off the blades as if a sunbeam shone directly on them—appearing more like a mirage one would see on a scorching day, with heat waves shimmering up into the air.

Pythius led his mount down the hillside and onto the swale that led to the brook. As he approached the water, grass swallowed up the cart road until it disappeared under his feet, and soon he was urging his horse to wade through tall, thick vegetation until he came to the sandy bank. A few lazy bees flitted over the grass flowers. Bird call punctured the draping silence. Time seemed thick, like molasses, as the sun beat upon his shoulders and he studied his surroundings.

He slid off his horse and stood in puzzlement. When he bent over, he saw his reflection scowling at him, and he would have sworn he was looking at a slab of ice had he not reached in with his hand and stirred the water. He pulled off his boots and took a hesitant step into the brook. The cool water soothed his hot, swollen feet as he waded knee-deep across to the other bank, then stepped onto dry ground.

What now? Where was the entrance to Elysiel? He scowled again, now realizing those men at the tavern had purposely misled him for a laugh. Surely he was nowhere near the border, and the thought of wasting his day returning to throttle those brigands sent a rush of utter weariness to his bones. Exhaustion and frustration dropped him to his knees, and he cursed loudly enough to startle his horse. With a deep sigh, he went over to the nag, who took long draughts of water between snatching clumps of grass in its teeth. He unfastened the cinch and let the saddle and bags drop to the grass, then removed the bridle to allow the horse easy grazing. At least one of them was happy.

After wasting the better part of an hour tromping around looking in vain for some sign of a trail, he kicked at the dirt and cursed once more. In minutes he was saddled up and riding again, going the only way he figured made sense—forward. After wading through the creek and galloping through the scrub grass until both he and his horse tired, he caught sight of rooftops over the crest of a hill. At last—surely someone there would redirect him properly.

But when he made out the wooden cottages and storefronts nestled in two rows with the dirt lane bisecting the humble village, his jaw dropped along with his reins.

"What witchery is this! It can't be!" He let his gaze travel the length of the buildings until it rested on the tavern where only last night he had sat with those two men. *How can this be? This village was directly south, not north.* He had stayed true to his course, the sun arcing the sky from his right shoulder to his left shoulder the whole way. He had not circled back.

Fury seethed out of his mouth in vacant grumblings. A few villagers walking along the lane stared at him but registered no reaction. Was this a familiar sight—having strangers wander lost through their village? Was this some trickery they perpetrated themselves?

He spun his horse around and galloped back the way he'd come. With the sun setting now in the west, he felt turned around. He should now be heading south, but the shadows cast along the ground as he rode made clear he was on a northerly route—just as he had been this morn. Ire smothered the consternation eating at his gut. He was so close, yet . . . Again, he wanted nothing more than to wrap his hands around Calli's delicate neck and crush her windpipe for withholding the secret to entering Elysiel. He let the delicious image of her gasping for air, her eyes rife with terror at her impending death, console him for the moment.

By the time he arrived at the creek—the same little brook he had first encountered at the end of the cart road—a sliver of curved moon was lifting up into the sky, giving little light. He stared at the moon's perfect reflection, unwavering on the surface of the water as if it were a painting on a sheet of glass, then kicked a rock into the brook, shattering the moon into a thousand blinking eyes that glared at him in derision. Even though he had not eaten all day, his frustration squelched his appetite, and he set about making camp and hobbling his horse, determined to go to sleep, hoping that when he awoke at sunrise, he would find this whole matter a bad dream.

"Well, what do we have here?"

Pythius threw his woolen blanket to the ground and grabbed his sword. Within seconds he was on his feet, ready to fight. The early morning sun's glare struck his eyes, and with his free hand he shielded them in order to see who had spoken to him. It took a moment to register that the deep voice had come not from a man but from a woman. And a beautiful one at that.

Her chestnut hair shimmered with golden light from the sun's caress, and her eyes met his with a piercing look that punctured his heart. Her appearance took his breath away and set him trembling. He had never seen a woman as magnificent as she—this creature before him who stood poised like a goddess and whose every feature was perfect and simple in its beauty. He tried to form words but they wouldn't come. No doubt she was from Elysiel; she had the same pale hair and complexion as Calli, and the same ice-blue eyes.

Joy coursed through his veins. Surely the king had seen or heard of his arrival and had sent this beauty to welcome him in!

He bowed deeply and said, "My Lady, I am King Pythius, from Paladya. I seek entrance into Elysiel. Will you escort me?"

To his surprise, the woman laughed and threw her head back. "You cannot fool me. I know why you have journeyed here. You are the lion come from the thicket."

Lion? Pythius stood inches from her scrutinizing face. Her stare unsettled him. How did she know his house sported a lion sigil? Was she a witch? Or somehow knowledgeable of his monarchy?

Before he could say more, she put a finger to his lips. Her flesh burned and he jumped back.

"My name is Lady Vitrella, and I have been waiting for you to arrive."

"Waiting? Did you see me coming?"

She laughed again and her mockery irritated him. But she paid him no mind and looked out over the brook. "I have been waiting ages for your appearance. Do you not know? You are the one fore-told—the lion from the thicket."

"Yes, yes, you said as much. But what does it mean?"

She walked around him, in deliberation. He smoothed his unkempt hair and clothes, neatening his appearance as best he could. He spotted his horse further down the meadow, munching grass, its left legs still hobbled.

She turned to face him, and her gaze paralyzed his heart. "You mean to say you have come, seeking the scepter, and you do not know the prophecy?"

Pythius's gut clenched. How did she know he sought the scep-ter? Had his scheme somehow been revealed? Just who was this woman? The hairs on his neck tingled, and he sensed trickery. Yet, as hard as he tried to wrest his gaze from her, he could not.

She laid a burning hand on his shoulder; he startled in shock at the heat, but he stood still and tolerated it, waiting for her to explain. She moved more like a cat than a woman, with grace and confidence, but slinking and wary. From time to time her eyes darted across the grass, as if watching for something or someone.

"The prophecy states, 'The lion has come up from the thicket. He has gone forth from his place to make your land desolate. Your cities will be laid waste, without life. And it shall come to pass that in that day that the heart of the king shall perish.' Have you not heard of this?"

"I . . . I do recall something about the king's heart perishing, but naught of the rest. I have no intention of laying this land waste and desolate." He now worried that the king of Elysiel had somehow uncovered his intention and sent this woman to trap him. He lifted his sword and took a stance, ready to strike. But she only laughed in response, and the jagged sound of it sent a chill across his neck.

"Is that so?"

She drew close to his face, and he caught a whiff of her exotic perfume. His breath hitched in his throat, strangling his words of protest.

"For centuries, the armies of Elysiel have attacked my kingdom in the north, a vicious war that has left my people ravaged and hopeless. I have yearned for this day—to see deliverance."

"Deliverance?" This was not how Calli described the Borderland wars. King Declan had joined armies with Elysiel to fight those wars, but nothing Pythius had gleaned from his research revealed an oppressed people. Perhaps Calli had lied to him yet again.

"The king of Elysiel is a ruthless killer. The cursed scepter corrupts each king and poisons his heart. For centuries the power in the scepter has been abused and mishandled, and so the prophecy must come to pass. The lion must remove the scepter far from Elysiel, and then my people will be able to once again live in peace."

Pythius sucked in a breath as Lady Vitrella stepped back and let her hand drop from his shoulder. A burning sensation on his skin lingered underneath his tunic. He tore his gaze from her enchanting face and pushed the engulfing feelings of longing for her out of reach. The bright sunlight glared off the brook, which once more looked like ice or glass. The meadow grew strangely silent. "I was told if anyone tries to take the scepter, in that day he will surely die."

"Were you truly told that?" She made a noise of disgust. "You have been lied to. Everyone here knows that in the day the usurper takes the scepter, he will not die but his eyes will be opened, and he will acquire great power. The power over good and evil. The divine knowledge of all things, good and bad. He will be like God, and none shall be able to oppose him. And he will live forever." She came so close to his face, her hot breath rubbed against his lips. "Do you desire such power?"

"Yes! Yes, I do. It is what I have come for."

"Good." She smiled but her eyes brooded, and to Pythius it seemed she trembled. Was she excited, worried?

"Tell me," he said, "what do I have to do? How do I get in and where must I go?"

"I will tell all, and you must listen carefully, for it will not be easy. But you are destined to succeed. You are meant for greatness, and great power. Few can wield such power, but you are the lion foretold. You are the one my people have been waiting for."

Pythius's heart raced at the thought of such power in his hands. The scepter—the craving eating at him all these months—was nearly his. No wonder he had been so obsessed with journeying to Elysiel and stealing the scepter. It was destined and foretold. His very life had been anticipated for centuries—to be a deliverer! How could that be? He cared nothing for delivering this woman's people—but if that was one result of capturing the scepter, what concern was it of his? In gratitude, he would aid her, using his great power to protect her land. He would make any promises she insisted upon if it meant she would help him to grasp his prize.

"I cannot risk entering the land, for the moment I cross the boundary King Cakrin would know. The king is the Keeper of the sacred site, and that is where you will find him at dusk, for every evening he enters the site to commune with his evil god. You must not linger long in Elysiel, for your true intentions will be revealed to the king. The scepter gives him this power to know all those in his land, to the very core of their soul. And so, should he catch notice of you, he will have you captured and tortured in ways that will make you regret you had ever been born. But that will not come to pass so long as you heed my words."

Pythius shook his head in amazement. Calli had described her king as a wise, compassionate man who cared deeply for his land and people. And here, Lady Vitrella painted much the opposite portrait of the man. Which was true? But did the truth concern him? Not at all. Good king or bad, he would seize the scepter. The thought of such power in his hand sent a thrill through his body. He could taste that power; he thirsted for it with a furious thirst. He must have it!

"Do not hesitate in your quest. When you arrive at the ice cavern and enter, you will find Cakrin in the center of the crystal circle, worshipping his god." Her face scowled in revulsion and she let out a long hiss. "He will not be apprised of your arrival, for when he is in communion with his god in the sacred site, his thoughts are closed off to all others. Strike him hard and fast with your sword and he will die, for he is just a man. Without the scepter, he is nothing, but take care—he is a seasoned warrior, and should he best you and lay hold of your sword, you will fall. Take the scepter and hurry back here, where I will have a fresh horse awaiting you. It will be hours before the king's absence at court is noticed. By the time Elysiel sends pursuers, you will be well beyond their reach."

Pythius nodded and fingered his sword. "And you—what do you want from all this?"

Lady Vitrella stroked his cheek with her hot fingers. He rolled his eyes and groaned. "Only your victory. Your brave act will set my people free. It is all I yearn for, and . . . I will be forever in your debt . . ."

Before Pythius could say a word, her searing lips were on his. He surrendered to her passionate kiss, and only after she released him did he dare open his eyes and suck in a breath. "I . . . I don't know what to say—"

"Just say you will do all I ask."

"Oh, of that you can be certain. It is I, My Lady, who am deeply grateful to you. I hope . . . one day when I am in my full power and ruling the known world, you will honor me with a visit." He touched her hot lips with his finger. "I will make it well worth the trouble of a long journey."

She smiled and blinked in pleasure. "I will cherish that day—of that *you* can be certain."

After she had given him directions to the site and assured him she would be waiting at their present location for him to return, she whistled and summoned a horse as black as night. Where it had come from, he couldn't guess, but the beast galloped up to Lady Vitrella and stopped before her. She then swept her hand in a wave before the brook, and in response the water grew a covering sheet of steaming ice, beginning at the banks and solidifying inward until a seamless mirror lay over the surface.

"Walk your horse onto the ice and stop," she instructed. "Gaze at your reflection and do not blink. Sit as still as you can and wait."

She then mounted up onto a silver saddle and gave a simple nod, then rode south and over the rise of hill. He watched her with equal parts awe and bewilderment.

He coaxed his horse onto the ice as she directed and stared unblinking at his reflection below him. Tendrils of steam hissed and swirled around his mount's feet. Pythius cooed to it to calm its nervous jitters. The thin veneer began to blur, and he resisted the urge to rub his eyes. Soon his sight grew faint and colors swirled before his eyes. Bits of creek and ice and grass all spun in a whorl about his head, but he kept his gaze fixed. Then the strange mist lifted and through the ice he could see himself as before . . . yet, as his horse shifted footing, the horse in the reflection did not. It was as if his image had been imprinted upon the ice, but he was free to move.

He turned and looked over at the far bank, expecting to see the grassy knoll as before, but instead his eyes met with a thick copse of spindly trees growing to the water's edge. The sky burned a deep indigo blue, and a faint warm breeze tickled his ears. He could not believe the land spread out before him: a wide undulating prairie blanketed with purple and white flowers stretching to a backdrop of majestic mountains, snowcapped and twinkling like diamonds in the sun.

How had he arrived here? He had the strange sensation that he had changed places with his reflection, and that the true king of Paladya was locked in ice in another timeless world. Would he again switch places with his reflection when he fled Elysiel? The thought was uncanny, yet he could conjure up no other explanation.

No matter. He had finally arrived in Elysiel—the hidden kingdom of myth and magic. A kingdom blessed by heaven and ruled by the king and Keeper of the sacred site. A king who wielded a magic scepter that held infinite power and granted immeasurable life and divine favor.

But not for long. The lion had been roused from his thicket, ready to stalk his prey, and soon . . . the heart of the king would perish.

SIX

AS HE SCRAMBLED over another jumble of granite, he finally caught sight of the cavern entrance tucked into a wedge of towering rock. He had pushed at a steady, hard pace the entire day, and exhaustion washed over him at the welcome sight of his destination. After taking a short break to gulp down water and cram some dry bread and moldy cheese down his throat, he pressed on, every nerve tingling in excitement. Already he could feel the scepter in his hand, and he let the vision of power surge through him. He regretted having to leave his horse below, but he'd had no choice. Only a mountain goat could climb over these crags. And a determined usurper.

Evening approached, and the air trilled with birdsong. Throughout the day as he'd ridden north, further into mountains that shone like polished white marble, he'd been awed by the prodigious life abounding in Elysiel. Herds of caribou grazed in grassy prairies, alongside dozens of other animal species that intermingled peacefully. At one large lake, thousands of beasts and fowl gathered to drink and cavort in the water. They created a brilliant tapestry of fur and feathers that undulated as they drank. Pythius wondered if men in Elysiel hunted at all; the creatures barely lifted their heads in curiosity as he passed, displaying no fear of him.

He drew close to the cavern, and only then did he see the ice framing the entrance, hard to distinguish from the underlying marble. A chill wind blew from the ragged hole in the rock, laced with the scent of winter and snow. A webbing of frost filigree bordered the opening, which was just large enough for a man to squeeze through.

Pythius drew in a deep breath of brittle air and tipped his head to clear the threshold. He lay one hand firmly on his sword as he peered into the dim cavern. An icy finger of wind rushed down his neck and he shivered. He stood still, unblinking, letting his breath slow and his eyes adjust. A high ceiling coated in ice curved far overhead, the ice extending down rough walls that opened into a gigantic cavern that Pythius could have fit half his army into. And most amazing were the thick ice crystals that hung from the roof of the cavern, some many times his height, dangling like tenuous swords of doom. If one broke off, it would no doubt spear a man just as handily as the sharpest sword. The thought made Pythius move in silence, aware that any loud sound might dislodge the icicles and cause them to rain down like heaven's vengeance upon him.

Something moved to his left! He spun and saw movement, then realized it was only his reflection in the wall of ice. He loosed the tight breath in his chest, listening intently for any sounds coming from the cavern. He wished he could light a torch to see better but knew that would be foolhardy. He would have to manage only a few steps at a time.

Soon he detected massive shadows deeper in the cavern. As he inched closer, he saw they were towering shapes with a mostly flat surface. At first he suspected they were giant rocks, but upon closer examination he noted they were partly transparent and fraught with cracks—giant crystals! With a glance left and right, he made out more in a line. But not quite a line. As he walked from one to another, he saw they formed a circle—but what an enormous circle it must be! It would take him the better part of an hour to walk this circle, from what he could surmise from the few giant slabs before him.

He stopped again to listen, gazing deeply into the strange patterns threading inside the crystal that mesmerized him by their shimmering beauty. Veins like those found in decaying leaves interwove throughout. The massive blocks seemed to be illuminated from within, with an ethereal light not found in the natural world. Still, he heard nothing but tiny drips of water, no doubt formed by condensation on the cavern's ceiling.

Curious, he touched the giant crystal before him, and jumped back when his fingers stuck and burned. He put them in his mouth, the pain just as searing as if they had been laid upon hot coals. And then something shifted within the crystal, as if it were alive.

Pythius stepped back and held his breath as some strange image formed on the face of the slab. Where his fingers had touched the burning surface, a hand appeared, as if his own hand had left an imprint, but as he watched, agape, an image materialized as if drawn by an unseen artist, the hand now connecting to a body, delineating a figure standing atop a wall with a hazy horizon in the distance. His heart trembled when he recognized the parapet the figure stood upon, and then the man himself, wearing his own royal robes with the lion banners flapping in the breeze behind him. A sickly feeling gripped his gut as the image grew more detailed and his tranquil harbor far below the palace walls began to churn with disturbance.

It was he himself upon that parapet, but he looked older, weathered, drawn. How could this be? Were these slabs enchanted? And what was it showing him? A horrid pain then gripped his left hand, a deep ache that caused him to moan aloud, despite his effort at restraint. A jolt of sickness made his head spin, and he felt terribly tired and weak, as if he had been struggling against this pain for an unbearable length of time. He felt the weight of difficult years upon his shoulders, a tremendous burden he could barely endure. Desperation and hopelessness engulfed him, and he fought an urge to run—run down to the shore in some mad pursuit, his mind filled with hate and fury and panic.

He stumbled backward and tried to wrench his gaze from the scene unfolding before him, but he could not turn his head. His eyes were riveted on the shape looming large in the disturbed waters of the harbor, undulating in a rocking motion and creating waves of such force they crashed against the battlements and sea-walls, pounding every ship into splinters. He could even hear the faint cry of terror arising from the city as one voice. What on earth was happening to him?

In a sudden shudder, he fell to the ground, his hand still throbbing from the residue of pain. He studied his upturned palm, touching it gingerly and unable to find any evidence of damage.

"You are seeing a piece of your future."

Pythius leapt to his feet and strained to see through the dark to the source of the voice. It was a man's voice—deep, calm, assured. His heart still pounded in distress, but he forced his mind to focus and think. No doubt this was the Keeper—the king of Elysiel! He must find a way to strike him before he could sense his intention. Lady Vitrella had made it clear he would not be able to fool King Cakrin or successfully mask the desire of his heart. And although Pythius was confident in his skills as a swordsman, he was shaken by what he'd just experienced. He would need all his wits about him if he hoped to best a king with centuries of fighting experience—prophecy or no.

"Who are you?" Pythius asked, crouched and waiting to see this king appear out of the gloom.

"You know well who I am, King Pythius."

Pythius could sense the man drawing closer. "How . . . how do you know me?"

"I knew you the moment you stepped into the realm of Elysiel." King Cakrin spoke evenly, and Pythius gritted his teeth. Lady Vitrella had misinformed him. How in the world would he be able to get the upper hand and slay this king? He could barely see two steps in front of his face, and no doubt the king had a sword at the ready, and eyes adjusted to the scant light. Cakrin had the advantage in his cavern of ice.

A chill soaked into Pythius's neck and traveled down his arms. He berated himself for touching the slab. It had been a foolish act that had rendered him vulnerable. If Cakrin knew all about him and why he'd come, what could he tell him? Any lie would be exposed. As he searched in vain for something to say to buy time and gain proximity to the scepter, Cakrin continued.

"And I have seen my future as well in the mirror of the sacred site. This very day. The day of my death."

Pythius gasped.

"Some believe the future can be changed . . ."

Now Pythius could make out a man striding slowly toward him, although he couldn't make out his features. Long hair fell over his broad shoulders, and to Pythius's surprise he carried no weapon in his hands, but there . . . the scepter! Even in the faint light Pythius could see the heart encased in the crystal handle, beating in a steady pulsing of unearthly light. His jaw dropped as an overwhelming longing consumed him.

". . . But it cannot. Here, the future is frozen in time, in these crystal slabs, like fish trapped in ice. You can break such ice into pieces, but the fish remains. You have come in treachery and out of a lust for power, but you have gotten a taste of the price of your action."

Pythius clenched his hand in remembrance of the unbearable pain. "You lie. Do not try to dissuade me from my path."

Cakrin came out of shadow and stood only feet in front of him, inside the circle, just on the other side of the slab where Pythius stood. "I cannot dissuade you. Our fates are sealed. But surely you have been warned. You cannot remove the scepter from Elysiel. Only the heirs can wield it and access the power of the *sha'har sha'mayim*. Your heinous act will only result in pain and death. Do you not know that the heart of the matter is a matter of the heart? Beware, oh King, of your own heart! If you allow it to harden, it will only crack and shatter. If you steal the heart of the king, you will lose your own. And that will mean your death."

The king raised his arm and Pythius stifled another gasp. The scepter shot a blast of vibrant blue light the color of sapphire into the cavern, illuminating the ice in a bath of surreal color. Crystal twinkled throughout the cavern—a million sparkling gems that throbbed with magnificent beauty. Pythius fixed his eyes on the solid piece of white crystal that was the scepter, so intricately engraved, housing the heart—a crystal heart beating with incomparable power and life.

Now he could make out Cakrin's stern face, and the lines around his eyes that caught the scepter's light and hinted at his age and agelessness. The king of Elysiel made no move as Pythius raised his sword and pushed the tip against his throat.

"I don't believe your lies!" Pythius spat. "Look at you—you are the fool! Standing here, defenseless, eager to go to your grave. It is you who will die, not I. I am the lion foretold! I have come from the thicket to seize the scepter and free the oppressed people of the northern Wastes—"

King Cakrin's laughter, as sharp as icicles, punctured the thick mood of the chamber. To Pythius's consternation, he continued to

---

chuckle, and shook his head, as Pythius pushed the point in harder until he drew blood.

"Why are you laughing?" Pythius screamed. His words reverberated off the cavern walls, and ice cracked and fell in large pieces to the ground. Pythius looked up and noticed the hefty hanging crystals shake from side to side. He forced his voice to a lower decibel. "I said, why are you laughing?"

"You have fallen victim to Vitra's propaganda. Oppressed people? Those in the northern Wastes are vile creatures that want nothing more than to skin their enemies alive and eat them without remorse. They have no reason or dignity. Vitra is only using you to retrieve the scepter for herself. And when you fail to deliver, she and her hordes will come after you with such vehemence, you will rue the day you ever heard the word *Elysiel.*"

"Shut up!"

"You saw your doom in the crystal mirror. What awaits you will not be thwarted. For there is another prophecy—one aimed at the lion from the thicket—"

"I said, shut up!"

"Of the serpent that will be spawned—"

With a roar of fury, Pythius plunged the sword deep into King Cakrin's throat. The cavern exploded in noise as ice shattered. The walls broke apart in massive chunks, and icicles fell from the ceiling like wayward spears. With a grunt, Pythius pulled his sword from Cakrin's neck, releasing the dead king in a slump on the ground. He covered his head with one arm as he dodged falling icicles, swinging his bloodied sword wildly above his head to deflect them. Icicles clattered in great dissonance as they speared the soft dirt, two impaling the dead king where he lay on his stomach, blood seeping alongside his head.

Soon, the clamor lessened, and Pythius watched a few more icicles dislodge and fall to the ground. Silence settled, and a chill ground fog enveloped his feet. He breathed hard, stunned and exhilarated, as he spotted the scepter a few feet away lying on the ground, undamaged. With his blood pounding his ears as noisy as ocean waves, he bent down, shaking and weak, and reached for the scepter.

It was his. All his. And the fool of a king had made no effort to protect it. Or his own life. What kind of king would go so willingly to his death—especially one who had fought his enemies for centuries?

Pythius hesitated. It made no sense. None at all. Still . . .

He refused to believe he had witnessed his future in the crystal slab. It had to be some trick. The future wasn't fixed; it hadn't yet occurred! At any moment one could alter course, change one's mind, take a different path. Cakrin had stupidly believed in fate, and because of that belief allowed a stranger to wander in and kill him. All that power, long life, dominion—he'd thrown it all away. For what? He hadn't even bothered to defend what he had sworn to defend. What a weak coward!

Pythius wrapped his hand around the scepter and waited. For what, he was unsure. He expected some surge of power or awareness or special knowledge to instantly fill him. But he sensed nothing. Yet the crystal heart still beat steadily in his grip. No matter. In time it would probably attune to him. He held it up to study it, marveling at the way it glowed an eerie blue, casting wide shadows. He looked over at the slabs and could now see the giant circle they formed.

He walked into the circle toward the center, and as he walked he chuckled. Calli had warned him if he touched the scepter he would surely die. Lady Vitrella was right. He had been lied to. King Cakrin had lied to him as well. And had called him a fool. And now the king lay dead on the cold ground in an icy cavern and he, Pythius, had the mighty scepter in his grasp. Who truly was the fool?

He took one last look at the sacred site, wondering just what power could possibly be trapped inside those monuments of crystal. Whatever secret they held would remain—at least for now. With the power he now wielded, he might find a way to unlock their mysteries. What if he could turn Paladya into a land as prosperous and fruitful as Elysiel?

Pythius strode to the mouth of the cavern, where the night lay draped across the landscape. A few stars winked in the sky, but the air outside blew warm—much to Pythius's delight. He hadn't realized how cold he was, and the warmth began to thaw his stiff fingers and the toes in his boots.

But as he stepped outside the entrance and onto the stone embankment, a howling wind kicked up from the north, riding fast and erratically over the mountains and sweeping down to where he stood, wrapping him in a frosty cyclone. The gritty wind whipped his hair and stung his eyes so that he could not see a thing. He tested his way, one step at a time, and edged along, burying his face deep in his cloak, which he wrapped tightly around his head. It was all he could do to stay on his feet and not topple down the uneven rock face to the jumble below.

He found some shelter under an outcropping of rock, but the wind did not relent. And the air, now freezing, burned his throat as he breathed in shallow spurts. He held the scepter out, hoping the blue pulsing light would better delineate his surroundings, but what it revealed sent a shiver of fear through his half-frozen limbs.

The ground beneath his feet had turned to ice, and he found himself stuck, unable to move an inch. With a determined yank, he managed to free his ice-encrusted boots and raced down the piles of boulders, aware of ice pursuing him, as relentless as the fiercest enemy. A quick glance behind him revealed the voracious ice had enveloped everything, turning the mountains to hoarfrost as it consumed rock and shrub alike. Breathlessly he ran, his heart hammering in his chest as he held the scepter aloft before him, using it to light his way in the darkness. Not surprised, he noticed his horse was nowhere in sight. The water squeezing out the sides of his eyes turned instantly to drops of ice that clattered at his feet. Was this strange weather the land's response to the Keeper's death? Would it last the entire night? He doubted he could keep running at this pace all the way to the boundary of the kingdom.

To his greater dismay, as he entered the lowland of vast prairie, the storm gained in fury. The grass turned brittle, then became buried in a sheet of ice. As quickly as a cloth soaked up water, the grassland became an ice-coated wilderness, more bleak and forlorn than any of the Barrenlands Pythius had traversed to arrive in Elysiel. Despite the cloak covering his head, his skull ached in pain from the cold, and he could no longer feel his fingers or toes. He had never experienced a wind this biting, gnawing at his bones and flesh and exhausting him as he battled against it to make headway across the open prairies.

Unable to press ahead without collapsing, Pythius lunged for the cover of a wide-spreading tree, its giant twisting branches full of leaves that created a thick canopy overhead. Leaning into the trunk, he caught his breath, but he found no comfort in his refuge. Ice quickly encircled the tree, then raced up the trunk to coat every bit of exposed wood. Within seconds, the leaves turned white and broke like glass in the snarling wind, dropping around his face and shattering into pieces. Soon, the tree was stripped bare, its exposed branches quivering as if in shock.

Pythius bemoaned this bad turn of luck. He squatted down and wrapped his arms around his knees, his teeth chattering so hard it made his jaw hurt. He didn't think he could be more miserable, although he reminded himself he had succeeded in his quest. The scepter was his! Surely once he made it across the boundary, he would leave the vicious storm behind. He would ride south to warmer climes, to his pristine harbor where his palace awaited him. Where he would then begin his crusade to dominate the known world!

Snow flurries swirled around his face as he dared a look out across what had been only yesterday a green, prodigious land drenched in heaven's blessing. Now, with its king dead and no Keeper to protect the sacred site, Elysiel was clearly vulnerable to the northern clime's harsh weather—although this storm smacked of more than just inclement weather. It was summer, and even the Barrenlands hadn't been this unbearable. Pythius could only conclude that heaven had withdrawn its favor, and perhaps was even punishing Elysiel for its years of hateful wars. How was that prophecy worded? The lion from the thicket would make the land desolate. Yes, that had to be the reason! The king's heart had per-ished, and the sacred site would no longer protect his people. They would pay for their centuries of evil. It had been foretold!

Pythius smiled even though his cracked lips throbbed in pain. It had been his destiny to steal the scepter. He had done heaven's bidding. Surely great power and reward awaited him back in Pala-dya. He tucked his head back into his cloak and closed his eyes to wait for morning. The wind no longer howled a threat but became a soothing song to his ears. He tucked the scepter tightly in his arms and pressed his frozen cheek against the smooth crystal, and the steady rhythmic heartbeat in its handle lulled him to sleep.

SEVEN

THE LADY VITRELLA reined her horse at the edge of the brook and slid off, careful not to fall. She chuckled at her clumsiness and the preposterousness of her form. She rather enjoyed this limiting human shape with all its foibles and eccentricities. And strange hungers. She had watched humans eat things like fruit and cheese, never understanding how such meager fare could appease hunger. But she had been so pleasantly surprised by the delight to her tongue—a delight that rivaled her enjoyment of raw entrails dripping with hot blood from a kill. And how gullible humans were! She had ambled into the tavern exuding human pheromones, drawing the riveted attention of every man in the room, aware of their increased pulse and excited imaginations. They practically drooled at her as she shimmied in between them and laughed at their flirtatious banter. If only they knew how she could tear them open with her teeth and spill their guts before they had a chance to even draw a breath.

It had been more years than she could count since she'd changed shape. As Vitra, the hated and feared *Tse'pha*, she wielded power and strength that no other shape would allow. But there had been times in the past when a disguise better served her purposes. And this was the most important time of all. Draining Cakrin's daughters of their collective beauty had been no easy feat.

Waylaying them on the southern road had not proved difficult. They often traveled together, without an entourage or bodyguards. Vitra had ensured all the roads south of Elysiel remained free from attack these last few decades—all in preparation for this one conquest. Endless hours she had schemed in the northern Wastes, in her baths of scalding water and mud, preparing for this eventuality. So it had only been a matter of time, a short wait, until those three had crossed the boundary unaware and unprepared for her attack.

She had restrained herself from mutilating and devouring them as she so greatly desired, for in order for the spell to work, their bodies had to become receptacles of exchange. Her vileness for their splendor. She let out a blustery laugh as she strolled along the brook, watching the first hint of daylight to ease over the horizon. Shame, though—for those princesses. The spell, when reversed, would return her to her own full form and power, but the damage would be done. No one tainted by her essence—not even for a mere few days—would ever truly recover. The marring was lamentable and couldn't be helped. Elysiel's princesses would never be called beauties again. Oh no, far from it. But at least they would have their lives. Or what was left of them. Surely they would be grateful for that.

Vitra stopped and listened. With her human ears, she had to strain to hear. Human senses were so deficient. She waved a hand in an arc over the rippling water, shifting the molecules to respond to her command. Water turned to ice, burning dry ice that steamed, and the surface of the brook became a mirror. In it she saw the king of Paladya, surrounded by snow and frost, running ragged and exhausted toward her. He was close now. She smelled his sweat and the residue of fear and excitement saturating his body.

Her eyes locked on to the scepter in his hand. He had done it—killed the Keeper and stolen the scepter from the gullible fool. One look at the ice-ravaged landscape told all. All life would now lay dormant and frozen in time—every human, animal, and insect—unless an heir to the throne appeared.

And she had made sure that could never happen. Every last heir was now dead. The binding of the scepter to the land had been finally severed, after agonizing centuries of waiting. When she killed the first Keeper, and King Lantas had given his heart in death to save his kingdom, she'd thought her victory to retake her land was complete. Then heaven had thwarted her yet again by placing that king's heart in the scepter and giving his heirs untold life and a binding to the land. But now! The power of the sites would be hers, and *her* land would no longer be under repression—by any Keeper of the site or by heaven. She and her kind could now return to their former dominion over the northern Wastes—unimpeded and unchallenged. And her first order of business once the scepter was hers and she unlocked its secrets would be to destroy the sacred site. She would summon all her power and channel it through the scepter, and those impermeable slabs of crystal would shatter as easily as panes of glass. What a thrilling sight to behold! One she had longed to see since the days heaven established the site eons ago to curb her power.

She squatted down at the edge of the mirror and looked at her true reflection. Her reptilian body shimmered with dark-green scales, and sharp claws extended from her wiry nimble hands. Her snakelike head rose up proud on a strong neck, and the fleshy tendrils of hair moved like hundreds of tiny snakes about her face, brown and green and gray, slithering over the scales of her cheeks and forehead and spilling down her crested spine. She was a beautiful ancient creature of the underworld, as old as time, spawned by the Great Serpent himself. She, in turn, had spawned thousands more over the centuries. And now, without the interference of either a Keeper or the guardians of heaven, she would loose her kind upon the world and devour it. Hers was the face of the Gorgon, feared the world over. One look directly into her unshielded eyes would turn any creature—man or beast—to stone. And that was all she would need to do to take the scepter from the simpleton Pythius from Paladya. She would revert to her true form, and in his horror he would stare at her face. She chortled in glee. His statue would make a nice entrance marker into Elysiel—now an abandoned, cursed, and frozen wasteland. A tribute and testimony to her consummate victory.

She laughed long and loud as Pythius, haggard and unsuspecting of his doom, arrived at the brook and stepped onto the ice.

Pythius fell to his knees on the smooth cold surface and stared at his reflection. His fingers stuck to the ice where he held them splayed. Contrary to his hopes, the morning had broken colder and the wind railed even more viciously. As he scanned the land around him, all of Elysiel lay buried under white, encased in a coat of frost. His parched throat ached for a drink, but there was no water to be found. He longed desperately to be rid of this storm, but now he worried he was somehow trapped. What if this brook was truly frozen and prevented him from exiting Elysiel? Just how, then, would he escape? Would he have to smash the ice, and if so, how? He had nothing but a sword and the fragile scepter.

He waited as before, sitting as still as he could, although his limbs trembled from exhaustion and cold. Fear gripped his gut as he envisioned himself turning into a block of ice, the scepter stuck in his tenacious grip for all eternity.

Then, as before, mist rose from the brook and swirled about his hands and knees. Colors broke apart and blended before his eyes, and Pythius stared, unblinking, as the sun appeared over the shoulder of his reflection, whereas the murky dark clouds of Elysiel hung over his head where he knelt. He smelled loamy soil and the perfume of wildflowers, the aroma intoxicating and welcome. Birdsong flitted on the air, tickling his ears and making him yearn for home.

Warm sun began to bake his shoulders, and he moaned in delight. The air around him brightened; the wind abated. Clouds gathered behind his reflection, and he stared at his own puzzled, frowning face as he watched snow pelt his mirror image and an erratic wind whip at his hair. He laughed in a roar and pulled his hands from the ice.

As he rose to his feet, his reflection remained fixed in place. All movement in the mirror froze as if Pythius looked upon a painting of himself in the midst of a turbulent storm. He wrenched his gaze from the disturbing sight and tipped his head back to drink in the warmth of a new morning outside the boundary of Elysiel. Ah, what a glorious feeling!

Stiff and sore, he stumbled off the surface of the brook, which slapped with riffles of water against the small boulders in its path as soon as his boots touched the sandy bank. He watched his footing as he clumsily crested the bank to the grassy knoll—and nearly ran into Lady Vitrella.

An uneasy feeling gripped him as he stood there, feeling strength and life return to his limbs. Her horse waited nearby, but no other. She was to bring him a horse so he could flee, or so he recalled. He studied her eyes, but they were veiled in secrecy. Without a doubt, he knew she was hiding her true intention. Oh yes, the power throbbed in his hand—a beacon to all. Who could resist its siren song? None.

He tightened his grip on the scepter and laid a hand on the pommel of his sword. A fierce rush of covetousness flared inside him at the thought she might wish the scepter for her own. At the thought of anyone desiring to steal what was now rightfully his.

The woman spoke to him but he could not hear her words. They sounded foreign, garbled. Their dulcet tones turned into a piercing screech, and Pythius resisted the need to cover his ears. He spun around and cowered at the noise, befuddled and enraged. Surely she was some kind of witch trying to bespell him!

He faced the brook once more and stared into its waters as he yanked his sword from his scabbard out of her notice. His jaw dropped in horror at what he saw alongside his reflection.

Coming down the embankment behind him was a repulsive, terrifying creature. A gigantic snake thing with reptilian scales and snakes for hair. The face, ugly and maleficent, sported long fangs dripping with slime, exuding a putrefying stench that made him gag. Whether this was an apparition or a dark creature summoned by the Lady Vitrella, he could not guess. But he wasted no time inquiring.

He flew around with a roar, squeezing his eyes shut, fighting the revulsion and nausea that gripped him in the creature's presence. With a hefty lunge, he slashed his sword in an arc through the air and felt the sharp blade slice through flesh. The ghastly shriek the beast emitted upon tumbling to the ground told Pythius he had not dealt it a death blow. But he had no desire to test the mettle of his foe; he wanted only escape.

As the creature lolled on the ground, gathering strength and seeking to raise its massive head, Pythius gagged and ran past it straight to the black steed, returning his bloodied sword to its scabbard. Lady Vitrella was nowhere in sight. Had she gone into hiding when she released this vile creature upon him? He threw the dangling reins over the horse's neck and leaped up into the saddle, gripping the scepter.

As he whooped at the horse and kicked its flanks, he felt the steady pulsing heartbeat rippling through the crystal shaft of the scepter, burning hot into the palm of his hand. He winced at the pain but had no time to strap it behind the saddle. Who knew what that creature was capable of? Pythius did not linger to find out. He prayed his horse could outride the evil that would surely follow.

Vitra wrapped her arms around her stomach, staunching the fountain of green blood draining from her body. Her fury squelched the pain. Every pore in her body screamed at the sudden transformation as her strained human shape reverted to its true form. She had forgotten the intensity of shifting and the temporary debilitation in summoning her innate strength. The human form limited her adeptness at wielding her power, and now hindered her body's quick healing properties. Having to call her true nature back from not one but three human receptacles at the same time proved much more complicated than she had anticipated.

She cursed her ill timing, knowing now she should have shifted long before Pythius stepped onto the ice. And she had no means of pursuit.

She rubbed her gut as the flesh began sealing closed, arresting the blood flow. She slithered down to the water and glared at her image, seeing bits of the glamour still tinging her flesh—a swath of golden hair, a patch of silky skin. She spat a glob of blood and green mucus into the brook, and the water began to boil and churn. Fish popped to the surface, belly up and panting for air, and Vitra stuffed handfuls of them in her mouth, the juices splurting over her face and running down the snaky tendrils of hair. When she felt sated and the water churned in a boil to drench her face, she slid into the scalding water and moaned in relief and frustration.

Her plan had failed. The fool king was off to his kingdom with the scepter. But it would do him no good—only bring pain and suffering, and he would curse the day he stole it. And now that he had incurred her wrath, his punishment would become unavoidable and absolute. For she had another plan, oh yes. One that would bring untold destruction and misery to the king of Paladya—for what she intended to unleash upon his city of weak and powerless men would bring terror into the hearts of all. And they would be powerless to stop her. She would exact a price Pythius would be unwilling to pay, and that would signal his ultimate ruin and the downfall of his short-lived monarchy. In one instant of time she could foresee the events laid out before her.

It would take many years of retreat in her den deep under the fires of the northern Wastes to spawn such great evil, drawing ancient power from the bowels of the earth to feed and nurture this one creature. She would have to pour every bit of her life blood and energy into its creation. But she would have it done—spawn a monster the world of men had never seen and would not be able to destroy. Pythius's demise would extend to all human flesh. And for that, she would bide her time willingly, gladly lay all her battles to rest and conserve her strength. She had tolerated humankind long enough. Why heaven favored such weak, impetuous, flawed bags of skin and bones, she could not understand.

Despite her contented resolve and anticipation of a future victory, she felt troubled by something inexplicable. At the moment King Cakrin had been slain, she should have sensed the land power dissipate. Elysiel should have grown instantly silent from the severing of the Keeper, and from the removal of the scepter. But a link still held—weak, yes, but undeniably there. Maybe it was Elysiel's last gasp at holding on to heaven's blessing. Perhaps in time it would peter out, the way a dwindling flame deprived of its oil gutters and then dies. Perhaps it was because the site still stood intact, Keeper or no.

She would not let this niggling warning distract her, though. It was time to put her next plan into action. And when she got the scepter back, she would shatter those crystal sentinels in the cavern of ice. Surely then her power would return in full measure.

Her wound nearly healed, she slipped under the surface of the roiling water, and with a flick of her long forked tail, swam upstream toward the northern Wastes.

Pythius squatted by his poor excuse for a fire, cradling his hands around the smoldering tinder and moss he had managed to gather from under piles of rocks that hadn't been drenched by the day's downpour. He had ridden hard through the rain, wishing he'd had his bags of dry clothes and oilcloth coat, seeming to recall they were tied behind the saddle of another horse he had ridden ages ago. At least the rain had finally abated. He raised his eyes to where his horse hung a tired head as it grazed without enthusiasm, then scanned the bleak expanse of flat empty land in the damp evening and sighed.

His journey was wearing on him. Even in the Barrenlands he could tell summer was losing its hold on the land. The coloration of the small shrubs and stunted birch and hickory testified to the encroaching fall, as did the colder nights that kept him hovering over his fires. At least the tundra he'd first encountered on his journey to Elysiel had dried enough to provide solid ground under his mount's hooves. With regret, he had traded Lady Vitrella's fine mare in one of the northern hamlets for a lesser horse in order to also afford stores, flint, and other necessities to get him through the weeks of desolate terrain.

As he rode, he worried that any moment he would be overtaken by that vile creature—or by some war band sent from Elysiel. He could only assume that the ferocious storm he'd left behind had blown through, and the king's subjects had discovered the body lying in the ice cavern—although his pursuers would have no idea of his identity. And if his days were troubled, his nights offered little respite, for that monster that had attacked him haunted his sleep, with its hideous face and fearsome fangs. In all his life he had never seen anything so terrifying and was glad he hadn't looked it in the eye, for he suspected the sight of its hungry gaze in such near proximity would have stopped his heart beating.

What concerned him most of all was the strange mark on his left palm that never ceased burning. He had thought that by now the pain would ease and the mark fade. He'd ridden with such urgency and concentration when he fled Elysiel, hours had passed before he realized his hand was inextricably clenched on the scepter—so that he'd had to painfully pry the crystal from his grip. When he finally freed it, the flesh had shredded and bled as if burned to the bone. Afraid to touch it again, he had wrapped the scepter in a piece of cloth and tied it to the back of the saddle. Why it burned him, he could not explain, for he'd carried it without trouble until he crossed the boundary of Elysiel.

With the small fire blazing and now hungrily eating the twigs and small branches Pythius fed it, he retrieved the precious bundle. He unfolded the cloth with care and stared at the scepter's beating heart that bathed the crystal shaft in iridescent blue light. The sight of its beauty made him suck in a breath. But it also set his hand aching, which made him race to retrieve his water skin and drench the wound, although the cool water did little to relieve his pain. Upon closer examination of his prize, it seemed to him that the heart beat a little fainter and the light shone dimmer than when he'd first beheld the scepter in the cavern.

A deep and abiding fear grew in his own heart. He did not want to believe the Keeper and his words of warning, that the vision he had seen in the crystal slab was a true portrayal of his future. He could only conclude that the Keeper had done something to the scepter to make it burn—enchanted it or coated it with some topical poison. And he'd somehow manifested that image on the crystal slab. He must have been a mage or trickster in addition to a king. But no matter. When Pythius returned to his palace, he would summon all those wise in medicine and magic and uncover the source of the scepter's shielding. And surely someone would have a balm to rid his hand of this infection or irritation or whatever it was.

He held his throbbing hand open and examined the mark. A dark gray heart sat in his palm, the center nearly black and so painful to the touch that Pythius groaned as he explored it with his fingers. He started at the realization that, rather than shrinking, the mark was spreading like a slow penetrating dye. Tendrils of gray now seeped into the base of all his fingers, making them difficult to bend. He reasoned that his hands were stiff from hours of gripping the reins; from too many days of arduous riding without gloves; from the harsh, unrelenting elements. Surely that was making the irritation spread.

He pushed his fears aside and warmed his damp bones by the fire. Then he stripped off his wet outer garments and laid them out on the small scrub bushes around his makeshift camp. In just a few more weeks he should be able to see a glimpse of the towering Paladin Mountains to the south, now that he was on the straight stretch of the Great Northern Road. And then a short journey over the King's Pass, and Paladya and Tranquil Harbor would come into view. What a glorious sight that would be.

He had thought the prospect of returning to his palace and resuming his rule would invigorate him the closer he neared the capital city. But instead, a growing apprehension spread in his gut just as steadily as the blotch on his hand. A malaise settled on his heart, like the touch of an icy finger. He would have been away most of a year—too long a time to vacate the throne. Yet if he discovered treachery had wormed its way into his palace, he would show no mercy. He had threatened Urstus with death should he allow any to usurp his monarchy. Still, he dreaded what he would find upon his arrival. Would his advisors think he'd tarried too long and assume he was dead? Well, no matter; he would soon find out.

The thought of Calli struck him suddenly. Surely she would have given birth by now. Long weeks had passed since he thought of her. Why, he barely recalled what she looked like. Had she obeyed his charge to mind Urstus? He frowned thinking of the deceitful way she had misinformed him about Elysiel and the scepter. Her independent streak was a challenge to his authority as well. He needed her compliance to keep his dissenters mollified, yet if she chose to resist him in any way upon his return, he would show no leniency—wife or no.

Perhaps the baby she'd birthed could be used as leverage. Didn't all mothers dote on their children? He wondered briefly if he was now father to a son or daughter. No matter. If having children kept his wife submissive and his enemies reluctant to attack his house, or gave him the appearance of a settled family man, then it would serve his purposes. His wife, busy with mothering, would leave him alone to unlock the power of the scepter, and he would turn all his attention on conquering neighboring lands and searching for more of those mysterious sites with their unlimited fount of power.

He glanced once more at the crystal scepter, lying near the fire, the heart beating steadily but faint. There had to be a way to access its power. To join the heart with his own. He refused to believe the lies Cakrin and Calli told him—that the scepter would only work for the heirs of Elysiel and only within the borders of that land. Power was power. And if magic locked the power within the scepter, then magic could *unlock* it. No doubt that was why Lady Vitrella had tried to steal the scepter from him by setting her vile monster upon him. She must have known the scepter could be wielded by one who was not a Keeper. It might take him years, but he would uncover the truth. And heaven help anyone who stood in his way.

EIGHT

CALLI PACED fretfully, holding her three-month-old son in her arms. She wished the babe wasn't teething and fussing; she so wanted Pythius to see his little toothless smile when he entered their bed chamber. For months she had dreaded her husband's return, unsure what his disposition would be. And when she heard the heralds sound the horns and watched Pythius ride into the courtyard below hours earlier, a sickening feeling of anxiety came over her. Would he be glad to see her? Had he missed her at all? She hoped upon seeing his new son he would soften, that his hard edges and brusque manner would give way to tenderness, not just for her sake but for the child's.

She looked with adoration upon Collin's sweet face. She had named him after her paternal grandfather, as was the custom in Elysiel. She hadn't thought to ask Pythius for his choice in a name before he left on his hasty quest. Perhaps he would choose another for their babe, but she didn't care. As long as her husband would love him and protect him—that was all that mattered. Surely he must want to see her and the child. No doubt Urstus had much urgent news, needed to fill the king in on the affairs of recent months during his absence. Despite rumors of unrest and secret uprisings, Calli had not witnessed anything unsettling from her perch high above the city. No doubt troubling affairs went on below these mighty stone walls out of her earshot. But during her pregnancy, her every concern was for the well-being of her babe. She'd even stopped visiting Caryn, and sent a carriage to fetch her aunt to bring her to the palace instead. She'd never felt unsafe before, walking along the seedy streets that led to the docks, but she had feared to take any chances now that she was queen. Before, she was a nobody, a young woman taking care of a sick aunt. But now she would be recognized as Pythius's wife. Who knew what enemies of the realm might be lurking, waiting to wreak their revenge upon her for the cruelties meted out to House Ardea?

So she'd spent most of the summer sequestered in the palace and in comfortable ignorance of the affairs of Paladya, whiling away the hours stitching needlepoint or knitting soft sweaters for the babe to come. When autumn brought its cold, brisk winds sweeping up through the palace windows, reminding her that the harsh northern winters must already be pummeling the Barrenlands, she wondered if Pythius would ever return. He had been gone so long.

More than anything, she wanted word from her father. All this time—nothing. No response to any of her letters. The silence boded something terrible. But surely, Pythius would have news for her. Maybe even a letter he'd been given to hand-deliver. There had to be a simple explanation for why she had heard nothing from Elysiel.

She stopped her pacing as the door blew open. Pythius strode in, wearing fine clean garb that hung a loosely on his frame. She noticed that he had lost some weight, and his face looked wan and haggard, despite his clean shave and neatly trimmed hair that fell over his shoulders. His eyes drank her in, and her heart fluttered as it had the first time they'd met. He was surely a handsome man, and his noble bearing and dark eyes reminded her of why she had fallen for him from the moment they'd met.

"My Lord," she said, and bowed her head. She hoped he would take her in his arms and tell how much he had missed her, but when she looked up, he was studying the babe.

"A handsome child," he said, appearing as if he might be afraid to touch his own son. "Have you given him a name?"

Calli wondered at his unemotional response to seeing his son. "I call him Collin, after my grandfather, but if you prefer a different name—"

"That will do. The child is . . . well?"

"Yes, My Lord." She held him out to her husband. "Would you like to hold him?"

Pythius hesitated, then took the bundle from her arms. A hint of a smile rose on his face as the baby stared curiously into Pythius's eyes. "He has your eyes," he said, "so pale, like . . . ice . . ."

"But he has your strong chin—and your thick hair."

"Yes," Pythius said, his thoughts wandering somewhere. "He will be a handsome child, no doubt." He gave her back the babe without another word.

He looked suddenly at her. "And you—how do you fare?"

"Well, My Lord." She bit her lip, afraid to voice the question tearing at her heart. "And my father. And brothers. Did you see them—were they well?" The fear made her throat close tight.

He waved a hand in the air and looked out the large window to the harbor. "Yes, fine. They were all fine and glad to hear of our marriage. They . . . sent their blessings and regards."

Calli's body trembled. Surely there was more, but she didn't want to press Pythius. He'd only been back a few hours. Maybe in the evening, once he'd had time to eat and rest, they could talk. And she could learn more of his visit to her land. She dared one more question.

"And how does King Cakrin fare? Did he welcome you with graciousness and celebration?"

"With open arms. I must say, Elysiel is an amazing land, bountiful and blessed. It is truly all you said it would be."

Calli wondered at his unenthused tone.

A knock sounded at the door and Urstus stepped inside. "Excuse me, My Lady. Sire, the seer is here, as you requested."

Pythius nodded to Urstus, and the advisor left.

Seer? Calli knew of no seer. Why would Pythius want to speak with someone like that? She glanced down and only now noticed his left hand covered with a thick black leather glove. She reached out to touch his wrist, but he swung around and yanked his hand away.

"What happened to your hand, My Lord? Were you injured?"

"It's nothing serious. Just a little . . . mishap along the way. The healer will look at it this afternoon."

"I see." Calli rocked the babe in her arms as he began to fuss again.

Pythius looked once more at his son. She asked, "Are you happy? You are now a father; you have an heir to continue your lineage. I have put off christening him until your arrival. Should I make the preparations for his naming?"

She watched him clench and unclench his gloved hand, as if it were stiff and painful. Another knock came, and Agatha, her attendant, peeked into the room. Upon seeing the king, her face paled. "I'm sorry to intrude, please forgive me—"

"No, it's fine, Agatha. Come in," Calli told her.

"Just bringing the fresh swaddling clothes and blankets for the babe, ma'am."

Pythius stepped back. "Well, Urstus is waiting." He nodded once, a perfunctory, polite gesture void of any affection. She had so hoped for more, but at least he had smiled at his son. Maybe in time . . .

Agatha placed her bundle atop the dresser and turned to Calli. "How does His Majesty seem to you, ma'am?"

Calli pursed her lips. "I imagine this is all so very much for him to take in—coming home after so long, seeing his son."

"Yes. 'T'would be, I am sure. But I hope he was pleased with little Collin." Her eyes brightened, and she came close and cooed at the babe, who made a little squeal of delight. "How could anyone not love you, you little muffin?"

Calli smiled, then remembered Pythius's appointment. "Agatha, the king has sent for a seer. Do you know who this seer is, and why the king might consult one?"

Her eyes widened, and Calli thought she detected fear. "King Declan had a seer, ma'am. Creepy, they are."

"How so?"

"All them seers, they come from a holding up in Torth, far to the west. Chosen when they're young, and kept in dark rooms. Or so word has it. They say they can see the future, and they're never wrong."

"Why does that distress you, Agatha?"

"Well, seems to me it's unnatural—to know what's to come. Wouldn't want to know things like when I'm to die, or if an accident was to befall me. Couldn't do nothing about it but watch it happen . . ."

"Yes, I agree." Is that what Pythius wanted—to know his future, in order to try to prevent anything disastrous from occurring? What had prompted him to seek out a seer the same day he arrived home? This news did not sit well. Something disturbing must have happened to him on his journey. And it seemed so odd—Pythius had met her father and brothers and said all was well, yet she had still heard no word from anyone in Elysiel. Surely the moment her father had heard firsthand of her marriage to Pythius, he would have sent his congratulations. Or a gift or letter given to Pythius to deliver to her upon his arrival home. But Pythius had presented nothing to her. This disturbed her greatly.

"Agatha." She signaled the girl to come close and whispered, "If there is any way you can busy yourself close enough to overhear the king and this seer, I would be grateful. I would like to know what it is that concerns the king."

"Yes, My Lady," Agatha said with a solemn nod.

"But take care and be cautious. It would not be wise for you to be caught listening."

"Yes, My Lady." Agatha's face showed she was very aware of the punishment that would await her should she be found eavesdropping.

"Thank you," Calli said. She watched her attendant leave the room and turned to stare out the window. Boats rocked like small toys in the swells of the harbor, and leaves whirled in the air, kicked up by the erratic fall winds buffeting the stone walls. She looked upon Collin's face—his sleepy eyes and gentle mouth. She never knew she could love anyone as much as she loved her small son. She hoped, in time, Pythius would grow to love him too. If he didn't, she feared what might become of Collin, knowing the viciousness of the lion that paced beneath the king's scrutinizing gaze.

"You are blind!" Pythius declared upon entering the library. He circled the aged man, who stood unmoving in the center of the room, his hands clasped behind him, his eyes white, as if all pigment had been flushed away by some strange illness. A long gray beard dangled down his chest like ragged cloth, and he wore a strange silver earring in his left ear. He seemed utterly serene, as if he were asleep on his feet. Pythius grunted. Perhaps he was asleep.

Urstus cleared his throat. "This is Xio Xsu. He is Declan's most favored seer—"

"Yes, yes, but how can he see if he is blind?" Pythius threw his hands up in the air. The old man didn't even flinch at his words. Was he deaf as well?

"Sire," Urstus offered, "all seers of note are blind. They are born that way, and chosen carefully for their gift."

"Gift." Pythius sulked. The seer apparently didn't mind being spoken about as if he weren't there. "Explain," Pythius said to the seer.

The blind man understood he was being addressed. "We are taught to heed the augury from the time we can speak, oh King. There, in the dark, and in silence, we learn first to see, and then hear. The augury speaks at will, when it knows a seer is waiting for a vision."

Pythius felt he was the blind and deaf one. Nothing this man said made sense.

"And this . . . augury—it tells you of future events. Can you ask it questions?"

"No, oh King. It will tell you what you must know, and no more. It shows a seer what will be and what must be said."

Pythius stifled a laugh. "And pray tell me, did this augury warn King Declan of the invasion that took his life? It does not appear so, for he was taken unawares that night my father raided this palace."

The seer said nothing in response. *This is foolishness. A blind man seeing what is to come.* But since the man was already here . . .

"Tell me, seer. Has the augury given you a vision or word for me?"

"Yes, oh King, it most certainly has. I was given the vision many months ago, and that is why I came to Paladya to await your return."

Pythius's heart pounded hard. "You knew I would summon you."

"Of course," the seer answered evenly.

Pythius grunted. "Well then, tell me this word you have for me." He turned to Urstus. "You may leave us alone now. And send the healer to my private chambers; have him wait until I am finished here."

"As you wish, Sire."

Pythius could tell Urstus wanted to stay to hear the seer's proc-lamation. Of course he would. If the seer had some bad tidings to declare, that nosy advisor would spread rumors throughout his kingdom. No doubt Urstus had spent these many months under-mining Pythius's monarchy, seeking alliances so he could gain power, although Pythius was certain it would take some effort to uncover his duplicity. Well, he had spent many nights while on his long journey thinking of a way to "dispose" of his father's leftovers. And that would be his next order of business, after he had this foul pain in his hand healed. First things first.

Once the library door clicked shut, he turned his full attention upon the seer.

"Speak, man, and tell me what you will." He smiled and wan-dered around the room, touching the heavy metal sculptures King Declan had collected and put on pedestals to display. They were of noble and mighty beasts—including a lion, lowered on its haunches, eyes fixed on some prey in the distance. *If only Declan had known in advance the lion had planned to pounce. Why wouldn't the augury have foretold that? Did Declan deserve his fate, and was that why he had not been forewarned? Or was this "seeing" just a ruse, a way to pander to royalty and be paid in gold?*

The seer spoke in a deep, clear voice not his own. "The augury says, 'What have you done, oh King? Great treachery leads to grim punishment. The sin of the father is visited on the son. As the son has done to the father, so shall be done to the son.' "

A chilling pain stabbed Pythius's heart. "What . . . this is gib-berish, man! What are you saying—speak plainly!"

"A seer can only speak what the augury tells him to speak. However, I can tell you what I see."

"Yes, yes! Tell me." He put his gloved hand over his heart, as if to still it. His palm throbbed mercilessly. *That healer better have something to rid me of this pain—and the blotch that is staining my hand.*

The seer continued to speak evenly, unemotionally. "I see a barefoot boy with a knife in his hand. He moves like a lion in the dark and comes upon his prey. With a swift slice"—the seer moved his arm in a sudden motion as if wielding a knife, and Pythius jumped back—"he cuts his father's throat. Blood drenches the bed-clothes and spills to the floor. He wipes his blade and returns to his bed, no one the wiser."

Pythius stood unblinking, his jaw slack. What witchery was this? How could this man have known he had killed his own father in his sleep? Or was he only guessing based on rumors? Surely rumors must have spread throughout Paladya—spread by Declan's previous supporters, wanting to shift the blame off House Ardea and onto his father's inner circle. Yet . . . the seer's description was too specific to be ignored. How he had padded in his bare feet to his father's bed, how the blood had splurted all over his bedclothes and he'd had to bury them outside the palace walls in the dark under a moonless night.

The seer remained still. "As the son has done to the father, so shall be done to the son."

Pythius nearly spit in the man's face, but the seer stood calm and unruffled. "What does that mean? You said the sin of the father is . . . what?"

"Visited upon the son. Oh King, just as you murdered your father in cold blood, so shall your son murder you."

"My son . . .?"

"The augury has revealed it. It will come to pass."

"You mean my son—the babe just born."

"You cannot run from your fate, oh King. You have set your heart as the heart of a god. You have stolen the heart of the king, and therefore you will lose your own."

Pythius choked. Those were King Cakrin's exact words! But was the seer speaking of the king of Elysiel or of his own father, Linys? Or both?

The seer, with his white orbs in his head, seemed to stare at Pythius in disdain. "The augury strikes where the heart lies. Where, oh King, does your heart *lie*?"

Pythius's mind jolted to the chest in which he had placed the scepter, now hidden under his bed and locked, away from curious eyes. That was where the heart now lay, beating, waiting, until he could find a way to harness its power. But he sensed the seer was not speaking of that heart. *Where does your heart lie?* The seer's words rang through his head. He thought of a proverb from his childhood: "Where your treasure lies, there your heart will be also." Was he asking what his heart was set upon, or did he mean lie, as in not telling the truth? His heart held many lies, and he would not stand for any of them to be exposed. Certainly not from some witless, blind, and senile spouter of doom.

Pythius let out a loud laugh. "You are making all this up, you old fool. I never murdered my father. And how can anyone predict what a mere babe will do years from now?" He took the seer's arm in a rough grasp and dragged him to the door. The seer complied without resisting.

"The augury has spoken. Oh King, it will come to pass."

We shall see about that! There was one sure way to prevent the seer's prediction from coming true. His son could never kill him . . . if he were dead. Then what would the seer's precious augury have to say? Pythius threw open the door to the library and looked for Urstus. No one was in the hall except the girl who waited on his wife. She was busy dusting the baseboards on her hands and knees. He held tightly to the seer's arm as he said, "Girl, go fetch Urstus for me."

"Yes, Sire," she said with bowed head.

She promptly jumped to her feet and ran down the hall.

When Urstus approached unattended, Pythius said quietly to him, not caring that the seer could hear him, "Take him far from the palace. Then kill him."

Urstus gulped as he nodded. "As you wish, Your Majesty."

Pythius scowled as he watched Urstus lead the seer down the long hallway and out through the double glass doors, the aged man unflinching and cooperative. *Truly a fool. See how he goes to his death completely unbothered?*

He realized he was holding up his gloved hand. Unbearable pain shot through his fingers, and he ground his teeth at the pain that was getting worse each hour. His mind flashed in memory at the terrible sensation he had felt when staring at the crystal slab in the ice cavern—the sensation that he had carried this awful burden of pain for years, and it had so worn him down he was beyond exhaustion. He shook his head trying to fling the memory away.

No matter. The healer awaited him. And if this healer could not find a way to remove the pain and rid his hand of the blight, he would summon every healer in the kingdom and beyond— even every herbalist and practitioner of magic. Whatever it took. He was the king of Paladya—he had ultimate power and wealth. No one would refuse him. Surely there was *someone* in all his realm who could cure him of this bewitchment or poison or whatever afflicted him.

He stood at the glass doors and looked out upon the garden, sensing an unnerving presence, as if the king of Elysiel were breathing on his neck. He spun around and looked about the room but saw no one. Yet . . . he was sure someone was there. King Cakrin's words echoed loudly in his head as if he were standing beside him, in that very room: *"You are seeing a piece of your future . . ."*

"I will not believe your lies, King Cakrin," he spoke aloud to the air with a bitter anger, spinning one way then another, searching for the source of the voice. "You are dead, and soon this seer will be dead as well. I will not stand for anyone to oppose me. I have the scepter; it is mine! And if it is destined for my son to kill me, well, he will not get his chance. Come morning, I will kill him myself, by my own hand. What do you have to say to that, *oh King?*"

A sharp pain raced across the back of his neck and down to his gloved hand. He gritted his teeth against the next wave of torment and tromped up the stairs to his private chamber, where the healer awaited him. Still, the words of the seer swarmed in his mind.

"The augury strikes where the heart lies. Where, oh King, does your heart lie?"

NINE

CALLI PATTED her son on his back as he sucked on his tiny fist, fighting sleep. She pulled the wool blanket she'd knitted for him up around his chin and rocked the cradle in a gentle motion until he finally drifted off. She would now have a few hours to rest herself; her nerves were frayed from worrying.

It took all her resolve not to pack and flee for Elysiel, back to where she knew she would find love and security in the arms of her family and under the protection of her king. More than ever before she felt unsettled, unhappy, and unsure of her future. She'd thought being the queen would afford her security and protection, but she felt vulnerable now with Pythius returned. Neither his presence nor his words gave her any comfort; rather, her dread and fear had only multiplied since he rode into the courtyard.

"My Lady!"

Calli turned at the frantic whisper. "Agatha," she said in an undertone, "what is it?" She had never seen the girl so afraid. Calli's own heart trembled in fear at the stricken look on her attendant's face.

"Oh, My Lady, 'tis bad, very bad."

Calli walked to the door and looked down the hall, then shut the door with a quiet click. She took Agatha's hand and led her to the far corner of her chamber, so they could speak without the possibility of anyone overhearing.

"H-His Majesty the king plans to kill the little babe."

Calli felt the blood drain from her face. She opened her mouth to protest, but no words would come.

Agatha grasped Calli's hands and squeezed them. "My Lady, you must go, now! I heard what the king said—that it was foretold his son would kill him. That Collin would one day do this deed! And so he means to kill the babe on the morrow." She gulped and shuddered. "He is mad, My Lady. Mad and wild."

"Where is he now?" Calli breathed out in terror.

"In his private chamber, seeing a healer."

Calli's mind spun with panic. *Leave, how? To where?* "Anyplace I go, he will find me." The stark truth of her words stuck her. No, Pythius would never let up in his search should she flee. There would be no safe haven anywhere in Paladya. And no doubt he would offer a large reward for her capture. All eyes would be on the watch for her.

"My Lady, I will give you some of my clothes. And help you pack a bag. Vinny, the stable boy, can get you a horse. He has no affection for the king, and he's a friend—"

"No, no one else can know. And a horse will be . . . too noticeable. I must . . . sneak out somehow . . ."

"Through the delivery tunnels, My Lady. They open out below the palace, down by the marketplace."

Calli nodded. "You'll have to show me." How suddenly her serene life had been upended!

"Of course, My Lady."

She took her faithful attendant's hands. "Agatha . . . you must come with me! You will not be safe from the king's wrath once I've gone. He will know you are an accomplice."

"Don't fear for me, Majesty. I'll be fine here, and perhaps I can . . . mislead the soldiers, tell them you've gone . . . somewhere."

"You cannot say my aunt's—they would surely kill her if she denies having seen me." *Oh, poor Carryn—when she finds out I've gone missing! It will break her heart.*

"I'll say you made for the coach—to take you to Yammer. That will send them east. Will that do?"

"Yes, oh I suppose." But where to go? The only place her heart longed for was Elysiel. Somehow she had to find a way out of the city and home. But wouldn't that be the first thing Pythius would expect? She would have to stay off the Great Northern Road, and avoid the King's Pass. She could follow the coast! The small dirt roads were difficult for carriages, and sometimes even for horses, as the tide often washed over the roads and filled the estuaries, forcing travelers to scramble over boulders and through brush from one village to the next. Or so she'd heard. She'd never visited any of the quaint hamlets outside Tranquil Harbor, but she'd heard of the village of Blunt, at the mouth of the Irt Estuary. She thought hard, trying to recall the maps she'd seen stretched out across the library tables. Blunt was situated on the southern shore of Buddle Bay. But how long would it take for her to walk there? Were there any marked roads or would she wander lost? She would need to procure a map. And she had to pack! The magnitude of her task overwhelmed her.

Fear coursed through her limbs as she thought of the way Pythius had held Collin in his arms, and had almost smiled at his son. How could any man murder his own child? It was unthinkable! Yet somehow she knew Pythius would not hesitate—if he thought one day his son would kill him. Only now did she realize what an evil man she was married to. The sooner she fled, the better. *Oh, Collin—how will I keep you safe?*

Calli hurried to prepare a small bag of clothes for her and the babe. She didn't need much; she could buy what she needed once she was far enough away. She went to her writing desk and pulled open the drawer, then took out parchment, pen, and ink, and a pouch full of gems and gold coins. Pythius had given her the gems and gold as a marriage gift. Little did he know she would use them to finance her escape!

Agatha appeared at her side with servant's clothes in her arms. "Put these on, My Lady, and the cap. If you tuck your hair up underneath, you won't be recognized. But hurry!"

In a flurry of despair and hopelessness, Calli threw off her garments and donned the plain garb Agatha had brought her. Then, as ready as she could be, she gathered up her son in his blankets and hid him under the cloak she draped over her arm. Agatha peeked out into the quiet hallway. Calli figured the servants were having lunch or busy with their chores. She hoped she could slip out of the palace unnoticed.

Agatha signaled her to follow. Calli kept a ways back, in case Agatha encountered anyone. *Please, God*, she prayed, *grant me safe leave of this place, and watch over this precious babe. Show me where to go, where we will be safe from the king's wrath.*

Thankfully, they met no one. Agatha led her down the stone stairs to the outside garden, then in through a small weathered side door, one Calli had never noticed before. Agatha shut the door behind them, immersing them in darkness. The scent of mildew and ocean spray assaulted her nostrils in the damp, confining space. Calli could make out Agatha reaching into her apron pocket and pulling out a flint. She rocked her son, who was beginning to fuss from being carried so hurriedly through the palace. *Please, Collin, go back to sleep. Don't start to cry!*

Agatha took a torch down from the sconce on the wall and used the flint. With a deft stroke of her hand, she set the torch aflame. "We keep these torches soaked in lamp oil, so we can use these tunnels on a moment's notice. Easier way to get to and from market."

Calli wondered if Pythius and his guards knew about these tunnels. Surely they must. She kept glancing back as they hurried through the passageway hewn from stone, careful not to trip on the rough uneven ground. Collin, much to Calli's relief, fell back asleep.

After what felt like an hour, Calli spotted light ahead. Soon a fresh breeze wafted in and she breathed deeply, wary but relieved to have come thus far. They emerged from the stone wall only yards from the edge of the street market. She scanned the crowded streets, packed at midday with shoppers and vendors. Perhaps she could pass unnoticed after all.

Her heart pounded at the realization she was truly leaving. Not just leaving Paladya, but her aunt, her life as queen, her marriage—everything—never to return. She fought back tears as she thanked Agatha with a tight embrace and handed her three gold coins.

"No, My lady, I couldn't take these—"

"You must. You may need them should your life be in danger." She closed Agatha's fist around the coins. "Please take care."

"Don't worry, My Lady. Just get someplace safe." Agatha placed a hand on the babe's head, then leaned over and gave him a gentle kiss. "Heaven be with ye."

"And with ye as well." Calli watched as Agatha hurried back to the tunnel entryway. *Safe? Was there truly anyplace safe from the king's rage?*

As she hurried through the bustling market toward the harbor, keeping her head down, she knew in her heart that no matter how far she traveled, wherever she went, Pythius would not stop until he found her and the babe. She thought of all the men at his command, not just in the palace, but stationed throughout the city. They would be looking for a woman and a baby. They would search every road until they found her. Who could she trust to help her? No one. Not with a price soon to be on her head. Anyone who had seen a woman carrying an infant would confess, and tell in which direction she had been headed.

Tears flooded her face as she hurried down one cobbled street after another, working her way north as the sun arced the sky. After looking back repeatedly, she trusted she hadn't been followed or spotted. Collin began crying, needing to be fed. She uncovered his blankets and looked at his sweet face. It broke her heart to know the danger he was in.

She ducked down a narrow street and hid on a recessed stoop of an old derelict wharf building to nurse her son. A few men walked the street, carrying ropes and boxes toward the harbor. They took no note of her. Now that she had stopped hurrying, the cold fall wind sweeping off the ocean sent shivers down her neck. Winter was coming, and from what she could tell, a storm was brewing over the sea. She would have to find some shelter for the night, but where? Would she be able to sneak her babe into an inn and take a room without being reported later? If Pythius offered gold as a reward, mouths would talk. She wished now she had brought some smaller coin. Her gold would be noticed, and suspect. A servant carrying gold? What was she thinking? They would accuse her of being a thief.

Hopelessness washed over her anew and made her knees collapse. In the shadow of the portico, she nursed her babe and cried. She would never get away, never be safe. Come morning, Pythius's guards would find her and drag her back to the palace to be punished. And Collin would be murdered.

Oh, dear God, show me what to do. Show me how to save my precious son!

Every muscle in her body ached as she stood and stretched. Her feet throbbed in the too-small ratty leather boots Agatha had given her. Clouds billowed overhead, and she heard the slosh of water against wooden pilings in the harbor. The squawking of the circling gulls jabbed at her like pointed warnings, as if telling all the world where she could be found.

It was no use. She was on foot. The king's guards would soon be searching for her on horseback, by carriage, marching up and down every street, knocking on every door. She could never outrun them. If only she could climb into a cart, hide unnoticed under boxes or goods destined for a coastal village. Or perhaps . . . board a boat!

Yes, if she could find a boat readying to leave, she could stow away on board. She'd never been at sea before, and the ocean looked menacing and treacherous, but she would rather face its terrors than the ones awaiting her on land.

She wrapped Collin tightly in his swaddling blankets and ran to the docks, keeping her bag hidden under her cloak in case there were unsavory men about. But when she arrived at the docks, the boats were tied at their moorings, and all the fisherman had gone home for the day. No doubt they'd seen the approaching storm and made for the harbor before the swells grew formidable. Fat, cold raindrops spattered her face as she stood on one dock and stared at the darkening horizon. The waves looked angry and menacing as water slapped against the stone seawall.

She fell in a heap on the rotted wood planking, her heart surrendered to hopelessness. It was no use. She may as well just throw herself and her babe into the sea and end this. She would rather die at the hand of God than at the hand of man. Maybe heaven would have mercy on her soul, and on Collin's soul as well. Her heart wrenched in the knowledge she had not even given him a proper name christening.

A strange calm resolve came over her as she settled into her decision to end their lives. The ocean seemed to beckon to her, lulling her with its power and strength. Her thoughts drifted like a tide, washing up images of her father and brothers onto the shores of her mind. Oh why had she left Elysiel? If only she had stayed. Then she would never had met Pythius nor married him. But then . . . she would never have been given this beautiful babe, and even though she knew she would soon be parted from him, she hoped heaven would reunite them in the kingdom awaiting all those who strove to be true and faithful.

Oh, what will you have me do? She raised her eyes to the tumultuous heavens; the sky roiled as if God himself were raging in fury over the injustice of her life. *Is there even a tiny chance for hope? Some way to save my son?*

Knees shaking in fear, she stood at the edge of the dock, holding Collin tightly in her arms, staring at the turbulent sea. She drew in deep breaths in preparation for the shock of the water and the end of her life. However, just as she meant to leap, something glinted in the corner of her eye. She turned her head and spotted a large box floating off the side of the pier, and heard wood smacking against wood as the object knocked against the piling.

A sliver of sun slicing through the cloud cover caught on the object's metal detailing. Calli walked over and bent down to find a large wooden trunk. The latches and hinges shone like gold, although Calli guessed they were only brass. The odd light from heaven illuminated the old trunk in a way that reminded her of the light in Elysiel—the way the sun lit up the countryside on a fresh spring morning, with a clear, unhindered sheen that almost seemed to glow. She'd never really noticed how unusual was the light that drenched Elysiel until she left her homeland and lived in Paladya. Here the sunlight was dull in winter and harsh in summer.

She pulled the trunk up against the dock and fumbled with the latches. Why she was bothering, she did not know. But she was nudged by curiosity at seeing the strange light bearing down, as if heaven were telling her to notice. Maybe there was something in the trunk that could help her. But what could that be?

Unable to grasp the latches as the trunk bobbed and pitched in the swells, she carefully set Collin down on her coat and leaned over to haul the trunk up out of the water. It was surprisingly light, allowing her to lift it up onto the dock effortlessly. How odd.

Rain now beat down in a steady patter, soaking her clothes as she worked at the latches. Finally, her numb fingers managed to pry up the metal clasps and she threw open the lid . . . only to find the trunk empty.

Her heart sank yet again. Well, what had she hoped to find? A means of escape? A bitter laugh escaped her mouth. She looked around at the large fishing boats clunking against their moorings. She did not know a thing about operating a boat. Setting off to sea would only delay their inevitable demise. And she didn't have the heart to steal what was another's sole livelihood.

She looked again into the trunk. Someone had spread pitch in all the places where the pieces of wood abutted, making the trunk seaworthy. Not a drop of water had found its way inside the closed trunk. She fingered the lid and noticed small holes. Why would someone put those there? She counted twenty-four, spaced evenly throughout the lid, yet no water had come through those holes, even thought the trunk had no doubt pitched and yawed in the sea's swells.

A loud shout made her spin around as she knelt on the dock. Her heart nearly stopped beating. Palace guards! Already groups of Pythius's men in their black-and-red uniforms were searching the harbor. How had they come so quickly? She watched them scouring the nearby lanes, keeping her head hidden as best she could. Soon they would find her. She had run out of time. Pythius must not be allowed to get hold of Collin!

Her eyes lighted on the trunk again. It certainly was too small to provide her with escape . . . but her son would fit inside just perfectly. Oh, how could she even think of sending her babe off into the sea? Yet . . . wouldn't that be better than drowning him? What if this was heaven's answer to her desperate prayer?

She heard more guards calling out in the streets as the rain now pelted her in a steady downpour. She had no other choice. Without another thought, she pulled blankets from her bag, then positioned her sleeping son in the center of the trunk. She tucked the pouch of gold and gems under his head, then pulled out a piece of parchment and her pen and ink and somehow managed to write a hasty note explaining who this babe was and how his identity must be kept secret at all costs. The ink ran from her tears and the invading raindrops, and she had no time to properly allow the parchment to dry. But it would have to do. She laid the note carefully on her babe's chest, hoping some kind fisherman might find the trunk once the storm passed, and take Collin home and care for him, raise him as his own. Oh, what a foolish thing to hope for! Surely she was sending her son to his death.

She kissed her babe lightly on his forehead, and as her tears mingled with the pouring rain, she closed the lid and fastened the latches, making sure they were secure. It felt as if all heaven was weeping with her as she lowered the trunk gently into the water and watched the swells carry it away and out of sight.

Please, dear God, send my son to a faraway land, a safe shore far across the sea, to a place where men live in peace and harmony, where Collin can grow up happy and loved, without fear for his life. He is in your hands and at your mercy. Be gracious and protect him.

Calli let her tears stream as she stumbled from the dock, her back turned away from her hated deed, her heart sinking as if weighed down with an anchor. Why even bother to escape? Maybe she should just return to the palace and say her son had died. As if Pythius would believe her.

But what if she could make it look like she had thrown herself and her babe in the sea? Maybe that would at least give Collin a chance of survival. If the king believed them both dead, perhaps he would call off his search.

Calli wiped her face and hurried off the dock, then headed along the shoreline, keeping an eye out for the guards, who seemed to be searching lanes farther away. The rain and blustery wind obscured visibility, and for that she was grateful. Maybe the guards would tire of the weather and hole up in a tavern with a pitcher of ale by a warming fire.

She came upon a wide stretch of sandy beach between two sea-walls, and there she pulled out clothes from her bag—her clothes and Collin's. She laid two piles at the water's edge and set her simple gold crown on top, just hidden from view. She took out her beautiful leather shoes, the ones she had worn on her wedding day, and set them out as well. That would assure Pythius the items were truly hers.

Calli took one long last look out to sea, and watched the tumultuous water churning as the cloud-choked sky drenched her with more rain. She shivered more from despair than cold, knowing it was foolish to hope, but it consoled her somewhat, knowing that Collin was now in heaven's hands, regardless of what might befall him. She knew there was no better place he could be.

She pulled her soaked hood down over her face and trudged over the sand to the dockside lane. The streets were empty, although she imagined at any moment the guards would come marching toward her. Yet, as she ambled down one lane after another, weaving through the wet city, drenched and unbearably cold, she saw no one. Finally, near twilight, she came to the last cottages, now few and far apart. Cobbles turned to dirt, and all she could find to follow was one muddy, rutted road that hugged the coastline.

This was it, then—she had left behind her life and her most precious babe. She would leave behind her name as well, and anything that might tie her to her life in Paladya. Who knew how many months or even years it would take her to arrive in Elysiel? Without coin or food or even water, would she even last a week? If she could make it to Blunt, perhaps she could inquire after work, something menial to earn her a bed and a meal for a time. And then, perhaps, she might find a compassionate soul who would give her a ride in his cart or wagon north. Little by little she would inch her way home. Although, deep in her heart, she dreaded what she would find upon crossing the boundary into Elysiel.

Calli lifted her weary eyes from the road. Up ahead stood a lone ramshackle barn, dark and abandoned. Beyond exhaustion, heavy with grief, she barely made it into the somewhat dry shelter before she pulled off her wet clothes, found something only partly damp to put on, and then collapsed into a deathlike sleep.

TEN

PYTHIUS SCOWLED as he stood on the seawall, cursing the rain that lashed at his face and the wind that whipped his hair into knots. He cursed Calli even more, berating himself for ever having married her. He knew all along he'd never be able to trust her. Treacherous she was—just like everyone else. And ungrateful to boot. He had given her everything she could ever desire, and this was how she treated him? When he found her, he would make her suffer. Oh, how he would delight in torturing her and hearing her pitiful cries for mercy—which would never come. Death was too good for such a traitor.

He watched his guards run up and down the beaches, scurrying like black ants, their torches jiggling in the darkening twilight. They had questioned dozens of citizens. How was it that no one at all had seen her? Were they protecting her? Had she bribed them into silence? Or were they all just blind fools? No matter. At the first hint of dawn, his soldiers would pound on every door and search every cottage. If he had to tear Paladya apart stone by stone and beam by beam, so be it. If Calli was hiding anywhere in his city, he would discover her. Already his mounted patrol were stationed at all the roads leading in every direction out of town. He didn't trust that handmaid of hers, stating her mistress had fled west on the coach to Yammer. No doubt she was lying, or Calli had lied to her. Well, his men were on their way now, racing on horseback to catch up with the evening coach. He would soon learn if his wayward wife was on board. His soldiers had questioned the aunt, but of course she denied any knowledge of her escaped niece. But that was to be expected. Calli would never endanger the old crone by seeking to hide in the first place she knew he would look.

He rubbed his aching hand and cursed the fool healer who had attended him with his tinctures and salves. Those useless formulas had only exacerbated the pain. He'd had the healer thrown in the stocks and beaten for his efforts. Maybe that would make the next charlatan hesitate before claiming he had skill! He cursed King Cakrin while he was at it, for bespelling the scepter. But he would prevail! Somehow he would find a way to undo the curse put upon that blasted stick of crystal. For Pythius was certain now that the affliction on his hand and his inability to touch the scepter without it burning him were the result of witchcraft. He had summoned Urstus before heading out into this ugly, miserable weather to find a witch.

Urstus had faltered, and Pythius was sure the old advisor had stifled a laugh.

"Where on earth would I find a witch?" he had asked.

"Do I know? Or care? Ask around. In a city this size, there're bound to be witches about. Just go! Find one tonight!"

Pythius blew out a frustrated breath as he strained to see what was transpiring on the far northern harbor past the docks. He hurried down toward the water as torches amassed, indicating a large group of soldiers gathering. They had found something!

As his boots touched sand, his head palace guard ran toward him, holding something in his hand. Pythius exploded. "The queen's crown!" How dare she discard such a treasure—on a beach where any peasant or beggar might find it? It was worth a fortune! Never mind the blatant disrespect Calli was showing for her husband and king. Once word got out she had "disappeared," the rumors would abound, with unpleasant consequences. How his enemies would rejoice to hear of it.

Well, he would not give them the chance to gloat or conspire. Once he found Calli and killed her, he would make sure all knew it was a tragic accident. Perhaps she could . . . slip and fall out her chamber window . . .while holding her child. With all the wet weather, a misstep on a slippery balcony would be believable. And, perhaps tossing her broken and beaten body over the railing would be a way to cover evidence of his torture. A perfect way of disposing of her . . . and killing the child. He laughed at his brilliance.

He glared at his guard. "Where is she—have you found her yet?"

"No, Sire. The rain and waves have erased all traces of footprints. Yet . . ."

"Spit it out, man! Tell me!"

His guard lowered his gaze with a polite tip of his head. "Sire, it's likely the queen drowned herself. We found clothes—"

Pythius snorted. Calli would never drown herself nor her darling child. He'd seen how she looked at the thing, with such adoration and devotion. More love than she ever showed him, for certain. Another ruse, no doubt. Did she think he was daft?

"Show me!" he demanded.

He followed the guard to the shoreline, where an entire contingent of his soldiers was milling about. He shouted over the whistling wind, "Why are you standing around? Keep searching!"

The men jerked to action and scattered about the beach, some heading toward the smaller boats tied to the older broken docks spaced sporadically along the harbor's northern edge and others climbing the seawall into the narrow lane that ran along the wall. He knelt down as his head guard held the torch aloft, spilling light over the pile of soaked clothing lying upon the sand. A few yards ahead, waves smacked the beach, and even in the murky dark

Pythius could make out whitecaps, and spindrift blowing on the easterly wind. He tried to picture Calli willingly walking into the icy sea, her head held high, stalwart and determined, clutching her child in her arms.

He chuckled at the thought and bent down to sort through the clothes. Yes, they were hers; he recognized her fine deerskin boots. He stood and swiped his wet hair from his face. He was already tired of this cat-and-mouse game. He'd gone out into the cold rainy evening driven by the thrill of imagining his hands around Calli's throat, sure his guards would have found her in no time and had her bound, awaiting his arrival in the heart of the city. But he saw now he would have to quell his disappointment and urge for revenge for the moment. She was trapped, like a mouse in a corner. It was only a matter of time. No sense wandering about wet and freezing in the dark. He'd had enough cold and snow and ice back in Elysiel to last a lifetime. A hot blazing fire with a glass of aged brandy awaited him back at his palace.

An icy spear shot through his heart—as if a cold hand had reached into his chest and squeezed with all its might—and he doubled over. They were occurring more often—these cold, horrible pains. And they were making him irritable and impatient. He was losing his composure at inappropriate times, and his thoughts were often distracted and interrupted by the incessant pain. This had to stop. He hoped Urstus had found a witch and had one waiting for him upon his return.

The words of the seer replayed in his mind. How his son would one day kill him. He looked at the small pile of clothes before him, trying to figure what Calli would have done to save her babe. She knew his guards would be searching for her—for a young woman with an infant. He could not take the chance his son was still alive somewhere. Would she have given the child away? Found some young couple willing to take him in and pretend he was their own?

Yes, that's what he would have done. That way she would be able to move faster and undetected. Perhaps in time she planned to return and retrieve her child, when she deemed it safe.

He wished he had gotten a better look at the babe. All infants looked alike to him. No matter. At first light, he would have his guards search the entire city. He would personally question anyone with a male infant in their home. Somewhere out there was his son, and he would find him. *Calli, you may think you have thwarted me, but I will not be made a fool of. I will find your babe and kill him. And then I will find you. However far you run, you will find no safe haven.* He knew her heart was set on Elysiel. If she made it to the border, what a surprise she would find there. No doubt, word would leak out from the southern hamlets of King Cakrin's death and the disappearance of the scepter, and the news would come to her ears. She would be even more desperate to return home, then. And there was only one main road leading north for over a hundred leagues.

If Pythius's soldiers failed to find her anywhere in Paladya, he would send a contingent north—with the express charge of hunting her down. They would not be permitted to return until they accomplished their task, no matter how long it took. He would send his finest soldiers on his fastest horses. Her capture was inevitable.

With that happy thought, he strode back up the beach to his waiting carriage and commanded to the driver to make haste for the palace. He could already taste the fine bouquet of brandy on his tongue.

The next day in late afternoon, Pythius motioned to the commander of his great army, Ka'zab, to take a seat across from him in the vast throne room, but the dark, brooding man declined and paced the marble floor instead.

"You have a report for me?" Pythius was glad for the interruption. For the entire day, he had been questioning the local citizens his guards had been rounding up, all with vague reports of Calli's whereabouts—some having seen her midday in the marketplace; others in the evening walking down the harbor streets. All with little description that would confirm their sighting, and no doubt hoping for some reward—the vultures! He had sent every one of them away with a lashing.

Ka'zab walked in a measured cadence with his hands clasped behind his back. He looked out the rows of windows toward the garden, but Pythius could not tell by the man's expression what was on his mind. He sat uneasy on his throne and rubbed his hurting hand.

"My scouts have returned from the north and west, Sire." He stopped abruptly and turned to face the king. Ka'zab's glare sent a strange shiver down Pythius's spine. Why did this man so unnerve him? He had a strange air about him, something inhuman, birdlike, the way his beady eyes shone black in his face, and the way he cocked his head. "As you are aware, during your long absence I sent out my best infiltrators, seasoned fighters and spies, and they have brought me . . . interesting news."

"Which is?" Pythius fought to rein in his impatience. It seemed he was waiting for everyone to give him what he wanted. A healer to heal his hand. A witch to be found to undo whatever spell had been cast upon him. His guards to find his rebellious wife and hidden child. A new seer summoned from Torth to appear before him. And now, here was Ka'zab, dangling news in front of him like a tasty tidbit offered to a starving man.

"An interesting development, Sire, in a farming region over three hundred leagues to the northwest." Ka'zab paused, as if deliberately withholding his news to irritate his king. Pythius gritted his teeth and waved him to continue.

"You asked for word of another . . . strange circle, similar to the one you reported you had seen in the north. You said that one was made of giant crystal slabs—is that correct?"

"Yes, go on."

"My spies discovered another site, but one made of stone. This one stands atop a giant knoll, overlooking a fertile valley. A spring gushes up from the ground in the center of the circle."

"Stone, you say?"

"Ordinary stone, Sire. But these slabs of stone are gigantic. No man or beast could have erected such things."

"And they stand in a circle?"

"For the most part. A few have fallen down; a few are missing. But a huge village has been built around them, with a thriving agricultural center. Nowhere near as large as Paladya, though . . . the spies reported back peculiar observations—of giant fruits and melons the size of wagon wheels, and figs and pomegranates as large as your head."

"I see . . ."

"If Your Majesty is interested in expansion, this is a choice region. And the villagers are merely peasants, living in ignorance, untrained in the art of fighting. They would be an easy conquest, should one choose to . . . acquire their land. However, there are other townships and hamlets much closer with desirable farmland. May I ask, what concerns you about this circle—"

"Assemble your best men, Ka'zab. I want you to prepare a long, extensive campaign against this land and its people. Start small, raiding and pillaging the outskirts. I want you to infect the region with fear. Use whatever brutal tactics you desire in order to put terror into their hearts and make them flee. Burn down their villages, slay their women and children, steal whatever wealth they are hording. Take whatever you wish to keep for your own—that will sweeten the pot for your men."

Pythius watched Ka'zab's eyes widen in delight. "This may take years, Sire—"

"Take as long as needed to chase every last man away. Make them run far, Ka'zab, and with such fear that they will never dare return to their . . . circle of rock. Is that understood?"

Ka'zab nodded, clearly thrilled at the prospect. Pythius shivered again at the bloodlust evident in his commander's eyes. "We will begin preparations immediately, Your Majesty. I delight to do your bidding."

Of course you do. "I expect regular reports by messenger, of your progress."

Ka'zab bowed. "Will that be all?"

"Yes. You will be duly rewarded upon completion of your assignment."

"Thank you, Sire."

Ka'zab turned and opened the door to exit, and the head of his palace guard slipped in as he departed.

"Sire, we've found a child that seems to match the age and description of your son. Shall I bring in the parents?"

Pythius let out a long exhale and reached for his chalice of wine. The drink did nothing to ease either the pain in his hand or his exhaustion. He hadn't been able to sleep, not even for a minute, last night—what with fuming over Calli and trying to find some way to make his hand stop throbbing. The only thing that seemed to take the edge off the pain was ice, and so he'd dunked his hand in a crock of chipped ice and tried to sleep that way, but to no avail. His hand burned so hot, the ice melted away within minutes, requiring his servant to come in and empty the water and refill the crock over and over.

He realized he was staring at his glove, and the guard was waiting for his answer. "Yes, yes. Bring them in!"

The guard slipped out the door, then returned with the couple in tow. A man and his wife, simple peasants, both near his age. They walked fearfully, with their heads bowed, toward the throne, as the guard led them along. The woman cradled an infant in her arms.

They said nothing as Pythius circled them; he knew his nearness wrought terror in their hearts.

"Let me see the child!"

The woman hesitated and spoke softly. "Your . . . Your Highness, please. This is our only child, our son. Please do not take him from us—"

"Be silent! Do you know the price of treachery?"

The man raised his head, trying to be brave. Pythius felt nothing but disgust over his pathetic expression. "We have done nothing . . . our neighbors can all attest that this babe is our—"

"Oh, no doubt they can." Pythius knew how those peasants stood up for each other, lied for each other. Calli could have bribed them all. Or even worse, rallied them to her cause, playing on their compassion and empathy.

"The child!" Pythius demanded.

The woman held out her arms, and Pythius pulled the blanket down to study the child's face. It did not look familiar . . . yet, it was about the size of his child, with similar wispy hair. Oh, if only he had taken a closer look at his son. But, no matter. He would do whatever it took to prevent a mistake. He would err on the side of caution.

He looked at his head guard, who stood at attention off to the side. Pythius summoned him and said, "Take the child."

As the guard reached to obey, the woman screamed. "No! Please, Sire, he is all we have. We love him—"

The man pushed at the guard, trying to get at the child, but the guard struck him and knocked him to the ground. The woman wailed in a shrill voice of anguish. Pythius covered his ears. "Oh, take them all. Kill them."

Pythius gestured to his guard to leave, but the man stood there with the child in his arms, a stunned expression searing his face. The so-called parents fell to the ground in shock, the woman carrying on even louder now, and her husband trying to quiet her as she grasped at the guard's legs, trying to pull him toward her.

"Enough of this drama! Go!"

The guard shook his head and drew himself to attention. "Yes, Sire," he said, then strode out the door with the child in his arms. Momentarily, two other guards rushed in and grabbed the young couple and hauled them away. When they were finally out of earshot, Pythius removed his hands from his ears. Although he normally enjoyed hearing the screams of panic of those at his mercy—or should he say, lack of—he was in no mood to enjoy it today. Exhaustion rippled through his limbs and made him weak. He would have to give in and take the sleeping compound his healer had prepared for him. If he didn't get some rest, his thinking would become impaired. It seemed he had yet to get a full night's sleep ever since he fled Elysiel.

After a few minutes, his head guard returned. Pythius questioned him and the guard nodded. "Your command . . . is being carried out as we speak."

Pythius noted the pained look on the man's face. "Do you have a problem with my decision?"

The man gulped. "No, Your Majesty."

"Good. I want you to find all the male infants in the city under the age of one and have them . . . disposed of. Do not bother to bring the parents to me. It . . . is a waste of my time. If any other parents resist, kill them as well. Do you understand?"

The guard nodded but did not look into Pythius's eyes.

"Then, go—carry out my order. Inform me when the task has been completed. I want soldiers searching the city around the clock. And report back to me any sightings of . . . the queen. Are the riders ready to leave for the pass?"

"They are assembled at the stables now, Sire. They needed time to say good-bye to their families—"

"Yes, yes, of course. Well, send them on their way. And remind them to ride fast and hard, and to inquire of everyone they meet on the Great Northern Road. Tell them they may not return without my wife. If perchance she is found within Paladya, we will send word and summon them back. Understood?"

"Yes, Sire."

"Leave now. And send in Urstus."

The guard mumbled something Pythius could not make out, then exited.

Pythius sat back on his throne and closed his eyes, but it did little to relax him. He had just begun to nod off when he heard the sound of someone clearing his throat.

Urstus walked toward him, leading another blind man by the arm. Pythius could tell this was a different seer; although the man was as old as the other, with a similar long beard and silver earring, he was noticeably shorter and heftier.

"This is Xio Xee, Sire, the seer sent from Torth—"

"Yes, yes, I see." *At least one of us can see.* He stood before the seer. "Tell me, Seer. What does the augury say? Will I find my wife? Is my son truly dead?"

"Oh King," the seer began, his voice thin and breathy, "one cannot question the augury. It speaks at will. It does not answer questions posed to it."

"Then of what value is it?" He turned to Urstus. "Isn't there some other mage or fortune-teller in the city who can answer my inquiries?"

"None as reliable as the seers from Torth. Their predictions always prove true and dependable."

Pythius's gut wrenched at the reminder. *"The augury strikes where the heart lies . . . the sin of the father is visited upon the son."* The memory of his hand wielding the knife, slashing his father's throat, burned in his mind.

He stamped his foot in frustration. He had to know if his son was dead—or if he was still alive and hidden somewhere. "Does the augury have anything at all to tell me?"

The seer stood unblinking, his white washed-out eyes staring at nothing. "No, oh King."

"Well, you will stay here in my palace until it does." He shook his head in frustration and said to Urstus, "Put him in some dark, quiet room—where he can listen and wait for a word from the augury. I must know if the child lives!"

The seer spoke so quietly, Pythius had to draw near to hear. "You may have to wait a very long while, oh King."

"Then wait, I shall. As will you. Take him away!"

Late in the night, Pythius removed his glove with tender care, sliding off each soft leather finger as he gritted his teeth. By lamplight he examined the black heart recessed like a brand into his palm. Now all his fingers had turned a sooty gray color; he could hardly bend them. Anger carried him like an errant wave and he lashed out in fury. He picked up an ornate vase and threw it across the room. It shattered as it struck the wall, and pieces of the porcelain flew into his face. With a growl he uncorked the jar of ointment the healer had left him and winced as he slathered the caustic oil over his hand.

He cursed Urstus and his feeble excuses. There were either no witches to be found in all of Paladya or else they feared coming forward. *"Word has spread,"* his advisor had scolded, *"of how you killed the seer. Do you really expect anyone to dare offer their services to their king, knowing what fate might await them? You should be building trust, not making more enemies, Sire."*

Building trust? That was no way to rule a kingdom. He would show his lazy advisor how to flush out a witch. At dawn he would call in his Eyes and Ears—two men who were adept at acquiring information. It often required some blood spillage, but Pythius cared not what such information cost or who had to pay the price. He would show Urstus how power trumped diplomacy every time. Why couldn't the old codger see this by now?

He stood and listened to the quiet. Down in the city below, his guards were relentlessly searching for Calli and the babe. He knew he should be patient. Something would show up soon. It would take nothing short of a miracle, some intervention of heaven, for Calli to escape his wrath.

His eyes shifted to his bed. The scepter called to him, tempting him in agony and frustration. He could not resist its siren song.

He knelt down and reached under the footboard for the wooden case, then pulled it out and opened the lid. With trembling fingers he folded back the silk cloth and sucked in a breath.

The exquisite beauty of the crystal never failed to awe him. The entire shaft of the scepter glowed with that faint blue light from within, and the heart in the handle beat slow and steady, the way a man's heart might while he slept. In the hand of King Cakrin, the scepter's light had been brilliant, far brighter than it was now. And the heart had beaten hard, punctuating the air with its audible rhythm. Surely it was now dormant, waiting to be wielded, its power also sleeping.

More than anything he yearned to grasp it again and demand its fealty, awaken it and summon its power. Here was his deepest wish, his most desired dream, his greatest accomplishment—inches from his hand, his for the taking. Contained within that crystal shaft were health, endless life, prosperity. So close—only a finger's reach away—but the scepter might as well be buried with King Cakrin for all the good it was presently doing him. Yet Lady

Vitrella had told him he was the one foretold to steal the scepter from Elysiel. She had seen him coming; the prophecy was explicit. He was the lion from the thicket come in a rush of destiny. He had caused the heart of the king to perish and yet . . . since that moment, he had been rewarded only with pain, betrayal, and the threat of death. This was not acceptable!

He narrowed his eyes and steeled his nerve. He would not be thwarted, not any longer. The scepter was his by all rights. It was destined to be his. He would claim its power and make it bend to his will.

A rumble rose in his chest, the roar of a lion, the lion's blood rushing through his veins and emboldening him. He grabbed the crystal shaft with his blackened hand and raised it high in the air, night swirling around him like ghosts breathing on his neck.

The roar turned to scream as pain jolted his heart like a lightning bolt. He fell hard to the cold stone floor and smacked his wrist, and the crystal scepter flew across his room, then clattered to a stop against a far wall. As the king of Paladya began to slip into unconsciousness, the last thing he saw was the encapsulated king's heart, pounding in a steady beat of recrimination and mockery.

ELEVEN

ARNYL QUAY pulled his coat tighter about him as he made his way carefully across the storm-littered beach. A streak of pink lay over the horizon as he gazed out at the Barebones through the shreds of fog. He could make out the first three islands in the dawn's illumination. Petrel, with its two ragged peaks, and Gannet and Cormorant lying in shadow behind it, low and flat like flounders. They should have been named after fish, not birds, he mused, not at all happy this crisp fall morn—and for good reason, he told himself.

The storm had been a big one, biggest he'd seen all season, and no doubt more to come. Like the saying went: "Storms as steady as labor pains." He hated to think how tangled his nets would be. *Only two things certain in life—fog and tangled nets.* Fog tickled his neck and pooled around his boots. Bleak Harbor indeed looked bleak on this dreary day. He raised his eyes and looked around. No one combing the beach yet, which was surprising. Plenty of odd treasures to be found. He bent over and picked up a broken glass float, deep blue, the glass etched and dull from being tumbled in waves and sand. He tossed it into a jumble of driftwood and shell and noticed a few rotting fish tangled in seaweed. The air smelled of fish and brine, and wood smoke from someone's hearth. Most days the aroma would have invigorated him, but not this day.

His stomach grumbled, complaining about his missed breakfast, but today he would fast. He made a solemn vow not to touch food or drink until the morrow, not that it would make a difference. Could he compound his grief any more? Depriving himself of a day's sustenance would do little toward relieving him of his guilt. His loneliness was another matter. And his regret—that was the worst. He'd run through that day in his mind endless times, thinking how he'd do it over, make it come out differently, but it only tortured him. There was no getting around it. He was to blame. He'd been drinking, and Emelee had warned him, like she always had, but he'd never listen, never. Overconfident and reckless he was—she'd warned him that would be his undoing. And he'd paid the price for it—they both had. But Jayden had paid with his life.

Arnyl's throat clenched closed as he approached the stone memorial he'd erected at Blight Point. One year to the day. And a storm much like this one—although he hadn't paid it much mind then. Others had—Bayley, and Gar. But he didn't listen, just figured he could ride it out like most other storms and pull in one last catch. Emelee had told him not to take the boy, but he snuck him away when she wasn't looking, needing a hand at the prow while he pulled in nets. The others were all busy with their haul, the biggest mackerel run they'd seen in years, the fish running just ahead of the tempest.

He had blamed it on the drink, as if that would excuse him. She always told him it would be the death of him, but it hadn't been; it had been the death of their boy. Just seven, seven years old . . . Arnyl wished he had died too that day. When Jayden had gone overboard, he should have just thrown himself in as well. He snorted in derision. He was the kind of fisherman who could catch anything he set his mind to, but as hard as he'd tried, he couldn't pull his son from the inky depths.

Arnyl fell to the damp sand as a pale light broke through the fog and shone on the stone. He'd erected a simple marker, a large piece of granite he'd bought from the quarry and hauled in his pull cart. Before he even had Jayden's name half-chiseled across the face of the slab, Emelee had packed and gone. Not two weeks after the tragic drowning. *"I'll never forgive you,"* she had spat at him as he sat on the beach, carving the letter *D.* She'd threatened many times to leave, but with nothing keeping her tied to him any longer, the boy having been the only rope binding them, she had packed a bag and left for Scuddle, where she'd grown up and where her family no doubt consoled her and welcomed her return. They never liked him, but now he understood why. Why she had married him was a mystery—a hardworking, clean-living girl like her. But maybe at the time he'd done a convincing job of pretending he had stopped drinking. His friends weren't fooled though. Alyck had told him it was only a matter of time before she'd leave him—if he didn't change his ways. He should have listened to his friends, listened to all of them—especially Emelee.

He let the tears fall as he ran his hand across the top of the granite marker. He'd made a vow after they buried Jayden, and given up the drink. Hadn't touched a drop since. Not that it did any good now. His friends applauded his decision, good friends they were. They stuck by him, despite what had happened. Their wives were another story, being friends with Emelee, but he didn't have to fish with *them* year in and out. But he hadn't stopped drinking to please anyone in Tolpuddle. He knew he had to repent of his ways and seek heaven's mercy. Not that he deserved it; he didn't. But how else could he go on? He hoped God would forgive him for what he'd done, but he couldn't see how. He surely couldn't forgive himself. *Will my heart ever heal?*

"Like fish caught in a cruel net, so men are snared in an evil time when it falls suddenly upon them." The saying was too true, but he'd brought the evil upon himself, through his careless drinking. Another saying came to his mind: "The sea gives and the sea takes." He'd heard that his whole life. Many met with tragedy at sea, but most fell victim due to no fault of their own. The sea was often a harsh and violent contender, one without care or compassion for those who plied her waves. She demanded respect, and most fisherman paid it. Arnyl knew he had not respected her that day, venturing too far from the harbor, staying out too long, challenging her with a bottle in his hand as his small boat rolled in the deep trenches and shimmied over the tops of the swells. And Jayden—his eyes full of trust, and fearless, the way Arnyl had taught him to be, already a steady sailor, like most of his mates. Just as comfortable sitting in a boat as sitting on a chair in his cottage. His bright eyes, cheerful smile, that silly laugh he would make when he'd be tickled on the bottoms of his feet . . .

A great sob burst out of Arnyl's chest. Followed by many more. He sat there before the memorial stone and wept, full of regret, letting one wave after another drown him with sorrow. How long he sat there, he couldn't say. But when he lifted his eyes, the sun had pierced the cloud cover and he could make out a few boats sailing out of the harbor, light glinting off the folds of their sails. No doubt many vessels tied to the docks had been damaged and needed repair. He would walk over later and see if he could help.

That was another vow he'd made—to be a good neighbor, though he knew he could never work off his mistake, or make amends for what he'd done. He'd always been the loner—drinking alone, brooding alone, fishing alone. After losing everyone and everything he loved, he'd vowed to be a new man. All who knew him commended him for giving up drinking, for being so neighborly. He now presented a cheerful countenance, eager to help, always ready to encourage. But inside, he was empty. He had nothing to live for, no hope, no peace. He fished, he ate, he swept his floor and mended his clothes, one day like the next. For what? He knew he should be grateful for heaven's provision, but it all seemed so pointless.

And today, more than ever, he felt like he was just treading water, waiting for the sea to pull him under, to peaceful oblivion. Some days he rowed out beyond the Barebones and thought to pull in his oars and just let the sea take him where it willed. He'd been sorely tempted many times, especially those first months after Jayden's death. But somehow he just kept on going. Without his wife and his son, his life was purposeless, meaningless. Was this heaven's plan for his life—to fish alone until he grew old and shriveled like a smoked cod? He knew the truth in the saying, "Accept the way God does things, for who can straighten what he has made crooked?" but he didn't *want* to accept the way things were, and that was the honest truth.

He got to his feet and brushed sand from his trousers. He let his eyes follow the mounds of burgundy heath and emerald-green ice plant growing thick up the hills to the promontory. He could make out the roofs of Bleak Harbor Inn, their black spires puncturing the blanket of fog still clinging to the seaside town. He imagined the marketplace would be busy, the way it always was after a big storm. Although few fishermen would have much to offer except what they found trapped in their nets. By dusk, the boats would come back in with their catches. The market would stay open extra hours this eve, with the promise of late offerings.

He took one last look at the stone, then, with a sigh, turned and walked around the cove to where his nets were stretched across an inlet, anchored onto the barnacled rocks. He'd been laying nets in this one spot for years, and without fail, he always found them full after a storm. But he dreaded what he'd find today, figuring most of the nets would be tangled and ripped, maybe even irreparable. He could count on many long, tedious hours with needle and twine, late into the night, for many nights to come. But at least that would give him something with which to occupy his hands, if not his mind.

Fish flopped in a giant writhing mass close to the surface. Arnyl whistled and shook his head. He'd need more than his small pull cart to haul this catch to market. He sent a silent prayer of thanksgiving heavenward as he drew closer to inspect both the haul and the damage. The weight of so many perthin struggling for untold hours since the storm had swept them into his nets had strained the jute, but he could make out few tears, much to his surprise. He climbed carefully onto the spray-slick rocks and ran his hand along the edge of the netting, noting the places that needed repair. Most of the larger rips were evident on the rocks, where net attached to the metal rings anchored there.

He watched the silvery-blue fish tussle in the morning light, their scales sparkling with iridescence. There had to be hundreds of perthin—more than he'd ever hauled in at one time. They would bring a good price at market too, with their rich flavorful meat—a rare fish, easy to debone, a good keeper for many days on ice.

Perthin. He hadn't seen a school of them in ages. They were found in warmer southern waters. Yet this storm had blown from the north, as most did, usually coming down from the Shivery Coast and barreling through Scuddle before hitting Tolpuddle and circling back east to open water. How strange to see them here, in Bleak Harbor.

He walked over to the wooden shack nestled into the wall of sandstone that wrapped around the small cove. He kept his nets and cart inside, along with his surf fishing rod and fishing line. When he opened the rickety weathered door, his eyes fell on the small bird carving Jayden had made for him two summers ago. His heart ached in sweet memory of his son straddling the large log that had tumbled onto the beach, sitting there with his head bowed in concentration, digging into a soft piece of driftwood with a carving gouge. Jayden had loved birds: gulls, pelicans, cormorants. As soon as he could walk, he was stumbling along the shore, waving his hands at the sandpipers, coaxing them to fly. Arnyl's own heart had soared watching his son and the joy he exuded for life. He looked at the now-empty beach, too keenly aware he would never see his son run across the sand ever again, never see him grow up, marry, raise a family. And it was all his fault . . .

Arnyl yanked the cart out of the shack and dragged it over the sand to the water. He hoped when he got to market he could enlist the help of some of the village boys to transport this fish. He'd need a few more carts, but Alyck kept extra on hand and wouldn't mind him borrowing them. He'd seen his friend's boat heading out of the harbor earlier, so he knew the carts weren't being used at present.

He climbed back up on a low rock and began tossing fish. Perthin wiggled and slipped in his hands as he scooped them up and fell into a rhythm, swaying back and forth, watching the mound grow in his cart. He let his mind empty and willed his heart to stop aching. *Fish, eat, sleep, fish, eat, sleep* . . . He let the words lull him, numb him to the import of this day, push away the memories drifting in of Jayden, of his drowning, of Emelee leaving, of her accusing tone that only drove home his guilt like a spike to his heart.

In the midst of his dance at the edge of the sea, his cold hands hit something hard underneath the soft, slimy bodies of fish. He stopped and pulled at his net, trying to get closer to whatever lay entangled at the bottom in seaweed. But his net would not give, so he lay across the flat rock and reached into the water, fish flopping against his cheeks and tickling his head as spray filled his nostrils.

He felt with his hands, outlining something boxlike, made of wood, touching upon something slick like metal. A trunk. With hinges. Had someone been forced to throw ballast overboard during the storm? Was this some pirate's treasure, or just a box full of coal? Whatever it was, it was stuck. And heavy. And would tear his net to shreds if he didn't find a safe way to extricate it.

He went back to his shack and grabbed a large metal pry bar, and after some maneuvering managed to free the trunk enough to pull it toward him. He stopped and listened. Surely he was imagining things; he thought he heard a sound come from the trunk.

Spurred by equal parts curiosity and worry, he positioned his feet into clefts in the rock and leveraged the trunk, lifting it with a grunt. With another hefty pull, the trunk slipped up over the stony ledge and landed at his feet. He pushed his hair out of his eyes and wiped his hands on his trousers. Diver gulls heckled overhead, eyeing his pool of fish. He used his shirtsleeve to wipe the water and tendrils of seaweed from the trunk's lid, then fiddled with the latches until, after some effort, he was able to flip them up.

The trunk cracked open. Arnyl raised the lid and his breath hitched.

A babe with pale gray eyes stared at him, calm, quiet, undisturbed, as if he'd just woken from a pleasant nap.

Arnyl rubbed his own eyes and looked around. Was this some prank? Surely this babe had not been drifting at sea during that violent storm? From where had it come?

Questions cluttered his mind as he stared in disbelief at the babe, who reached out a small hand to touch Arnyl's face. The babe looked no worse for wear.

With a shaky hand, Arnyl reached in and picked up the child. It had been too long since he'd held a babe this small. It must be . . . three, maybe four months. Only wearing a swaddling gown, drenched, yes, and smelling of urine. Arnyl could only guess how long the poor babe had been at sea. Why would someone put it in a trunk like this? Who would do such a thing?

He stripped the babe of its wet, clammy clothes and set him—he soon assessed it was a boy—on the warm rock to dry. How strange that the babe wasn't crying. Surely he must be hungry. Or had he lost his hunger after so many days at sea? Arnyl had no way to feed an infant. He would need to get the babe some milk, and soon.

Bayley. His friend's wife had just given birth to their second child. He would take the babe to her. But what would he tell her?

Arnyl stared at the child in awe. Of all things to pull from his nets. *"The sea gives and the sea takes."* The words struck Arnyl with a strange significance. The sea had taken one boy from him . . . and now had brought him another.

He shook his head at the preposterous idea. Perhaps a mother, in her panic and fear of sinking at sea, had set this babe in the trunk, hoping to be reunited, by some miracle. She could be searching for her babe at this very moment, distraught and forlorn.

He would have to take the babe, then, to the town magistrate. Someone there would know if a mother was looking for her child.

Arnyl sat on the rock and stroked the babe gently on the cheek. "What a beauty you are, a treasure found in a net of fish." His heart ached at the touch of soft skin, rekindling memories of when Jayden had been an infant. *So long ago, but seems only yesterday . . .*

He returned his attention to the trunk, thinking maybe it would hold a clue as to the name of its owner. To his surprise, he found a velvet drawstring pouch under the nest of wet blankets. He set that on the rock beside the babe and pulled out all the wet bedclothes, then found a damp sheet of parchment.

Arnyl held it up and read the few scant lines. The ink had run and grown faint, but he could clearly make out the simple script. What he read shocked him.

"To whoever finds my child: know that he is the son of King Pythius of Paladya, who seeks his life. If word should ever reach the king that his son lives, the babe will be killed. If heaven has spared my poor babe and delivered him into safe hands, you must raise him as your own, or find someone faithful and capable to do so. He must never be told who he is or how he was found, and no one must ever know. I pray you will raise him with love and give him a good home. Christen him with whatever name you see fit; he is now yours. Queen Calli of Paladya."

Arnyl's jaw dropped. He picked up the pouch and opened it, astonished at what he found. Gold coins, and gems of all colors. Surely a king's fortune. Or a queen's, in this case.

Well, now some of his questions were answered. A king's son! He had never heard of this Pythius, or of a land called Paladya. But he had never ventured more than a day's journey from Tolpuddle, where he'd been born and raised and lived his entire twenty-five years. Never had any interest in lands beyond, either. Perhaps someone in the village would be able to tell him where this land was. But—no. He must not utter the name of this place, or of its king. He knew it would only lead to questions he could not answer. And he most certainly could not discuss this with his own parents. Their taste for gossip was only exceeded by their love of drink. He was glad they'd moved to Spratt years ago and hardly ever wrote him.

He reread the note once more, contemplating all the while what to do with this babe. He knew no one who might be willing to take him. And he couldn't risk leaving the babe on some doorstep or turning him in to the magistrate. This babe's life was in danger, and if some powerful king somewhere was seeking to find him, he must do just what this queen requested. He could tell no one. Heaven had delivered the babe into *his* hands.

But surely he could not keep this child himself! He was in no position to raise an infant. Of course, he knew how to clothe and bathe and feed one. But what would people say? How could he explain the babe's sudden appearance in his life? More to the point, he had proved himself untrustworthy; he had caused the death of his only son. No, it would be better to find someone else to take the child.

But heaven sent him to you.

There was no denying the miracle of the babe caught in his nets, alive, well, unharmed. On such a portentous day. Still . . .

He looked upon the child and his heart swooned with love. A sudden desire to protect and care for this babe filled his soul and soothed the constant pain that haunted him day after day. Was heaven showing him a way to heal his heart? Was he being given a second chance? Did he dare try to be a father to this child?

He picked up the babe and pulled him to his chest. He closed his eyes and let the tears fall. He had found many treasures in his nets over the years, discarded or lost items that had somehow landed in his hands. But this was the greatest treasure ever, more valuable than all the gold or gems in the world. He knew at that moment, while holding this small babe in his arms, that he had been chosen by heaven for this responsibility. He already loved this babe as if he were his very own, and he knew he would never be able to part from him.

He looked at the huge school of perthin struggling in his net. *Perthin.* That's what he would call his son—who had eyes the silvery-blue color of the fish in his nets. A simple name, certainly not a royal one—nothing that would call attention to his nobility. He would raise him to be a fisherman, to work with his hands and live an honorable life, but there was one thing he would not allow. He would never let his son go out to sea. He vowed before heaven as he sat there with this babe in his arms that Perthin would stay on land and never step foot in a boat. He couldn't bear to worry that he might lose another son to the deep. He didn't dare tempt the sea to take back what had been given.

He lifted the babe, turned him around, studied every inch of him. Underneath his pale wispy hair, on the nape of his neck, Arnyl found a birthmark. Strange—it was in the shape of a perfect star, although one leg and one arm of the star were a little longer than the others. He had never seen a birthmark quite like it, so perfectly shaped, the size of his thumbnail.

Perthin began to fuss and nuzzled at his neck.

"So you *are* hungry, sweetling. Well, then, let's go find you some milk." Bayley's wife, Nella, had a goat or two that she milked, and would no doubt have a bottle fashioned for a babe to drink from. And some clothes for the babe as well. But what would he tell her? He would have to think of something as he walked to her cottage at the edge of town. Tongues would certainly wag upon hearing his news. Nella was known to be a talker. Well, he would just have to come up with something believable.

He looked at all the fish. The ones in the cart were already drying out. He pulled the rough tarp up and over them, hoping they'd keep. But if they didn't, it wouldn't be too great a loss. His biggest catch of the day was in his arms. He would pay the market boys extra to take the carts to the beach and load up all his fish. He had a jar full of coppers on his mantle. The pouch of gold and gems he would hide and never touch. They belonged to Perthin.

Maybe one day he would hear of this king's death, and then it would be safe to tell Perthin his true origin. But what of the babe's mother? If the king was searching to kill his son, would he kill her too? Arnyl's heart ached thinking of how she'd had been forced to send her babe off to sea, trusting heaven to watch over such a helpless thing. He mouthed a prayer that heaven would watch over Perthin's mother as well, this tragic queen of some faraway land. *Keep her safe. Perhaps one day she will be reunited with her son.* Although Arnyl could not imagine how that could ever happen.

He unbuttoned his shirt and wrapped Perthin in it. Then, with the warm morning sun on his shoulder, he carried the babe in his arms as he clambered over the piles of driftwood and seaweed and up the dunes toward Bayley Tettenhall's cottage.

Calli felt a hand shaking her shoulder. She lifted her face from the cold sand and tried to open her eyes. Where was she? Thoughts flitted like moths in her head, too fast for her to catch. All she could remember was . . . the furious storm, blowing so hard it took all her strength to keep moving, one foot in front of the other, wind beating her down, her tears emptying into the sea until she had cried herself dry. Collin's sweet face intruded and her grief rushed anew. *Oh my poor babe. Will I ever see him again?*

She wiped her eyes and jumped to her feet. Pythius's men must have found her! But when the shape before her came into focus, she saw a young girl holding out her hand.

"Miss, are you ill? Here, have some water." She handed Calli a water jug. As Calli gulped down the water that soothed her dry throat, she noticed the girl carried a large burlap sack over her shoulder.

"Where . . . am I?" She looked around and saw a long stretch of sandy beach, and off in the distance something that glistened like a river.

"Not afar from Blunt, miss. That's Crook's Head, over there." She pointed back behind Calli, but Calli had no strength to turn her head.

"Have you . . . seen any soldiers about?"

"Soldiers? Why, no, miss. We're far from any garrison." She studied her curiously. "Are you hurt? You should come back with me."

"Back where?" Calli shook from the thought of anyone from Paladya recognizing her.

"To Blunt. It's a bit of a walk, I'm afeared. By the Irt, over there." She pointed at the slow-moving water in the distance. "Can you make it?"

"I . . . I think so."

"Here." The girl pulled a dark roll from the pouch of her smock. "It's got a bit o' sand on it, but was baked fresh this morn."

Calli took the roll. "I'm grateful, thank you. What is your name?"

"I'm Addie, miss."

"And what's in your sack?"

"Oysters, miss."

"Oysters? What are those?"

"You've never had 'em? Why, they're the most delicious things in all the world. I've been gathering them for my auntie. She's shorthanded, what with the ague that's been knocking everyone down. Can you cook?"

"Why . . . yes, I can—"

"Well, if you need a job, she'll be wanting to hire you. I'm s'posed to be in school, but the teacher is out sick too, so I'm helping my auntie."

"And she's a cook?"

"At Blunt Tavern. She makes the best fish chowder—with celery and ale. Though she don't tell my mum it's got ale in't.'"

Calli's stomach grumbled. How many days had she been lying on the beach? At least the storm had passed. Now only a few thin clouds drifted overhead in the calm, cool morn. Somehow she had eluded capture by Pythius's guards—until now. There was no telling how far and wide their search would reach. She would have to keep moving, not stay long in one place. But she did need to eat and regain her strength. Maybe she could work at this tavern for a week, and do what she could to change her appearance. She could chop off all her hair, for one thing. And she'd have to come up with a new name, and a story that no one would question. She didn't dare ask about news from Paladya or Elysiel. Better if she appeared uneducated and uninformed.

She fell into step beside Addie, who walked in a slow manner, hauling her bag of oysters. After half an hour, they came to the wide, smooth estuary that flowed into Buddle Bay. Addie told her of the flower farms and orchards up the Irt River, and named many of the marsh birds she saw flying overhead. Water sparkled in the bright sunlight, and the air smelled fresh and clean.

The simple beauty of this peaceful region gave Calli a glimmer of hope. Perhaps she could blend in after all, bide her time, slowly work her way back to Elysiel. Maybe she had fooled Pythius, and he had concluded she and Collin were dead. She didn't dare relax her guard, though. One slip and word could get to him as fast as a crow. She only hoped that in time he would forget about her and about that warning the seer had given him. Collin—grow up to kill his father? Yet the idea was not as preposterous as she had first thought. With a man as evil as Pythius for a father, it was not unlikely Collin would have grown to hate him, and even want to kill him. Maybe the seer was only predicting the inevitable, had she stayed and raised her son in the palace. But the prophecy was now moot, wasn't it? Her son was no doubt dead, either drowned at sea or dead from lack of nourishment. She had sent him to his death.

She choked back tears as she trudged in silence. Now what did she have to live for? She did not know. But at very least she had to discover how her father and brothers fared. She would have no peace in her heart until she stepped foot across the border into Elysiel and felt the welcoming sun of heaven's blessing upon her face once again, even though it would never truly heal the ache in her heart.

If she could make it that far without being caught.

• PART TWO •

"Do not rejoice . . . that the king is dead. For from that snake a more poisonous snake will be born, a fiery serpent to destroy you!" (Isaiah 14:29 NLT)

TWELVE

PERTH COULD feel Danyl laughing at him behind his back. He scowled and squatted again, wiping his slimy hands on his apron, and drew in a long breath. With a grunt, he managed to heft the crate partway off the dock, only to have it slip out of his hands and back onto the wood planks with a thud.

"Out of the way, tadpole." Danyl poked him with his elbow, chuckling as he pushed him out of the way.

"I can do it," Perth protested.

"Trolls be hanged! We'll be here all day if I wait for you to get these stacked. Go help Tanin with the rigging, small fry. You *can* carry a length of rope?"

Perth made a face and purposely bumped the older boy as he passed, but Danyl only laughed harder. Older by only three years, Danyl was maybe twice Perth's weight. He noticed Tanin's pa, Alyck, shaking his head and nudging Gar Scrimshire as they loaded the crates onto the wagon. He strode down the dock, eyes locked ahead to where Tanin stood coiling rope into spirals on the wet deck.

"Don't let 'im goad you, Perth. You'll grow." He exchanged amused looks with Gar. "One day."

Perth wished he could put his hands over his ears as he passed the laughing men, but he didn't want to let on how much they irked him. His dad always told him to ignore their barbs, insisting they meant no harm, that they were just teasing. "Don't take yourself so seriously, Perth," he'd say. "A man's *heart* reveals the man—not his height. You won't be a shrimp forever."

But it felt like forever. He was already fifteen, and still shorter and skinnier than boys years younger. Danyl and Tanin were a head taller, having shot up last summer, now as tall as their fathers. It wasn't fair. He was braver than both of those scamps put together. But he'd show them. Once he put his plan into action, they'd stop calling him names and treat him with respect.

He ran up the ramp to Tanin.

"Hey," Tanin said, "I thought you weren't allowed on a boat."

Perth made a face and picked up the end of one of the ropes strewn about the deck. "It's docked. Or hadn't you noticed?" He began pulling and twisting the heavy rope so it played out in a large even circle as he fed it through his hand.

"Well, it's probably a good thing you weren't out on this run. The waves were monstrous. Someone as light as you—you would have flown over the railing. We'd 'ave had to tie you to the mast."

Perth raised his eyes and looked out to sea; the horizon was flat and serene. "You're pulling my foot. There's no swells out yonder."

"I'm telling you—the waves were pouring over the railings. Ask my pa. That's why we come in early. Plenty of fish to be had but Pa worried for the boat."

Perth shook his head. He wasn't going to fall for another of Tanin's tales. He exaggerated worse than Danyl—the two always bragging. But after tonight, he himself would have something to brag about—when he brought back a sackful of treasure.

"Is it true your pa spotted some trolls out in the garbage dump yesterday?" Perth worked to keep his voice flat as he finished up with one length of rope and started in on another.

"'Tis the truth. He and three other big men went out there last night and guarded the road into town—just to make sure the mob of 'em didn't get any smart-alecky ideas."

Perth threw Tanin a look. "You know they always travel in threes. No one's ever seen more at one time. No more, no less."

"Says who? My pa says there was a whole passel of 'em, sitting in among the fish guts and trash and stuffing their faces with muck and manure. Disgusting!"

Perth had never seen a troll, although he had no doubt they existed. He'd heard tales his entire life of the ugly creatures—gigantic things with saggy flesh, sharp tusks growing out of the lower jaw, hair stringy like fishing line, and eyeballs that bulged out of their faces like bloated fish eyes. Folks said they were so ugly they made you chuck up your breakfast. No wonder mothers threatened to throw their children to the trolls if they were bad. His own pa had told him plenty of bedtime stories about them, although Perth doubted any held a spark of truth. How they loved to eat cow dung and rubbed it all over their skin. How they made flowers shrivel up as they walked past—their smell so putrid everything within sight wilted. How they foraged from village to village, digging up gardens and stealing anything shiny. Gar had told once how his whole string of silver fishing lures had disappeared from his porch one night. He blamed it on the trolls. He said someone had spotted a few trolls later on with the lures festooning their hair. And then there was the claim that they couldn't resist beautiful shoes. Why on earth would a troll want a pretty shoe? They certainly didn't wear any. From what Perth had heard, trolls had gigantic hairy feet, covered in warts and boils. Maybe they used the shoes for digging tools.

As much trouble as the trolls caused, no one had ever gotten close enough to them to hurt them. It was said they could move as fast as lightning. One fisherman, angry the trolls had stolen all the trays of fish out of his smoker, chased after one, intent on beating it senseless with his shovel. He'd been found unconscious the next day with both his arms broken, the busted shovel lying next to his head, and a lump on his noggin the size of a melon. He could barely speak for a week, and when his words did return, they were filled with terror. This was long ago, when Perth had been a babe. The few accounts Perth had heard over the years of those who dared confront the trolls revealed them to be vicious, uncannily strong, and violent. So folks stayed away, let them be. So what if they stole a few things, took a few fish or a pair of shoes? You were the fool if you left things lying around that the trolls could get. They never went inside anyone's cottage, but more than one villager claimed he'd heard them on his roof, tromping like a herd of horses across the sod. Why they'd climb over someone's roof, Perth had no idea. He figured that was just another tale told for a laugh.

No one had mentioned a sighting in many months, until yesterday. Some figured they went further south in winter. But now that it was spring, they'd returned, and from all accounts were causing more trouble than ever. And the latest rumor was that all of Grinda Gannet's fine linens had been stolen off the clothesline at the inn. She was particularly upset—or so Gayla said at the market this morning—because each piece had been hand-stitched and trimmed with lace filigree—years of painstaking work. Perth didn't know anything about stitchery, but the way Gayla had carried on, a great tragedy had occurred. Grinda was so beside herself no one could coerce her to come out of her drawing room—and she had guests waiting on her. Or so Gayla had moaned. Now she had to find fabric and lace and help replace all the pieces that had been taken. By trolls, of course. What would trolls do with a lacy tablecloth? Spread it across a pigsty and set four places for supper? Perth laughed and shook his head.

"What's so amusing?" Tanin asked, finishing up with the last bit of rope.

"Nothing," Perth answered, clamping his mouth shut. He looked out to sea and thought about what Tanin had told him.

"Did you see Bayley's ship while you were out?" His pa was on *The Sea Farer* with Bayley—a big sailing ship with at least fifty hands. They were due in by evening.

Tanin shook his head. "They went south of the Barebones— toward Scoria Point." He looked at Perth and his face softened. "I'm sure they'll be fine. If they ran into the same rough seas we did, they'd make for Battered Beach. They hadn't set out that far."

Perth nodded. He hated that his pa forbade him to go to sea. He wouldn't even let him row a boat around the harbor. He said he'd made a vow to God when Perth was born—because of Jayden. Perth scowled. His pa had quit drinking fifteen years ago. Ale was the reason he'd tipped the boat in the storm and lost Jayden. It was an accident, but Perth was the one having to pay for it, wasn't he? As if the moment he stepped into a boat, it would sink. But he knew if he disobeyed his pa, it would bring him grief. Although Perth suffered enough grief himself, what with the teasing and name-calling he got from everyone around him. As if he were a coward or something when he was left behind on the docks as the crews set sail. Yet he respected his pa's vow, and to this day had never felt the sea move beneath him. He often looked with longing as the ships unfurled their sails and sped along, pushed by the wind. There seemed nothing more exciting than skimming over the water and feeling the ocean spray on your face.

But he would just have to find other ways to fulfill his need for adventure. He was so tired of hauling fish and tying lines and carting groceries up to the inn. He was tired of living in Tolpuddle, where nothing exciting ever happened. And worse, Bayley Tetten-hall teased him every time he had to deliver something to his cottage, saying he was almost old enough to pick one of his four daughters to marry. That he was almost of an age to settle down and raise his own brood of young'uns.

Marry? That was the last thing he wanted. He planned to see the world, travel to faraway lands, seek his fortune. Doing what? He had no idea. He just knew if he stayed here, he would end up as lonely and empty as his pa. He'd asked his pa again just last night why he didn't remarry, seeing as how his wife—Perth's mum—had died years ago of the ague, off in Scuddle where his pa never ventured. But he'd only laughed and said no one would want an old crusty man like him. Old? Why, he was only thirty-nine. Perth thought his father was plenty handsome, although a bit rough around the edges, like any fisherman. But he was strong, healthy, and women seemed to notice him—at least Gayla Kedge did. Perth had seen the way the two looked at each other when they passed in the market or spoke at the inn. But when Perth had mentioned her name last night, his pa had nearly choked on his potato.

He could picture having Gayla as a mother. She was kind, funny, always giving him a hug or tousling his hair. He knew most boys his age didn't like their mothers fussing over them, but Perth had never had a mother to speak of, and he kind of liked the show of affection. From what Tanin had whispered to him, back when he was about ten, Emelee—his mum—had showed up a year after Jayden's death and left his pa with a basket with a babe in it. "He's yours," his mum had told his pa. "But I don't want anything of yours anymore. So take him." And then she had left and gone back to Scuddle. When Perth went to question his pa about it, he said he shouldn't listen to talk. But his pa would never tell him the truth. Every time he had asked him what happened to his mum and whether the story was true, his pa just clammed up. "The past is past. Finishing is better than starting," he always said. Implying that it didn't matter where you were born, or who birthed you. What mattered was how you lived and what people would say about you when your life was over. Better to be an honorable, kind peasant than a rich evil king. Or something like that.

Since he wasn't needed on deck any longer, he said good-bye to Tanin and headed back down the dock. Alyck Rowe was loading one last crate onto his wagon; this was Perth's chance to find out the truth.

"What's up, stripling?" Tanin's tall, lanky pa leaned down and glared in his face.

Perth gulped. "Well, sir. I was just wondering . . . about those trolls."

Alyck straightened and repositioned a crate, then strapped the lot down as he spoke. "What's to wonder about? They're back. They seem to come back every spring, like a patch of annoying weeds."

"Did you really see them in the garbage dump last night?"

"See them? Could smell 'em from halfway across the village. They made a big enough racket with their snorting and chortling. Didn't you hear 'em? You live a rock's throw away from the dump."

Perth shook his head.

"Well, you must have salt in them ears, small fry. But I'm sure they'll be there awhile, if you've a hankering to get a look. But you better not get too close. They get a whiff o' you and you'll be their next meal. You know how much they like fish flesh, *Perthin*."

For the millionth time, Perth cursed his pa for giving him that ridiculous name. Perthin! Whoever named their babe after a fish? It was a constant embarrassment for him, every time someone new learned his name. There'd be a laugh, and then, without fail, some stupid fish joke to follow. Well, one day he'd leave Tolpuddle, and the minute he did, he would give himself a new name. Something . . . regal and fancy. A name that would impress folks—not make them laugh at him behind his back.

"Are you teasing the poor child again?"

Perth spun around to see Gayla Kedge setting down a basket overflowing with flowers, the wind tugging her hair, a scowl on her face. Her eyes reflected the stray grays and greens of the sea as she threw her rope of long hair over a shoulder.

"Didn't mean any harm, Gayla." Alyck lowered his head and pulled the strap tight over the crates, then led the cart horse around to head back to town. Gayla kept her eyes pinned on him as he climbed up on the bench and jiggled the reins. He mumbled a polite good day and left Gayla shaking her head and stifling a chuckle.

"I think he's afeared of you," Perth said with a grin.

"He should be." Gayla patted Perth's head, then nodded at her basket. "How 'bout you help me carry these back up to the inn? I have a cake to pick up at the baker's, and I don't think it will fit in there."

"T'would be my pleasure," he said, glad for an excuse to get away from the stinky docks and the incessant teasing. He knew his pa wouldn't mind. Pa always told him to be eager to lend a helping hand to those that needed one. Besides, at this hour of day, so close to teatime, there was bound to be a bogberry tart hot out of the oven he could finagle. Freya, the cook, could never say no to what she called his "sad puppy face."

He bent over to pick up the basket, when Gayla's voice stopped him.

"Perthin Quay! What's that in your pocket?"

Before Perth had a chance to spin around, Gayla had already pulled the flask from his trousers and had the top uncorked before he could utter a word of protest.

He reached to grab for it, but she held the glass to her chest. "It's just some cider."

She took a whiff and frowned. "Not the kind of cider a boy your age should be drinking." With a brusque motion, she upended the bottle and poured out the contents onto the dock.

Perth hung his head. Trolls be hanged! If his pa found out, he'd be punished from one end of Tolpuddle to the other.

Gayla drew close to his face and spoke in a quiet, harsh tone. "You should know better, Perthin. If your pa heard you were drinking . . . why, it would break his heart. You *know* what drink did to him!"

"But I'm not him! I only take a sip from time to time—"

"That's not the point. Maybe you have better control than your pa—there's no saying if that'd be so. But you're a child, and still living in his home. You have to respect his rules. And don't tell me he's never lectured you on drinking, because I've heard him—numerous times."

So has the entire village. Perth stood unmoving, feeling the chastisement as painfully as if she'd just struck him. He knew she was right. And it wasn't as if he really liked the stuff. He just wanted to show the other boys he was as grown up as they were. Danyl had dared him to drink in front of his other friends, and he'd done it without making a face, although the stuff burned his throat and made his eyes water. He figured if he carried the flask around and drank a bit from time to time, he'd not only get used to it—the bigger boys would leave him be. Gayla just wouldn't understand, so he didn't bother to explain it.

He said nothing as she slipped the flask into the pocket of her sweater, hoping she wouldn't tell his pa. He doubted he'd ever see that bottle again.

A sudden commotion broke out on the far end of the dock. Men shouted and pointed out to sea, but Perth couldn't see past the boats and stacks of crates blocking his view. Gayla said to him, "Leave the basket. Come, something's happened."

She ran ahead and Perth followed at her heels. He nearly crashed into her as she stopped suddenly halfway to the railing.

Chugging around Blight Point was the bow of *The Sea Farer*. Or what was left of it.

Gayla put a hand over her heart. "Oh, dear God, what happened?" she said, the color drained from her face.

Perth could only stare in shock as the rest of the ship rounded the point. She was listing hard to port, and huge chunks of wood were missing from the gunwales. It was almost as if some giant creature had . . . taken bites out of the hull. The bow was smashed in, and one of the large masts was broken in half, leaving the sail flapping like a sheet on a clothesline. Had the ship crashed into some cliffs? Perth couldn't imagine how, without her going down.

He stood off to the side as men rushed past, pushing him out of the way. Others ran toward town, crying for help. Perth felt useless as strong hands caught the mooring lines and secured the ship, its battered hull clunking against the dock. His gaze skittered back and forth along the ship's decks. In a flurry of movement and mayhem, he caught sight of his pa and he sucked in a breath of relief.

His pa spotted him but turned and ran off toward the foredeck. Gayla grabbed Perth's sleeve before he could sprint on board. "We'd best stay here, out of the way."

Perth fidgeted, annoyed. He had to find out what had happened. He watched the ramp slide into place, and men spilled down it, like rats scurrying from a fire. Then he spotted his pa—with his arm around Bayley Tettenhall.

Bayley walked hunched over, and even from where Perth stood he could make out the blood. Blood streaming down Bayley's arm, and soaking the side of his head. His black hair shone with blood. From what Perth could tell, his pa was all right.

Gayla rushed up the ramp to help. "Perth, go fetch Lisal—at the apothecary's shop. Tell her to bring her bag of bandages and ointments. Hurry!"

Perth nodded and took off. But as he ran, he listened to what the men were saying around him. Rumors were already flying like gulls, winging toward the village as men ran down the dock and up the cobbled road across the heath-draped hillside. He heard one fisherman say two men had been knocked overboard. He claimed they'd been attacked by a knucker.

Knucker? Perth stopped and turned to see who was talking behind him. He didn't recognize the older man who was hobbling along, hanging on to the sleeve of a young fisherman Perth only knew by sight.

"What's a . . . knucker?" Perth asked.

The man trudged up to Perth and shook his head. Fear darted wildly in his eyes; he resembled a crab caught in a trap. "Never seen the likes of it in all my life . . . a knucker it was. No denying."

The man turned to his companion. "Must 'ave been twice the length of the ship—and near as wide. With fearsome eyes that burned with fire." The man clutched at his heart and would have fallen down had his friend not held him up.

"I don't understand," Perth said.

The younger fisherman propped the old man up against his shoulder and glared at Perth. "Oh, brine and bother! What's to understand? They were attacked by a sea monster! Can't you see them bites it took out of the hull? Nearly pulled them under, but the captain managed to poke one of its eyes with an oar. The beast about ripped off his arm for the effort. Poor Bayley. Doubt he'll be able to use that arm ever again."

Perth gulped past the heavy lump lodged in his throat. His stomach churned and he felt sick. It was one thing to brave a storm, knowing the danger you were facing. But to be out fishing on a clear, cloudless day, the ocean a sheet of glass—only to be attacked by some beast large enough to sink a ship? And why would such a creature attack a ship anyway?

"Where'd the thing come from?" Perth asked, anxious to get to the apothecary's, yet unable to get his feet moving.

"Who knows?" the young man answered him. "From the deep, I s'pose."

The older man waved his arm in the air. "No, not that one. That one's from the north—where all manner of evil is bred. I heard told once, by my great-grandpa, of the giant sea wyrms that once swam under the ice, blowing fire from their nostrils—"

"Fire?" Perth said in disbelief.

"So the tales go. In a place where ice burns and fire freezes. In the northern Wastes, far, far away."

Perth shook his head. Tales conjured in an old man's imagination. But . . . there was no denying the holes in the hull. He would just have to wait and ask his pa what he thought. Now, he'd better hurry and get help for Bayley Tettenhall or he'd be severely rebuked by Gayla.

Perth said a hasty good-bye to the men and ran up the road. When he reached the promontory, he waded through the flowering heath to look out across the harbor stretched out below him, Blight Point curved like a finger around the sparkling bay. The water was so calm, it shone like glass.

But out beyond the harbor . . . Perth saw a strange turbulence. In one place only, the water was disturbed, undulating as if something was astir below the surface. Perth tried to focus, but it was too far away to tell if his eyes were playing tricks on him in the late afternoon glare.

The sight caused an odd feeling to well up in his heart. Righteous indignation paired with anger and an uncanny desire to stop this threat. He stood there fuming, both surprised and fueled by a sudden urge to best the creature. Why he felt these things, he couldn't say. But something was endangering his village, and it had to be stopped. Yet what could he do? He was just a boy—who had never handled an oar or a sail. Who could only throw a rock halfway from his cottage to the water. Who couldn't even push off a couple of bullies who tried to intimidate him.

With a sigh, he forced the urge down, then turned and did the only useful thing he could think of at the moment—run for help.

THIRTEEN

I T HAD BEEN easy enough for Perth to sneak out. His pa, exhausted from the chaos of the day's events, had almost fallen asleep in his soup. Fishing was tiresome enough, and the crew of *The Sea Farer* had begun their day before dawn, setting out to bring home a hold of silverfins by day's end—only to have encountered the sea monster. After fighting the thing off and hobbling back to port, the crew learned there were over a dozen injured men that had needed tending, and his pa had stayed late after dark helping. Which suited Perthin's plan just fine.

The tales of the monster had the village in a fret by eve, and if any still didn't believe, all they had to do was take a good look at the ship's damage to realize the truth in the talk. On his way back from the inn, after crossing the headlands, he'd dallied in the marketplace and listened. No two villagers seemed to be in agreement on what they'd seen, but no one doubted the beast had a menacing intent. When he asked his pa to describe the knucker, he only said two words: *huge* and *terrifying*. He couldn't get any more out of him. No doubt his pa wanted to keep from frightening him—as if such a thing *could* scare him.

He kicked a rock on the road and snorted. His pa still thought him a helpless little boy; he was always overprotective, never allowing him to do half the things his friends were allowed to do. When he whined about the unfairness of it all, his pa would only shake his head and repeat his usual lecture of how he'd vowed to God to keep him safe. But his pa was smothering him, and didn't want to admit that soon his son would be a man. As much as Perth loved his pa and wanted his approval, he yearned for freedom, for adventure. And he was never going to get either by nodding his head and being dutiful.

And that's why he was heading out in the dark, after moonset, to the village garbage heap. A thrill of danger spurred him to run across the rickety bridge that spanned the slough and up over the bluff to the outskirts of Tolpuddle. No one would be out guarding the lane his feet were pounding hard—not tonight, after the harrowing affair with the sea monster. What were a few noisome, stinky trolls in comparison to a sea monster? No doubt all the able-bodied men of the village were snoring in their beds like tired rumphogs.

As he neared the end of the road, Perth could make out the huge smelly piles of trash. Every bit of waste and garbage—rotted vegetables, fish guts, broken furnishings, irreparable wagon parts, threadbare clothing—ended up here to rot. He winced at the stench but kept a stoic face. If those trolls were watching, he wanted to make sure they knew he was fearless. During the day the gulls swarmed the piles, squabbling over their findings; anyone could see the flocks winging around the piles all the way from Bleak Harbor Inn. Perth pictured the trolls doing much the same—sitting smack dab in the middle of a putrefying mass of waste and sifting for treasures they could use to adorn themselves. Or stuffing their faces with whatever they found tasty.

He wondered about the tales of their strength, but he had no intention of fighting them to suss out the truth. He was no fool; even if they revealed themselves as wimpy and cowardly, there were three of them and only one of him. Instead, he planned to use his wits and cunning to trick them. He only needed to steal something from them, something to prove he'd actually bested them. He could always make up some story of a valiant fight—although he doubted Danyl and Tanin would believe a word. Even if he came back beat up, they'd just laugh and say he must've tripped in his clumsiness. So the only way they'd believe him was if he stole back some of the baubles the trolls had taken from the villagers.

Where they kept such things, Perth had no idea, but he figured, since they moved about from village to village, that they must carry sacks of their treasures. Or have a hiding place they retreated to after a night's foraging. Perth would only have to follow them in secrecy to learn just where they hoarded their booty. Maybe they had a cave or hollow somewhere. Someone said trolls lived under bridges, and would come out if they heard boot steps on the boards above, then attack and eat the unwary traveler, or their goats or sheep. But Perth didn't believe such a tale. No one had ever gone missing in the vicinity of a troll and turned up half eaten, as the stories suggested. No one's munched-up bones had ever been found thrown atop a trash heap. Fact was, no one had ever been brave enough to learn the truth—until now.

He figured if he were a troll and he saw some angry farmer running after him with a pitchfork, he'd turn and thrash the poor sod in defense. Maybe the trolls weren't evil after all. What if they were just misunderstood? Busily minding their own business, just trying to find food enough to fill their stomachs, and there folks were—chasing them down and calling them names. He'd be upset too. As far as them stealing all those shoes and linens—well, he still couldn't figure that out. The trolls were blamed for everything that went missing from the village. Or for anything that had mysteriously broken overnight. Easier to blame a troll than your neighbor, truth be told.

Perth stopped at the edge of the first heaping pile of refuse. He set down the burlap sack he had brought, laying it flat on the ground so the trolls would see nothing was in it. He lifted his arms to show them he harbored no evil intent, carried no weapon.

Night grew thick, amplifying every sound. He could hear rats scurrying about the piles, and other small creatures. Maybe badgers or porcs. Trolls weren't the only ones that thought a pile of rotting fish made a good meal. His heart pounded hard as he listened, and he pushed down the fear threatening to make him run back home. Now that he was here, he felt vulnerable and exposed. His clever ideas for tricking the trolls flew from his head as he heard the sound of something clearing its throat. Shivers raced up his back and across his neck, and he willed himself to stand calmly, but he couldn't control his jitters as three giant shapes lumbered toward him.

He hoped the trolls couldn't smell his fear—or see all that well. He groaned inside, now greatly regretting his foolhardy idea. These trolls would see a small boy putting on a brave face. They would make mincemeat out of him. He was as good as dead.

A deep grumbling voice came from one shape. "*Wellll* . . . look what we have here—a minnow."

"Ooh, a tasty minnow . . ." another shape muttered.

Perth shook uncontrollably as the three trolls drew nearer. They cautiously took a step or two, then sniffed the air. Perth, for his part, wished he could plug up his nose with his fingers. They stank so bad, his eyes watered and tears ran down his cheeks. But he stood still, afraid the slightest movement would send them into a rage. And he didn't like that remark about being tasty.

"I-I'm just a boy," he said, "and a skinny one too. Don't have any meat on my bones to speak of."

The third troll laughed with a grating sound that hurt Perth's ears. It came close enough to point a gnarled, filthy finger at him. "True, cousin. You speak truth."

The troll towered over him, larger than even Tanin's pa by a head or more. In the darkness, Perth couldn't see much, but the tales of their ugliness were no exaggeration. Warts erupted from the troll's face, and its hair was all atangle, like bent wire. A triple chin sagged under a hideous mouth full of crooked blackened teeth, and two sharp tusks protruded from the lower jaw, curving up alongside the blubbery lips that now smacked in delight. Perth noticed this one was cross-eyed.

The troll drooling over him waved the other two over. Perth's gaze locked on the slime dripping down one of the tusks. "Come see this brave minnow!"

Perth tried to keep still as the trolls' hands pinched his waist and pawed at his clothes. He couldn't get over how huge they were—wide as cows, and they wore shreds of clothing in a hodgepodge fashion. Why did they wear clothes at all? And one actually had a tattered, grimy hat atop its head, although Perth couldn't tell what kind of hat it had once been. Another had at least a dozen necklaces around its neck, all encrusted with slime and mold and mud so that Perth could not make out whether they were made of gold, silver, or decorated with jewels. These were strange creatures, to be sure.

"Tell us, cousin, why did you come seeking us?" the troll with the hat asked in a cooing, grating tone.

To his surprise, he found his voice, although when he spoke, he cringed at the wavering and pathetic words. He'd hope to sound braver. "How is it you can speak? Who taught you to talk?" Did they think humans were some kind of relation—is that why they called him cousin?

His comment set off a volley of hysterical laughter. Spittle flew at him and coated his face. He used his sleeve to wipe off the sticky goo. He wished they would step back a few feet. Their smell was making him gag, and he put his hand over his nose.

"What's so funny?" he said through his hand, trying to see them through his stinging tears. For some reason he was no longer afraid, and his curiosity was emboldening him.

"You are, cousin," the cross-eyed troll said. "Coming here to challenge us. You mean to steal some of our treasures, don't you? Well, you can't have them."

"Can't have them!" the one with the necklaces added in a mean, throaty voice. "Maybe we should tear off a few fingers and stuff them in those baggy trousers of yours."

"Or munch on a foot. He might not have any meat, but I'll wager those bones are crunchy. So young and fresh—"

"Yes, fresh!" the cross-eyed troll said, a wild, hungry look growing in its eyes.

"Yes, fresh!" the one with the hat parroted.

Perth tried to wiggle out of their circle, but they closed ranks, leaving him no means of escape. His heart pounded hard in his throat.

The troll with the hat laughed so hard that Perth felt waves of sour wind blow against his face. It laid a huge hand on Perth's head and gave him a brusque pat that almost pounded him down into the dirt. The other trolls joined in, and soon, in their merriment, they were guffawing and rolling in the dirt like rumphogs. Perth edged back slowly, hoping to take advantage of their gaiety to make a hasty escape, but as he started to turn, he felt a painful clamp on his ankle. One of the trolls had grabbed him.

Perth cried out. "Your nails are sharp, and they're digging into me. Kindly let go!"

"Ooh, you didn't say *please*, cousin."

"Please!"

The troll released its grip. All three creatures fell onto their backsides and roared with laughter.

The cross-eyed troll wiped its eyes, and the mud caked across its cheek broke off in bits. "Oh, you have to hand it to this little minnow—he's braver than fifty big, strong men." It put its face so close to Perth's that their noses touched. Perth shook, more from disgust than fear. If they were going to torture and eat him, they would have done so by now. Or so he thought. Then again, they could just be playing with him the way a cat toyed with a bird or a mouse before killing and eating it. He gulped.

The troll with the hat sat up and glared at him. "Tell us the truth, now, cousin. Did you come to rob us? If you lie, we will know."

"Yes, we will know," the other two chimed together. "Know, we will know! Know, we will know!"

"Fine!" Perth yelled over their chanting. "I did come to rob you—"

"There, see!" the cross-eyed troll said. "I was right. I *told* you—"

"I was the one who said it first," answered the troll with the necklaces. It had picked something up and was waving it in the air. It looked like a woman's shoe, although it was full of mud. Mud splattered Perth's face. *Great.* Soon he would be as filthy as they were. He had to get out of there, but how?

"No, I said it first—"

Perth yelled as loud as he could. "Does it *really matter* who said it first?"

The trolls grew suddenly quiet and looked at each other. The first troll grumbled under its breath. "No, s'pose not . . ."

"But what to do with the minnow?" the one with the hat asked, now circling Perth and waggling a finger at him.

"He's just a minnow," the cross-eyed one said. "We should throw him back into the sea."

"Yes!" the necklaced troll said. "Let's throw him in the sea!"

The troll with the hat glared at the others. "Now, that's not a polite way to treat a cousin. We should offer the minnow some tea and crumpets and send him on his way."

"Crumpets! With clotted cream!"

"And jam. Don't forget the bogberry jam!"

The troll with the hat plopped down in the garbage heap and sighed. "Oh, how I miss clotted cream! It would taste so divine on a bowl of grubs!"

Perth stood listening in disbelief. Carrying on about tea and crumpets? These trolls were odder than he ever imagined. "I could get you some clotted cream," he offered without thinking.

All three trolls craned their necks and stared him down. The one with the hat smiled—the sight of its crooked, rotted teeth made Perth shrink back. "Could you, now?" It then scowled. "It's a trick. We will let you go, and then you'll never return."

"I give you my word."

The first troll spat, and its spittle grazed Perth's cheek. "Man's word. Worth nothing. Not even a bucket of fish guts."

"My word is true," Perth insisted. "If you release me, I'll bring you back a pot of clotted cream tomorrow night."

The three trolls grumbled, but Perth couldn't make out their words. The one with the hat said, "We don't trust any man's word. But we know we can trust you, cousin. You are trustworthy and honorable among men. We will let you go."

Perth felt relief wash over him. Why they thought him trustworthy, he had no idea. But he knew better than to waste his time trying to make sense of anything these trolls did or said. They were whackier than old Mrs. Shrubble, who always threatened to bonk him with her broom every time he passed by her dilapidated cottage near Blight Point. He should leave before they changed their minds and decided his feet were crunchy and delectable after all.

"He should show those big brave men of his village how fearless he is," the cross-eyed troll said with a grin. "We should give him a token to take back with him."

The other trolls nodded. The one with the hat said, "No man has ever dared face us. You may be a minnow, cousin, but a brave one indeed. Tell us—what would you take from us had you robbed us?"

Perth clammed up. What should he say?

"Would you care for my fine hat—?"

The cross-eyed troll slapped at the one pulling the hat off its head. "The minnow doesn't want a smelly old hat, do you, cousin?"

A fierce itch started working its way up Perth's back—no doubt these heaps were infested with fleas. "Just give me something one of the villagers can identify, so they'll know I've spoken the truth when I tell them you gave it to me." Although he now wondered if his claim would be answered with derision. His friends might say he found it along the road, by chance. Or even accuse him of having stolen the object in his possession. He realized now his plan to impress his friends was never going to work.

"There!" The troll with the necklaces said. "A smart minnow! I'd love to see the faces of those lugs when they learn this little fish has more courage than they." It took hold of the strands of necklaces and draped them over Perth's head. They hung heavy on his chest. "These should do. Someone will be missing these pretty baubles. I stole them just last fall. Although I shall miss them dearly!"

The troll with the hat smacked the other and said, "You have buckets of jewelry. What are a few necklaces?"

"But I so love them all!" It patted Perth on the head and fiddled with the necklaces. "There, my, don't you look lovely?"

Perth shook his head. He was now covered from head to toe with mud, drool, and slime. He would have to dunk in the slough and scrub all this muck off before slipping back into his cottage.

He hoped that would get rid of the smell. He hoped his pa was too tired to wake when he came in. Maybe he should just throw the necklaces in the slough, to avoid being labeled a thief.

Before he could protest, the cross-eyed troll grabbed him by the neck of his shirt and lifted him effortlessly in the air. Was it going to throw him? Perth clenched his eyes shut and waited, but nothing happened.

"We'll be waiting for that clotted cream."

"And a crumpet—can you bring me a crumpet?" the one with the hat asked.

"Ooh, crumpets, yes crumpets," the third troll crooned.

"I'll do what I can," Perth said, hoping Freya would let him have these things if he snuck into the inn's kitchen tomorrow afternoon. He hoped she didn't ask a whole lot of questions. He certainly wouldn't tell her who they were for.

"Then be off with you, cousin," the first troll said. "We'll be waiting." The other two waved.

"Yes, waiting, waiting!" the one with the hat said with a laugh. Perth watched it leap around in glee. He walked away from them, leaving them all dancing around the garbage heap, making obnoxious, loud noises that could wake the dead.

He wondered if he would wake up in the morning and discover this had all been a dream.

FOURTEEN

ARNYL LOOKED up and saw Gayla walking purposefully toward him. He lowered his eyes and fiddled with his stack of fish, hoping maybe she'd pass by. He knew his feelings were plain for her to see, and just that thought tangled up the words in his mouth worse than any storm-battered net. He wouldn't be surprised if, when he tried to say good morning, he'd look no more intelligent than the sea bass lying on his table with their mouths hanging open and their eyes glazed over.

He wished he didn't care for her so much. Surely she could never reciprocate his feelings; she seemed so much more refined and educated than he, although he knew very little of her background other than she'd that moved to Tolpuddle six years ago from Bluster, way up along the Shivery Coast. She and a handful of others had made their way to his village with little more than the clothes on their backs one early spring, declaring a huge nor'easter had destroyed their seaside town. She soon got a job at Bleak Harbor Inn, helping Grinda entertain the guests and see to the food and pleasantries needed—although Arnyl had the impression, from Gayla's efficient and organized manner, that she practically ran the inn herself, since Glinda was wont to suffer from emotional . . . episodes, as they were called in polite circles. Not that Arnyl listened to gossip. But he couldn't help overhearing a thing or two as he sold his fish in the marketplace. Not too many folks in Tolpuddle could refrain from gossiping, seeing as there wasn't much else exciting to pepper a conversation. Although today, the only talk was of the knucker.

He lifted his eyes and found Gayla staring at him. His gut twisted in knots, but he made sure to keep his mouth shut as he smiled a greeting at her.

Gayla frowned. "Arnyl, maybe you can sort out the true tales from the tall ones for me. Just what did attack *The Sea Farer* yesterday? Did you perchance get a look at it?" She sat down on the stool Arnyl vacated for her.

He was glad his voice came out without a hitch. Having her this close flustered him terribly. He walked a few steps and busied himself adjusting the canvas tarp overhead, retying the cord so that it stopped flapping in the morning breeze. "I only saw the back of the monster, but that alone showed how gigantic it was. Scales the size of . . . cows, a dark green, but shimmery as the sun hit it. It moved like . . . a huge eel, but I never did see its face, thank the heavens."

Gayla sat listening with keen attention as Arnyl went on to describe the attack, the way the beast threw itself against the hull over and over, and the awful cracking sound of the wood buckling under its strength. He felt himself tremble anew at the memory, but when Gayla laid her hand on his wrist in an attempt to comfort him, her touch only made him shake even more.

He sucked in a breath and walked to the other side of his stall and began stacking his crates against the wall of the large wharf building beside him. He wished more customers would come over, which would give him an excuse to look busy, too busy to chat, even though he wanted nothing more than to sit and talk with Gayla the whole day. But trolls would sprout wings before she'd take a man like him seriously. He was just a fisherman with nothing to offer a fine woman like her. He had to accept that fact, although he noticed she always seemed to seek him out whenever she saw him around the village. Perthin teased him about her, said she had her eye on him, but Arnyl chided his son, saying Gayla was just one of those friendly types. She spoke to everyone. Perthin only shook his head, laughed, and said, "Pa, you're a blind fool." Said he should hear the gossip going around, but Arnyl would not suffer gossip. Listening to folks' rumors only dug up trouble and created a big hole you fell into.

Perthin. The thought of his son set off another ache in his gut. He looked over at Gayla, whose soft eyes rested on him. He cleared his throat and came alongside her. "I'm worried about Perthin," he said. "I know he's taken a liking to you. I see the two of you talking at times. So . . . I'm wondering . . ."

"If he confides in me? Tells me his secrets?" When Arnyl shrugged, Gayla chuckled. "Pulling secrets from a boy that age is like getting a troll to take a bubble bath. Is there something you've seen him doing that worries you?"

Arnyl looked around the market at the other vendors selling their fish and vegetables and crafts. The lanes were finally filling with people. Any other morning villagers would be out early, buying what they needed for the day, but the knucker had no doubt kept many a family up with worry all night, depriving them of sleep. Arnyl noticed more than a few yawns.

He turned back to Gayla. "He snuck out last night, thinking I wouldn't notice. He's never done that before, and I have no idea where he went. Only, when he returned well after midnight, he was wearing just his trousers, carrying the rest of his clothing in his arms. And he was soaking wet—and smelled like he'd been rolling in fish."

Gayla erupted in laughter. "Well, that could imply a number of possibilities. He might have stumbled in the dark and landed in a manure pile, then tried to wash off in the slough—"

"Yes, but where would he be going so late at night, and not wanting me to know?"

"Oh, no doubt there are many places a boy his age might want to explore out of sight of his pa. Let's hope though, if there was a girl involved, he fell into the manure *before* he made it to her window."

Arnyl groaned at the thought that Perthin might have snuck out to see a girl. Gayla laughed again and made a face.

"You look like you've seen a troll! Why, your face has gone pale."

"A girl? He's only fifteen."

"And plenty old enough to start courting."

Arnyl pursed his lips. "I've never seen the boy lay eyes on any girl."

"Not in your company, I'd venture," Gayla said. "Did you talk to your own pa about the girls you liked?"

Arnyl thought back to when he met Emelee. His pa had been too busy with his drink to even notice his comings and goings, and hadn't cared a whit when Arnyl had told him of his engagement. Emelee had been the one sneaking around and not wanting her folks to know she was dating him. But he knew why, even at the time. No one wanted their daughter to be out with a drinker. He'd already gained a reputation before he was Perthin's age.

Arnyl sighed and leaned back against the building. "I really don't know what to say to him, Gayla. I've tried to raise him right, taught him to be honest and upright, hardworking, humble and God-fearing—"

"And you've done a wonderful job. Perthin may be a bit impetuous and restless, but that's his age. He's soon to be a man, and will want to make his own way in this world. He may not want to spend his life fishing in Tolpuddle—not when there's a big world out there to explore. You can't blame him for feeling a little trapped, can you?"

"No, I s'pose not." For some reason her words reminded him of the day he'd found the trunk tangled in his nets. Arnyl had released Perthin from his trap that day, set him free, saved his life. Did Perthin now feel trapped in his own cottage? Arnyl didn't want the lad to feel that way, but maybe Gayla was right—maybe it was just his age.

He looked at her and asked, "Well, what should I do then? Talk to him about it? Ignore him and turn a blind eye to his sneaking? I just don't know what to say to him."

Gayla stood and moved closer to Arnyl, and he smelled her fresh, clean scent, laced with a hint of lavender. His heart beat double time, and he was sure she could hear its loud pounding. "I'm no expert, Arnyl. I've never raised a child. But I can tell Perthin's a good lad, with a good heart. You've laid out a straight course for his feet; I'm sure he won't turn aside from your teaching. Just keep doing what you're doing."

"He's angry that I won't let him go to sea."

"But he knows you made a vow. Your keeping that vow shows him your integrity. Even if he resents it now, he'll respect you for it—in time." She lowered her voice and leaned close to him. "What a terrible loss you suffered, with Jayden. No one can criticize you for your decision. You took a bad situation and turned it around, turned your life around. I'm sure that wasn't easy, and few men have the strength and heart to raise a child on their own. How his mother could have left him with you and just walked away . . ."

A strangled sound came from Gayla's throat. Arnyl looked at her and saw tears pooling in her eyes. He startled at her abrupt shift in emotion; he had never seen her cry before. Maybe she regretted never having married or raised children. Arnyl realized he'd always assumed that had been her lot in life. But what if it wasn't? It was more likely she'd had a husband and perhaps even a babe and had lost them in the storm that ravaged her village—why had he never considered that? She never spoke about her past, and maybe that was the reason. How stupid of him! He always sensed she was carrying some deep pain underneath the cheerful countenance she showed all the long day. Who knew if she cried herself to sleep at night in the privacy of her room at the inn?

Arnyl felt a sudden longing to pull her into his arms and hold her, but he knew he could never indulge in such feelings. Instead, he took her hand and squeezed it, hoping she'd take it as a kind, neighborly gesture. Although just holding her hand sent his heart soaring with the gulls.

Gayla rallied a smile and used her free hand to wipe her teary eyes. "Well," she said, raising her chin, "I should be getting back to the inn. Grinda will need help with lunch, and Orsyn is trellising the grapevines. I promised him I'd keep Grinda company and greet the arriving guests. And I've still got stitching to do on the new linens, although they are nothing like what she had before. But they'll have to do in a pinch. Trolls be hanged! I can't figure why anyone would steal sheets and pillowcases off a clothesline."

Arnyl smiled at her talk, the gaiety of it lightening his heart. He was glad she had changed the subject. "Thanks for your advice about Perthin. I think, though, if he keeps sneaking out, I'll be tempted to follow him."

Gayla frowned, but her eyes danced in merriment. "Be careful, then, that you don't fall into that manure pile as well. It's awfully dark out there on the road without a lantern." She turned her head and looked to the east, as if seeing something far away. "I hope we've all seen the last of that sea monster. I've never heard of anything so terrible in all my life, and it gives me a chill to think about it. I hope it has moved to deeper waters far away, or gone back home—wherever that may be."

Arnyl nodded as Gayla started down the lane. She turned and said, "Be careful, out there, Arnyl. I'd hate it if anything happened to you."

Arnyl's breath caught at her words. He managed to say, "I will," then could only wave good-bye as she smiled wistfully at him and headed up the cobbles toward the promontory.

Perth dangled his feet over the edge of a large rock as he smeared clotted cream over a cold crumpet. He'd gone to all that trouble to get a sackful of the pastries, having been forced to promise Freya he'd help her tomorrow in the garden thinning carrots and beets in exchange for the treats, then had snuck out again after dark and run back to the garbage heap—only to find the trolls had gone. Why? They had made him promise to return, and they sure seemed eager to get hold of some crumpets. Perth couldn't figure it out, but he'd called to them for most of an hour, circling the mounds of smelly garbage, careful not to trip and have to bathe in the slough again.

Well, he'd kept his promise, but there was no sense letting good crumpets go to waste, so he sat there enjoying his midnight treat under the blanket of bright stars. The heather blooming all around gave off a faint perfume, and the breeze sliding off the sea and sweeping up the hillside hinted at the coming summer, gusts of warm air mingling with the traces of winter that lingered. Behind him, high up on the bluff, sat the inn, all the lamps now extinguished and the windows dark. Below him, the village spread out in a scramble of lanes, the shops and cottages also dark, as if a stupor draped over the whole world. He felt an odd sensation, as if he perched on the edge of time, his childhood behind him and his uncertain future calling him, a stronger pull than the sea's tides, making him stir with restless need. His heart heard a call to adventure, some destiny tugging at him, some wave of fate carrying him along toward an unknown shore.

He stood and gazed at the sea, utterly dark and foreboding, and felt the urge to run—run far from its foam and spray and vast emptiness. An image, then, materialized in his mind, of a strange and beautiful land with snow-covered mountains bathed in light, sparkling with an uncanny brilliance. He realized with a start that he'd been dreaming of this place for months, and his heart called to it, although he had no idea if it even existed. Just thinking of this serene land of vibrant green rolling hills and lakes that reflected the passing clouds like silvered mirrors filled him with a poignant longing, the way he imagined someone might feel after catching sight of his homeland at the end of a long, tiresome journey.

Maybe he had only conjured it in his imagination, but the magical land held sway over him, as if he'd been there before—as if it were his true home and he ached to return. Or maybe his longing to leave Tolpuddle and see the wide world was fashioning this dream. Regardless, he felt like the agitated sea, churning and rolling, unable to stay still.

Movement in the sea, close to shore, caught his eye, but in the dark of night, without a moon to illuminate the waters, he couldn't tell what he was seeing. He watched the sea grow calm again while he finished the last crumpet, then wiped crumbs from his face and stood to leave. At least if his pa caught him coming in, he wouldn't have to lie. He would say he went to sit and look out at the harbor to watch for the knucker.

As he took a step down the trail, a loud explosive noise made him jerk his head up and look back out across the harbor. He froze as the wooden docks along the coastline broke and shattered into the air, the pieces of the wood flying like dark shadows, but there was no mistaking the source of the destruction. An undulating shape rose up from the water, sending waves smashing against the pilings, and now joining the splintering sound of wood were the faint screams and shouts of the villagers below as they ran from their cottages toward the harbor, their tiny lantern lights bobbing in the air like frantic fireflies.

Perth's jaw dropped as he watched one dock after another break apart and burst into shards, the monster hugging the shoreline and raising its massive head as it swam. Torches swarmed the shore and lit up the knucker's iridescent scales as its back crested, and a tail whipped out of the erratic waves, then slapped the water so hard a giant spout of spray flew into the air, soaking the thatched rooftops of the cottages closest to the bay.

The creature was monstrous! Perthin held his breath as every limb shook. What could a mob of villagers do to stop something so powerful and bent on destruction? And why in heaven's name was it attacking his village? As Perth raced down the hill, crushing heath underfoot, he thought of all the waterside shops and cottages that were under attack and worried for his neighbors. From his vantage point, he could see turbulent water race up the lanes and flood the market square, and not a few roofs went flying when the beast's tail lashed out in a sweeping arc as it swam by. His own cottage lay out of the way of the monster's attention, but Perth did not hold out hope his home would be spared. He only hoped his pa had fled to safer ground.

The screams and yells grew louder as he arrived in the center of town; the swollen noises of sorrow were louder than any crashing wave. Water sloshed knee-high against the buildings, swirling and eddying in a chaotic dance as Perth waded through its cold embrace, searching for a sign of his pa in the crush of villagers running hither and thither. A madness had overtaken one and all. People were crying and running, carrying loads on their backs and dragging frightened children by the hand. Huge pieces of rafters and splintered posts bobbed on the water, smacking into unwary villagers and knocking them down.

Perth rushed over to help one woman who had fallen and was being pulled in the current toward the thirsty sea. He managed to help her past the inflow of surge to a higher spot on the hillside, where she joined dozens of others huddling together in fear and cold, most drenched with their clothes and hair dripping. A few shared dry blankets, but it was clear to Perth that his neighbors had been caught unawares with no time to grab any belongings at all. A few babies howled, adding to the cacophony that filled the night, a growing mournful sound of wailing that cut Perth's heart.

There was nothing else he could do here to help. He needed to find his pa, and see if anyone had thought of a way to stop the sea monster from leveling the entire village of Tolpuddle. Unable to think of anything consoling to say to the whimpering villagers, he ran back down the hill and through the center of town, striding as quickly as possible through the heaving water, dodging debris and flotsam, the remains of his neighbors' furniture and clothing and pieces of what had once been their simple, safe homes. At least the inn stood high enough on the promontory to remain untouched, a lone structure that Perth thought might very well end up the only one remaining in the village after this beast's attack. He hoped Gayla had stayed put, although, knowing her, she was probably down at the ruins of the harbor seeing if she could help.

He snorted as he thought about the trolls. Maybe they had known that knucker was coming and had fled. No doubt the garbage heaps had been inundated with water and swept into the sea. Perth hated to think of all that refuse contaminating his pristine harbor. But that surely was not to be the worst damage from this monster's ravaging. Perth dreaded what he would find as he neared the docks, fearing the news that many of his neighbors may have been killed. One look at the flattened streets where rows of cottages once stood told him some might not have gotten away with their lives in time. He hoped he was wrong.

He steeled his nerve and made for a large group of men huddled on the shore where the main ship dock once stood. Not a piece of wood remained standing, nor could Perth see any boats up and down the coastline, although in the dark he could not see very far. The dozen or so torches held aloft revealed total destruction of what had once been the seaport for his village.

Perth stopped and gaped, aghast at the sight, his thoughts suspended. He hadn't noticed Alyck Rowe until he felt someone grab his arm and shake him out of his mesmerized stupor.

Perth turned and looked in the fisherman's face, and what he saw in Alyck's eyes made Perth jolt in fear. The distraught man wasted no words. "Your pa; he's been hurt."

Before Perth could ask the questions that assaulted his mind, Alyck marched across the littered beach toward Perth's cottage, moving with deliberation. Perth, following wordlessly, stole a glance at the now-quiet sea. They passed crowds of people at the water's edge, who waited numb, shocked, disbelieving, no doubt hoping the knucker's fury had ebbed with the receding tide.

Perth followed Alyck over the dunes, silent the entire journey, until they reached the door to Perth's home, which, to his great relief, remain intact and undamaged. Alyck turned to him. "I'd best be seeing to the others. So many missing . . ." His voice trailed off, as if all the strength in his burly body had leaked out. Perth nodded. He didn't want to ask just who was missing. No doubt he would learn at dawn's first light, a dawn he had no desire to see come.

He watched the fisherman hurry off, then with a deep breath pushed the door open to face what had befallen his pa. His mind went blank, the night's events swarming him in a flurry of confusion, as he realized that his life—no one's life—would ever be the same from this moment on. Would his village survive, or would those left homeless and bereft of all worldy possessions leave and start anew elsewhere—just as Gayla had done years ago with a small group of stragglers from the Shivery Coast?

He stepped quietly into the cottage and smelled a strong scent. Eucalyptus . . . and mint. He wasn't surprised to find Gayla standing next to his pa, who was stretched out on the sofa, a cloth wrapped around his head. The oil lamp's glow revealed deep creases in his pa's face.

Perth hurried to his pa's side, catching a glance from Gayla, whose expression told him he needn't worry. "What happened, Pa? Where are you hurt?"

"Oh, Perthin. Thank the heavens you're all right. When I heard the commotion, I ran to your room, but you were gone." His pa tipped back his head and winced. "I . . . I thought I'd lost you . . ."

"I'm fine, Pa, fine. I was up on the promontory." He added, "Just sitting and looking out over the harbor, checking to see if that monster was anywhere around. I . . . I saw it attack the harbor." He came alongside his pa and picked up a steamy cup of tea that sat on the table beside him. "Here, drink this." Perth was glad Gayla was there, seeing to his pa.

Gayla stepped back and looked at Perth. "I should go. See who else might need help."

Perth watched his pa and Gayla exchange looks. He could almost hear the words form in the moment between them. Finally, his pa spoke. "Thank you, so much, for seeing me home and wrapping my head. I'm sure with Perth here . . ."

Gayla nodded, her eyes swimming with tenderness. Perth wished she would stay, but she rushed out the door before he could say good-bye.

Arnyl tore his glassy gaze from the door and found his son. "I ran to the harbor, looking for you, when the first big wave swamped the village. I never saw it coming, only heard loud crashing in the distance. The force of the water knocked me against Rickard's Dry Goods. I blacked out, but heaven be thanked—Alyck chanced upon me and got me to my feet. That's when I found I could barely walk. I think my leg might be broke." His pa drew in a long breath and shuddered, as if his ribs ached from the motion. "Alyck and Gayla managed to get me home but I'm afeared I won't be up and around for many a day."

Perth heard his pa's voice choke up. "I don't want to be a burden on you—or on anyone. I can't bear the thought that I might be stuck on this couch for a fortnight or more—"

"Pa, I'm just glad you're alive. I'll tend to you, don't you worry."

His pa stared wistfully toward the window, where the dark night encroached. "So many hurt, their homes gone, swept away. What will happen to Tolpuddle?"

"I don't know, Pa. But come morn, I'll head to the marketplace. I'm sure that's where everyone will gather . . . whoever's left . . ."

Perth stared at his pa. His whole life, he'd never seen him sick or hurt, and the sight of him lying there tore at his heart. "Just rest," Perth told him. "Drink your tea, and I'll get you comfortable."

Perth gathered up blankets and a pillow from the bedroom, and after repositioning his pa and leaving him to wrestle with sleep, stepped outside onto the wooden porch. He gazed along the dunes to the shore and listened to the night settle into a deep quiet. But Perth knew much pain lay just below the surface of the night's silence. The harsh morn would reveal all, and grief would gush in the bright light of truth. He knew he would get no sleep this night.

An anguish rose in his heart, surprising him with its intensity. He walked out to the closest dune, far from the warmth of his home, far from the ravaged village. There, under the dome of stars twinkling for all the world as if they knew nothing of the troubles of humans on earth, he let the tears pour down his face, glad none of his friends were around to see him so weak and pitiful. Yet along with his despair came another feeling, rising in him like its own kind of monster, a mix of outrage and fierce determination that made him raise his eyes to heaven and cry out.

"God of the heavens, of the vast star field, I implore you! Do not leave this village and its people at the mercy of such a beast. Show me what I must do to stop it from destroying us. Let me avenge my village. If you would but show me how, and provide the means, I vow to not rest until this threat has been vanquished. I know I'm just a lad, but let me prove my worth. I'm not afeared of this monster."

Perth gazed up at the stars, knowing the One who created such magnificent lights had unlimited power and wisdom. His pa had taught him of God's mercy as well, and Perth hoped heaven would shower him with that mercy, and have pity on his poor village. There had to be some reason the monster had attacked, and if he could but learn that reason, he knew that it would provide the key to stopping it.

A strange chill danced across his neck. Perth spun around, sensing someone near, but he saw no one. The air thickened, the way it often did during a thunderstorm, and Perth held his breath. Something was coming toward him, but no one appeared among the ice plant trailing across the sand. Yet he knew he was not alone.

"Who's there?" he demanded, looking left and right and behind him. His arms shook, yet more from anticipation than fear. He sensed a presence so potent, he felt he could reach out a hand and touch it. But he saw nothing—nothing at all but the diaphanous mist clinging to the sand.

After a moment of imposing silence, Perth heard a noise. A soft sound, like a whisper, close to his ear. He waved his hand, swatted about his head, but encountered nothing.

Then a shape—gray and unformed—slid through the air and coalesced into the semblance of a man. It floated inches off the ground, and stood taller than Perth by a head or more. Perth could make out what looked like a face, but it was featureless, yet words came from where its mouth would be.

"You would do well to fear such a creature," the voice said, low and sonorous. Its words dissipated in a glitter of moonlight.

"Who are you?" Perth said, his own words barely a breath of air.

"I've come in answer to your plea."

Perth strained to see this apparition closer. "Are you an angel sent from heaven?"

The shape laughed with a gentle lilt. "No, but I once was a young lad, like you . . . so very long ago."

Perth stood unmoving, watching the thing with narrowed eyes. "What do you want?"

"To help you."

"And why would you want to help me?"

The shape lifted higher off the ground, and Perth followed it with his eyes, not wanting to let it leave his sight. "Because I know where this beast has come from, and who has sent it."

"You do?"

"And there is only one way to stop it."

Perth's curiosity trumped his tremble of apprehension. "And what is that?"

"I will tell you, Perthin Quay. But once you hear my words, you may wish to recant your vow." Now Perth could see the unremitting dark of this thing's eyes, yet he sensed nothing evil about it. Much the opposite—Perth felt an aura of genuine kindness and sympathy.

He straightened and lifted his chin. "I would not. Once a vow is made, it must be kept. I will not break my vow made before God and all heaven."

Perth watched, unblinking, as the gray shape shifted and gelled into the form of a man. Now he could clearly see the man's features, although he was still ethereal and a wisp of cloud. A dim glow came from the man's eyes and lit up his noble face. Perth had never seen anyone like him—with eyes so pale, like ice, yet filled with gentleness and compassion. Perth felt strangely drawn to this man or ghost or whatever he was, and if he'd at first felt any inkling of fear, it was now gone. "Please . . . tell me who you are and from whence you've come."

The man smiled, and just that simple gesture warmed Perth's heart as if he stood by a blazing fire. He let the warmth radiate into his soul and yearned to hear all this strange visitor had to say.

"My name is Cakrin, once king of Elysiel, but now dead."

"What is Elysiel . . .?" But as soon as Perth asked the question, he knew. Knew in a rush of awareness that Elysiel was the land of his dreams, the place his heart cried out to see. And in some uncanny way, he recognized this king as well, as if he had always been there in his dream, somewhere in the background, or behind him—a strong but gentle presence.

The king said nothing, only nodded, as if he knew what Perth was thinking and feeling. But how could this be? Was he imagining all this? Maybe the shock of the night's horrors was unhinging his mind. He reached out a hand to touch this king but met with only air.

Cakrin's smile dropped. "If you are keen to fulfill your vow, I will help you. For I am in need of your aid, and we share the same enemy. Come to me here, tomorrow night, prepared to leave. You have a hard journey ahead, but must travel light. No human in all the world has the power to stop the evil behind this destruction, yet I have gifts to give you that will aid you to be victorious. Gifts kept in the crypt of kings, held in secret for this day, a day long foretold. But you must be certain, Perthin Quay. You face a very dangerous foe."

Perth gulped, but he knew now, deep in his heart, he had to go. He did not know why, but he felt it as surely as he knew he was alive. This was his destiny, what he was born to do, and this truth filled every pore in his body. He suddenly felt older, much older, as if this king had infused him with the wisdom of the ages, opening his mind and heart to a greater understanding of the world and his place in it.

Yet he had to ask. "Why me? Why did you come to me—a lad of fifteen—instead of to someone big and strong, with years of battle under his skin?"

"Because, Perthin Quay, a matter of the heart is at the heart of the matter. Man judges by the outer appearance, but God sees the heart, and yours is true. Guard your heart, lad, for it is the well-spring of life. If your heart is true, you cannot fail." He added, "I have heard your prayers in the night, all of them."

"How?" Perth mouthed.

"That is the way it has always been. The way of Elysiel."

Perth stared into the king's moonstruck eyes that radiated with a shimmering light. He then looked across the dune to his cottage, where his pa lay in pain, needing his help. How could he leave on the morrow? He surely couldn't tell his pa his plans. He knew just what his pa would say if he recounted his conversation with a ghost—one claiming to be a dead king come to fetch him—Perthin Quay—to save not just Tolpuddle but perhaps the known world. He would say he was daft and threaten to punish him for such foolish talk. And then—when his pa discovered him gone, what grief would fall upon him? Would he fear he had lost yet another son? How could he inflict such grief upon his pa? Doubts assailed him, making him wonder if he'd been foolhardy to make that vow. His divided loyalties rent his heart in two.

"Perthin Quay," the king said, "I know your heart aches for your father. But he will be well cared for. Should you undertake this quest, you must leave this life behind and set your sights on the task before you. Will you do this?"

Resolve settled in Perth's heart, ushering in a calmness and certainty. He knew now there was no turning back. "Yes. Yes, I will go. I will meet you here on the morrow at night."

The ghost nodded once, his ephemeral shape fading until nothing but mist swirled around Perth's feet.

—FIFTEEN

PYTHIUS WATCHED Ka'zab eat as he sat at the head of the massive oak dining table in the empty banquet room. His mercenary commander attacked the wild boar haunch with fervor, as if he hadn't tasted meat in months. Juices dribbled down his cheeks and soaked his beard, but Ka'zab kept eating, and Pythius's servants kept bringing platters of meat, roasted ears of corn and potatoes, boards of fresh-baked bread, and tankards of ale.

Pythius was impatient to hear his commander's report, but he reined in his ire. Ka'zab had never been one to acquiesce meekly to his king, and Pythius, upon hearing of the man's long-awaited return to Paladya, summoned him to report on the recent months' raid in the northwest. Ka'zab sent back word agreeing to come to the palace—on the condition that he first be served a hearty meal. So Pythius made sure the fare brought to his faithful leader of his dark army would demonstrate his gratitude.

He emptied his own chalice of wine, hoping the herbal tincture his latest healer had infused in the drink would work better than the last potion. Fifteen years of unabating pain had worn him down to the bone. He silently cursed the scepter—still encased in the box beneath his bed. All these years, he'd found no one able to unlock its power. Each mage and witch he summoned to study it had concocted theories and formulated opinions and waved their

hands muttering strange words, but they'd all failed. He saw little choice other than to put them to death. He couldn't take the
chance of loose tongues alerting his enemies to his bane. And due
to their failures, the pain in his hand had never subsided. Instead,
it had grown steadily worse, until his entire left arm had become
useless and stiff like an old tree limb, the agony never ebbing. The
terrible suffering weighing upon him in the vision he'd seen in
the crystal slab was now, all these years later, a daily reality. Yet he
refused to believe Cakrin's words, although they haunted his every
waking moment and even seeped into his dreams: *You saw your
doom in the crystal mirror . . ."*

Ka'zab wiped his sleeve across his face and pushed his plate
away. He narrowed his eyes at his king and spoke. "Our attack
upon the villages in the northern lands has been met with some
opposition. But it is nothing we cannot quell."

"Explain," Pythius said, corralling his impatience. He wanted
this conversation to reach its end quickly so he could dunk his arm
in ice in the privacy of his chambers.

"Around this stone circle, a city has grown. Refugees from our
skirmishes are pouring into this place, and now word tells of a
leader that has risen up to organize the villagers and form an army."
Ka'zab snorted and laughed. "A pathetic lot. Farmers, herdsmen,
untrained and unequipped."

"And have you attacked this city and taken control of the
sacred site yet?"

Ka'zab looked into his empty tankard and signaled the servant
waiting near the table.

Pythius steamed but held his tongue. He must have access
to that site and its healing waters! He could not endure another
year of this torment. He had gritted his teeth for so long due to
the chronic pain that they had worn down and were hardly fit for
chewing anything tougher than dried fruit.

Ka'zab upended the tankard and drank down the ale. "The leader—a self-proclaimed regent named Sherbourne—is erecting a massive stone wall around the city." Pythius opened his mouth to protest, but Ka'zab threw up a hand to silence him.

How dare you show your king such disrespect? Pythius wondered why he tolerated this man's insolence, but he needed Ka'zab. No other man in his army was so driven, so eager to ravage and plunder those lands. And his campaign over the years had proved successful beyond Pythius's expectations. The whole region to the northeast lived in terror and chaos—exactly what Pythius had hoped would result from Ka'zab's brutal attacks. But surely—fifteen years should be plenty enough time to achieve victory. He suspected Ka'zab was taking his time, enjoying the spoils of war, and not feeling the sense of urgency Pythius felt for a swift and complete victory.

"You have not answered my question," Pythius said evenly. He dared not show his irritation.

"Sire, there are thousands in that city, and much plunder for the taking. But these things must be planned with care. Each skirmish takes us closer to the walls, but Sherbourne is amassing an army and forging weapons. I have returned to ask Your Majesty to provide more men and arms. For us to lay siege properly in an open assault—which is what must be done, and soon—we need to at least double the forces now in position."

"And once you have your armies in place, how much time will it take until victory?"

Ka'zab chuckled, and Pythius wondered what his commander thought was so amusing. Was he laughing at him? He scowled and rubbed his arm.

"Not long at all, Sire. I have already infiltrated their battalion and have learned of their weaknesses. Upon my return, I will take my place as a guard in Sherbourne's regiment in order to learn of their strategies and plans. It is as good as done."

"Splendid! You shall have all you need. But time has run out. Be about your business as quickly as you can, for I want to march into that fallen city before winter. Have you had any word of the Keeper?"

Ka'zab pushed back his chair and stood. "No, Sire. If there is such a person, no one in the land has heard of him."

Pythius frowned. Maybe this site had no Keeper. But surely someone in that land knew something about the sacred circle and the healing properties of the water that bubbled out of the rock in the center. Ka'zab's informants had heard of ancient tales hinting at the magic waters, yet none seemed to pay much heed to them. Could they be only stories without any basis in truth? Pythius knew from experience that legends often had their roots in truth. Just like the crystal scepter.

The thought of the scepter drove a spike through his heart. By now, he should have been ruler over the known world! The Lady Vitrella had promised him great power, but she obviously had lied. No doubt she wanted the scepter for herself, and had sent that vile snakelike creature after him to take it. He seethed thinking about the prophecy she had spouted to him. If it indeed had been foretold that he would take the scepter, then why was the blasted thing still in a case under his bed? Why in all these years had none of the mages and wizards and wise men of his kingdom been able to unlock its power—or heal his hand? Yet Pythius knew there was power to be had. Well, if Elysiel's crystal slabs were out of his reach to control, then perhaps this other site would suffice. Surely if it had been erected by divine appointment, then it, too, must have great power waiting to be harnessed.

"Sire, if there is nothing more, I should be on my way."

"Yes, yes of course. Meet in the morn with Argabus, the city commander of Paladya's regiment, and tell him your needs. He will provide all the men and arms you require."

Ka'zab bowed. "We will depart the city as soon as we are equipped. You shall not be disappointed, Sire. Before the year is out, this Sherbourne and his city will fall, and the sacred site will be yours for the taking."

"Excellent." Pythius forced a smile past the pain throbbing mercilessly up his arm. When the door clicked shut behind Ka'zab, he fell back in his chair. He longed to thrash and break every piece of furniture in the room, but the very thought exhausted him. It took all the strength he could rally each day just to get out of bed and dress, then attend to his many affairs. He was wearied beyond tolerance. In some ways he regretted having put Urstus to death under the false charge of treason. The old man had, admittedly, been adept at handling all the kingdom's affairs and excelled at diplomacy—something Pythius refused to employ. The new advisors in his cabinet had proved even worse than old Urstus—self-seeking and groveling, and just as duplicitous. No matter how much he paid those in his confidence, he had failed to find one incorruptible man he could trust. But no matter. The lion still roared, and the people still cowered. Even after all these years.

Pythius turned at the sound of the door creaking open.

"Father, what is it—what's troubling you?"

He wiped the grimace from his face. A glance at the ornate mirror taking up half the wall showed how utterly haggard he looked.

"Inaya, my sweetling. It's nothing—"

She looked down at his gloved hand. "How unbearable it must be to live with such constant pain. Has your new healer done nothing to quell it?"

Pythius stood and wrapped his good arm around his fourteen-year-old daughter. "The pain ebbs and flows. No matter. I've lived with it all these years. All great kings must bear their war wounds."

Pythius forced a smile, hoping to assuage his daughter's concern. He pulled back and studied her. How had she grown up so quickly? Why, it seemed only yesterday that he'd married Samira, a year after Calli's disappearance. He still refused to believe Calli was dead—or his son, even though he'd had every male infant within the kingdom disposed of, every road watched, and there'd been no sight or word of them anywhere. After two years, he had called back his soldiers from the Great Northern Road, when their effort to uncover the wayward queen's whereabouts failed to succeed.

He thought about the startling news their commander brought to him upon their return—news of Elysiel. Pythius had secretly instructed the man to inquire in the northern hamlets about the hidden land, and what he learned had shaken him to his core. Elysiel was still encased under a giant sheet of ice! None had been able to cross the boundary once the great storm had ravaged the land. It was truly as Lady Vitrella had foretold—Elysiel was now desolate, without inhabitant. Would it remain that way forever?

"What brings you here?" he asked Inaya.

"You weren't at supper. Mother asked about you."

Of course she did. Her jealousy and suspicion know no bounds. "I had to dine with one of my commanders. And I am afraid I will be busy most of the night." He gave his daughter as sympathetic a smile as he could, hoping that would appease her. "Now, Inaya, I have important matters—"

Inaya stood on her tiptoes and pecked her father on the cheek. "Yes, yes, I know. Matters of State and all that. I'll see you in the morn, then." She glanced once more at his hand and frowned. "I wish there were something I could do to help."

"Your concern is touching, as always. Be a good girl, now. Tell your mother I will be in the library should she need me."

Pythius watched her leave and sighed. He had thought he would never grow to love a child, but, well, there was no getting around the truth. He had married Samira for political alliance with Rushbrook, and to keep his dissenters at bay. Samira was at first nothing like Calli—entirely submissive and agreeable. Never a word in defiance; she knew her position at his side. He thought her a bit of a bore but pleasant enough to look at, and for the first few years she served her purpose and did her duty, and he gave her token attention. But as she got wind of his various affairs with women about town, she grew petty and critical. He didn't deny his dalliances but defended them. He was the king of Paladya. He could do what he liked, and who was she to voice any complaint? He provided her riches and comfort to her heart's content. But that wasn't enough for her. She demanded his faithfulness, and her ranting at his affairs drove him farther from her. Now he slept in his own chamber and only sat at her side to keep up appearances. He would have gotten rid of her years ago if it hadn't been for Inaya, who loved her devoted mother. And he would never do anything that might hurt his precious daughter.

Inaya—she brought him immeasurable joy. The moment he had learned of Samira's pregnancy, he sought out the seer, to determine if this child would pose a threat to his rule—or his life. But the seer assured him the augury was silent, and insisted it would be wise for him to love his daughter. For years he had prodded the seer, demanding word from the augury regarding Calli and the boy, but—nothing. He hoped it meant the boy was truly dead, yet he dared not believe it or let down his guard. His Eyes and Ears still patrolled the kingdom, listening for any word of a young man who might claim to have connection with the king or be plotting an uprising. But apart from the usual grumblings of dissent, they'd heard nothing.

Pythius retreated to the library, desiring quiet and wanting to avoid facing his prying wife. Only last week she had learned of his latest affair—with a seamstress in the mercantile district. Samira had seen the woman entering the palace grounds, escorted by his seneschal, Ramus—a man whom Pythius thought to be discreet and trustworthy—and somehow had followed them through the secret corridor to his bedchamber. In contrast to Samira's slight frame, this woman had all the right curves; she was a voluptuous specimen he'd noticed from his carriage one morning as he journeyed through the city to meet with the local magistrate. And what a pleasure she proved to be! Despite the seamstress's embarrassment at being discovered in the king's bed by the queen, she seemed to quickly forget the intrusion once Pythius had his wife hauled off. He let his thoughts wander in memory of their affections, hoping to distract himself, if only momentarily, from the pain rippling up and down his arm.

He turned up the wick in the oil lamp and pulled out the large map of the northern region. He noted the areas marked in red— the villages Ka'zab had destroyed. As he stared at the spot marking the new city with its wall, he felt a presence in the room. A chill ran across his neck.

He trembled as the familiar presence grew closer. *Go away! You are just a figment of my mind!* He tried to close off his thoughts, focus on the map, but as always, he could not push this thing away. He feared his pain was driving him to madness, for as the years went on, this *thing* seemed to haunt him more often. Yet it never spoke to him. Why he sensed it was Cakrin's ghost, he could not say. He concluded Lady Vitrella had something to do with this—the witch! She surely had bespelled him, and was attempting to torment him from a distance. There was no denying her great power—he saw the way she had enchanted the water of the brook to allow him entrance into Elysiel. And summoned that evil snake creature to attack him. None of his mages or healers knew of this additional affliction, though. He dared not voice his fear that he was being haunted by a specter; he knew how that would look.

But he was not mad! Something or someone was in the room, beside him. He could almost feel breath blowing in his ear. He swatted the air and jumped to his feet.

King Cakrin's face imprinted in Pythius's mind—such that it seemed the king was standing right before him, staring at him with those ice-blue eyes, vacant, unreadable. Pythius shook his head, trying to fling away the vision, but when he reopened his eyes, Cakrin remained before him. Pythius could stand it no longer.

"Go! Depart from me! What do you want?"

The library door opened. "Sire," his seneschal said, peeking inside with caution. "Do you need anything?"

"No, no, I'm fine." He tried to wave the man away, lest he witness his odd behavior. He shouldn't have spoken aloud; the palace was full of ears and those ready to find fault with him. But the man cleared his throat and spoke.

"Your Majesty . . . the seer is here—"

"The seer? At this late hour?" His heart hammered in his chest.

"Yes, he has just arrived by carriage from Torth. He says he has a word from the augury."

Now? After all these years of silence? Pythius's gut soured and bile filled his mouth. His injured hand pained him anew, as if someone had plunged a knife into his palm. He moaned and doubled over.

The seneschal ran to him and took his good arm. "Sire, here, sit." He lowered him gently into the padded chair. "Should I have him wait . . . until you feel ready to receive him?"

Pythius shuddered and sucked in a breath. He looked past Ramus to the fireplace hearth, where the ghost of King Cakrin stood, a slight smile on his face and judgment in his unblinking eyes. Pythius groaned and squeezed his eyes shut. He knew he would never be ready to hear what the seer had to say. But there was no avoiding it. Maybe, he hoped against all hope, he would be given good news this time.

Pythius pushed a laugh out his mouth. Those foolish, blind seers. Declan's old seer had predicted Pythius's death at the hand of his son—and that had yet to happen. After all these years, the prediction now seemed a joke, or something that had been said to frighten him. No doubt his enemies had bribed that seer to say the things he had. To make Pythius buckle in fear. Surely the old seer had been well paid and prompted to "foretell" Pythius's murder at his son's hand in order to upset his rule. Well, it hadn't worked—even though it had caused his traitorous wife to flee. But no loss there. If Calli hadn't run off, he never would have married Samira, and Inaya would never have been born . . .

He supposed he should be grateful, then, for the seer's dire warning. For, now that he had Inaya, he couldn't imagine life without her. Something good had come out of that prediction after all. Maybe the same would prove true with this new pronouncement.

"Bring him to me," Pythius commanded.

The seneschal bowed. "As you wish, Sire."

Pythius searched the room with his eyes as he waited for the seer. The ghost had gone. He loosed a sigh of relief. But then, a voice whispered close to his ear, chilling his blood and causing his knees to give out from under him.

"Prepare to meet your doom, Pythius!"

SIXTEEN

PERTH SPOTTED Alyck over by the breakwater, but there was no sign of Tanin, Alyck's son. The morning sun heated his shoulders, but Perth's heart shivered in despair. His pa had sent him out early to help with the cleanup, but when Perth had learned Tanin hadn't come home last night, he joined the search parties that were scouring the shoreline looking for the missing. Over three dozen were still unaccounted for, and just minutes ago Perth had looked on, horrified, as a child's body had been hauled out of the water and carried to shore.

He stopped to rest and looked at the devastation around him. Tolpuddle was utterly destroyed. A few buildings remained partially standing, but Perth figured those would probably have to be razed and rebuilt to be of any use. A makeshift tent camp had been erected up on the promontory and was growing in size by the hour. Survivors hauled broken beams and pieces of planking up through the heather hour after hour, fashioning framing they overlaid with sheets and netting and tarps—anything they could salvage from the ruins of the village. He'd heard Orsyn had come by at dawn, loaded with a cart full of blankets and supplies from the inn. With apology, he explained he couldn't spare much for these poor souls, with the inn now a refuge for dozens of parentless, frightened children. No doubt these meager dwellings did little more than provide a scant reprieve from the winds scurrying up from the bay that blew inhospitably upon the necks and hearts of his neighbors. Would everyone in his village leave to find a new home? Would his pa heal, and what would he do? He couldn't imagine his pa living anywhere but Tolpuddle. Perth's quest lay heavy on his mind and heart as he caught up with the other searchers and listened to them talk.

He turned to Alyck. "Any sign at all of Tanin?" he asked hesitantly. Perth saw the answer in Alyck's tearful eyes. He had never seen the fisherman so distraught and wished there was something more he could do to help. However, he knew that destroying the knucker was what would help the most, and so felt even more resolved to fulfill his vow and set off on his journey. But to where would it lead? King Cakrin had told him he had gifts for him that would help him be victorious. He still didn't understand why the king had come to him, but he realized it wouldn't do any good to question it. In his heart of hearts, Perth understood this was his destiny, and today he felt it even more powerfully, looking out on the wreckage and ruin that was once his cheerful little seaside village. Even if the villagers chose to rebuild, they would never feel safe unless they knew the sea monster had been vanquished.

After a few more hours of aiding in the cleanup along the bay, Perth headed back to his cottage, exhausted and downhearted, to make lunch for his pa and himself. He knew his pa would be antsy and frustrated, wanting to be out helping with the rest of the villagers. Guilt and trepidation wore upon Perth; he knew how upset his pa would be once he learned he'd run off. He should write a note to soften the blow, explaining why he had to leave, but what could he say? Maybe he should confide in Gayla? Bad idea. He knew what would happen if he did. She would lecture him about his responsibility to tend to his pa. Maybe even say he was daft to believe he'd spoken to a ghost.

It did sound ridiculous. If Tanin or Danyl had told him they'd been chosen by some dead king's ghost to go after the sea monster, he'd think they were daft too. No, he had to keep this a secret—otherwise he'd never slip away. Somehow he had to manage to pack a bag and sneak out without his pa noticing. Maybe the pain formula the apothecary had prepared would make his pa sleep. Regardless, he would not fail to keep his appointment with the king after dark. He had made a vow.

"Is that you, Perth?" his pa called out as Perth stomped sand from his feet on the front porch.

"Yes, Pa." He threw open the door and found his pa propped up on the sofa, his eyes ridden with pain. "I thought I'd make us some lunch."

"How bad is it?"

Perth glanced at his pa on the way to the small kitchen. He knew he couldn't hide anything with a forced smile. "It's bad, Pa. Lots of folks are missing." He gulped past the rock in his throat. "Tanin too."

His pa moaned and shifted in his spot. Perth watched a new wave of pain sear his pa's face. "I hate it that I can't help! How can I just sit here and do nothing? And I just don't understand why such a thing happened. Why would God above allow such a fearsome beast kill innocent folks? There's no rhyme or reason to it."

Perth nodded. "You always say the ways of God are mysterious. That people can never predict when hard times might come. 'Like fish in a net, people are caught by sudden tragedy.' That's what you always say, Pa."

His pa nodded solemnly. "And there's another old saying that goes, 'Accept the way God does things, for who can straighten what he has made crooked?' "

Perth nodded; he'd heard his pa spout that plenty of times before. But he wondered at God's apparently crooked ways. There was no making sense of them. He cut a slab of cheese and stuck it on a plate with a loaf of bread he'd gotten from the bakery yesterday. A bakery that was now a pile of splinters, Perth thought with great sadness. Now there'd be food shortages, what with the fishing boats destroyed and the gardens flooded with seawater. That alone would force people to move away. With a sigh, he threw some bogberries onto the plate and brought it out to the den.

As he set it down, he realized he hadn't seen Gayla at all. "Pa, I should go up to the inn and see if Gayla is all right—"

"She came by right after you headed out this morning. Brought me another tonic. She's fine, Perth. Making rounds to those who . . . survived."

Perth blew out a breath in relief. Thank the heavens for that mercy. He could see his pa, too, was relieved to know she was safe. Perth couldn't bear thinking that she might have been killed. Which made him wonder if any of the missing would be found alive.

Once more righteous indignation and the desire for retribu- ⏎ tion filled him to overflowing. King Cakrin had told him he knew *who* was responsible for this attack. That meant there was someone intent on recklessly destroying lives without remorse. Perth could hardly imagine someone so evil. And who had the power to control something as enormous and monstrous as a sea monster? Surely not a mere human. But, if not someone human, then . . .

Perth trembled all over at the realization of the danger he was about to put himself in. Cakrin had said he would face a dangerous foe. Yet . . . the king had confidence in his ability to succeed. For some reason he believed this ghost king.

Elysiel. Ever since the king had spoken the name of his land, Perth could not shake it from his mind. It flitted in his head like a beautiful note of a song, the way a plucked harp string would linger on the air. Or how a wind chime shimmered with bright sound. Without thinking, he turned to his pa, who chewed distractedly on a piece of bread.

"Pa, have you ever heard of a land called Elysiel?"

"Elysi—what?"

"Elysiel, Pa."

"Where did you hear of that place?"

What should he tell him? "Uh, just heard someone talking about it down by the shore. A beautiful faraway place . . ."

His pa grunted. "Don't know anything at all about it. I've lived here my whole life and never traveled farther than Scuddle nor cared to learn about other lands. The only places I hear about are the villages up and down the coast, as boats come from afar into the bay to sell wares or fish. No doubt this Elysiel is a ways from Tolpuddle." His father narrowed his eyes at him, and Perth did all he could to erase any emotion from his face. "Now, don't run off thinking life's bound to be better someplace else. Everyplace has its trials and heartaches, Perth. You make your own happiness in life, and you have to stick with those who love you."

Perth nodded, picturing the sparkling mountains he saw in his dreams. "Yes, Pa." He popped a handful of bogberries into his mouth and let the sublime landscape of Elysiel fill his mind. He could almost smell the snow-tinged air and the fragrance of flowering meadows. A meandering stream glistened in the afternoon sun, and a lazy hawk circled overhead. Birdsong erupted from a dense forest of majestic trees as sunlight splintered through the branches and illuminated a shady path that beckoned him. Suddenly the longing to leave was unbearable. He got to his feet.

"I should go back and help more. There's so much damage, so much cleanup. It will take weeks."

"Then go, Perth."

Perth studied his pa's frustrated face. But more than frustration laced his features; a deep misery lay heavy upon him. Perth felt it too. "The villagers have rallied together. It will be all right. You'll see. We can rebuild, and Tolpuddle will be back in business in no time. The sea monster may have destroyed the village, but it can't destroy its spirit."

His pa mustered a smile and patted Perth on the arm. "You're right. And as soon as I'm able, I'll be out there helping to rebuild."

"Maybe you should get some sleep, Pa." He pointed to the small corked jar on the table. "Will that tonic knock you out?"

"It packs a punch. I don't want to take too much of it; I can handle the pain—so long as I don't try to get up too suddenly."

"Well . . . I think you should take some tonight—to help you get a good night's sleep. You always say sleep is the first step to healing."

He watched his pa finish off the lunch, then took the plate into the kitchen. "I'll be back with some supper." *If I can find something. Maybe there'll be fish trapped in the wreckage of the boats floundering near the shore. And if not, I can always fry up some corncakes.*

His pa nodded and Perth left, torn between wanting to help the villagers and wanting to start on his quest. *Elysiel . . .* Once he finished his quest, he knew where he would go. He had yearned for years to see the world and seek his fortune, but now only one dream consumed his heart—to step foot in Elysiel. Wherever it was.

Perth stood at the threshold of the front door, watching his pa snore away on the couch. The moon rising in the east cast a soft light through the window, and the glow settled on his pa's face, showing his peaceful countenance. Perth was grateful for the tonic's strength, and although his pa had told him to put just one teaspoon in his tea, Perth had put in three, hoping the increased strength wouldn't be noticeable in the taste. But if his pa did notice, he didn't say anything. He'd been too busy listening to Perth recount the day's activities—and was especially overjoyed to hear Tanin had been found, none too worse for wear.

One of the search parties had found Perth's friend half buried under a pile of broken boards near the south docks. From the lump on the back of Tanin's head, Alyck figured his son had been knocked out for some time. When he asked Tanin what ailed him, the only big complaint Tanin had was his grumbling stomach, which made Alyck laugh heartily and slap his son on the back.

Perth had watched the two head home for supper with a grin on his face. At least that was some good news. The other good news was that two small fishing boats had put in at harbor, boats that had been feared lost, and they'd reported no further signs of the knucker—much to everyone's relief. Maybe the beast had moved on . . . yet that might only portend more danger and destruction for the next village along the coast. It had to be stopped!

Perth had fed his pa supper—he'd found no time to look for fish, so he just scrounged through the icebox, threw a bunch of withered vegetables in the pot, and called it stew—and then gave him his tonic. As he recounted the day's events, he watched his pa's eyes start to close. By the time the snores grew even and deep, Perth had a bag packed with a few changes of clothes and some small things he thought might prove useful, like his whittling knife, a bit of rope, some flint, and a water flask. He figured if he needed anything else, King Cakrin would tell him. He tiptoed to the door, grabbed his heavy coat, and put on his sturdy boots. With one last glance at his sleeping pa, he closed the door behind him and trekked across the dune to the place he'd encountered the ghost last eve.

A quarter moon rose up from the sea, splattering creamy light over the swells. Perth felt an unexpected twinge of homesickness assail him—as if he'd already left. Already he missed his pa, and standing there, looking out at the serene bay, he realized how much a part of this place he was. Everyone he knew lived in Tolpuddle. He, like his pa, had lived here his whole life. It was all he knew.

And now he was about to venture out to new lands fraught with danger.

He thought about the two notes he had left. He sure hoped his pa wouldn't open and read the one to Gayla. Arnyl Quay was nothing if not honorable, and Perth trusted he wouldn't give in to temptation or anger and overstep. Not like Perth had said anything too personal—he had only asked her to look after his pa and hinted a bit at how much his pa cared for her. He assured them both he would be careful and safe, although no doubt they would scoff at his words. He didn't say where he was going or why—only that he had been asked to help stop the sea monster, and the one who had asked him was trustworthy. He would send word when he could and would return as soon as possible. He'd torn up three different letters he'd started to write, for every time he tried to give a lengthier explanation, he only sounded more and more foolish. Simple was better, he decided. The less said, the less they'd worry about. Or so he reasoned.

As he stood on the moonlit dune, Perth worried the ghost would not appear, and after some time wondered if maybe he had imagined the whole encounter. He sat on the damp sand under the stars and prayed. Prayed heaven would favor his quest and hear his cry to avenge his village. Prayed for God to watch over his pa and Gayla and all those in his village who had suffered such loss and looked to heaven to provide and comfort. Prayed for the courage to face his destiny head-on—even if it proved to be as dangerous as the ghost had implied.

When he finished praying, he opened his eyes and saw King Cakrin standing before him.

Once again, Perth marveled at the strange apparition wavering in the night air. The king nodded at Perth and asked if he was ready.

"You mentioned I will have to face a dangerous foe. What . . . or who is it?" Perth asked.

The king nodded again. "You have seen her face. She is an ancient evil, with a long history in many lands over the world. Tales of her evil have seeped into fables and fairy tales over the ages, but none have truly depicted how treacherous and fearsome she is, for her wickedness is beyond measure or definition. You may have even heard her name mentioned; in some places along these coastal villages she is called the Gorgon."

An image appeared in Perth's mind—of an ugly creature with scaly skin and snakes wrapping around its head. Perth realized by the texture of the image that he was looking at ochre stone. The seawall! He had walked by it thousands of times and never really looked at the weather-worn carvings in the stone, but he recognized the creepy face. All along the seawall, every hundred feet or so, this face stared out at the sea with its wide-open eyes and snarling mouth. He hadn't noticed the hair before, thinking the strands were made of the type of cable rope used on ships, but now he understood they were snakes. How odd.

"Those who followed the old religion, eons ago, felt that if they put the *Tse'pha*'s image on the doors of their cottages and storefronts, and everyplace she might try to enter, it would protect them from her," the king said.

Instantly, other images filled Perth's head—of the Gorgon's face on the iron knocker of the tavern, in cobbles mortared at the edge of the lane heading into the village, carved in old barn doors. Why had he never noticed before? Even at the entrance to the village cemetery—the Gorgon's face lined the stone archway he passed on his way out of town to the refuse dump. He shook his head in awe at the realization he had lived in Tolpuddle all this time and never noticed.

"You used another word for her—*Tse'pha*?"

"In the oldest language the word means serpent. She is one of the oldest creatures in the world, spawned by the Great Serpent himself. My people have battled with her for centuries, without success."

Perth gulped. If she were that ancient and powerful, what chance did a lad—and a shrimpy one at that—have against her?

King Cakrin obviously knew his thoughts. "Fear not, Perthin Quay. A massive army may not have victory over such an abomination, but a small, unnoticeable boy just might. She has been dormant for many years, working her evil in the bowels of the earth, but has now arisen for a last, great fight. She will not see you as a threat, and she will not expect one so young and seemingly insignificant to dare try to kill her. You will have both the element of surprise and, more importantly, heaven's favor on your side.

"Centuries ago, a prophecy was spoken and recorded in the annals of Elysiel—of the serpent that the *Tse'pha* would spawn, that would attack and destroy the world of men. But this final attempt of the *Tse'pha* to destroy humankind will bring about her own destruction. She has set herself against heaven and unwittingly against the Keeper of the sacred site, and because of that she has incurred heaven's great wrath. It is no matter to heaven that you are but a boy. In God's hand you are a vessel of wrath, and you go in his power and strength. Trust heaven and be faithful, Perthin Quay, and fulfill your destiny.

"So . . . how am I to vanquish her?"

"I will send you to the crypt of the kings. There, you will find the crystal sword—fashioned out of the same crystal as the sacred site. The crypt is guarded by the three trolls—"

"Trolls?" Perth rolled his eyes, recalling his encounter with the trolls in his garbage dump. "Why trolls?"

"Do not scoff. The trolls fiercely guard the sword and allow none to enter the crypt." The king sighed and his face turned melancholy. Perthin wondered at his shift of emotion.

"I don't understand—where is this crypt and how will I get there? Won't it take me ages to make my way on foot?"

The king smiled. "Look down, Perthin Quay."

Perth glanced down and saw he had on a pair of strange boots. He hadn't even noticed they'd been put on his feet. They felt so light and airy, he would have thought himself barefoot as he wiggled his toes. "Where did those boots come from?"

"I put them on you. They are the shoes of swiftness, and they will take you to the crypt without delay. If you journeyed on foot without them, it would take you most of a year to reach Elysiel—"

"Elysiel! I'm going *there* to retrieve the sword?"

"Yes. But my fair land is under a curse, buried in ice. And closed to all incomers. But these shoes will take you to the crypt's entrance, and there the trolls await."

"But . . . won't they attack me or send me away?"

The ghost chuckled. "Tell them I sent you. They will give you the sword; do not fret."

Trolls. Why would a king like Cakrin use trolls to guard his sword? How strange.

"Once you have the sword in hand, speak to your boots and tell them to take you to Vitra. That is the *Tse'pha*'s name in the northern Wastes. Here is where you must be extremely careful."

Perth clamped his mouth shut and stared at Cakrin. His heart pounded hard in his chest. "Why can't you get the sword and kill her? You're already dead; she can't hurt you."

Cakrin chuckled again. He swung his arm toward Perth, who leaned back at the sudden motion of the king's advance, but the arm went right through Perth's stomach and came to rest at Cakrin's side.

The king continued, his face calm and reassuring. "As you see, I am not corporeal. I cannot wield a sword. You must do this. Only the crystal sword can kill Vitra. You will find it lightweight and easy to handle, as it will adjust to your strength once you wield it.

But take care—once you grip the sword, you must not let it touch the ground, not even the tip." He pointed to a dark cloth sack resting on the sand a few feet away. "When you cut off her head—"

"Her head?"

"You must put it in this sack and pull the string closed and knot it well."

"I have to . . . c-cut off her head?"

"It's the only way. But you must be careful. You cannot look at her face—not even for a second. Even after she is dead, you must not look at the face of the Gorgon, for anyone looking directly at it will turn to stone."

Perth threw up his hands. "How, then, can I kill her if I cannot look at her?"

"When you hold the sword aloft, you will see her reflection in the crystal. Use the sword as a mirror. The sword will let you know when she is near. You will have to strike her with your eyes closed. Only look at her or her head by using the sword to reflect her face. If you perchance gaze directly at her for even one second, you will be turned to stone. The northern Wastes are littered with soldiers and other hapless victims who have been thus changed."

"Will they remain that way forever?" Perth asked, feeling suddenly sick to his stomach at the thought of spending eternity as a statue.

"It is uncertain. Perhaps when she is dead, they will return to their former state. No one knows, and the prophecy does not speak of it."

"And what about you—what will happen to you when she is killed?'

The king's eyes filled with sadness. "My life is over. I have gathered with my ancestors. Once I am no longer needed, I will take my place in the crypt and sleep with all those who have gone before me. Until the great day of release."

Perth's head swam with Cakrin's words. He wanted to learn more, hear of Elysiel and these kings, learn about this sacred site and ask more about the Gorgon, but the king held up a hand.

"It is time. One day, all your questions will be answered, but for now you must be patient and focus on your quest."

Perth blew out a breath. "All right. So, after I cut off Vitra's head and stuff it in the sack—then what?"

"Then you search out the sea wyrm. The only way to stop the beast from its raging fury is to turn it to stone. Once you have the head in the sack, tell your boots to take you to the village of Sprat. There you will find a ship waiting for you. When you catch sight of the monster, summon it—"

"How do I do that?" Perth doubted he could just whistle to the thing as if it were a dog.

The king smiled. "It will sense the Gorgon's head. Just hold the sack high in the air—it will find you. Then avert your eyes and pull the head from the sack and hold it aloft. The serpent will turn to stone and thus will meet its end. Then, for your sake, and the sake of all living things, toss the sack with the head into the deep and rid yourself of it. It will settle on the bottom of the sea and molder until it becomes a harmless bag of bone."

The ghost grew quiet, allowing Perth to mull over all the things he'd been told. Shoes of swiftness? A sword of crystal? A head that could turn man and beast to stone? It was too fantastic to believe. Yet he knew the king was not tricking him. The boots were on his feet by some act of magic. He only had to tell them to take him to the crypt to see if they truly had the power the king claimed. Of all the things Cakrin told him, the most disturbing was his mention of a ship awaiting him. As much as Perth wanted to be sailing on the sea, the prospect filled him with guilt and worry over what his pa would say if he learned he'd gone to sea against his wishes. But he was being foolish—boarding a boat would prove to be the least of his dangers!

Finally, the king spoke once more. "Do you have any questions, Perthin Quay?"

Any? He had so many he thought he would burst from the load of them. But only one question needed an answer before he left. "Will you look after my pa? Make sure he recovers and doesn't fret too much about me?"

The king smiled. "Your father is in good hands. Elysiel is watching over him."

What does that mean—how could a cursed land be watching over his pa? But he knew that question would only lead to more questions. King Cakrin was right. It was time to go; questions would wait. He felt keenly the urgency to begin his quest.

He picked up the sack and sucked in a deep breath. It felt strange in his hand—heavy but somehow insubstantial, as if it lingered in some netherworld between reality and imagination.

"Fear not, Perthin. I will be with you, watching over you and helping you. And heaven is with you. You are the one foretold."

Perth watched in the cool night, with the stars sparkling like thousands of diamonds overhead, as the king disappeared. He stood on the sand, sack in hand, and let out his long-held breath.

Looking down at his boots—the strange dark boots that adorned his feet and felt like air—he sucked in a breath and spoke, feeling a bit silly talking to his shoes.

"Take me to the crypt of kings—in Elysiel."

In a sudden flash of light and whip of wind, the world vanished before his eyes, and he felt as if he were flying high above Tolpuddle, above his life, beyond the stars. Blood pounded his ears as time skimmed through his flowing hair. Joy coursed through his limbs and his heart pounded in excitement as snow-encrusted mountain peaks called to him, drawing him to the place of his dreams, to his destiny.

Elysiel!

SEVENTEEN

PYTHIUS'S STOMACH clenched in pain as he watched his seneschal escort the seer away from the library. He had barely seen the doddering old man out and heard the door click shut before collapsing into his chair. The seer's pointed words tormented him. *"Oh King, there is no other way. You have something of hers and she demands it. If you do not return it, she will destroy your kingdom. The augury has spoken."*

Never! He would never allow his enemy get her hands on the scepter. It was his, by prophecy and right! How dare she threaten him? And just how did the Lady Vitrella think she could mount an attack against his fortified city? Even if she sent ten legions of those vile snake creatures to overrun his land, his massive army would hack them to pieces. Fortresses lined the borders of Paladya like an iron chain. His arsenal of weapons could vanquish any approaching army within days. Just let her try!

All those years of fighting in the northern Wastes against the king of Elysiel had failed to produce a victory for her—how could she think to best him? He was no silly superstitious fool like the king of Elysiel—a man who let his usurper stroll right into the ice cavern and slit his throat without even defending himself. He was a powerful conqueror and strategist. Neither she nor her army would be any match for him.

Pythius rubbed his arm and poured himself a drink from the decanter on the side table. He threw back his head and let the pungent liquor burn his throat. If only he had uncovered the secret to the scepter—then he could draw upon its great power and worry no more about dissenters and enemy attacks and threats. Fifteen years! And all this time, the pain never ebbed, only grew more intolerable with the passing years. How dare she pair her threat with a temptation? That once he complied, his pain would vanish. The thought that she might hold the key to ending his pain infuriated him. And how did she know what he suffered? He knew the answer. Surely she had informants in his own city, perhaps even within the palace.

He'd never forgotten those few words King Cakrin had uttered to him right before Pythius had sliced his neck. Something about another prophecy, about a serpent that will be spawned. He summoned up the strange vision he had seen in the crystal slab, of the waters roiling in Tranquil Harbor, and Cakrin's words. For fifteen years he had tried to stash that memory in the back of his mind, but now the image shown to him in the ice cavern was all he could see, as if it had been burned into his eyes with a fiery brand. He refused to believe he had seen his doom, as Cakrin had put it. Still, it gave him pause, causing him to wonder just how many ships he had in position in the harbor. No matter. He would speak to his sea commander in the morning, assess the strength of the forces guarding the entrance to the bay.

Yet knowing his enemy must have someone inside his circles made him fidget with fury. He knew whom he needed to speak with and when. Now was not soon enough.

He called for his attendant and instructed him to ready his horse. The servant knew better than to question why he planned to head out into the night or where he was going. He smirked. No doubt Samira would suspect a dalliance in the city when he failed to go to bed. Even though her chamber was down a long hall from his, he knew she spied on him at every turn. The times he'd caught her, she handed him a lame excuse of needing to stretch the tightness from her legs or fetch a cup of warm goat's milk. But what did he care what his nag of a wife thought?

He strode to his chambers and dressed warmly for his ride across the city. No doubt the docks would be freezing at night from the northern spring gales blowing across the water. Ever since that storm had engulfed him and iced over all the land of Elysiel, he could not abide the cold—and cold always made his arm streak with terrible pain.

After gathering his things, he peeked in on Inaya, sleeping so peacefully in her ponderous bed of goose-down-filled comforters. He'd amassed his mighty army and trained his fighters not just to protect Paladya and himself—but to ensure that his precious daughter would always be able to sleep this peacefully in her bed, without fear or worry of her safety. And he intended to keep it that way.

He didn't know the names of the two men who had served as his Eyes and Ears in the city all these years—ever since he'd taken the throne. Ka'zab had been the one who'd brought the two beady-eyed men to him late one night by the docks, assuring him their services would prove invaluable. And they certainly had. Due to their information, he had stopped many insurgencies before they'd gotten out of hand. Without question, he put to death every person they named as traitor. They spoke little, but every word from their mouths revealed their diligence and keen observation. He assumed they themselves had a network of spies that reported back to them, but he never asked questions, and they did not like making small talk. They just did as they were told, and he made sure he paid them very well—in gold, no less.

Pythius jiggled the pouch of gold he had stuffed into his vest pocket. He hoped the extra coin would loosen their tongues more effectively than the finest brandy. And perhaps they would be forthcoming with a name or two. If not tonight, then before the new moon. The seer had been clear that the scepter had to be delivered to Lady Vitrella's contact before the new moon—to the barkeep at a seedy tavern wharfside. Pythius knew better than to storm the place or interrogate the owner. He had no doubt Lady Vitrella planned for one of her minions to be there, ready to carry out her wishes. Surely the tavern was just a meeting point.

An hour later he rapped on a peeling wooden door, nondescript among many in the smelly rutted lanes fronting the harbor. Two sharp knocks, followed by two sets of three. He pulled his cloak tighter around his neck as he waited, wondering if he'd made the trip for nothing. Perhaps the men were out, doing their job—listening and watching for traitorous activity. He rarely sought them out; most often they sent word to him regarding pertinent tidbits they'd discovered.

He kept one hand on his shortsword, glancing about in case thieves were trolling the district, but all he saw in the darkness were two mongrels tearing at something with their teeth and growling as they tussled in a stagnant puddle. Well, if any deviants dared try to rob him, they'd be sorry—although they wouldn't live long enough to feel such remorse. Pythius chuckled, then stopped as he heard footsteps approach on the other side of the door.

He stepped back as the door opened to darkness, unsure who he'd met with until he recognized the voice. In a hoarse whisper the man said, "Ah, Sire, do come in, come in . . ." He ushered Pythius in and waited. Soon, Pythius's eyes adjusted enough to spot a dim lantern at the end of the hall. "This way," the man said, turning and expecting Pythius to follow him, which he did, in silence.

As the man slid into one of the overstuffed chairs in the small sitting room—a room Pythius had sat in on numerous occasions over the years—his partner, a much smaller and leaner fellow with eyes as black as coal, came in and sat beside him, unspeaking and only acknowledging his king with a slight nod.

The late hour and his cold, throbbing arm taxed his patience. He got straight to the point. He knew those two wouldn't mind bypassing the pleasantries, and he doubted they would offer him something warm to drink—even if he commanded that they comply.

"I'm interested in any information regarding one Lady Vitrella. Who she has in the city, who is relaying information to her. She is . . ." Pythius considered how he could describe her, recalling the stunning beauty that had gripped his heart and made him breathless. How her finger had been hot to the touch, nearly melting him where he stood. And those eyes . . .

The small man cleared his throat. "Sire, we are well familiar with the Lady Vitrella—"

Pythius jumped to his feet. "Why wasn't I told?"

The two men exchanged a look. "Why, Sire," the bigger one with hunched shoulders said, "we had no cause up till now to alert you to her—or of many in the city whom we have eyes upon. There is no reason to bring so many names to your attention unless they pose an immediate threat. We watch and listen, sift truth from lies—"

"Is she here, then? In Paladya?"

The bigger man continued. "We have never laid eyes on her, nor have any of our informants. And we know little about her. Yet she does have those in the city who gather information and report back to her. We have caught and tortured more than one such messenger." He exchanged another look with his companion, and Pythius wondered at the expression. The man continued, "Her spies are . . . particularly resilient to torture; some even . . . seem to relish it."

Pythius frowned. He tapped his foot and the sound echoed down the barren hall. "I was paid a visit by a seer from Torth—" Pythius noted the evident rise of interest on the men's faces at this. He went on to tell them the seer's pronouncement, then hesitated. Oh, why not? He may as well tell them everything, as the more knowledge they had to work with, the better able they would be to assist him in stopping his enemy.

The two men sat motionless and unblinking as he told them his tale of traveling to Elysiel. He left out no detail, but described how he had encountered the Lady Vitrella, the prophecy she had spouted to him, and her instruction to kill the Keeper and take the scepter. Pythius had told no one his story until now; he'd kept it as secret as the box under his bed. For some reason, relating this long-hidden tale brought him a rush of relief—although he purposely omitted the hiding place of the scepter.

After he related it all—the ice cavern and the vision he'd seen in the slab of crystal, murdering the king, the horrible snake creature he'd seen in the brook's reflection, the mark caused by gripping the scepter—he grew suddenly exhausted and sank back into his chair. The men waited as he produced a flask from an inside pocket of his cloak. He grimaced as he took a long drink of the potent formula his healer had mixed with his brandy. Pain rippled up and down his arm like a whip, and he suppressed a groan.

The scrawny man nodded slowly and said, "This explains much, Sire. Only hours ago were we contacted by someone who . . . is a seer in her own right. For years she has faithfully shared her visions with us, and they have proved true."

"A witch?"

"A soothsayer . . . from the old religion." He smiled and his eyes turned even darker, reminding Pythius of a raven eyeing its prey. "But one with a fondness for coin. Yet she sought us out, agitated by a vision and even insisted upon speaking with you. We had planned to send word to you at dawn's light."

"What did she see?" Pythius rubbed his arm harder, trying to focus past the pain to the man's words. The room suddenly seemed chilled.

The bigger man answered, "Why, something very much like you described seeing in the crystal slab. The harbor churning, and some . . . creature smashing against the docks and shattering ships. She said something about your doom . . ."

Pythius clutched his heart and the man shut his mouth. "Yes, yes. What else did she say?"

Again the two men looked at each other, and Pythius sensed hesitation. The scrawny man cleared his throat and spoke. "She saw something else in the water."

"Something?" Pythius held his breath. He did not like the look coming over the man's face as he deliberated whether or not to continue.

"Some*one*, Sire."

"In the water . . ."

"Strapped to a post, a piling, I believe, erected out in the harbor."

Pythius shook his head, confused. "Someone put there? A captive?" *Or bait, perhaps?* Why would anyone do such a thing?

The bigger man read his thoughts. "The soothsayer said this would be the only way to stop the creature from destroying the city—a high cost, indeed, but the only way. She was certain of this."

The other man added, "A terrible price to pay, but she made it clear, Sire. The only way to prevent ruin would be to sacrifice her to the beast."

Pythius trembled. "Her?" He gulped. "Who?"

Neither man spoke.

"Who!" Pythius demanded.

The two men exchanged one long, last look before the scrawny man found his voice. "Why, your daughter, Sire. The Princess Inaya."

Arnyl stood on his front porch leaning on the makeshift crutch Alyck had fashioned for him, staring out over the dunes. He thought of Bayley Tettenhall and his useless, ripped-up arm, and of Alyck's twisted ankle. They were a fine lot—all of them injured in one way or t'other and doing no good for no one. The village destroyed, people fearful and leaving by the droves, and his own son up and gone. The brilliant sunshiny day seemed to mock them all, casting a glow over the sand on a morning that should have been rife with thunderheads and driving rain.

Just what in the blazes did Perthin mean by that note? That he'd gone off with someone trustworthy to stop the knucker? Had some addled self-made hero with a death wish rallied up boys from the village to take them on this foolhardy and dangerous quest? Had any other lads taken off? Why would Perthin believe such a thing? No one could stop such a monster—and how would anyone track it if not by sea? Perthin would never board a ship—or would he? The thought made his blood boil—more from fear than anger. And how in the world could he have left his own pa like this, knowing he was needed to tend to not only him but so many others suffering in Tolpuddle? It made no sense at all.

He'd hobbled over to Bayley's cottage late last night, fed up with worrying, aching for a drink for the first time in years. And if he'd had something stronger than tea in his cottage, he would have drunk it all down in one long guiltless gulp. Not once since he'd found Perthin in the trunk that day had he wanted a drink, but now, today, he couldn't get the urge out of his mind. It was a good thing he could barely walk, for if he could manage it, he'd be searching through the piles of broken timber in the village looking for an unbroken, overlooked bottle to ease his worries.

He had shown Bayley the note Perthin had left on the dresser, but upon reading it, his friend only shrugged and said, "The boy's a faithful, careful lad. He'll be back. I wouldn't worry so."

As he stood in the morning light, waiting for Gayla to appear over the dunes, he hoped his friend was right. His heart ached with hopelessness. Trolls be hanged! He would take off after the lad if he could. Perthin was only fifteen! And a shrimp at that. He couldn't bear the thought of something bad happening to his son. To his other son.

Thoughts of Jayden pressed in on him, pummeling him with memories all tied up with guilt. If he lost Perthin too . . .

A shimmer of light caught his eye. The sun's rays glinted off something shiny Gayla held in her hands. Arnyl watched and grumbled as she walked toward him, her skirt swishing in the morning breeze and her long hair flowing out behind her. His throat tightened. He rarely saw her hair loose like that, and it made her appear so young. Just the way she walked reminded him a little of Emelee, back in the days when he'd courted her, back in his drinking days . . .

He shook the memory away. He felt like he was dodging a hailstorm from the past, and he didn't like it one bit.

"Ah, Arnyl—you're up and about!"

Arnyl held his breath as Gayla drew near, her smile the brightest ray of light he'd seen in days. How could she be so cheerful?

He hated to ruin her mood—no doubt her hopeful spirit was lifting many a villager and giving them reason to press on. That was perhaps what he loved most about her—her indomitable spirit.

Although he doubted a large dose of her cheeriness would do him any good. He'd rather have a dose of that devil liquor . . .

"What is it, Arnyl? You look like a troll just walked over your grave." She studied his face and frowned; no doubt his consternation was as easy to see as a wart on a troll's nose.

"The lad's taken off." Arnyl hrumphed. "Left a note saying he joined some fella, off to stop the knucker."

Gayla's countenance sank, and the brightness seeped out of her eyes. "Oh dear . . . Arnyl, did he say where he was heading?"

He shook his head, then remembered something Perthin had said . . . what was it? "He mentioned some land afar off. I didn't pay it much mind at the time, but maybe that's the place he was heading to. Although I've never heard of it."

He tried to avoid looking in her eyes; they were like crab traps. If he wandered in, he knew he'd never find a way out. She was standing too close, and her floral scent wafted up his nose and made him lightheaded. He backed up a step and stared over the dunes, trying to recall that name.

"Something like . . . Elysum . . . Elisal . . ."

A little noise from Gayla's throat made him turn back to look at her. Her face seemed to have paled, but he couldn't rightly tell in the bright spring sunlight.

"Was it perhaps . . . Elysiel?"

Arnyl could tell she was trying to maintain her composure, but there was no doubt the word had been difficult for her to say. He narrowed his eyes in curiosity. "You know this place? Is it far from here?" He spoke more to himself than to her. "I should rig up a cart and horse and go on after the daft lad—"

Gayla stopped his fidgeting with her hand. "Arnyl, Elysiel is a thousand leagues away . . . and, surely, that is not where Perthin is headed."

"You don't seem all that sure to me," Arnyl said. "And just what do you know about such a land?"

Gayla turned and faced the dunes, her face drawn in thought. "Up on the Shivery Coast, in Bluster, we . . . heard tales of that strange land. It was reported to be a magical land, hidden from all but those invited in. Of course . . . who would believe such stories . . .?"

A silence settled uncomfortably around him, making him fidget. "Oh, the lad left you a note too." He reached into his pants pocket and pulled out the crumpled paper sealed with sealing wax with her name written upon it. She took it from him and slipped it into the pouch she had clasped around her waist.

"You're not going to read it?"

"I will," she said, her eyes dancing. "In private. If there's anything you need to know in that note, Arnyl, I will be sure to tell you."

With a wistful expression, she took his hand as he leaned against the side of his cottage. He felt his face flush with heat, and his heart thumped hard. Her closeness was unbearable, but she fixed him with her gaze, allowing no retreat. In a soft voice she said, "Perthin will be all right. I'm sure heaven is watching out for him. He's a good lad; you've taught him well. He won't do anything foolish."

Arnyl's breath came out wobbly. "I . . . I hope you're right—"

"Why, Arnyl—you're shaking! Let's get you inside and let me make you some tea." She held up the shiny object Arnyl had seen upon her arrival. It was a small silver box, beautifully scrolled. "I've brought you a special healing blend—from the north. I've kept it all these years. It's made from delicate flowers that only emerge from the ground every ten years—in the snow. They bloom for just a day, and then their petals wither. As you can imagine, they are rare and highly treasured—"

Arnyl pulled away from her touch and reached to open his front door. "Oh brine and bother! Then you shouldn't waste them on me! I've got plenty of—"

"This is my gift to you, Arnyl." Her words fell upon his ears as softly as the softest flower petals. He stopped and stilled his heart. He hoped she couldn't tell how befuddled and flustered he felt.

"I'm sorry . . . I do feel a bit weak. Maybe it would be best if you left and tended to others more needy."

She held open the door and urged him through. He gripped the crutch and hoped she would leave; he was unable to bear her company a moment longer. Jayden gone, then Emelee. Now Perthin. He couldn't abide letting his heart be hurt again. He wanted Gayla by his side, in his arms, sharing his home and life. This he longed for more than anything—other than Perthin's safe return. Yet he would lose her too. Even if she would deign to love him—which seemed an impossibility—he couldn't take the risk of losing anyone else he loved. Better to push her away now, seal over the hole in his heart with a heavy stone. He would have to face the truth—he was now alone, more than ever before.

This was heaven's punishment, no doubt. Giving him people to love, and then taking them away. It was no less than what he deserved.

"Go," he said, not even turning to speak to her. He didn't dare for a second look into her riveting eyes. "Just go."

He felt her hesitate, afraid to cross the chasm he'd just carved out between them. From the corner of his eye, he watched her set down the small silver box on his side table, then, without a sound, she left like a faint breeze, leaving a trace of her perfume behind her to tease and torment him.

EIGHTEEN

PYTHIUS KEPT his face burrowed down in his cloak. Wind seared his cheeks raw, and his arm screamed in pain. It took every ounce of effort to put one foot ahead of the other as he threaded through the sewage-filled lanes and breathed through his mouth so as to not gag from the stench. His Eyes and Ears had agreed to making the arrangement, and they'd asked no questions. He only hoped the man would show up—and had done as he commanded—whoever this foul brigand was. Well, he didn't want to know and he didn't care about the particulars, as long as he had acquired what he needed.

A week until the new moon. That's what the seer from Torth had said—and what the aged soothsayer had confirmed. He had ordered his two informants to take them to that old hag the moment they shocked him with their pronouncement. Sacrifice Inaya? Nothing on heaven or earth would make him do such a thing! But the hag had only looked at him with her one good eye and cackled. Her other eye—an eerie and disgusting glass one—roved in its socket, as if seeing worlds far and near. Pythius could barely stand to listen to her voice, for as she spoke, her words grated upon his ears in such a painful manner he forgot about his afflicted arm. Even now he heard them ring out in his head, sounding like the cracking of ice on a winter lake: *"It is the only way to stop the attack from the north. You must erect a pole out in the harbor, just beyond the high-tide line. And on the eve of the new moon must tie your daughter to the pole as a gift to the gods. The gods will only accept a sacrifice of what is dearest to your heart, and since you refuse to relinquish the one, you must lose the other."*

She had glared so deeply into his eyes that he felt her scurrying around in his soul. Her look told him she knew about the scepter, and it was that of which she spoke. He would never give up the scepter—but how could he bear to lose Inaya? As he headed out the hag's door, she had called to him, "I see your pain. And your need. You must make a choice. Pain either way. But it is the only way to save your kingdom." Her laughter had stabbed, as sharp as icicles, and it took all his control not to strike her for such rudeness.

Pythius grunted as he turned a last corner in the dark and approached the dock where he was to meet this man. Exhaustion darkened his mood such that if this man failed to appear, he would find some hapless soul and cut him to ribbons. His thirst for blood roiled within him, the need to strike out and slash someone into unrecognizable pieces. Why should he listen to that old fool—either of those old fools? He should have run both the seer and the witch through with his sword. Maybe that would have satisfied some of his bloodlust. It had been too long since he'd killed for pleasure. Maybe that would take his mind off the pain.

He had ordered his Eyes and Ears to kill anyone with a connection to Lady Vitrella. Perhaps that would stall—if not eliminate—her access to information. And though he did not fully trust the seer nor the hag, he could not take the chance there was some truth to their too-similar visions. Yet, he had formed a plan. No doubt when he failed to show up with the scepter on the appointed night at the tavern she would unleash her evil, but if the hag's words were true, then maybe there was a way to stop the attack coming to his harbor. He shuddered, more from memory than from pain and cold. What *was* that thing he'd seen in the crystal slab, churning up the waters? Surely no living thing could cause such disturbance and destruction! It had to be witchcraft of some kind. But, no matter. Certainly his plan would work. It had to . . .

He raised his eyes from the warmth of his cloak collar and saw the shape of a man in the shadows of the dock. With a hand on his sword, he drew close, but the man said nothing. He was a giant of a man, arms as thick as logs, and he towered over Pythius by more than a head. Pythius followed the silent man into a dark alley, keeping a few paces back in case of treachery. But the man only stopped at an alcove and swung open a door.

"She's in here," he said, then put out his palm. "My payment."

"Not until I see her. Is she as I described—young, long fair hair, slender—"

"I did as ordered. Always do." The giant spit to one side and Pythius's anger was aroused, making him finger his sword with an itchy grip.

"You will be paid once I see her."

The man spit again and scowled. Perhaps he did not know he was speaking to his king. Regardless, Pythius's hackles rose at his rude insolence. The pain racking his body made him tap his foot. "Hurry up, man," he hissed. "Fetch her." He had no intention of going into that dark room without a torch.

Pythius waited in the dark alcove for the man to return. In no time at all, the giant emerged holding on to a wriggling, squealing girl with her hands bound behind her back and her mouth gagged with a rag. Even in the dark her eyes shone with terror, which brought a wave of pleasure to Pythius's heart. Oh, how he loved to see such fear. He breathed in deeply, feeling empowered and inspired, as if her fear nurtured and fed him. Ah, he would prove victorious over that deceiver from the northern Wastes! One look told him the girl was a good match. No one—not even Lady

Vitrella's best spies—would be able to tell the difference—especially not after he'd done what he planned to do to her. With a battered, swollen face, she would be unrecognizable.

Pythius felt a grin rise on his face. How long had it been since he felt this confident, this victorious? He would prevail! His plan could not fail. He would thwart Lady Vitrella and all of the gods above. He was the lion from the thicket, the one foretold. He would stop her threat and rule the known world—scepter or not! Now that Ka'zab was weeks away from victory over that land in the northwest, Pythius would finally have access to one of those sacred sites. He would find the Keeper and learn how to harness the magical waters spewing out of the rock in the center of the circle. He had tolerated this pain long enough, and now it was time to act decisively. He realized he had let the years of pain whittle him away to nothing—which was just what Lady Vitrella had been waiting for, no doubt. Why she had waited this long to give him this ultimatum. Well, she had a surprise waiting for her, and whatever threat she was unleashing on his kingdom would be stopped!

The giant pushed his meaty paw into Pythius's face upon releasing the girl into his custody. "My pay. I got it coming."

Pythius let out a laugh and pulled out his sword. "Yes, you do—and here it is!" With a quick stroke, Pythius sliced through the man's throat. He backed away as blood spurted, but to his disgust some of it splattered his face and neck. The giant fell with a loud crash to the ground, and the girl backed up against the wall in shock. She was so frightened, she shook like a rat cornered by a cat.

Pythius wiped the blood from his sword and sheathed it. He took the girl's arm and she flinched, then fought him. Although his blood raced with the thrill of his kill, he had no energy to drag the girl along. He raised his arm to strike her hard across the face, intent on battering her into submission, but she swooned and fell to the ground instead. No matter. He had picked this meeting place specifically for its proximity to the nearby secret tunnel. He might be in grueling pain, but he was still strong and virile.

He threw the girl over his shoulder like a sack of coal and marched steadfastly down the street under the murky night sky. He saw no one as he slipped between two crumbling stone buildings and down a corridor so narrow he had to twist sideways to ease himself and his load through. The path grew dark as he ducked under a low stone archway that blocked out the night's dim light.

He dropped the unconscious girl onto the hard stone pathway as he felt for a key in his vest pocket. A quick glance at the sliver of light filtering in from the street where he'd entered told him no one was watching. He wiggled the key in the rusted lock; the stickiness and dirt in the hole confirmed that no one had used this secret entrance to the sea tunnel since his father had invaded Paladya all those years ago. He laughed as he pushed open the resistant squeaking rotted door and marched ahead in the dark with his load once more draped over his shoulder. He could almost taste the blood of that giant in his mouth, and he let the memory of his brutal murder tickle his mind and invigorate him as he headed for the pinprick of light ahead.

The tunnel was saturated with the smell of bracken and salt, and Pythius sucked in a deep breath of the sea air. The old algaed stone walls dripped with moisture and dankness, but the chill did not discourage him. All was going according to plan.

He pushed open the barred door to a small chamber that had a tiny high window facing the sea. He could hear the breakers crash against the seawall just outside the damp and secluded space. Even if the girl screamed at the top of her lungs for help—and Pythius was certain she would—no one would hear her. She was far away from any ears other than those of the seals barking effusively out on the rocks below—and their cacophony would only add to the smothering of her cries.

As he ripped off her gag, she came to, and just as he expected, she began to scream. He backed away from her cater-wauling and said, "Save your voice, my sweet. No one can hear you." He looked at the wet, cold dirt floor and frowned. He still had a week until the new moon, and he needed her alive and well. It would not serve his purposes to have her succumb to the cold. "I suggest you make yourself as comfortable as you can. You will have a chill night ahead of you. I will return tomorrow with blankets and food and water. But don't waste your energy trying to escape. You cannot fit through that window up there, and these bars are thick iron. Unless you can shrink to the size of a mouse or turn into a gull, you will have to remain here, I'm sad to say."

The girl pulled in an attempt to loosen her hands that were still bound behind her back. "Who are you? Let me go! What do you want with me—I've done nothing—"

"No, of course you haven't. But you will do something for me. In time. For now, accept your fate—"

She lunged at him, but he chuckled and pushed her to the ground. "A brave one you are." She had watched him murder that hulk and yet still dared attempt to wrest her freedom from him? He smiled. "I like your spirit," he said, reaching over and caress-ing her cheek. She jumped back and screamed. "I do have to be on my way, but . . ."

He drank in the growing fear in her eyes as if it were a tonic, an elixir that assuaged the pain that throbbed mercilessly up and down his arm. Yes, he could use a diversion, a little distraction . . . and she was quite a comely specimen. He wouldn't hurt her—too much. But he did need a few bruises and swelling to mask her true identity. He had thought to wait until the new moon to inflict his damage, but why postpone pleasure?

He unclasped his cloak and set it neatly on the ground. He noticed a few stray blood spatterings on his vest and cravat as he removed them. No matter. He'd learned long ago a trick to remove blood from his fine clothing—toss them into the incinerator.

He laughed and watched the terror grow in the girl's eyes as she pressed herself into the corner of the small cell. No doubt she wished she were a mouse or a gull right now. But sadly, she was not. Poor thing.

NINETEEN

PERTH FELL with a hard thud to cold ground. He felt around him as his spinning vision began to clear and his fingers met with ice, freezing ice. He got to his knees and stared down from the icy promontory to which his boots had brought him. Stretched out before him in the strange haze that lay like gauze over the land was a vast ice field—cursed, no doubt, as King Cakrin had described. *This* was Elysiel—the sublime land of his dreams? Yet, underneath the thick sheath of ice, Perth could make out color—faint greens and lavenders, as if this vibrant, flourishing wilderland had not been destroyed but was merely frozen in time. What had done such a thing to Cakrin's great land? Would killing the *Tse'pha* undo all the damage done to this hidden and bewitched kingdom?

Again, Perth felt a grievous weight on his heart as he stood torn between wanting to restore Elysiel to its former splendor and fearing the thought of facing the kingdom's greatest enemy. Yet, even buried in ice, Elysiel touched a strange nerve in his heart. He could sense somehow that untold numbers of living creatures—beasts, birds, and men alike—lay alive but dormant underneath the icy sheet. The feeling disturbed him greatly; it was as if he could almost hear their slumbering thoughts, their dreams, as they endured—unmoving, unblinking—the passage of time as it flowed around and past them, leaving them behind. And their captivity stirred an unexpected sentimentality inside him, giving him the urge to cry. He blew out a breath and started exploring.

The speedy journey that had whisked him to Elysiel had left him lightheaded. He sought to find a place to sit, but not a rock showed through the glacial landscape. He resigned himself to searching out the entrance to the crypt of kings, worried it would take him all day—if it were indeed day. He had left in the dark of night, but a light infused the sky, akin to sunlight filtering through a thick veil of fog. Perth wondered if any day had dawned in Elysiel since this curse had been draped over it. But his worries quickly fled as he neared the towering wall of rock. One sniff confirmed what his eyes failed to find—the entrance had to be close . . . and no doubt, so were the stinky trolls.

Before he even stepped through the narrow crack in the outcropping of iced-over rock, his eyes began to water. He threw a hand over his nose and entered with hesitation. Even though Cakrin had assured him the trolls would help him, he did not relish another encounter with those vile creatures. Would these trolls be just as ugly and horrifying as the ones he'd spoken with in Tolpuddle? Would they tease and taunt him, or just give him what he asked and let him be off on his way? He did not think he could stomach another round of ridiculing and poking and filth. Perhaps these trolls would be more mannered and reserved—seeing that they held an important position guarding the crystal sword in the crypt.

He took slow steps, sucking breath in through his mouth and wiping tears from his stinging eyes. A long, narrow hallway hewn of stone seemed to lead to darkness. Icicles hung overhead like dragon's teeth, some so low Perth had to duck under them to pass. In the recesses of ice-covered rock, he made out carved forms that he presumed were the likenesses of men. These stood heads taller than him, flanking him on both sides of the hallway, lined up as if at attention. No doubt he was in the crypt of kings. Were all the past kings of Elysiel buried in here, behind the carvings? What a dismal place! Even after many minutes of passing by these silent sentinels, he could still see no end to the hallway or any other way out of this chamber. He wished he'd brought an oil-soaked torch. How did the king expect him to navigate in the dark?

Suddenly a loud crashing noise sounded ahead, followed by a flicker of light. Perth froze in his steps. Heavy clomping drew nearer, and the light grew in brightness until Perth could make out large bulky shapes approaching him.

"Ah, he's here, he's here," one raspy voice shouted in a gurgle that sounded like excitement.

"I told you he would come!" another voice answered.

"No," the first voice insisted, "I said it first."

"No, it was I—"

Perth rolled his eyes as the trolls lumbered toward him, keeping a hand over his nose. He tried to still his shaking but couldn't help but feel a ripple of terror come over him as the trolls—and there were three—touched him all over with their grasping, clutching hands. At least they weren't covered with dung and mud as the other trolls had been. No doubt they would roll in a refuse heap— if there was one nearby. Still, they stank to high heavens. Maybe even when clean they exuded a stench. And it seemed true that trolls always traveled in threes. Why was that? Perth wondered.

"Speak up, minnow. Rumphog got your tongue?"

Perth noticed this troll looked just like one of the ones he'd seen back in Tolpuddle—with crossed eyes and a giant wart on the tip of its nose.

"I . . . the king . . . King Cakrin sent me—"

"Yes, yes," another of the trolls said. This one was huge, nearly as wide as the narrow hall. "Of course. That's why we were expecting you, minnow."

The third troll pushed its way through. Perth's eyes widened upon seeing the hat on its head. It wasn't the same floppy hat as the one sported by the troll in the refuse heap but rather looked to be made of straw—although it was mostly in shreds. As was all their clothing. Perth could swear these trolls were wearing the same strange bits of garments as the other trolls had. And they called him minnow. Wasn't that what the trolls had called him back in his village?

"Now, sisters, you are being rude—"

Sisters? Surely these creatures weren't female . . . yet, that would explain the previous trolls' fascination with hats and necklaces and linens . . . Perth gulped. If these were females, how large and ugly would the males be?

The largest troll continued, "We are crowding our poor cousin in this tiny space. Let's entertain him in the drawing room."

"Yes, let's! Yes, let's!" the other two trolls trilled.

Perth shook his head as they dragged him through the hallway, around a corner, and into a larger but empty anteroom—empty except for the puzzling piles of ladies' shoes lining the walls in haphazard fashion. Beyond lay a shimmering chamber, but from where Perth stood, he could not peer inside. Strange light seeped from the farther room, casting a dim blue glow upon the three trolls as they stood and studied him.

"You are here for the crystal sword," the cross-eyed troll said, circling and smelling him, and running her gnarled pointy fingers over his clothes. He hoped it—she—wasn't looking with longing at his attire. Her wiry hair bounced around as she spoke. "How fares the king?"

Perth scrunched his face as he removed his hand from his nose. "Uh, the king is dead."

The trolls, much to Perth's surprise, began to wail—all in discordance and sounding like cats with their tails caught in a closed door. The troll with the hat smacked the two others. "Of course he's dead—do you have to remind us?"

Then why did you ask? Perth was already growing weary of their company and the closeness of their smelly bodies. "I didn't know that trolls traveled so far north—"

"Why, silly cousin," the giant one said, "this is our home."

"Elysiel!" the cross-eyed troll moaned.

"Elysiel!" the troll with the hat echoed, then sneered and shook her face, flinging slime from the pointed tips of her tusks. "It's her fault! All of it. Evil Vitra!"

"Evil! Evil!" the other two trolls chanted. Perth covered his ears until their ruckus died down.

Perth wished to hurry them but didn't want to upset them again. They seemed quite unstable and apt to fly into hysterics at the slightest prompting. "Um, do all trolls come from Elysiel?"

The three grew quiet as if confused by his question. The cross-eyed troll put her hands on her wide hips and said, "Whatever do you mean, cousin? We just told you Elysiel is our home."

"Why, yes, you did say that. I was just wondering about the other trolls—"

His words set off another round of uncontained chortling, followed by a fit of guffaws and snorting. Perth stepped back and pressed himself against the wall as more slime flung from tusks.

The troll with the hat threw her thick, lumpy arms up in the air. "We are the only trolls there are!"

"But," Perth objected, "how can that be? Only days ago I saw three trolls in Tolpuddle. Surely my village is hundreds of leagues—"

"*Thousands* of leagues away, silly cousin."

"Yes, silly, silly!" the other two sang.

Perth frowned.

The cross-eyed troll said, "We get around, cousin."

"That we do!" the troll with the hat added. "We travel with much speed!"

All three trolls broke out into a dance—if such feet stomping and spinning could be called dancing. Their careening bodies merged into a blur. Perth ached from standing in the cold chamber. His feet were turning into blocks of ice, and he could no longer feel the tips of his fingers. "Please, would you just bring me the sword of crystal so I can be on my way?"

The trolls stopped dancing. The one with the hat narrowed her eyes and drew close to him; the sour odor exuding from her body made tears run down his cheeks. He held his breath and hoped she would back away before he had to take his next breath.

"The king must trust you, minnow. You are indeed trustworthy and honorable among men—"

"Yes, and you must slay the evil one and cut off her head!" the cross-eyed troll added with a finger poking his chest.

"Vitra! It's all her fault," the largest troll said.

"Did she cause this curse? Turn the land to ice?" Perth asked.

The trolls humphed as one. "No, that was not her doing—that was the evil king of Paladya—but he will get his comeuppance soon!"

"I don't understand . . ." Perth began.

"Us!" the troll with the hat said. "She did this to us! Stole our beauty and turned us into ugly trolls."

"We are the princesses of Elysiel. And she did this to us!"

"Yes, us!"

"Yes, us!"

Perth threw his hands over his ears to snuff out the wailing and whining that followed. Princesses? Were these trolls King Cakrin's daughters? How could anyone wield such power to be able to turn humans into vile creatures such as these?

Finally, the trolls' wailing turned to sobs and sniffles. Perth cleared his throat and said the only words he could think of: "I'm sorry." Now he knew they were misunderstood, even though they inspired fear in the hearts of men—and for good reason.

"But you will kill the evil Vitra—and we will have our beauty back!"

"Yes, we will be beautiful again."

"But you must be careful!"

"Yes, must!"

"Yes, must!"

Perth waved his arms to shut them up. Their grating voices were giving him a horrible headache. "I will do what I can—to kill the *Tsépha* and restore Elysiel—if it can be done. I made a vow to your king, and I never go back on a vow."

"See, sisters," the large troll said. "He is truly trustworthy and honorable."

The troll with the hat smacked her sister forcefully on her head. "I already said that—"

"No you didn't!" The large troll struck her back.

"Yes, I did!"

"Please!" Perth yelled over the din. "The sooner you give me the sword, the sooner I can kill your enemy and restore your beauty."

The trolls settled into a dull silence as they thought this over. "I will fetch the sword!" the troll with the hat said.

"And I the shield," the cross-eyed one announced.

The two trolls fled into the far chamber. The remaining troll sighed and plopped to the hard ground. Her gaze drifted longingly over the piles of shoes along the wall. "Oh, I long for the day when I can wear all my pretty shoes again!" She turned to face him, thoughtfully stroking the long tusks protruding from the sides of her mouth. "You must succeed, cousin. Do not forget—you cannot look the *Tse'pha* in the eye; she will turn you to stone."

"Yes, the king told me—"

"And you cannot let the tip of the sword touch the ground. If you do, it will lose its power—"

"Yes, I know—"

"And before you depart, you must visit the ice cavern and look into the crystal slabs."

An unexpected fear gripped Perth's heart. "Why? What is that place? The king said nothing about my visiting—"

"You must. It will show you what you need to see. It will show you your future. Prepare you."

"I don't want to know my future." Perth turned as the other two trolls came running back into the anteroom, one carrying a sword that appeared to be made of glass and the other a shield of dull copper or some similar metal.

He turned and studied her face. Somehow, even despite all its ugliness, he sensed something tender and kind underneath. Maybe being in Elysiel brought out some residual beauty the princess had beneath her offensive appearance. He could understand now why the trolls were such a disagreeable lot. If he'd been turned into a troll against his wishes, no doubt he would be testy and irritable too.

The troll hissed in Perth's ear. "You must visit the cavern. The king will speak with you there."

"Why? Does the ghost live in the ice cavern?" The king had called this place the crypt of kings. Maybe all the ghosts of Elysiel's kings haunted this place. The thought sent a shiver up Perth's spine.

"It is the sacred place, the sacred site. The kings of Elysiel have been the Keepers of the site for untold ages. Our father will speak to you there, in the presence of the other kings."

"Other kings? Why?"

All three trolls fell quiet, almost as if in reverence. He sensed a great sadness fill the room.

The troll with the hat handed the crystal sword to him, along with a worn leather scabbard. She gestured for him to put it on and waited while he did. The old leather was supple and cracked, and when he fastened it around his waist, it fit his hips perfectly—as if it had been made for someone his size. The sword felt light in the scabbard, as if made of air. He wanted to study it, for it had strange markings engraved along the handle, and he'd never seen such a sword before—made of a solid piece of crystal. Well, he had never truly seen a real sword before—only in his picture books of fairy tales. He wondered how something so light and made of crystal could actually cut off a creature's head. He would have to get very close to his enemy to do the deed. The thought made him tremble.

"The ghosts always speak," the hatted troll said, as the cross-eyed troll handed him the copper shield. It, too, felt light in his hand, but he sensed it had seen much warfare, so he trusted it was more resilient than it looked. He looked at the three trolls, standing in solemn assembly, and he sensed that all their hopes and dreams rested upon him and his impending task.

The large troll laid her gnarled hand upon his shoulder, and, for once, her touch did not make him cringe. "That is the way of Elysiel, cousin. The way it has always been . . . and always will be."

TWENTY

PYTHIUS HESITATED at the narrow entrance between the two buildings before slipping out of sight. He was sure someone was following him, although he could see no movement up the cobbled street, only flickering shadows cast by a lamp in a window here and there. Each of the last three nights he had managed to sneak out of the palace unhindered, with a parcel under his arms. Tonight, he carried a jug of fresh water and a loaf of bread. He smiled thinking of his impending encounter with the girl imprisoned in her cell. The last three nights of torture had been a delightful distraction from his unbearable pain. Strange, but it seemed that ever since the seer had announced Lady Vitrella's demands, his pain had doubled, even tripled—if that were possible. He hadn't slept in over a week—not even for a minute. His healer had given him every potion under the sun to try to quell the stabbing pains that came now in more frequent and stronger waves, but those foul elixirs did no good. In his rage, he had the healer disposed of—the third this year. They were all useless, posturing idiots.

He could have just left the girl with some stores and blankets and returned tomorrow—the night the sliver of new moon would rise in the sky—but after battling her ardent resistance that first night, which impassioned him with fury and desire, all he could think of each day was how to inflict more subtle pain upon her to hear her cry louder and more fervently. Even her curses were music to his ears. Her unbreakable spirit was a refreshing change from so many other weak women he had tortured in the past—women who swooned and gave up fighting after realizing their efforts were hopeless.

After another minute of scanning the dark street, he unlocked the door and proceeded through the tight space, feeling along the walls slick with seawater until he arrived at the stone landing where the locked and barred cell stood. He found the lantern he'd left hanging on a protrusion of stone on the wall, then located his flint. He listened for sounds coming from the cell, but the girl was silent. Either she was sleeping or she was holding her breath in fear of him. He snickered. And rightly she should fear. Each night he had increased his inflictions of pain, so that last night she had fallen unconscious in a heap on the cold ground. Such a disappointment! He'd probably broken most of the bones in her face, and perhaps even her jaw. Maybe she would be unable to eat or drink now, but no matter. She only needed to remain alive one more night to serve his purposes. And now no one would be able to recognize her face—not even her own mother.

After a moment, he managed to get a spark to catch on the oil-soaked wick, and the glare of bright light revealed the girl curled up in her blankets in the far corner under the tiny window. He stood a moment and listened to the waves that crashed in erratic rhythm against the wall and echoed down the tunnels. His palms began to sweat in anticipation of the things he planned to do to her tonight. He would hold nothing back, allowing his pain to flow out of his body and into hers. Ah, blessed relief!

He reached into his vest pocket and produced the key, but just as he put the key into the lock, he heard a voice behind him.

"Pythius! What are you doing?"

He spun around and dropped the lantern. It shattered in pieces on the wet stone, oil spreading in a pool about his feet. Flames guttered, then snuffed out as oil met with water. But even in the dark, he recognized the voice. Samira! His own wife had followed him! And now she would see the girl, her injuries, and there would be no end to her mad ranting. How could he explain this to her? He swallowed, enraged by her intrusion that had complicated things. Well, her impetuous, nosy action left him no choice.

He pasted on a smile. "Samira, my love. Why did you follow me here?"

She came close to study his face in the near dark. He smelled her lovely fragrance, recalling the first time he'd held her in his arms all those years ago. Oh, how things had changed since then. Now her scent made his stomach roil. He would have killed her years ago if it hadn't been for Inaya. How distraught his precious daughter would be when she learned of her mother's demise. He would have to console her, take her into his arms, and comfort her. *She will take the loss hard, poor thing, but in time she will get over it. In time.*

Samira's voice was hard and accusing. "Just what have you been doing down here? And what is this place? This looks like . . . a prison. Is someone in there?" She leaned up against the bars trying to see inside the cell.

Pythius grabbed her arm forcefully and she shrieked. "I've had enough of you, woman. Enough of your prying questions. I made you my queen, and this is the gratitude you show me?" He squeezed harder, wanting to break her arm, and she screamed.

"Let me go! You're hurting me!"

He took no pleasure in her pain; she only made him sick. He had tolerated her long enough. Inaya would fare better without her mother's constant pandering and coddling anyway. He was wasting his energy and wasting his words.

He pulled out the shortsword sheathed at his side and plunged it into her heart. His wife emitted a brief cry, then fell into his arms. He pulled out the blade and pushed her away. She collapsed onto the stone pathway and Pythius exhaled. Excruciating pain shot up his arm, and he stumbled over to the wall and fell against it. He listened to the sound of waves, punctuated by an occasional seal barking, as he stilled his pounding heart and tried to even his breath. After a minute, he felt his strength return despite his exhausted, weakened state.

Well, good riddance, he thought as he walked over and hefted his wife's body over his shoulder. He trudged, teeth clenched, to the far end of the tunnel. Water swelled against the platform's edge three feet below, surging in and out as the tide wandered through the hidden waterways leading in from the sea to where he now stood. He dropped to his knees and leaned forward to flip the body into the black water. The ebbing tide would take her out to sea. Maybe, he thought as he watched the shape bob on the swells, some sea creatures would devour her and leave no trace. Or she might wash up onto a beach somewhere. Someone might even be able to identify her. But, no matter. Speculations would fly as to why the queen had been out alone, late at night, unescorted. He could blame his enemies, maybe claim that the band of black marketers had kidnapped her while she had been out strolling the gardens late at night, seeking a breath of fresh air. He'd been meaning to squelch that suspicious group of outspoken rebels for a while. Now he had the perfect reason to publically flog and hang them.

He grinned at his ingenuity. But a frown formed on his face as he turned back around and considered the locked cell. Without a light, he would have to continue his tortures of the girl in the dark, and what fun would that be? He would not be able to see the terror in her eyes or the poignant rage that so delighted him. Dealing with his wife had put a damper on his excitement anyway. Now he would have to face Inaya and listen to her worries over her missing mother. He would have to assure her he would do everything he could to find her. Then he would have to send out guards to search the city, and the palace would erupt in a bout of melodrama—none of which he had the patience for. He needed to focus on his primary task—and that was to have the girl tied to the post after dark tomorrow.

Through his Eyes and Ears, he had commissioned the erecting of the pole in the harbor, with ropes already attached and waiting. He had wanted to keep his plan a secret, but realized he couldn't possibly do what was required by himself. The two informants had heard the hag tell him how to stop the attack to come, and when he confided in them, they thought his idea a clever one. They assured him all he need do was bring the girl out to the street and they would take care of the rest. Everything was in place. Whatever evil was about to attack his harbor would be stopped—if that old soothsayer was right. And if she wasn't? Well, he had spent the last two weeks mustering and preparing his guards to protect and defend the docks. He had over two dozen large vessels with cannons at the ready. His commanders had questions in their eyes when Pythius told them what needed to be done, but they knew better than to voice them aloud.

Perhaps they were all wrong—King Cakrin, the seer, the old soothsayer with the glass eye. Maybe the threat in his harbor would never materialize. Maybe Lady Vitrella had been scared away and had given up her attempt to seize the scepter. He would welcome that outcome. But if his enemy had sent some evil to attack his kingdom, no matter. He would prevail! And then all in Paladya would see the lion roar and know his teeth and claws were still as sharp as ever.

He leaned down before the cell and felt carefully for the key he'd dropped in amid the bits of broken glass; he found it in a puddle of oil. He stood and inserted the key in the lock, then swung the door wide open. The shape of the girl remained the same, from what Pythius could make out in the darkness. He grabbed her and rolled her over, but he didn't need any light to see that she was not unconscious but dead—already she had begun to smell.

Pythius scowled, then kicked at her. "I need you alive!"

Now what was he to do? He would need to find another girl quickly, and he surely could not do this himself. He would have to go to his Eyes and Ears and have them find someone else. He cursed and stomped, thinking how his perfect plan was now in ruins. But, no matter. He would pay those men double for their efforts. And he would brush aside Inaya's worries for the moment. Maybe say her mother took off on a sudden trip—back to Rush-brook. Some relative had died, he would say. How true that was! He just needed to face tomorrow—and see if the vision he had seen in the crystal slab fifteen years ago was truly foretelling his fate. And then, come what may, he would turn his attention to what now consumed his heart—that sacred site with the healing waters that Ka'zab had discovered. For he knew if he did not finally get relief from the pain racking his body, he would not be able to bear it much longer. Ka'zab had assured him by missive that victory would come soon. That the Regent Sherbourne within his walled city was about to lose the battle.

Pythius thought about the scepter in the box under his bed. Maybe the scepter would respond to another sacred site? What if he took it to this new kingdom? Maybe the power of those slabs would unlock the power of the scepter. It was worth a try. He would never give up. Somewhere, someone knew the key to unlocking the scepter's power. He hated to believe that the Lady Vitrella might know the secret. Surely she wouldn't be demanding it from him if she didn't. So there had to be an answer to this mystery. If he could capture *her*, that might give him his answer. Why hadn't he thought of that? But then, his informants told him that in all these years, they had never seen her inside the borders of Paladya. Yet someone must know where to find her.

As soon as this ordeal was over, he would assign a large garrison of soldiers to seeking her out—while he headed northwest to the sacred site with the bubbling fountain of healing waters. Yes, that would be his next step, rather than waiting for his enemy to return with stronger forces. He would go after her just as he'd gone after the king of Elysiel. After all, he was the lion in the thicket! And just as he had vanquished one powerful ruler, he would another. The Lady Vitrella might be as crafty as a snake, but she was no match for him and his army!

He stormed out of the cell, leaving the barred door ajar, leaving the body of the battered and tortured girl to rot in the sea tunnel. He thought of his wife's body floating in the harbor at the mercy of the tide and the creatures feasting upon her flesh. And then he thought of his sweet Inaya, sleeping soundly in her bed, unaware of the grief to come in the days ahead. His heart hurt for her, but she would just have to learn that in life, disappointments sometimes cannot be avoided. This he knew all too well.

TWENTY-ONE

THE AIR IN the cavern was fresh and invigorating—a welcome respite from the stench of the trolls. *Princesses!* It was hard to imagine what they must have looked like before they had been transformed, but he suspected they had been beautiful and graceful, with noble bearing like their father. Was their lunatic behavior natural, or had it been caused by their curse?

He walked slowly, awed by the soft blue light emanating from the walls of ice. By that light he could make out more icicles dangling from the remote rock ceiling above him, and beneath his feet he could see far down, into splintered shadows and crevices that darkened into nothingness. His boots tapped quietly on the ice as he stepped with care, feeling he could slip with one misstep. With his pack on his back containing his few belongings and the sack for the *Tse'pha*'s head, he headed for the adjacent room the trolls had told him he'd find—a massive cavern that contained the sacred site—although he couldn't imagine what the place would look like.

He was not prepared for what he saw as he entered the chamber. The small entryway opened to a massive ice cave, making him feel miniscule and insignificant. Crystals glittered, and their sparkling multiplied as the rainbow slivers of light bounced off the icicles and walls and sparked like fire. He sucked in a breath as his jaw dropped, for he had never seen anything so beautiful. And a quiet strain of melody, like the tinkle of chimes, filled the cavern and set his heart racing, for it seemed to fill him with joy until he wondered if he could contain its measure without bursting.

Why did this stark beauty so move him? The emotions welling inside him puzzled him, for a longing sprang up like a wild weed, entangling him and his thoughts. He couldn't imagine ever leaving; the need to remain here, in this strange place, anchored him. He no longer felt the penetrating cold; rather, warmth infused him, spreading down his limbs to his fingers and toes, like being immersed in a hot bath. Every muscle relaxed, every fear and worry dissipated. His thoughts roamed to home, to Tolpuddle, to his pa, to his quest, but they all seemed so distant and detached. The only thing that mattered was here, now, in this chamber.

"That is because your heart is one with Elysiel."

Perth turned at the voice. The ghost of the king hovered a few steps away, gesturing ahead. "Why?" Perth asked. "I don't understand."

The ghost only smiled and said, "One day you will. But now that you have been here, you will never be the same, Perthin Quay. Come."

Perth followed the ghost as it crossed the great chamber drenched in blue light. The floor seemed made of giant blocks of ice and yet felt as soft as grass under his boots. He had the eerie feeling he and the king were not alone, but when he glanced around he saw only his reflection staring back at him from the ice-covered walls. Yet, he could sense others walking alongside him—three, four, six . . . Without seeing anything, he could make out the presence of now nine in step with him as he drew close to a line of gigantic slabs of ice. He felt their solemn regard for this place, their majesty and wisdom, their integrity and honor. They were there to support him, bolster his courage, reassure him. How he knew this, he couldn't say. Maybe he was under a spell, imagining it all—maybe he wasn't even here but at home in his bed, dreaming.

A chuckle shook him from his thoughts. "You are not dreaming, Perthin," King Cakrin said. "But you should dare to, for he who dreams can change the world. You dreamed for a better life for your father, for your village, and so you are here."

Perth loosed a shaky breath, thinking of what the trolls told him. "Why do I have to see my future? Why can't I just go after the *Tse'pha* and kill her?"

The king waited in silence. Perth looked at the slabs rising up from the ice floor and realized they weren't ice at all but crystal—milky and veined like the sword at his side. They were three times the height of a man and at least half that in thickness, and he could tell they formed a circle although he couldn't see to the other side of the cavern in the faint light. Upon nearing one, he sensed a vibration of energy, as if the thing were alive. Odd. He reached out and touched it, and suddenly . . .

He was on a hill covered with flowers in colors so brilliant he had to squint. Sunlight streamed around him, but it radiated a peculiar tint—he had never seen light of that quality before, almost as if it were otherworldly. And the smells! He drew in a deep breath and let the fragrance of the flowers intoxicate and fill him. He let him eyes roam, taking in the panorama before him that he knew was Elysiel—the way it had once looked. And yet, he knew he was not in the past but the future. He felt older, much older, but still infused with youthful strength. How he knew this he could not tell, but years had passed and he was now a man. And most startling of all was the deep-seated joy that rushed through his soul, a feeling of utter contentment and peace. It nearly knocked him over with its potency.

He tried to remember Tolpuddle, but the images he tugged at were wisps, as if that life he had lived was long past, nearly forgotten. Even the images of his pa were sketchy, and as he tried to summon up memories of his days with his pa and his friends back home, a strange sadness overcame him. It wasn't as if he had lost them—it was more like he had drifted away in time, the way a boat out on the horizon grows smaller and smaller until you can no longer see it. Yet the sadness was a sweet one, accompanied by a knowing that one day he would reunite with those he loved.

He became instantly aware of the presence of the nine others. They were there with him, on that hill, looking out over Elysiel, and he felt their joy as well, as if it seeped into his soul. He knew then it was not a joy from within him or them—it was coming from the land itself. And then an even stranger sensation overtook him. Life buzzed around him in profusion. He sensed bees and birds, ants and worms—felt them move and breathe and sing. And then he heard thoughts, thoughts of countless people, and images of them flitted through his mind, one after another, yet he could clearly see and hear them all at once . . .

The shock of so much life invading his mind made him jump back, and as he pulled his fingers away from the crystal slab, he was back in the ice cavern, in the dim light and cold air, and his heart sank in sorrow. He wanted more than anything to return to that place of peace and joy. He knew he would never find those same feelings in the world and life he knew. Was this to be his future? It must! He would do anything to see it come to pass, to have that to look forward to one day.

"That is why you were brought here, Perthin," King Cakrin said, his form drifting near the wall of the cavern. Perth could barely make him out. "For you will need to draw on that promise in the evil time you face just ahead. Even in the darkest of dark, Elysiel will be with you."

Perth could say nothing. He felt suddenly empty, lonely, sorrowful. He turned and walked to where Cakrin waited.

"It is time. The sword and shield will aid you in another way, for they radiate power from Elysiel. They can obscure and confound the minds of those near, making things appear as they are not, which will allow you to get close enough to Vitra to kill her. Shield your eyes at all times, and do not turn at sudden noises, for if you chance to look upon her . . ."

Perth nodded. The king's words did not frighten him as they had before. A lingering sensation from his vision stayed with him, the memory of what it had felt like to be much older, a man with many years of life and experience behind him. It was the stuff of dreams, the way centuries might pass in a deep sleep. In all his dreams of Elysiel, time had stood still, as if it no longer existed, as if he had lived with an eternity stretched out behind and before him, life with no end. He felt some of that now, standing there, readying his heart for what he must do.

He looked at Cakrin and saw a pool of warmth in his eyes. "I'm ready."

"Heaven goes with thee, Perthin Quay. You are the one foretold."

Perth nodded, overcome by a gratitude so humbling he could not answer.

He looked down at his boots and the words came out of their own accord. "Take me to the realm of the *Tse'pha*," he commanded.

In a whoosh, the ice cavern disappeared.

Pythius stepped up on the seawall as the setting sun behind him lit up the sky in an eerie orange glow. Heavy clouds gathered above, rumbling with thunder and pregnant with spring rain. Far out in the harbor, his armada of warships waited, and although the sea seemed calm, Pythius felt it.

Something was coming. And as if to confirm his intuition, the ground shook under his feet. At first the tremor was slight, almost unnoticeable, but in seconds it grew to a steady shaking, requiring him to place his hands on the wall's ledge to steady himself. He had felt earthshakes many times in Paladya, but he knew this disturbance had nothing to do with the shifting land masses beneath his feet.

A contingent of armed soldiers lined the shoreline a league away at the central docks. He could make out their shapes on the northern crescent of shore as one great shadow upon the sand, ready to face whatever was coming. He had arrived just in time to watch the events unfold. Inaya had detained him with her concerns over her mother's strange disappearance, and Pythius had tried to convince her that Samira had gone suddenly to Rushbrook. He'd seen her leave, he told her, and had promised to pass on word to Inaya, letting her know her mother would return in a fortnight.

But Inaya had fretted over his explanation, certain her mother would never have left—even on as urgent a matter as he'd claimed—without first informing her personally. As much as he wanted to stay and reassure her all would be well, he'd had no time for such niceties; the hour was late. He gave her a quick peck on the cheek and told her they'd talk in the morning, that he had something important to tend to that would keep him out most of the night.

Once his daughter had retired to her room, he had taken his seneschal aside and told him to lock Inaya's door, imprisoning her for the evening. If Inaya resisted or complained, Ramus was to say the king was worried for her safety—that there had been reports of some of the black marketers seen on the palace grounds, and some may have even slipped inside the living quarters. This would add weight to the accusations he planned to pronounce the following morning. Under no circumstances could he allow Inaya to show herself anywhere where spies might recognize her. After all, that girl now gagged, bound, and tied to the post out in the water before him—away from the notice of his soldiers—was supposed to be his daughter. He grunted in anger. How would offering up his daughter appease an evil sent to destroy him and his city?

But, no matter. He wasn't taking any chances. His Eyes and Ears had found a suitable substitute at the last minute. To avoid possible trouble, Pythius had had her drugged with a sleeping elixir—just enough to make her groggy and compliant in her haze of confusion. He hoped the "gods," or whoever was to be appeased by his action, would accept this girl in Inaya's place. The whole affair seemed foolish, after all. To think a strange creature would be quelled by one human sacrifice—and of a specific person at that! Yet he was willing to hedge his bets and do what the old hag told him he must do. No doubt one girl was the same as any other, in the gods' eyes. A frown formed on his face. Wasn't it possible that one-eyed witch was one of Lady Vitrella's spies? Why hadn't he thought of that before? What better way for his enemy to strike at his heart than to trick him into killing his darling?

The thought soured his mouth and gave him an uneasy sense— as if there were enemies on all sides of him, hiding behind the cottage walls, laughing at him, and plotting against him. He spun around and heard laughter, but no one was near—only his personal guards, and they were far back barricading the street and preventing any from crossing the seawall and heading to the beach. He climbed down from the wall and walked to the water's edge as thunder broke out in a rattle overhead. The ground shook again, more violently this time, and the laughter resumed. This time he was certain he'd heard it, just behind him.

He spun once more and—to his horror—found himself looking into a face that had haunted his sleep the last fifteen years.

"Cakrin!" he muttered, swiping a hand at the nebulous vision materializing before him. Surely all his sleepless nights and constant pain were the cause of this hallucination. The shape was only a wisp, nothing substantial, with sketchy features—although there was no mistaking the visage and form of the king of Elysiel.

"Go away, begone!" He continued waving, but the form kept laughing. Pythius's rage propelled him across the sand as he chased this chimera, covering his ears to keep the stabbing laughter out.

Then the ghostly shape lifted an arm and appeared to point out to sea. Pythius stopped, breathing heavily, sweat trickling down his neck and back in the chill evening air.

"There," the ghost said, "meet your doom!"

Cakrin's shape vanished in a *whoosh*. Pythius stood with his back to the harbor, fear riveting him where he stood. Without turning, he heard it—whatever it was. First, a quiet rumble, growing to a roar. And then loud sloshing, followed by faint cries and screams of alarm coming from the northern entrance to the harbor. And then, the unmistakable sound of wood breaking in loud explosions, one crash after another, coming closer and closer.

Pythius forced his body to turn around and face "his doom." What he saw sank every bit of hope he had.

Every one of his warships was either gone or sinking out in the middle of the harbor—broken, battered hulls that stood no chance of rescue. Water heaved in massive waves, undulating toward the northern shore and engulfing the seawall. Pythius watched in horror as one whole section of docks, wharfside buildings, and cottages was buried in water, broken into bits and swept out to sea. And then . . . he saw what had caused such inexplicable destruction.

A massive scaled head lifted from the waves, sporting a long, wide snout and gigantic eyes filled with fury. Following the head, a powerful neck curved up, and then a ridged back. Pythius gasped. The creature was massive! The length of many city blocks—larger than his entire palace. What manner of beast was this? It resembled a snake, but its head was square-shaped and . . . fire spurted from its nostrils!

Fire? Was he hallucinating again? How could any creature breathe fire? And in water no less! He rubbed his eyes in disbelief as more shouts erupted around him, this time closer and louder. He watched and waited, mesmerized, as the beast submerged under the water's churning surface. Someone grabbed his arm and he spun, only to see one of his bodyguards tugging on him.

"Sire! You must get off the beach. You'll be drowned!"

His feet refused to move. He couldn't wrest his gaze from the sight before him—as dock after dock shattered and the creature came closer, hugging the shore and headed pointedly for him.

"Sire—"

"Let go of me!" Pythius yelled. "Go back to your position on the street!"

The man, although surprised and confused, obeyed, leaving Pythius on the shore as water rushed up to his feet and the harbor rocked from the creature's movements. The ground shook so hard that the seawall behind him began shattering. Pieces of rock broke off and fell onto the sand, only to be swept away by the onrushing current of water swirling about Pythius's feet.

Suddenly, he was back in the ice cavern, his hand stuck to the crystal slab, watching himself stand on the stone promontory, his arm in horrific pain, and witnessing the destruction of his harbor. Yet . . . it was not quite the same image. The banners. The red banners with his lion sigil were flapping in the wind behind him. And he was standing . . . not on the seawall but on the parapet of his palace wall. And something was missing . . .

At that moment the furious beast rose once more from the water and lifted its head. But this time it appeared directly in front of the beach upon which Pythius stood, and appeared to hesitate.

Water encircled Pythius up to his knees, but he paid the cold invasion no mind. His eyes locked on the post and the squirming girl—now obviously aware of her terrible plight and struggling to get free.

Pythius held his breath as the beast eyed the girl and drew close. He could tell she was now screaming, although he could not hear her, gagged as she was. And the noise of a city in alarm coupled with the waves' eruptions made hearing anything beyond a few feet impossible.

Pythius stood riveted. The beast seemed to be sniffing the girl, and then, in an instant, it dove beneath the water and disappeared.

Minutes passed; the beast was nowhere in sight. The waves began to calm. Pythius looked along the beach at the wreckage left behind as the debris-filled water vacated the harbor-side streets and returned to the sea. Half the dock area was gone—ships, buildings, lanes. A large portion of the seawall lay in ruins. At least a dozen or more cottages were missing. Crowds of people gathered in the streets, watching the harbor, waiting.

Then, without warning, a shape rose again near the post erected in the harbor, but instead of a head, Pythius saw it was the beast's tail, a thick pronged mass of scales and ridges, flicking water as it whipped in the air. With a clearly decisive motion, the tail sliced the air, targeting the post, and with one fast sweep demolished both the post and the girl tied to it. Not a ripple marred the surface of the water then, and within seconds there remained nothing to show anything had ever been there—girl or beast.

Pythius sucked in a breath and trembled. What could this portend? He turned and saw his soldiers looking at him and waiting nervously for instruction. He glanced back at the harbor and watched the waters settle; the sounds of crying and moaning filled the air around him as night descended. He thought of the hundreds of his men now dead at the bottom of the harbor amid the bits and pieces of his finest ships.

He had been wrong. This beast his enemy had sent was an insuperable force that he had no idea how to kill. But kill it he must! Unless . . . he dared hope that the beast accepted the sacrifice of the girl. Maybe his offer had appeased the monster. But there was no guarantee it would not come back. The soothsayer had been right. She had foreseen this beast and had foretold accurately. He would just have to ask her, then, if his efforts had succeeded. If the monster was mollified.

His gaze was drawn once more to his ruined docks. Countless boats and buildings had been destroyed or swept out to sea. In just a few short minutes, the beast had taken a chunk out of his harbor city as easily as one takes a bite from a loaf of bread! It would take little effort for it to return and finish what it started—and destroy all of Paladya.

The image on the crystal slab rushed into his mind, and he now realized what was missing. In the vision he had seen, he stood on the palace parapet—but in his hand he wielded the scepter, the crystal scepter! Why would he take it out of hiding, and how was it possible for him to hold it? It must mean something—but what? Was it time for him to try to claim the power of the crystal scepter? Is that what the vision implied?

A sudden urge came over him—to rush back to the palace and take out the scepter. But no—he mustn't be hasty. The last time he had tried to hold the scepter, years ago, he thought he would perish from the burst of pain. He knew if he should experience that again he would surely die. But he had to know! And he had to learn if the sea beast had left for good—or if it had just given a taste of more to come.

Weary and anxious, exhausted from the lack of sleep and unremitting pain, he stumbled across the sand to where the commander of his city guard stood watching him from the edge of the lane. People ran through the streets in frantic hysteria, calling the names of missing loved ones and bemoaning the damage to their beloved city. None took notice of him—the king of Paladya, the ruler of their kingdom—trudging up to the lane, numb and in shock.

When he reached his commander, he looked around and got his bearings. It had been dark that night his Eyes and Ears had taken him to see the soothsayer with the glass eye. The streets in that seedy section of town bore no street signs and looked much like all the other drab and dreary streets down by the docks. But as he looked down a far lane, he spotted a rotted porch with three cats milling about on the railing—skinny, sleek cats that turned and, as one, all studied him as if they sensed he was staring. The same way the old hag's cats had stared at him that night as he stood in the dark entryway and listened to her warnings.

He turned and told his commander, "Go, take your men and join the guards stationed at the north end of the harbor. Assist them in conscripting every able-bodied person you see to begin cleaning up the damage from the attack."

The man nodded, then cleared his throat. "Sire . . . what was that creature? Where did it come from?"

Pythius knew what the man's next question would be—would the beast return? And that was what Pythius intended to find out that very moment. "I cannot answer your questions as of yet, but I will find the answers and stop that beast from doing any more harm to Paladya. You can be assured of that." He hoped his confident and authoritative tone would assure his men. He could not afford to let fear and uncertainty regarding his monarchy foment a rebellion. Not now—when he was so close to claiming one of the sacred sites.

When the man did not leave his side, Pythius said, "Why are you stalling? Go!"

"But, Sire. Should I arrange for soldiers to take you back to the palace?"

"No. I have other matters that need seeing to. Meet me back here, on the corner, at the start of the fifth watch. Have a carriage waiting."

The man bowed and dismissed himself without a further word. Pythius watched him gather his handful of guards and run down the lane as a thundershower burst open overhead. Cold rain poured in streams from the heavens, drenching Pythius's clothes and soaking the already drenched harbor town with more water. He removed his cloak and held out his throbbing arm, letting the water beat down on the pain, hoping the coldness would give him some measure of relief as he kept his head down and walked up the lane to the cottage with the cats. But he knew better than to hope. He had been hoping for fifteen long years, and now his hope had run out.

He stopped at the porch and glared at the cats blocking access to the front door. They held warnings and chastisement in their yellow eyes. He kneaded his arm and closed his eyes against the barrage of pain. He had done everything he could to eliminate Lady Vitrella's informants and nullify her threat. He had sent out his fleet and positioned his best men—more than a thousand of them—to stop her invasion. But he had failed. Now he was desperate. Desperate to find a solution, and to end his pain. Once and for all.

He rubbed his burning arm, but it only made the torment worse. The thought of slicing it off with his sword was now a real temptation. He could take this no longer. There had to be something he could do to save both his kingdom and himself. Of all those in his kingdom professing wisdom, only the witch with the glass eye seemed to truly have knowledge and be able to see what must be done. And she held no fear of the king's wrath to prevent her from speaking the truth.

As he pushed aside the meowing cats and reached for the door knocker, he made a terrible, unavoidable decision, lodging it into his heart like an anchor. He would do whatever the hag told him he must do to end this. No matter what it was. He hardened his heart against any sentimentality, preparing himself for whatever fate awaited him.

Words drifted into his ear as he stood there waiting for the door to open. Even though he knew it was Cakrin's ghost, he didn't care anymore. He didn't even flinch as the ghost's warning rang in his head like clanging church bells. His body felt hard, hard as the hardest stone, as if the ice overlying the golden land of Elysiel had encased him as well—rendering him void of feeling, care, or thought. The words only smacked against his spirit and fell lifeless to the cold ground.

"Beware, oh King, of your own heart! If you allow it to harden, it will only crack and shatter. If you steal the heart of the king, you will lose your own. And that will mean your death."

TWENTY-TWO

PERTH BLINKED, then realized his eyes were open. He was enveloped in utter darkness. Both an intense heat and a noxious odor hit him at once, causing him to choke on the hot, acidic breath he had sucked in. By the muffled echo of his cough, he determined he was in a cave or some other natural enclosure. His hand met with a rough, hot wall as he moved gingerly up sloping ground, testing the hard dirt with his feet, careful not to trip.

He kept one hand on the hilt of his sword and readjusted the shield that he had slung over his shoulder as he inched along the uneven wall, listening. Afar off, he heard sounds—voices, perhaps. But if these were voices, they spoke a strange language of rumbles—the sound rocks made when tumbled in a crashing wave, or boards being dragged over gravel. He tried to still his shaking, calling to mind his vision in the ice cave to calm himself. Although the king's words were meant to impart courage to him, in this strange, lonely place, they felt dull and powerless. The burden of prophecy weighed him down. Maybe King Cakrin held confidence in Perthin's heaven-directed destiny; maybe he had even seen Perth's victory in the crystal slabs. Still, the task before Perth infused him with a fear he couldn't squelch.

Yet there was no denying the odd feeling he had as he touched the sword at his side. It was as if the sword and shield had been made for him, for this moment. He had the strange sensation he had been here before, and as he clenched his eyes against the railing blackness and heat that forced cooling tears to run down his cheeks, he saw scenes flit before him, one after another, not unlike a memory of something that had happened eons ago.

One of him walking through this very cave. Another of horrible, terrifying creatures—birdlike, but with long spindly limbs, that moved with the speed of spiderbanes—running in masses over rocky crags. And yet another—of something hideous and frightening, its shape wavering in ice blue, as if reflected in the crystal of his sword . . .

Perth sucked in another hot breath and felt blood pound his temples. He *had* seen these images before. Not on the crystal slab, but in his own mind—as memories, not visions. They had been there, floating in the back of his thoughts, as he stood gazing out over the magnificent land of Elysiel, in what Cakrin told him was his future. He hadn't noted them then, in that vision, with the joyful aura of peace permeating every pore in his body. Those disturbing images had been stored and nearly forgotten, like the faint memory of a nightmare, no longer capable of triggering fear or sadness. Whatever pain those memories had once held had been erased.

But now—those pictures carried with them a potent dose of terror. For he understood what was to come, what faced him around the dark corner. If only he knew more—then perhaps he would know just what to do and how to ensure he would not fail in this mad, impossible task set before him.

He stopped at a bend in the corridor. A stream of cooler air wafted over him from his left. Air that was fresher and less caustic. Surely that would be the way out to the open. Just as he meant to step around the corner, he heard footsteps—many of them. He dared not run or make any noise at all, for he did not know if those approaching would hear him. All he could think to do was press himself into a narrow crevice in the wall as a faint light grew brighter down the length of what he could now see was an endlessly long passageway leading upward at a steep angle to his left.

Within seconds, blazing torches lit up the space as bright as day, their smoke stinging his eyes even more. Perth gulped and knew he was trapped. He could never outrun the horde emerging out of the darkness! As the shapes neared, his throat tightened in fear. Those were the spindly creatures he'd seen in his mind! They moved like spiders on their thin legs that bent at sharp angles, and they seemed to grab hold of the rocky ground with elongated feet. Their lean, recessed faces were partly hidden by hoods, and cloaks draped over their black uniforms that, from where Perth stood, seemed made of dull metal, making them resemble beetles on the march. They each bore a long knife at their side, and carried a quiver of bows up high on their backs.

Perth could think of nothing he could do other than draw his sword and wait for them to attack. Maybe the sight of the crystal sword would frighten them. Perth smirked in despair. And maybe trolls would sprout wings and fly! He was a goner. If King Cakrin truly believed Perth would prevail and live to see a long future, it would be nice to know what he would recommend to get out of this fine mess he was in.

Rows upon rows of these creepy soldiers approached. Perth could now see the faces of those in the lead, and the sight made him pale. They looked like dead men, skulls attached to thin necks of skeletal bones, yet not human. They were akin to birds, with beaked noses and small chins, but their hands were the most frightening of all—if he could call them hands. They were more like claws. Long, pointed claws—eight of them on each hand. Their eyes were so sunken in their sockets they looked like holes in their heads, yet Perth could tell they could see and see well. They took notice of everything as they marched, their heads darting quickly from side to side, up and down, alert and watchful.

Perth half-closed his eyes and waited. He withdrew the sword from its scabbard and held it in front of him, pressed against his chest, and oddly, the contact of the crystal against his shirt sent a wave of comfort through his heart. The blade felt alive with moonlight, translucent and radiating a faint blue light. His breathing slowed, and the sweat that had been pouring down his neck and back dried up—as if a gentle spring breeze had blown through the tunnels of the chamber and lightened his heart with a taste of spring.

He listened as the pounding clatter of footsteps arrived, not willing to even peek out at the sight of the descending army. Yet, he could tell row after row of soldiers passed him by without hesitation, without stopping. Minutes passed and the marching continued endlessly. Perth let his mind linger on images of Elysiel— images from his many dreams that had both soothed his soul and made him ache with longing. Now that he was away from his cherished land, he felt the ache as a true pain in his heart. And then he thought of his pa, lying on his bed, worrying over his son. He knew his pa had to be angry, but more sad than mad. And that made him hurt even more. The last thing he wanted was to hurt his pa, and in that moment, deep in the chamber of rock and heat and stench, homesickness grew like a shadow cast over his ephemeral peace.

He opened his eyes. Only a dozen or so rows of these intimidating creatures had yet to pass by him. He couldn't understand why they didn't see him, but the ghost had told him the sword radiated power and could confound minds. That must be what was happening—and Perth was glad. He didn't relish the idea of trying to fight his way through a large army of horrible creatures—magical sword or no.

After the last row passed him by, he let out a long pent-up breath, then tiptoed along the steep and narrow passageway toward fresher air and what he hoped would be escape from the confines of this cavernous maze of tunnels. Where they led, Perth had no interest in finding out. He only hoped once he arrived at the surface he would find a place to hide and observe his surroundings. He had no idea where he was other than someplace called the northern Wastes. Just the name conjured up images of inhospitable wasteland and barrenness.

He walked on and on, listening, stopping, expecting to hear more voices, but he heard nothing but the sound of his own soft steps and the occasional fall of pebbles from the crumbling walls. He wondered at this tunnel; it seemed hastily dug, and the earthen walls had a loamy stale odor that mixed with the ever-present acid tinge to the air.

Finally, he saw a soft smudge of light ahead and made his way for what he thought would be open air, but instead he found himself at the entrance to a large cavern. The glow was coming from another opening on the far side. But between him and that beckoning exit stood at least a hundred spindly creatures standing erect on their long, many-jointed legs, their cloaked backs facing him. The sight puzzled him. Why were they all facing the opening to the cavern? An eerie silence draped the chamber, so loud in its quiet that it seemed to bounce off the walls. Not a creature stirred as they stood at attention, rapt and waiting.

Perth had a bad feeling about this. He dropped back a few feet into the passageway and thought of the long journey he'd taken just to get this far. He had seen some small side tunnels on his way but hadn't considered investigating them. All he'd wanted was to get out; the stifling heat and closeness of rock was making him claustrophobic. And who knew where those side tunnels would lead? He could spend days wandering in the dark and never get anywhere. He certainly wasn't going to turn around and follow that army down into deeper passageways.

And his stomach was grumbling, making him wonder when he'd last eaten. Back at home, in Tolpuddle, but how long ago was that? He'd lost all track of time flying across leagues with his magic boots, then in his encounter with the trolls and the crystal slabs. He felt as if years had passed in that ice cavern, as he looked out over the Elysiel of the future. But now, thinking about food triggered a voracious hunger. He was famished! And thirsty. His tongue was sticking to his mouth, and his throat felt stuffed with cotton from the biting hot air he'd been breathing in all this time.

Suddenly, he had to have a drink. Thirst gripped him with such force, he couldn't think of anything other than getting his water flask out of his pack. But maneuvering with his sword and shield in this dark space so close to creatures that would tear him apart with one swift slice of their claws gave him pause. Yet he must have a drink! Dark spots swam before his eyes as his knees began to weaken. He tried to concentrate, but everything fuzzed. His head felt as thick as a block of ice. Just the thought of ice made him moan. Cold ice, cold water . . . oh, how he yearned to feel such refreshment against his hot face.

With his sword still in hand, he reached around and slid the shield from his shoulder to the ground. A rumble of noise began in the roomful of creatures, but when he looked over, he was relieved to see they still had their backs to him. But now there was movement, and Perth sensed agitation by the way they were beginning to fidget. Just what was going on—and how in the world would he get out? He couldn't stay trapped in this tunnel forever!

He wiped the back of his hand against his now sweaty forehead. But as he lowered his hand, he brushed against the shield leaning against the wall and it tottered to the ground with a *clang*. He cringed as the rumble in the room ahead grew quiet. Heads turned, and much to Perth's dismay, a few of the creatures began walking toward him!

Again he pressed himself into a crevice and held his sword up against his chest. His ravenous thirst blocked out all thoughts of Elysiel. He tried hard to calm his heartbeat, sure the noise of it would alert the creatures to his presence, but he couldn't concentrate. More black dots floated across his vision, and as the strange soldiers drew closer, his knees began to buckle. Every ounce of strength seemed to seep out of his body through the soles of his boots. Every nerve tingled with terror as the creatures, only a few feet away, slowed and looked in his direction. Surely they must detect him!

Something like shouting broke out amid the throng of creatures, but Perth could not see what the commotion was about. He could feel the heat radiating from the bodies of those coming close to him. All he could do was squeeze his eyes shut and pray. *King Cakrin—I need your help!* He didn't know whether the king's ghost was somehow with him or if he could hear his cry for help.

He raised his eyes heavenward and prayed. *"God of the starfield, Maker of all—deliver me from this evil!"*

Perth opened his eyes and gasped. The passageway was moving as if alive! The creatures stood only inches away from his face now, but their feet were buried in a sea of writhing shapes. In the darkness Perth could only guess what covered the ground from wall to wall, but whatever it was—or they were—wound around his own legs in a slithery, steady movement. They were like gigantic snakes!

He tried to sidestep them, but his legs became engulfed, and the force of them pulled him away from the wall and toward the large cavern ahead. The three soldiers ignored the snake-things and sniffed the air. Perth felt himself start to black out as the snaking mass tightened around his legs and squeezed. He tried not to cry out from the pain, but soon the pressure became unbearable. As a stifled squeal broke from his mouth, the three spindly creatures as one locked their empty shrouded eyes on his, as if seeing him for the first time.

As they reached out with their claws, nearly touching his face, he dove down into the writhing sea of snake-things and held his breath. He tried to push through them but they were impenetrable, and their smothering closeness prevented him from being able to use his sword in any fashion to cut his way through. Sucking what air he could, Perth rallied against the hot, slippery shapes that he deduced must be monstrous snakes. But as they tightened their ranks and pulled him downward, he fought in desperation to breathe. He no longer cared if he was detected; he thrashed and struck at the snakes, frantic to force open some breath hole as he began to black out. And then he dropped his sword.

Suddenly, he felt something grab his throat and lift him as he snatched his sword from the ground. The sea of snakes parted, and he drew in air like a drowning man surfacing from the deep. In a flash, one of the spindly creatures relieved him of his sword and shield, and another pulled the pack from his back. Perth fell against the wall, his mouth agape and fear hammering his heart. The snakes slithered away toward the cavern, drawing Perth's attention to the commotion only yards away. Something had entered the chamber—something huge and hideous. All Perth could see over the mob of soldiers' heads was something like a nest of giant shimmering green snakes, all wiggling in the air, but attached to . . .

Perth lowered his gaze, suddenly aware of what—or who— had just entered the cavern. He had seen that same sight in his memories, reflected in a blue haze in the crystal of his sword—the sword he no longer wielded and that radiated no more with the power and protection of Elysiel. He dared not glance up as the rumbling noise of soldiers quieted and a voice, ancient and terrifying, boomed across the chamber.

Perth did not understand what was being said; the language was foreign and grated on his ears. But he didn't need any interpretation. He knew what the words portended, and when he sensed the entire army of cloaked creatures turn and look his way, pinning him with their fierce attention, he didn't need anyone to tell him whom the words were directed toward.

The *Tes'pha* had captured him—here in her lair, encircled by her army.

So much for King Cakrin's reassurance that a small boy would go unnoticed. He was about as invisible as a troll at a tea party. And now, without his sword or shield, he was as good as dead.

He may as well be.

· PART THREE ·

"The king's heart is in the hand of the Lord. Like the rivers of water, he turns it wherever he wishes. Every way of a man is right in his own eyes, but the Lord weighs the heart." (Proverbs 21:1–2 NKJV)

TWENTY-THREE

PYTHIUS LAY in his bed in physical agony that he bore with a detached mind. He was too weak and worn down to even sit upright. The words of the glass-eyed witch swirled in his head, prompting him to form a plan, but he could barely string his thoughts together. All morning his servants and commanders—and even Inaya—had pounded their fists on the bolted thick door to his bed chamber, demanding entrance. Not even Inaya's pitiful cries roused any emotion in his now stone-hard heart. He felt nothing. He cared for no one. He barely even cared anymore for his kingdom. All he wanted was to die.

He had ordered the witch to speak the truth, to tell him what he must do to save Paladya and find relief from his suffering. She had only laughed. On any other day, at any other time, he would have whacked her head from her body with his sharp sword at such insolence. But he only sat there, cats climbing on his lap and winding about his legs, and let her tell him what was soon to come.

She chastised him for failing to listen to her previous warning. The gods demanded he sacrifice that closest to his heart—his daughter. And because he had tried to trick the gods, his doom awaited. She told him there would be no reprieve, no second chances. All was lost.

He had watched her as she looked afar, as if she was peering through walls and forests and mountains. He sensed her spirit leave the room and travel to other lands. After some time, she returned and faced him—her glass eye cold and haunting. Her grating words landed on his heart with the finality of a stone rolled across the opening of a tomb, leaving him in utter, irreconcilable darkness.

"The newly formed kingdom of Sherbourne stands. Your army, oh King, has been defeated. They are returning home like curs with their tails between their legs. You will have to concede to the regent and pay him homage. The waters of healing will forever be out of your grasp. So the gods have spoken."

He had no doubt the scoundrel Ka'zab had somehow betrayed him. How?—he doubted he would ever learn. But no matter. Nothing mattered now. Not even Inaya. She was dispensable—and his last mad chance.

Pythius had left the witch's cottage, kicking cats from his path, without a word. He did not doubt her proclamations—no, not one bit. They dripped with truth and appropriate condemnation. He had come to the place of surrender—surrender to his fate and his culpability. And even more so to acknowledging his stupidity in listening to all those who had prodded and nagged and manipulated him all these years. Lady Vitrella, Calli, Urstus, Artus. The list of traitors and deceivers could fill a whole sheet of parchment. *That cursed scepter!* If only he had never heard the legend of Elysiel's kings and the sacred site! If only he hadn't been so desperate for eternal life. He could have ruled Paladya in power and supremacy for decades if he hadn't gone off on that fool's errand.

He threw off his covers and leapt from the bed. Restlessness and suffering agitated him so that he could no longer sit still. He paced, back and forth, driving the pain into the floor with each pounding footstep, anxious to end it all. And if he failed with this last desperate attempt to mollify the gods, he would gladly face his doom. The witch did not say when the monstrous sea wyrm would return, but she did not need to. He sensed it with every muscle in his body—a tightening anticipation that alerted him to its coming. Oh yes, he felt it—and knew his destiny lay with that creature. But what destiny? He would soon discover.

Someone pounded again on the door.

"Father, please, let me in. I must talk with you."

Pythius opened to his distraught daughter; her bloodshot eyes attesting to hours of weeping. He showed her in, and she breezed past him to gaze out the window to the harbor. "Father, I'm frightened. The seneschal says black marketeers took Mother—from the palace! Have your soldiers found her? Does anyone have any word at all?"

She wrapped her arms around him and wept shamelessly into his shoulder as he stood there, wooden, holding her. He wished he could drink in the wonder of her, this very last time he would hold her, cherish her precious love. But he felt nothing.

"There, there, my sweetling. I am sure she will be found. No one would dare harm the queen. No doubt they want a ransom or some reward for her safe return. Do not fret." He pulled back and looked sternly into her eyes. "But you must stay inside, and in your bed chamber. I must be assured of your safety, for . . . if anything happened to you . . ."

He turned away and hoped his gesture would be interpreted as one of a concerned and worried father. He needed her in her room so he could find her at the appropriate time tonight. Without turning, he added, clearing his throat in an attempt to infuse some emotion, "Please promise me you will stay there, and await my announcement when it is safe to venture out again."

Pythius turned at the sound of another knock. His palace commander stood waiting, and Pythius could tell by the man's guarded expression that he bore bad news, but Pythius cared not what the man had to say. "What is it?"

The commander looked from Pythius to Inaya. "Sire, it . . . pertains to your wife, the queen."

Inaya rushed the soldier, nearly knocking him down. "Have you found her? Is she hurt? Tell me!"

"Commander, please have one of the guards escort Lady Inaya to her chamber—"

"No!" She pushed the man away and ran back to her father's side. "I must know what has transpired!"

Pythius nodded to the commander to speak, though his face told all. Clearly, he feared what repercussions his words would have. Pythius tried to look interested and concerned, for Inaya's sake.

The commander spoke with compassion in a soft voice. "The body of Her Majesty the queen has been found on a stretch of beach, near where the monster destroyed the harbor. No doubt . . . wherever she had been held captive for ransom . . . the buildings in that area were all destroyed. Sire . . . Lady Inaya . . . my condolences."

He stood stiffly, awaiting a response, but Pythius merely gestured with his head to tell the man to leave them alone. The commander readily complied without more than a "Yes, Sire," and was gone.

Pythius turned and looked at Inaya's horror-stricken face that had turned white in shock. She barely voiced, "Oh no . . ." before she swooned. Pythius barely caught her before she hit her head on the floor.

At least he wouldn't have to listen to her scream and cry in grief. He lay her down on the tiles and summoned one of the guards positioned down the hall.

"Take her to her chamber and lay her on her bed. Send the healer to tend to her, but under no circumstances shall you allow the princess to leave her room. Is that understood?"

"Yes, Sire." The burly man swooped Inaya up and gently folded her over one shoulder as if she were a sack of flour.

"I want at least three guards watching her chamber. Only the healer may enter. Is that understood? Keep her door locked at all times."

The man nodded, then exited.

Well, at least he would not have to waste his army's time looking any longer for the queen. Nor try to convince Inaya that he had done all he could to ensure the safe return of his wife. Not that any of that mattered now. For although the witch hadn't said so, Pythius knew she saw in her glass eye what he knew in his bones—that the sea monster was returning. And this time not just one section but the entire kingdom of Paladya would be destroyed. This would be his last and only chance to stop it.

He fell back onto his bed and began to laugh. As if he cared. What did it matter if the beast came and gobbled up every street and house in the land? He should welcome it! Yes, he would.

Laughter swept him up from where he sat upon his bed. He knelt down and, with painful effort, reached under the wooden frame until his fingers met with the latch of the chest. He slid it along the floor and pulled it to his knees. Dust covered the lid like cotton gauze.

He wiggled the stubborn latches until they popped open, then raised the lid and unfolded the aged velvet cloth wrap. The sight of the scepter once more took his breath away, and as he knelt there, staring, he heard his own heart pound hard in contrast to the slow, weak beat of the heart in the handle of the scepter. Barely any blue light radiated from the crystal, but the heartbeat was steady. It lay in quiet judgment of him.

"You are still mine," Pythius hissed to it, "even if I have failed to unlock your power. Even if the gods deny me forever. But I will command you. I have seen it! The vision will prove true, and I will wield you!"

He closed the lid and latched the box. Then listened.

A commotion was rising. He could feel it more than hear it. His palace stirred with agitation and alarm, and it was only moments before another of his guards rushed into his open room.

"Sire!"

"What is it?" he asked, although he already knew the answer.

"It's the sea monster. It's returned!"

Pythius let his eyes wander from the guard to the simple wooden chest on the floor.

"Yes," he said. "So it has."

TWENTY-FOUR

PERTH SHOOK all over, cringing and staring down at his boots as the horrible creatures reached out and grabbed him by his sleeves. At any moment he expected to feel those sharp claws rake through his arms and rip his flesh to shreds. Surely they would take him before the *Tse'pha* and force him to look at her.

Please, he pleaded to heaven, to King Cakrin, *help me!*

The fog muddling his mind cleared in the midst of his raging thirst, hunger, and terror. *His boots!* How had he forgotten?

Just as he felt the pain of claws piercing his flesh to yank him from where he cowered against the wall, he stared at his feet and cried, "Take me out of this cavern—and a league from these creatures!"

As if the walls disintegrated before him, Perth stumbled through open air and fell on his face against hard ground. The coldness slapped him awake as he rubbed his bruised cheek and sat up, using an outcropping of black rock as his backrest. The eerie hush of being alone, outside in this woebegone land, slowed his heartbeat, and although the chill air still carried a sour, fetid odor, it was much cleaner and fresher than inside those rock chambers. He took a quick look around to be sure no creatures were after him, then, realizing he was safe for the moment, blew out a breath and closed his eyes. Relief gave way to misery in short order, though, as he remembered he no longer had his sword, shield, or pack. Food he could do without, but his throat screamed for water.

Getting to his feet, he found his balance while leaning against the towering sharp crags surrounding him. What a strange terrain met his eyes—rock so dark and shiny it almost reflected the dim haze of sunlight filtering through the heavy cloud layer above. He ran a hand along the smooth glasslike surface that felt as cold as ice. The towering crags cluttered the landscape, and Perth knew one slip and he could slice his feet open—boots or no. And there was no water anywhere in sight on this gloomy day. But at least he had gathered a few of his missing wits about him.

He looked at his boots again and commanded, "Take me to the nearest clean, drinkable water source—away from any living things!"

Nothing happened.

He looked around, waiting for the *whoosh* to carry him to his requested place. What was wrong? He gave the command again, using different words, thinking perhaps his boots didn't understand. Again, he remained where he was.

He swallowed a dry gulp and shook his head, at the end of his patience. Maybe he should just tell his boots to take him home to Tolpuddle—if they would. What if their power had run out? King Cakrin never said anything about that. He thought longingly of the spring box next to his cottage near the harbor—he could almost taste the delicious water trickling down his throat. Even greater torment, he could hear in the desperation of his mind the bubbling of the refreshing water as it spilled over the rocks and ran down the little creek to the sea.

He perked up and listened, sifting through the quiet to a sound he welcomed with excitement. He wasn't imagining that sound! Water!

He climbed over jagged rocks and boulders, making his way to the other side of the giant wall he had rested against. His imagination had not tricked him—for there before him a clear spring bubbled up from a sloping pool made of the slick rock. He dunked his head in the warm water and then drank his fill, slurping water that tasted better than any he'd ever enjoyed.

When he was sated and the pain in his throat had eased, he sat and looked around. Amid the sloping shapes of black rock were pools of mud, boiling and burbling and emitting a horrible stench of molding things and stinging gasses. Vents of hot air blew in sporadic bursts high into the sky through fissures in the rock. Perth sensed the earth beneath him shift as if alive, the heat and gas exerting great pressure against the shell of the world and cracking it open as one would an egg. His gaze snagged on what looked like the shapes of men scattered here and there—some frozen in a standing posture and a few prone on the ground with what looked like arms stretched out to heaven. A pang of fear caught in his throat. Were those some of Elysiel's warriors Vitra had turned to stone?

After taking one more long draught of water, he walked with care to more solid ground and away from the mud pools. Now what? He had to get back the sword and shield—but how? He imagined those magical gifts were now in Vitra's possession. And guarded by hundreds of those creepy spider beasts. The thought of having to throw himself into danger once more did not appeal to him. If it weren't for his vow, he would leave. But it wasn't just his vow; it was his pa . . . and Tolpuddle. He thought back to his ravaged and ruined village, to the faces of the disheartened villagers—his friends—and their hopelessness and fear. And then he thought of Elysiel . . .

Just the word in his mind gripped him with fervent longing. Elysiel would never return to her former glory and beauty if he failed. The dead kings would remain in their silent crypt surrounded by ice and would never walk beside him across the rolling hills and fragrant meadows. The people of Elysiel would remain dormant under ice, trapped in time and space, never to awaken.

He had seen the future; he knew he would succeed in his quest. And yet . . . how could such things be fixed in time? He had been given a choice, and each moment he could choose to either face his destiny or walk away and abandon it. Oh, how he wanted to believe the king truly had shown him the future to come and not just the one he hoped for.

His body felt stiff and sore, and although the water had refreshed him greatly, he longed to eat something. As he walked to stretch his legs, he toyed with telling his boots to take him to the closest inn, letting the image of corncakes drenched in syrup and topped with bogberries make his mouth water in longing.

A noise startled him. He ducked behind another large black spire of rock and found himself in a strange open area—like a field, or a large arena, but without grass. He'd seen a drawing of one in his children's storybook—a place where great knights in faraway kingdoms fought each other from the backs of horses, with long spears. A wide sweeping circle of dirt lay enclosed all around by walls of uneven black rock three times his height, almost a perfect circle as large as the marketplace in his village. By the scuffed-up ground, he could tell this was a gathering place of some sort. And across the open expanse stood something that looked like a raised platform of rock, not entirely flat, but wide and sloped, that would allow someone to stand and look out upon a crowd. No doubt the walls, with barely any space between them, created not just a private enclosure but a place where a voice could carry out to a mob.

Perth tucked himself into a deep crevice between two of the giant formations as the noise grew louder. His eyes soon confirmed what his ears heard—that Vitra's army was approaching—thousands, by the sound of it. The soldiers chanted something with fervor in a marching rhythm, accompanied by the booming of drums. Two openings suddenly appeared on the far side of the enclosure. The spindly creatures in their cloaks and wielding their weapons poured through and, in minutes, filled the expanse—every inch of it. Some of the creatures carried flaming torches, and those soldiers lined up along the back of the raised rock. One lit a large pile of what looked like wood in the center of the platform —which must have been soaked in oil, for it flared in an explosion that shot a great burst of light across the arena, followed by ripples of heat. At least that was something to be grateful for; Perth's hands were quickly turning into blocks of ice in this freezing clime.

Now Perth could get a better look at the soldiers' features in the overcast light. Their eyes shimmered like dark mirrors, like fly's eyes, deeply recessed in their heads. Yet they didn't look much like eyes; they had no pupils to fix on anything. Perhaps, Perth thought, they really couldn't see—not the same way people saw. And maybe that's why they didn't turn to stone when they looked upon their leader, the *Tse'pha.*

From where he hid, he could barely see over the tops of the creatures' heads, yet what he now saw on the raised rock across the sea of bodies was unmistakable. Placed on a flat slab were his sword and shield—the sword unsheathed and lying there on display, as if tempting him to come claim it. The shield lay propped up against the protuberance of wall behind the platform. Thankfully, Vitra was nowhere in sight, but Perth suspected she would soon arrive by the way the soldiers stood at attention, grumbling quietly among themselves.

A soft voice spoke from behind him, startling him so suddenly that he almost cried out.

"Shhh, my young friend."

Perth craned his neck in the tight space and saw the ghost of King Cakrin beside him. At least he was far enough away from the milling throng to be heard.

"What's going on here?" Perth asked.

The king answered in a sonorous whisper that blew into Perth's ears like wind. "Vitra is gearing up for an invasion. She means to march down the coast to the kingdom of Paladya and overthrow the king."

"Paladya—where is that?"

"Thousands of leagues to the south," Cakrin answered. "An evil king has roused her wrath, and she has sent the wyrm to destroy his fair city."

"The wyrm? You mean the knucker?"

The king nodded.

"So if her ire is with this evil king, why did she send her sea monster to destroy my village?"

The king looked past him, out at the mob of creatures, his face thoughtful and calm. "She means to destroy as many as she can, so she can once again rule over vast lands as she did eons ago. Your village is only one of many that have been attacked. But there are numerous villages along the shores of the sea, and with both the wyrm and her armies, I fear few will survive."

He now turned and met Perth's eyes. "So, Perthin Quay. The time is now. You must go seize the sword and shield, and when the *Tse'pha* enters within these walls, you must cut off her head. It is up to you to save not only Tolpuddle and your father but the world."

Perth shook his head. "Are you mad? Do you see how many are before us? How many stand between me and the sword? And my pack was taken from me; I no longer have the sack, so if perchance I did find a way to battle through all those creatures and their awful claws, I would turn to stone the moment I killed her."

The ghost smiled. "Your pack is there, beside the shield. You cannot see it from where you stand. Everything is in place. Go."

A shiver raced from Perth's neck to his feet. "Alas! What can I do? I am only one small boy!"

"Do not be afraid, Perthin Quay. For there are more with us than there are with them."

The ghost waved his hand in a slow arc and raised his eyes to heaven. "O Lord, please open his eyes that he may see."

Perth stared in wonderment as a sight materialized all around him. The kings of old, of Elysiel, appeared in all their splendor, dressed in royal garb and wielding swords—dozens of them standing against the stone wall and radiating the shimmering light from their land. Perth put a hand over his eyes to block out the ubiquitous glare but could make out more shapes. Alongside the kings appeared hundreds—perhaps thousands—of warriors in armor, brandishing swords, shields, bows nocked with arrows, and other weapons. They entirely surrounded the unknowing mass of Vitra's loyal creatures, who clearly could not see what Perth saw.

"Is this some kind of trick—an illusion?" Perth asked.

The ghost smiled once more, gesturing widely with his arm. "All of Elysiel's past has rallied to help you, Perthin Quay. Watch!"

Those of Elysiel began to glow with such radiant light that Perth had to squeeze shut his eyes. Through a tiny crack in his fingers, he watched the light of Elysiel illuminate the gigantic circle brighter than a summer sun at midday, and now the creatures stirred, aware of the presence of their enemies. Soon, they fumbled about as if blind, thrashing their arms and yelling in low grumbling tones. Perth could tell they were afraid and distressed. With fear on their faces, they turned to gaze at the circle of black stone that surrounded them, and what they saw caused them to huddle in a squirming mass in the center of the arena.

The walls became mirrors reflecting the army of Elysiel in all its glory, revealing thousands upon thousands of encroaching warriors bearing down on Vitra's brood. King Cakrin spoke loudly in Perth's ear, over the noise of rising alarm. "Go—take your sword, for the *Tse'pha* is coming!"

Inspired by the sight of Elysiel at his side, Perth pushed his way through the mob of soldiers, who stumbled as if wandering in the dark. He dodged their swinging arms and trampling limbs, nimbly weaving through their bodies the way he often ran through the marketplace on his way to the docks or the inn. He felt invigorated and let his love for Elysiel and his pa spur him on as he pushed and shoved and ducked—impervious to the wildly swinging arms—until he finally made it to the platform, where his sword lay there for the taking.

In a quick motion, he scooped up the sword and held it aloft, hoping it would once more confound the minds of the creatures nearest him. And then he reached for his shield—just as he heard a loud roar close behind him.

As in a dream, time slowed. Perth shook in terror from the sound and sheer volume of the creature behind him. He had never heard a voice like it in his life, and it chilled his blood. The sound was pure evil, infused with hate and venom and ill intent. And its presence was stifling and oppressive. Perth had no doubt who was coming up behind him, and he wasted no time.

He lifted the sword to eye level and gazed into the crystal shaft. Blue light shot out from within it, bathing his arm in color and showing him a sight he wished he did not have to see. For the vileness of the thing behind him was so hideous he almost dropped his sword. Writhing snakes surrounded her massive head, which sat upon a body that looked like a giant snake. His jaw dropped as he gaped at the sight of her, now so close he could feel the heat of her body like the blazing bonfire consuming the wood in the center of the platform. Her stench reminded him of rotted flesh and refuse—worse than the garbage dump in Tolpuddle.

He readjusted his sweaty grip on the sword and sucked in a rancid breath. He waited one second, two . . . then clenched his eyes and jaw and spun around, flinging his sword arm out in an arc, aiming for where he envisioned her neck to be . . . but he only sliced the air.

Stumbling back, Perth regained his balance and grip and once more held up the sword to find his foe. How had she moved so quickly?

Another loud roar came—this time from his left. He ducked instinctively and angled the sword to see the monster barreling down upon him, her scalelike skin glinting in the blue light of his sword, which now bathed the entire enclosure around him. None of the spindly creatures seemed to see either of them or made any effort to come to her aid.

She stuck her neck out, and as her head neared his leg, she opened her mouth and revealed two gigantic fangs the length of his hands. This was the horrific face he had seen in the carvings on the walls of his village, on the tavern door, and in the cobbles of the streets—the face of the Gorgon! He tightened his grip and snarled with his own foaming rage. Well, her ugly face would never terrorize another village—not anymore!

A flash of searing pain shot through his leg as he swung with all his might. In one hard blow, he felt the sword meet with hard flesh and then . . . cut through it as swiftly as a hot knife through a block of butter. He toppled over the massive body that had crashed beside him, smacking his head against the hard rock platform. Woozy, he raised his eyes and saw the army of Elysiel, bright and mighty, raising a boisterous cheer, their forms ringing the arena, while the hundreds of Vitra's soldiers cowered, still blindly shaking in fear and confusion.

Perth reached down and felt his injured thigh; his hand came back bloodied. He eyed his pack, fearful of turning around and spotting the *Tse'pha's* head—which he knew had to be somewhere close by. From the exuberance of his ghostly supporters, he knew he had done the deed—chopped off her head with the crystal sword. Elation filled him, replacing the last tinges of worry and hesitancy.

He set down the bloody sword with a shaky hand and fumbled with his pack to remove the large cloth sack. With his eyes closed he felt around and located the head; the snakelike hair still wriggled as he got a good grasp on the tendrils and hefted the thing and stuffed it in the sack. By feel, he pulled tight the drawstring and tied a double knot. Only then, when he knew he had secured his prize, did he open his eyes.

King Cakrin's ghost floated inches above the rock floor beside him, a triumphant smile on his face.

Perth blew out a breath and submerged himself in the deep joy bathing him. He could hardly comprehend what he had done—but he hadn't done it alone. He never would have been able to vanquish the evil enemy of Elysiel on his own. Truly, he realized, he was not to be praised for Vitra's downfall; it had taken an entire kingdom to bring her down, and heaven had only used him for one small part. For this honor, he was humbled and grateful.

Perth collapsed on the rock, ignoring and uncaring of the vocal distress of the army of creatures who had lost their leader and still could not see. Now that he had done what he came to do, all his strength seeped right out, leaving him weary and faint.

The ghost drifted beside him and laughed. "Perthin Quay, you may be a great deliverer, but you are only human—and a growing boy at that. Before you tackle any other great feats, there is something pressing you must do—before all else."

Perth's heart sank a little at the thought that he would have to do anything else this day. "What is that?" he asked, almost too weak to say the words.

"Why, eat! Tell your feet to take you to the Ravenswood Inn, and there you'll find a hearty meal awaiting you in the hamlet of Firth, just south of Elysiel."

Perth's heart began to race. "Is Elysiel restored from her curse? Can I not return there?"

The king said evenly, "No, the land is still buried in ice. For there is an appointed time for her restoration, and she awaits her king."

"Her king? I thought you were the last king."

Cakrin smiled, and Perth felt the warmth as strongly as the sun in his vision of Elysiel. "There will always be a king on Elysiel's throne, Perthin Quay. And you will see that day . . . soon. Vitra's army is now without a leader, and without vision, so they will no longer pose any threat. But there is still the sea wyrm to attend to, and it is heading for Paladya. Go, eat, Perthin Quay, renew your strength, and then go fulfill your vow before heaven. Stop the sea monster from destroying the world, and return to your village and to your father, who is anxiously awaiting your return."

Food. Yes, he would eat, and *then* go after the knucker. His pa had always said, "Finishing is better than starting." Well, Perth had started something, and now he was bound to finish it. He bowed to the ghost. "Thank you, oh King, for helping me—for bringing Elysiel's army to my aid."

The ghost smiled once more with affection and longing in his eyes, as if he wished he could wrap his arms around Perth and hug him. "Elysiel is with you. She will always be with you. That is the way of Elysiel, and the way it will always be."

With a happy heart, Perth picked up his sword, and after strapping the belt around his waist, sheathed it. He slung the shield across his shoulder and then picked up the sack containing Vitra's now lifeless head, which although weighty was manageable. He glanced over at the huge snakelike body of his enemy and grimaced. She was enormous! He could have never, ever, done such a thing on his own.

At the prompting of a loud grumble from his empty stomach, he gave a quick nod to the ghost, then spoke to his boots, telling them where to take him—envisioning a huge bowl of mutton stew, a loaf of dark bread, and a slice of bogberry pie for dessert.

TWENTY-FIVE

ARNYL HOBBLED along the bustling street in the marketplace trying to avoid plunging his crutch into the puddles made by the recent rainfall. The sight of his neighbors attempting to restore things to proper order encouraged him some, but it also made him ache for Perthin, for he could picture him standing at the fish stall, haggling prices with customers and wrapping purchases. The lad had been gone for more than a week! And upon inquiring, Arnyl had learned that Perthin seemed to be the only one from Tolpuddle that had run off. Had his son lied about going off with some "worthy" fellow to stop the knucker? He couldn't bear to think Perthin had lied to him, but what if he had? What in heaven's name could the lad be up to—and was he safe?

Every waking moment he worried himself sick, wondering if he'd ever see his son again. But then he reminded himself—Perthin wasn't truly his son. Never had been. Maybe heaven had taken him away just as easily as it had given the lad to him in the first place. *The sea gives and the sea takes. The same goes with heaven—to be sure.* He reminded himself of the proverb yet again: "Accept the way God does things, for who can straighten what he has made crooked?" And this certainly was a crooked business—the lad rushing off in some heroic attempt to save Tolpuddle—if that truly was what he'd hoped to do.

He stopped at Alyck's new makeshift stall and leaned his crutch against the siding. "'Tis looking good," he said to his friend.

Alyck nodded. "Seem's a fool's efforts, though. If the knucker has a hankering to come back."

Arnyl lent a hand as Alyck steadied a board to cut through it with a hand saw. "Well, we can't live as if the moment were to come. We'd all just stand on the hillside watching the water—and starve."

"Right about that. I've taken the *Petrel* out twice this week, once as far out as Seaduck Isle and halfways to Flounder. Saw nothing— not a ripple on the horizon. No one else has seen hide nor hair of the beast."

Arnyl chuckled. "I don't think the knucker has any hair, but hide—yes. I can't get those whopping glittery scales out of my mind. Never seen nothing like 'em in my life."

Alyck gave Arnyl a funny glance. "What?" Arnyl said.

"Just haven't seen a smile on yer face for a while now."

The smile fled. "Well, I s'pose moping about and complaining doesn't make for good company. Not that I ever am the best company . . . at least not these days."

Alyck gave Arnyl a friendly slap on the back after laying the pieces of cut wood down on the ground. He picked up his hammer and stuck a few nails in his mouth to hold them there. "Arnyl Quay," he said through his clenched teeth, "you've always been the one to lift others up. You're allowed to be morose on occasion. Just don't go reaching for any bottles." He gave Arnyl a serious, stern look that meant business, then picked up a short length of board and held it up against one of the posts.

"I won't," Arnyl declared, trying to convince himself. The urge for drink had lessened over the last few days as his leg started to feel stronger and he could get about easier on his crutch. And Gayla's regular evening visits finally broke through his crust of despair and pulled him out of his dark mood. She was one persistent woman—determined to make him hopeful despite all the signs that Tolpuddle would never recover.

"What's that on yer face?" Alyck asked, holding the hammer in midair, about to strike the nail he positioned against the board.

"What?" Arnyl answered, perplexed. What was wrong with his face?

"I'll bet you are thinkin' of Gayla. That's it, in't it?"

Arnyl felt blood rush his cheeks. His neck heated up like a brazier, threatening to roast his chin. "Wh-what makes you say that?"

Alyck only chuckled and pounded home the nail. He pulled another from his teeth and set it in place.

Arnyl watched his friend pound nails, waiting for the flush to subside. And it nearly did—until Gayla appeared, coming down the foot path from the inn. The spring breeze played with her hair as she looked around with interest at the building going on in the marketplace. Her beautiful face shone in the morning light. Arnyl tucked his head, hoping she wouldn't see him.

"When are you going to stop hiding and just tell her how you feel?"

Arnyl gave Alyck a scowl, but his friend only laughed, causing others in the lane to turn and look their way. "Oh brine and bother! If you breathe a word . . ." Arnyl threatened. After a moment his neighbors returned their attention to their tasks.

Alyck only shook his head and laughed more.

Out of the corner of his eye, Arnyl saw Gayla heading straight over. *Oh, trolls take me!*

Alyck busied himself, so Arnyl took it as an opportunity to be on his way. With a perfunctory wave, he grabbed his crutch and left his friend, walking with his face set toward the harbor and home. Maybe Gayla wouldn't follow. No doubt she had other people to encourage and visit with.

When he reached the end of the cobbles and the beginning of the rutted dirt lane leading to the shore, he dared a look back. Gayla was busy talking with a woman and her child, gesturing animatedly with her hands. Arnyl couldn't help himself. Although he knew he was plenty visible, he stood there and watched her as if mesmerized. Sunlight tangled in her long thick hair and wind played with her skirt. She looked like an angel sent to brighten the gloom of day. He'd never known anyone like her—so cheery but sincere—not that phony kind of smiling that only covered up other feelings. Her inner strength and beauty just oozed out of her, as if she couldn't contain it all. He wished he could share her optimism. Each evening she assured him Perthin would come back, that he shouldn't worry. And last night she added, "Heaven is watching over him, have no doubt." How could she be so sure heaven cared that much?

His thoughts went to the day he'd found Perthin in the trunk. No doubt heaven had been watching over that little helpless babe back then. He was the son of a king, his Perth. Arnyl hadn't thought about that truth for many a year. Perhaps the lad was now even the heir to the throne in Paladya—wherever the place was. He'd wondered for years if—when—the time would be right to tell Perthin about his true identity and lineage. Would the lad have run off anyway had he known the truth . . . or even run off sooner? There was no telling how he'd react to such outrageous news. Probably wouldn't believe a word of it—not even if Arnyl showed him the letter and the jewels.

Did Perthin have a great destiny? Is that why heaven had spared him fifteen years ago, carrying him across the sea to land in a lowly fisherman's nets? Was it heaven's leading or foolishness that had made Perth take off to be a hero? Would Arnyl ever find out? Maybe Gayla was right and heaven was watching over Perth. Maybe the lad's disappearance wasn't so much heaven punishing *him*—Arnyl Quay—but about Perth seeking his destiny. He'd never considered that before. Still, he couldn't help but somehow feel responsible for the lad's behavior.

Arnyl watched in curiosity as two fishermen he knew from the village ran over to Gayla. Their movements showed their agitation, and they waved their arms as they spoke. Arnyl turned to the sea and scanned the waters, thinking the monster had returned and the men were running about warning the villagers. But when all three turned their heads in his direction and Gayla pointed at him, his heart sank like an anchor dropped in the sand. The men had news, and it concerned him. Which meant it most likely concerned Perthin.

Arnyl sucked in a breath and held it as Gayla ran toward him, the two men following at her heels. He studied their faces, hoping to read the emotions upon them, but he failed to discern if they were upset, fearful, or happy. He would have to wait until they reached him, although the suspense was more than he could bear. If anything had happened to the lad, he would set off in his little boat and let the sea take him where it willed. He would have nothing more to live for. Even now, only the single thread of hope for Perthin's return was tethering him to Tolpuddle and life itself. Should that thread snap . . .

"Arnyl," Gayla called out breathlessly as she ran onto the dirt road in her nice boots. He thought how she would get them all muddy as she reached him and grabbed hold of his arm. The two fisherman, panting, caught up with her and let her talk. They looked at a loss for words.

"Arnyl," Gayla repeated, "these men have seen Perthin!"

Arnyl spun and gripped the arm of the nearest man. "Where? Where did you see him?"

The man he was holding shot a wary glance at his friend, as if he knew what he was about to say would not be welcomed.

Gayla spoke for him. "These men were at sea—out by Scoria Point earlier this morning." She gave the two men a serious glare. "Tell him."

When they kept silent, Arnyl demanded, "Tell me. Where's my son?" The last word lodged in his throat. "Is he . . . dead?"

The other man answered, "Oh, no. He's ever' bit alive. But he's commandeering a sailing ship—"

"A ship?" Arnyl said.

The man nodded. "I seen him. At the prow. And he was heading south, toward Buddle Bay—"

"How can you know this? How can you be sure it was Perthin?"

"I know yer son, Arnyl. T'was him." He looked at his companion, who nodded with vigor.

"Perthin would *never* go to sea. He made a vow—"

Gayla gently took his arm. "*You* made a vow. Perthin never did."

Arnyl glared at her, disbelieving what he was hearing. "But he promised me. Said he'd respect *my* vow. He would never go to sea. And where in blazes would he get his own ship, anyway? Buy it? With what money? Steal one?" He shook his head and waved a hand in the air. "You two just saw some mirage or illusion. Or your minds are addled."

"He did have a ship," said the first man, shaking off Arnyl's arm. "A beauty of a vessel too. Fifty foot at the least. Three mainsails."

Arnyl grunted. "And who was with him—his own crew? Or do you mean to convince me that he was sailing all by himself?"

Gayla pulled him back, no doubt sensing his rising hostility. But he couldn't help the anger flooding his veins. They must be toying with him! Perthin—captain of a ship? Heading where? Why? It made not a lick of sense.

He waited for an answer, but when the two men looked at each other again and pursed their lips, a horrible sense of dread washed over him. There was something they weren't telling him.

He said quietly, "There's more, then. May as well spit it out, since I don't believe the first part you've told anyway."

The other man gulped and said, "He did have a crew—a full crew, all dressed up, like they was kings or something. Wearing robes and such. But . . . they weren't human—"

"They . . . what?" Arnyl said, the dread rising into his throat and sticking there.

"It was plain to see, as we drew near her bow. Arynl . . . the crew—they were . . . ghosts."

TWENTY-SIX

FATHER, WHERE are you taking me?" Inaya yelled from behind him on his horse.

"To the harbor!" Pythius answered over the noise of the horse's hooves and outcries in the palace. Without warning, he had gone to his daughter's room as the sun began to dip into the western sky, mindful of the sea monster's approach. By the time he had saddled up his stallion and strapped the scepter behind the seat, word had spread from the harbor to the palace of the sighting. The monster had returned.

One look at Inaya told him she had been crying endlessly for hours in grief over her mother, and now she was drained and exhausted. *Good. That will make it easier to handle her resistance.* He had interrupted her evening meal as well, so perhaps her hunger would also weaken her. He dared not involve anyone in his scheme, yet he didn't want to have to give her a blow to force her into submission. A small piece of him somewhere deep inside still loved her—although that mattered not.

Once Inaya realized her words were being whisked away on the wind as they galloped through the city, she grew quiet and held tight with her arms around his waist. No doubt the sight of her countrymen in a wild panic—rushing through the streets and screaming in fear—distressed her greatly, but Pythius was inured to their plight. All his thoughts were on the harbor and the new post his Eyes and Ears had erected for this terrible, final purpose.

As he came down from the crest of a hill on the long, winding slope to the harbor, he could make out the agitation in the waters, far off. The beast had not yet entered the harbor, but its roiling and surfacing created massive waves that were crashing hard against the seawall and flooding the already ruined lanes in one great surge after another. The thing was toying with him, seeking him out in challenge to defy him. But Pythius had no more ships to send out against the beast, and even if he had, he'd already seen the result of such foolhardy effort.

Upon reaching the edge of the sand, he reined in hard and slid off his horse. He helped Inaya down and she stood alongside him, gaping at the sight of the imposing waves drenching the beach and running up toward them. He led her onto the sand and felt the ground shake violently under his feet.

"Father, why are we here? What do you mean to do?" Her voice quavered, and Pythius was touched by her fear and her vulnerability in some small refuge of his heart that still had feeling. But he did not want to feel any tenderness toward her. He musn't.

He turned to her and took her hands in his own, soaking in her youthful beauty and perfection. He knew he, in contrast, looked haggard and gaunt and older than his years, worn down to the bone by pain and disappointment. He could lie to her, but at that moment he felt he owed her the truth. She had always doted on him, but would she willingly let herself be sacrificed to save her kingdom? He thought not. He did not relish the idea of having to hurt her, but he was ready and willing.

"Sweet daughter, there is only one way to stop this monster from destroying Paladya." He would not meet her eyes any longer. He was a rock, hard, uncaring. He was the king, and she was but a girl. His heir, yes. But without a kingdom, she would have no throne upon which to sit. He was doing this as much for her as for Paladya. Perhaps the gods would accept his gesture and spare her life. Perhaps the vision he had seen in the crystal slab had not been complete. It only showed the impending doom awaiting him, but it did not show the aftermath. There was still hope of success. Hope that he would somehow wield the scepter and vanquish this beast.

He clung to that tiny hope as he said to Inaya, "The gods have demanded I give you to them, my most precious thing in all the world. If I do, they will send the beast away—"

"What do you mean—give me to them?" she protested.

He kept his voice even and unemotional. "See that post there? I am to tie you to the post as an offering to the sea wyrm—"

Inaya pulled back from him and glared incredulously. "Are you mad? You would give me to a sea monster? As an offering?" Her voice rose in hysterics to match the timbre of the city's screams. "Whatever gave you the notion that such a heinous deed would please the gods—or a sea monster?"

Pythius noted the fury in her look—the same look Samira had often given him. That look of condescension and judgment. Suddenly his own fury rose to match hers. How dare she defy him? So much for being a trusting, dutiful daughter. No doubt she had only pretended all this time to care for him and appreciate all he'd done for her—all these years. She was just like her ungrateful mother. Why had he expected any reaction other than defiance from her?

As Inaya tried to run back toward the street, Pythius seized her arm and swung her back. She fell onto the sand with tears streaming her cheeks. Horror streaked her face. "Father, let me go! You are mad, truly mad!"

She attempted to get to her feet, but in his rage, Pythius smacked her hard across the face with the back of his hand and sent her reeling once more. He leaned over her and put his hands around her throat and squeezed, choking out her cries and words of condemnation.

"You *will* obey me—if I have to choke you unconscious and drag you out into the water."

She went limp, no doubt aware she was no match for him. "That's better," he said. He watched her warily as he pulled out the rope he'd kept hidden in the large pocket of his coat and tied her hands behind her back. She did not resist, but shot him a look so vicious he had to turn away. He had reveled so many years in the warmth of her affection—she was perhaps the only person in his life who had truly ever loved him. But now she would love him no more. But no matter. Chances were she would soon be dead, drowned or eaten—whatever fate was to come for her. So be it.

He threw her over his shoulder and winced at the coldness of the water as he waded up to his waist. The pain in his arm made his head wobble, but he narrowed his eyes and pressed forward, trying to keep his footing against the swells of water riding over him. One wave buried him momentarily, but he leaned against the current and slogged ahead until he reached the post. A board had been attached for her to rest her feet upon, and so he propped her up against the post and she stood there, quiet and compliant. He wondered at her manner, but then chanced a look in her eyes. She was heartbroken by his betrayal, and seemed to no longer have any will to live. She had lost her mother and her father in two short days, and it was more than she could bear. Pythius grunted. She had always been too soft and weak. She would have made a terrible queen—a deficient successor to his throne. No doubt he had coddled her too much and this was the result. Perhaps her failings were all his fault.

He fastened around her waist the chain his servants had mounted to the post, and then secured the rope knots, tying her hands and feet to the post, and after checking them one last time, he waded back to shore without a glance back. He knew where he had to go to watch the unfolding of his destiny; in his mind's eye he was already there—standing on the parapet with his red banners flying behind him and the scepter in his hand. The thought of holding that shaft of crystal with authority made him shake all over. It was time. More than time.

He mounted his horse and kicked it into a run, galloping through the panicked city and up the cobbled lanes as twilight bathed the streets. He lost track of time as the image of his daughter tied to the post filled his mind. That was how he would remember her for the rest of his days—if he had any days left to him. Well, he would soon find out.

He gave the stallion over to a groom at the stables, then marched across the tiled terrace and up the eastern steps to the promontory overlooking the harbor, carrying the small case containing the scepter.

As soon as he stepped foot on the ochre stone, the vision from the crystal slab struck his mind with gale force. Just as in the image on that day in the cavern, he was on the parapet of his castle, where he paced upon the ledge, his arm screaming in pain, his body beyond weariness. The red lions on the banners fluttered in the wind behind him as the sea wyrm tore up his kingdom, churning the sea and lashing out with its mighty tail.

And then he had raised the scepter with his other hand—raised it in defiance and challenge to the heavens.

As he stood there remembering, words from a long-forgotten time floated to the surface of his memory like bubbles from a sunken wreck.

"Oh King, just as you murdered your father in cold blood, so shall your son murder you."

In his vision, he was looking down at the beach, but not at the sea monster. Someone stood in a small boat not far from shore.

A young man. Why had he not remembered this from his vision? Yet, at this moment, he knew the recognition of this stranger had been the true source of his distress. For as he looked off toward the harbor—or what was left of it—he knew in his heart whom he was gazing upon. Knew without a doubt . . .

No . . . it cannot be!

He rubbed his eyes. There was no one on the beach or in a boat near shore. His imagination was playing tricks with him—as were his submerged fears. All had fled to higher ground for safety. He pulled out a small spyglass he had pocketed before leaving the palace, knowing he would be too far away from the harbor to see as much detail as he would like. He dared not remain on the beach— not just because of his vision, but so as not to be subjected to his daughter's cries. From here, at least, he would be spared that. He checked the shoreline to see if the man was anywhere about, but he saw nothing moving.

He gripped his wooden arm, letting himself truly feel the pain he normally tried to blot out every second through sheer will. It coursed through every pore in his body with agonizing penetration. He let the waves of pain pummel him as the waves from the approaching sea monster pounded the shores of his great city. They pulsed as one over him as he waited and watched.

Perth stood at the prow of the mighty ship, face to the wind, as he chased the sea monster into a beautiful half-moon harbor. It was the largest bay he had seen so far, and he and his "crew" had caught sight of many on their way south in pursuit of the beast. How many hours had passed since he stepped aboard this ship, he could not say. But every moment upon the ocean was a glorious one— even though his task lay heavy on his heart. But he could not help but be enthralled by the endless sight of water and the marvelous feel of the boat plying the waves, the wind pushing against the sails as the salty air filled his nostrils.

This is what he had longed to experience his whole life and now—here he was on a ship filled with the ghost-kings of Elysiel and graced with heaven's guidance. Perthin let the hand of heaven direct the vessel as he kept watch for the monster. They had followed in its wake, seeing the destruction it had wrought in one seaside village after another without spotting it. But moments ago, King Cakrin had shouted from the mainstay and pointed, and Perthin got his first good look at the creature the *Tse'pha* had spawned.

From his glimpses of its terrible head and gigantic body, Perth believed it was even more horrible than Vitra had been. Its dark green scales glowed in the dusky light, and each time its head emerged from the water, it spurted fire from its nostrils. It was just as the villagers and his pa had described. Perth wondered at the power the *Tse'pha* must have had to be able to create such a beast. And then, for the hundredth time, marveled that he had been able to kill her. Only courage and power from Elysiel could have enabled him to do such a thing, and the moment replayed over and over in his mind, inspiring and awing him.

After having experienced such divine favor and aid, he held no fear of the knucker. He only wanted to finish his quest and head home to Tolpuddle to see his pa and watch the expression on his face when he learned what a hero his son was! And then . . . The green hills of Elysiel still beckoned him as strongly as ever. He knew that after returning home he would have to leave once more—but maybe this time he would convince his pa to come with him. King Cakrin had assured him a time was coming when Elysiel would once more have a king on its throne. Perth wanted to be there to witness that glorious event—and wanted his pa to be at his side to see the restoration of the land of Perth's dreams.

As the ship entered into the harbor, the beast rose up from the waters in a great roar. Flame shot from its nostrils as it dove and surfaced again and again in a rolling fashion, churning great waves that Perth could tell were completely engulfing the cottages and shops near the shore. He could hear faint screams that carried across the sea to his ears, but one cry made him turn southward and scan the shore.

There, just yards from the beach, something protruded from the water. He craned his neck to see what it could be, then made out a shape that could only be human. But how was it hovering over the water? And who was it?

Although Perth knew his goal was to get close enough to the monster to turn it to stone, he couldn't ignore the pathetic cries coming from this person. And his curiosity pressed him to discover just what was making that noise. Yet he could not chance sailing the ship that close to shore, where it could run aground.

He turned to King Cakrin, who floated in the air near him. "Is there a small rowboat on board?"

The king led Perth down half the length of the ship and stopped. Three ghosts watched him as he lowered a small craft down the side of the sailing vessel until it touched water. Perth wondered if he was doing the right thing, but the look in the king's pale eyes confirmed it.

"We will set anchor here and await your return, Perthin Quay."

Perth nodded. He felt for the sword at his side, and then retrieved the bag with the head, which he had kept in the cold storage by the wheelhouse. Returning to the railing, he listened and heard another cry ring in the air and recognized it was a girl's voice. He wanted to ask about her, but Cakrin gestured to the dinghy below. "Go. Do what you must. Heaven is with thee, Perthin Quay."

As Perth slid one-handed down the rope and tumbled into the rowboat, a strange feeling came over him. Once more the sensation of agelessness and timelessness enwrapped him, and as he found his seat and grabbed the oars, a calm clarity set him at ease. He slipped into his destiny as if slipping into a worn and comfortable pair of slippers. Every move his muscles made as he rowed toward the girl, every breath he took in and let out, felt part and parcel of destiny. He had a faint remembrance of this moment too—it was lodged in his mind as he stood in the future Elysiel and gazed out at the beauty of the land. He had been here, he now recalled. And he knew now what was to be done.

The startling realization of the scope of his actions shook him, for now he understood there was more at stake than just one kingdom, one throne. A sweep of history rushed over him, larger than any wave, reminding him he was but one small piece of one greater story—the story of more than Elysiel and Tolpuddle and the northern Wastes. He was part of a story that stretched beyond time, beyond the stars, to the dawn of creation and to the end of all time. The awareness of this humbled him and energized him with joy.

As he rowed toward the girl, he saw she was chained and tied with ropes to a post protruding just above the high-tide line. He called out to her, since her back was facing him and she couldn't see him. Hearing him, she tried to twist her head, but it was evident she had little ability to move. Perth rowed harder, the raucous waves lifting his little boat up on crests, then dropping him in troughs with a thud. He searched the bay but did not see the sea monster, yet he knew it was near.

Finally, he reached the post, and he maneuvered close enough to grasp it with one hand and steady his boat as it banged against the wood in the swells. He could now see the girl, who seemed to be about his age and looked cold and exhausted.

She gasped upon seeing him. "Oh, who are you? What are you doing out here? Don't you know you're in danger?"

Perth smiled as he stood in his boat and found his balance. He saw the girl was quite beautiful, and although dressed in a simple gown had a noble air about her.

"I should ask the same of you. Who put you out here in the sea? And why?"

"My father—the king of Paladya. He has done this. He means to appease the sea monster by sacrificing me!"

The king? Perth took a quick glance behind him. The water churned, and it was evident the monster was now coming his way. He pulled out his sword as he said, "Why on earth would your father think such a mad act would stop this creature?"

She only shook her head. Her lips were blue and she shook all over.

"Hold still," Perth said. He moved his boat behind the post and bent his knees, then took a hard swing with his sword at the chain. It broke and fell into the sea. With two more strokes he sliced through the ropes binding her hands and feet to the post, and caught her before she fell facefirst into the water.

"I have you," he said, managing to sheathe his sword as he rolled her into the boat. She wiggled to sitting as he unbound her hands and feet from the knotted pieces of rope still constricting her.

"Thank you," she said with earnestness as Perth removed his warm cloak and wrapped it around her shoulders. "But whoever you are, we should leave quickly. The beast is coming!" She pointed and shrieked as the monster broke the surface of the sea only yards from them. The fierce, massive head rose up from the waves and seemed to be sniffing the air.

Perth recalled what King Cakrin had told him—that the monster would sense the presence of the terrible head in his sack. Now was his chance.

"What is your name?" he asked the princess.

"Inaya," she said with chattering teeth, her gaze riveted on the sea monster, whose head bobbed up and down as it continued to stare at their boat.

"Then, Inaya, I ask you to lie down in the bottom of this boat, and under *no* circumstances open your eyes until I tell you it is safe to do so."

She did as she was told without a word or question. Perth said, "Don't be afraid. Heaven is with us and will protect us. Be brave."

Perth undid the knot on the sack and took a deep breath. At that moment a wave swelled and tipped the boat sideways. The sea monster's back rose alongside them, high into the sky as it undulated, but its head was nowhere to be seen. Perth turned from side to side, watching the creature as it flanked the small rowboat and circled behind it. He held tightly onto the sack for fear it might fall into the water. Inaya whimpered but kept down and buried her head in her arms.

"Show yourself!" Perth commanded, but the sea grew strangely calm.

Perth held his breath.

All he could do now was wait and hope the beast would not upend them.

TWENTY-SEVEN

PYTHIUS HELD the small spyglass to his eye and stared in shock as he watched the strange man rescue Inaya and put her in his small boat. Was this the man from his vision? Could he truly be . . .? Pythius refused to believe Calli's son had survived all these years and had returned to kill him. What utter nonsense! But whoever the man was, he was interfering and ruining the only chance Pythius had to save his kingdom and his soul! He had to do something to stop him.

In the storm of his anger, his mind cleared in the realization that this was his moment! He had caught up to his vision in the ice cavern, and now was the time of reckoning. The red banners behind him snapped as the wind kicked up and threw grit into Pythius's eyes. He pushed hair from his face and bent down to open the case containing the scepter.

Even though he feared another jolt of the unbearable pain that had met him last time he attempted to wield the scepter, he sucked in a breath, grasped the shaft of crystal, and lifted it high in victory. His shining hour of power had come!

Suddenly, he was surrounded. Dark shapes encircled him—shapes that took the forms of men that towered over him. His mind and body went numb as his eyes locked on the one who materialized in front of him—none other than King Cakrin of

Elysiel! The dozen or so ghosts that hemmed him in all wore regal garments and crowns similar to King Cakrin's.

"Wh-what do you want?" he demanded with as much authority as he could summon. He held the scepter high above his head, aware that he felt no pain, but neither was there any special power emanating from it. Once again he reminded himself he was only hallucinating. These specters were not real; they existed only in his mind.

Cakrin merely looked at him calmly and said, "You have stolen the heart of the king. Your heart is now forfeit. A hardened heart cannot but turn to stone."

Upon uttering those words, the shapes vanished without a sound. A stab of pain struck Pythius's chest, sharp and brief. Then, his entire body exploded in pain, as if every drop of blood in his body had solidified. Unable to keep a grip on the scepter, his gnarled fingers let it drop to the stone ledge, where it clattered to a stop at his feet.

A scream erupted from the deepest place in his soul. He tipped his head back as it projected out of his throat into the evening sky, shaking the foundations of his palace and his world.

A strange jolt of awareness rocked Perth's spirit. He balanced with wide-spread legs as his attention was drawn to shore . . . and up, far across the city, to what looked like a great palace built into the side of the mountain. His heart began hammering in his chest as he craned his neck and tried to see past the watery mist churned up around him by the sea wyrm. What was it? Something . . . was calling to him, something powerful and compelling. He fought the urge to row back to shore and run with all his strength to find the source of this summoning, but he wrenched his gaze from the towering edifice above the city and searched the waters around him for the beast.

Through the dark-green water, he saw it—now only yards away and swimming with intent directly to their small, unprotected boat.

"What's happening?" Inaya muttered, still cowering on the floor of the rowboat with her head hidden in her arms.

"Shh, it's coming," Perth answered.

He reached into the sack and grabbed hold of some of the snakelike tendrils of hair, then waited. He could almost see the beast move under his boat, as if he were somehow linked to it, mind to mind. He closed his eyes and prayed, letting the peace of heaven and the promise of Elysiel fill and pacify him. He thought of his pa, of Tolpuddle, of Gayla and Tanin and all of the villagers awaiting deliverance and assurance the beast would never threaten their shores again.

Come, he whispered in his mind to the creature, *come get what awaits you!*

Water sprayed his face and the boat rocked as Perth felt the beast surface beside him. He could feel the heat of its skin, but Perth kept his eyes clenched. He pulled out the *Tse'pha*'s head and held it above his head and let out a wild cry of attack.

Pythius stood on the stone parapet and listened beyond the boundaries of his pain. His body reeled in agony and he stumbled about, wondering at the sound assaulting his ears. Was it his own cry coming back to torment him? Where was this voice coming from? He was alone, high above the city, yet this cry sounded as if it came from his own throat. Were those ghosts back with more taunts? Surely he had imagined them; he conceded he must be going insane, as the hallucinations had been more real than ever before.

In a daze, he looked around at the stone bricks he stood upon, trying to focus as his head throbbed mercilessly. The spyglass was lying at his feet. He picked it up and looked through it, strangely curious to know what had become of his daughter. He moved in a slow rotation, looking for the beach and the post out in the water.

There! The boat was still close by, but he could not see Inaya. Where had she gone? Pain tore his limbs apart as he stood there trembling, trying to hold the spyglass steady as he watched the man in the boat reach into a sack and pull something out—just as the horrid sea monster raised its head out of the water and opened its mouth, revealing fearsome teeth!

What is that thing he's holding? Pythius squeezed his other eye shut to try to make out the big, bulky object the man was pulling out of his sack. It looked like a head . . .

He gasped and clutched his heart. He had seen that head before, that horrible head. It had haunted his sleep for years, with its sinister face and sharp teeth, and those snakes that wrapped around its face. He would never forget that head—never! But what was that man doing with the creature's head in that boat . . .?

Another piercing pain ran through his heart, and he fell to the stone, onto his knees. He tried to suck in a breath, but the pain spidered from his chest down to his waist and up to his scalp, paralyzing him until he could not even draw in a whisper of air.

"Help . . . me . . ." he mouthed as his jaw locked and his lips froze open. All he could do as the pain spread to his fingertips and down his legs to his toes was glance to his side as a shimmering blue light caught his failing attention.

There, on the yellow stone in the fading light of evening, beat the king's heart in the chamber of the crystal scepter—a strong, steady beat that shot beautiful, mesmerizing light into the night and shone in brilliance under a canopy of stars that paled in comparison.

As his life sputtered out as quietly as a flame at the end of its wick, the heart in the scepter beat on, *ka-thump, ka-thump*— drumming the rhythmic sound of King Pythius's doom.

All grew strangely calm as the night settled in around them. Not just the sea, but the sounds of the city—as if a magical spell had put all to sleep. After waiting many minutes, Perth stuffed the head back into the sack and tied the string. Only then did he venture a peek out of the boat. What he saw made him laugh with joy.

"What is it?" Inaya asked from her spot on the bottom of the boat. "Are we out of danger?"

He took her hand. "Yes, you may open your eyes. Look!"

Perth smiled and pointed at the massive head of the sea monster—now a dull green stone protruding from the water a few feet from their rowboat. Inaya got to her feet, using Perth's shoulder to balance herself, and studied the giant face of the beast staring at them from high above, now a statue in Paladya's harbor.

"Oh my . . ."

Perth laughed again, and Inaya joined him. She then narrowed her eyes and said, "However did you manage that?"

Perth pointed to the bag and explained about the head. When he was through, he added, "And now, to make sure no one else gets turned to stone . . ." He hefted the bag to his shoulder and then tossed it overboard. They both watched as the cloth sack became saturated with seawater and then sank out of sight. "There. It will rest and rot on the bottom of the sea, harmless to one and all."

The princess shook her head and smiled. "You never told me your name."

"It's Perth. Perthin Quay."

"Perthin? You mean like the fish?"

Perth readied himself for a teasing joke about his name, but the princess only leaned over and kissed his cheek. Perth felt his face heat up. "Well, Perthin Quay, you saved my life, and for that you shall get a great reward." But after saying these words, Perth noticed her face darken and she scowled.

"What's the matter?" he asked.

"My father. He meant to kill me. He won't be likely to welcome me home."

"We will see about that," Perth said, feeling a bit ready for another tussle. He would like to say some words to this king about his actions. "But first, we should get you into some dry, warm clothes. The night is growing cold, and you'll get sick if we sit around much longer in this little boat. Plus, I'm starving, aren't you?"

"Yes, I am!"

"Well, I have lots to eat on my ship."

"Your ship?"

"Yes, it's out there." He pointed. "It's a bit hard to see in the dark, but that's where we're headed. Do you like corncakes and bogberries?"

Her eyes widened. "That's my favorite dish in all the world!"

Perth chuckled. "Mine too. So let's have at them!"

He repositioned the oars in their locks and started rowing. He asked Inaya about her city and her life in Paladya, and she asked him about his village and his dreams. When they neared the ship, he stopped rowing and said, "Have you ever heard of a land called Elysiel?"

She pursed her lips in thought. "I'm sure I've heard Father mention it, but I know nothing about it. What is that place?"

Perth heard the catch in Inaya's throat. He set down the oars and studied her face in the scant light. "What's wrong?"

Without warning, she began sobbing. Perth wasn't sure what to do or say, but figured she'd been through a bit of a scare, and sometimes when that happened, girls got all emotional. Or so Bayley's daughters did. After all, Inaya might be a princess, but she was still a girl—although a very brave one.

Inaya wiped her eyes and sucked in a few shallow breaths, trying to compose herself. "It's just . . . I thought my father loved me.

And then he did that . . . I don't understand. How can anyone be so cruel . . .?"

Perth frowned, wishing he had wise and comforting words to give her, but he didn't. For the life of him, he couldn't imagine any parent tying their child to a post so a sea monster could eat her. Again he felt his ire rise. He would speak a few words to that Pythius—king or no.

"Come, Inaya," Perth said gently, offering his hand. "Let's go make those corncakes."

A rope ladder had been draped alongside the ship, and Perth watched to make sure Inaya could manage the climb, but she scooted up the rungs like a tomboy. After she clambered over the railing and looked around, she said, "Where is your crew? Surely you didn't sail this vessel all on your own."

He noticed she had sloughed off her mood and was putting on a brave and cheerful face. "No, I have a crew, but . . . well, it's a long story. Why don't I tell you all about it in the galley—while I make us some corncakes?"

"Splendid! But you have to let me help."

He frowned. "But, you're a princess. Do you even know how to cook? Don't you have servants for that kind of thing?"

She smacked his arm playfully. "Of course I can cook. And I can sew and climb a tree. And wield a sword quite adeptly." She squinted at him in a fierce manner. "Do you want me to show you?"

"Ouch, no, thanks!"

She turned and looked back out to sea, although it was too dark to see anything other than the twinkling lantern lights in the windows and streets of the city. "Seeing as you've saved Paladya, I would like to give you a royal escort about town and show you my kingdom. If I can calm the wrath of my father."

"I'd like that very much," Perth answered, thinking he could wait a day or two before heading home to his pa. "There are plenty of spare bunks aboard, and it's too late to make for shore in the dark. Let's just get a good night's sleep and deal with your return and your father in the morning."

"Good idea," Inaya answered.

Realization hit him then—that he had done it. He had killed the evil *Tse'pha* and destroyed the knucker. His quest was over. He had fulfilled his vow to heaven. And even though he knew he could have never done it without King Cakrin's help and his army of ghosts, he couldn't wait to see the look on Tanin's face when he told him what he'd done—although, Perth thought with a sigh, he probably wouldn't believe a word of it.

TWENTY-EIGHT

PERTH WAITED in silence on the side of the road as Princess Inaya walked up to the iron gates barring entrance to the magnificent palace behind them. Perth had never seen such a sight in his life. The size and scope of the city had left him breathless as they rode in a hired carriage through the winding lanes, past countless shops and homes and parks in the bright early morning sunshine. He marveled at how so many people could live so close together in such a huge community. So many shops selling things he'd never seen before in his life, and buildings and structures made of different colors of stone and polished wood. It sure made his humble village of Tolpuddle seem so drab and plain. Yet his village called to his heart, and as fascinating and impressive as Paladya was, he yearned to see his pa and sit on the heather-draped hillside overlooking his own little bay.

As two guards pulled open the imposing gates to give them entrance, Perth watched an old man hurry down the wide cobbled lane from the palace toward Inaya. Perth laid a hand on the hilt of his sword, but then relaxed when the princess threw her arms around the man in a tight embrace. He joined the two and Inaya introduced him.

"This is Ramus, my father's seneschal," she said to Perth, then turned to Ramus. "Perthin Quay saved my life, and I mean to reward him. Tell me—where is my father?'

Perth noted the slight quiver in her voice, but she spoke with authority and composure.

The man's distress came out in his speech. "Your Highness, no one has seen the king since last evening. Guards are searching the city, but there has been no word . . ."

Perth watched Inaya's shoulders relax. "I see," she said. "Well, then I suppose we shall wait until he is found."

Perth followed Inaya and Ramus up the long ornate carriage lane to the front doors of the magnificent palace. He couldn't fathom how anyone could live in such a sprawling, imposing structure of such elegance. He felt funny tromping inside on the polished marble floors with his ratty old boots and dressed in his old tunic and trousers with the hole in one knee. But Inaya didn't seem bothered by his garb and disheveled appearance, although the servants gave them funny looks as they marched down the long gold-trimmed hallway into what looked like a gigantic library full of books and large carved sculptures of strange beasts. Inaya sank into a roomy upholstered chair and sent Ramus to have a servant bring a pot of tea and some biscuits.

Perth stared at the towering shapes of metal and wondered if these animals were patterned after real creatures or imaginary ones. He had never seen any like them in the land where he lived, but then again—the only creatures he was likely to run into in Tolpuddle were porcs and raccoons and trolls . . . although he doubted he'd ever again see those trolls sifting through the garbage heaps. The thought of the three princesses gave him pause. Now that Vitra was dead, had they returned to their former beauty? He hoped so—not just for their sakes but for the sakes of every village in the land. Folks would be relieved to be rid of the trolls and their thievery. He chuckled at how they had teased and tormented him and called him cousin. What a strange lot!

Perth's musings were interrupted by conversation down the hall. Someone was coming toward them, talking in a loud, stern voice, and the seneschal was saying something as well, but Perth could not make out the words. Inaya got to her feet, and at the sight of an old man with the longest beard Perth had ever seen, her jaw dropped.

Perth rushed to her side. "What's the matter?" he asked her.

She gestured at the man, who stopped inches before her, Ramus holding one arm to steady the ancient fellow, who had a large silver earring dangling from one ear.

"This . . . is the seer," she said with barely a breath of air.

"The augury has spoken, oh Princess," the seer said evenly, his hands clasped behind his back. Only then did Perth notice the man was blind.

All in the room grew silent, but Perth had to ask. "What's a seer? And an augury?"

Inaya let out a breath. "They have a special sight. The augury shows them the future. They are never wrong." She looked at Perth with worry swimming in her eyes. "The augury hasn't spoken in years—not since I was a young child."

Ramus cleared his throat. "But it has now spoken again—is that right, Seer?"

The blind man nodded and raised his chin as if staring at the ceiling. "The lion arose from the thicket and took what was not rightly his. It was decreed by heaven that, in that day, the heart of the king would perish. And so it has come to pass."

"What heart?" Inaya pleaded. "What king?"

"Why, Princess, the heart of your father, King Pythius."

The seer grew silent as Inaya stood unmoving, open-mouthed.

After a long moment, the seer continued. "It was foretold years ago that the sin of the father would be visited on the son. As the son has done to the father, so shall it be done to the son."

After a moment of silence, Inaya said, "I don't understand. What does this mean? What son, what father?"

The seer tipped his head as if thinking. After a moment, he felt for Inaya's arm. Perth grew strangely disturbed at the seer's enigmatic words.

Upon grasping Inaya's arm, the seer said, "Lead me to the western wall—to the stairs that climb the wall."

Inaya looked at Ramus. "Does he mean the parapet overlooking the sea?"

Ramus answered, "I believe so, Your Highness."

She nodded and Ramus led the way. They walked in silence out of the library doors and through a perfectly manicured and colorful garden of shrubs and flowers. Ramus held the seer's arm and carefully helped him step up onto a spacious terrace tiled with the design of a giant roaring lion. From the back of the raised platform, a set of tiled stairs wound up the curved yellow ochre wall to a high ledge. Perth could hear the sea from where he stood.

Perth followed last, behind Inaya, but as they neared the top of the stairs, Ramus held up his hands and yelled, "Sire!"

Inaya rushed onto the wide ledge that overlooked the tranquil, expansive harbor, but Perth gave little attention to the commanding view. For, a strange sight met his eyes.

Inaya had thrown herself down next to a stone statue of a man on his knees. "Oh, Father . . ." Perth heard the ache in her voice.

"Oh my . . . heavens," Ramus uttered. "'Tis the king . . . it seems . . ."

The seer, still standing and facing the sea, said in a firm tone, "It is. The augury has spoken." He turned in Perth's direction and seemed to study him with his vacant eyes. "The king murdered his father, and so it was foretold. As the son has done to the father, so shall it be done to the son." He added with a hint of a smile, "A man's heart reveals the man. Oh King, it is no secret where *your* heart lies."

Perth frowned and walked to the edge and looked out, uncomfortable with those empty eyes drilling into him. Why did the old man look at him as he said the words? And he quoted the saying his pa liked to recite—how would the seer know that? And why would he speak to the dead king—who was now just a lump of rock? This was all so peculiar!

"Wh-what happened to him?" Ramus asked.

Inaya answered in a sad manner. "He must have been looking at the sea monster when you pulled the head from the sack," she said to Perth. "Look—his spyglass." She leaned down and picked it up from the stone. "But, what is that—over there?"

Perth dropped his gaze to his feet, where Inaya was pointing. Something that looked like a long staff made of ice lay on the parapet. But . . . wait! He bent down and saw the most peculiar thing. A pulsing blue light was coming from the handle of the thing. Through the translucent rock, a fist-sized object thumped in a steady beat—almost like a heartbeat. Was the strange shaft alive? How could that be?

Perth grew aware of the morning breeze stilling, and a heaviness filled the air around him. He sensed King Cakrin's presence but did not see him. The moment felt pregnant with anticipation, and the only sound he could hear was his blood pounding in his ears. Perth picked up the staff and was surprised by the warmth it emitted. And the moment he closed his fingers around it, a blast of brilliant blue light shot out and lit up the air around them all. Perth heard Inaya and Ramus gasp, and he turned to see astonishment on their blue-tinted faces, but the seer's visage was unchanged.

As Perth studied the strange object in his hands and marveled at the loud, steady beating in its handle, the seer—to Perth's surprise—laid a hand on his shoulder and said to him, "The heart of the matter is a matter of the heart. You, Oh Perthin Quay, are a king twice over. You are the son foretold."

Perth swallowed and stared at the seer. "I don't understand. A king? Twice over? What do you mean?"

The seer said, "When you were born, the augury foretold you would one day kill your father—"

"My . . . father?"

Inaya shuddered and grabbed Perth's arm. "Oh, I understand! My mother once confided in me about something her attendant confessed in secrecy. The maid had been the servant of the previous queen—Queen Calli. Father had married her before my mother, and she had given birth to a son. This maid had overheard the seer telling my father this pronouncement upon the birth of . . . his son . . ."

She looked wide-eyed at Perth, blinking. "You, Perth . . . are my brother!"

"Your brother?"

They both looked at the seer, who merely nodded.

Ramus held up a hand. "Then, this is Calli's son? It was said he had died in a tragic drowning at sea."

Perth shook his head. "You are all wrong." He turned to the seer. "I mean no disrespect, Seer, but I was born and raised in a fishing village far, far away from here. My mother's name was Emelee, and she left me and my pa when I was just a babe. My pa raised me in Tolpuddle. I am no son of a king; I am the son of a humble fisherman. You are mistaken."

The seer only stared into the air. After a moment he said, "The augury speaks the truth; it does not lie." He added, "Your Majesty."

Inaya looked just as puzzled as Perth felt. "Well," she said, "we have a strange mystery on our hands. If it's true you are Pythius's firstborn, then you truly are king of Paladya. But what does he mean you are king twice over?" She looked to the seer for an answer, but he remained silent.

"I'm no king," Perth said. "I'm just an ordinary boy from a simple village."

"Surely there must be someone who can shed some light on this, someone who would know the truth," Ramus muttered.

Perth suddenly thought of his pa, and all the times he had refused to tell him any details of his birth and his mother's leaving. How he always told Perth not to listen to gossip and stories. He realized his pa had never once revealed the true story to him, despite all the times he had prodded him to do so over the years. His pa had always changed the subject and brushed him away with the words, "The past is past. Finishing is better than starting." Perth smirked. Well, his pa had some finishing to do—telling Perth the whole tale. And then he would know if the augury was right. A king? The thought boggled his mind. Could he truly be king of Paladya? He looked out on the vast city below him, but the thought only made him more homesick.

Now, more than ever, Perth felt the need to return home. He had no desire to be king of this kingdom. He looked at Inaya, who stared at him as if seeing him for the first time. Perth had to admit they shared a likeness, although her hair and eyes were much darker. But they both had the same shape face and chin—and the love of corncakes and bogberries!

"Inaya," Perth said sternly, "I need to return home. Maybe in time we can make sense of the seer's words—"

"I will come with you!"

Perth shook his head. "You need to stay here. You are queen now, and your subjects will be looking to you to lead them."

Inaya grunted. "Ramus can take care of things while I'm gone. He did while my father was alive, for the most part. I want to see your village, and I have a feeling that is where we will learn the truth about your parentage, Perthin Quay. Surely your father is hiding something. If you are truly king of Paladya—and my brother—I want to know!"

And so do I! Perth thought with a smile. "Well, then, I have no idea how to get to Tolpuddle from here, but I do have a sailing ship and a crew of ghosts. I imagine they can take us back as easily as they brought me here." Although he could only imagine the horror in his father's eyes upon seeing him arrive on a ship. He would surely get an earful when he stepped ashore. But what other choice did he have? He had no idea how to reach Tolpuddle by land, and it would no doubt take many months of travel, and he couldn't bear to wait that long to get home.

Inaya said to Ramus, "Please be sure the seer has a hearty meal and a good rest, then send him back to Torth in the king's carriage." She turned to the seer. "Thank you for coming and revealing what needed to be shown. Does the augury have anything more to say?"

"No, oh Queen. May your rule be long and beneficent, and may heaven shine its light upon your glorious kingdom of Paladya."

"Thank you, Seer."

"Excuse me," Perth said to the seer, "Can you tell me just what this object is that I hold in my hands?" The blue light still bathed them all, and the pulsing beat against the palm of his hand in a synchronous pulse with his own. It felt oddly soothing and comforting, resting there in his hand.

"Why, oh King, it is the crystal scepter."

Perth wondered where the king of Paladya had gotten such a strange and enticing object and what purpose it served.

Inaya nodded at Ramus, who took the seer by the arm and led him carefully down the tiled steps and back inside the library.

"And you, *brother*" she said with a giggle. "You are not dressed in proper fashion to make a grand return to your village! Perth, you are a hero! We will make sure you arrive in style."

"What do you mean?" Perth asked, a little worried over the idea of too much fanfare on his behalf. But then again, a little fanfare might ensure Tanin and Danyl would believe the stories.

"First—a long, hot bath, and then into some regal clothes—clean ones!" she said. "Then I will conscript what remains of my father's navy to sail the ship back to Tolpuddle. I do not think it best to pull into port with a crew of ghosts—it might send your villagers into a tizzy. I will see to it that the ship is stocked with not just food and drink but with treasures, supplies, and gifts to help rebuild your village."

"Oh, thank you! They'll be so grateful!" Perth's heart warmed at her queenly generosity. He could see already how she would be a fine, just, and gracious monarch for Paladya. The thought made him smile. Even if he were truly heir to the throne, this was her city, her kingdom, and she deserved to rule it. His heart cried out to another place. Why, he didn't know, but he would not ever rest, not truly, until he stepped foot in Elysiel. But, first things first, as Inaya said: a bath, clean clothes, and the journey home.

Inaya started for the stairs, but Perth looked at the scepter in his hand and asked, "What should I do with this?"

She shrugged. "Keep it, I suppose. I have no use for it. And now—to pack!" she said with glee.

Perth chuckled and studied the scepter in his hand. A crystal scepter. *Just what is your story? I wonder.* He spotted a small wooden case nearby lying open on the stones and put the scepter inside it. As he closed the latches, the blue light dissipated from the air.

He looked out on the warm spring day, at the tranquil harbor and the calm horizon, letting the last few days run through his mind—the encounter with the trolls, the vision in the ice cavern with the dead kings of Elysiel, his fearful time in the northern Wastes with those creepy spindly soldiers, the victory over the *Tse'pha* with the help of Elysiel's armies, and the besting of the sea

monster and rescue of Princess Inaya. Not to mention the pronouncement from the seer that he was a king—the king of Paladya.
The weight of all he had gone through came crashing down on his
head and heart. All he wanted in that moment was to crawl under
some warm blankets and sleep. But that he could do on the ship. It
would take many days to get home, and he could use that time to
rest before facing his pa.

He thought of kindly King Cakrin and how he had helped him
all along the way. Where was he now? Why had he not appeared
since they had left the ship early this morning in Paladya's harbor?

"Are you here?" he whispered to the air around him. He waited
a minute, but sensed nothing. Maybe the king had finished with
him and returned to his crypt, to wait with the other kings for the
day of their renewal. After all, Perth's quest was over; he was done.
He had killed the *Tse'pha* and turned the sea monster to stone.
Paladya, Tolpuddle, and all the seaside villages were now safe from
harm. Perhaps he would never see the friendly ghost again. The
thought made his heart sad.

What about that vision, though? In the ice cavern Cakrin and
all the kings were with him—in Elysiel. Maybe once he finally
made it to that glorious land the king would appear again. At the
very least Perth knew that one day, some day in the future, he
would walk the verdant hills of Elysiel with the kings by his side.
That was his future—of this he had no doubt. And he would do all
in his power to make that future come true.

With that comforting thought glowing deep in his heart like
the scepter, he skipped down the stairs to find someone who might
draw him a hot bath.

TWENTY-NINE

ARNYL WORKED in silence, away from the other men who were hammering the siding back on Bayley Tettenhall's cottage. He stopped for a moment and sipped the tea Bayley's wife had brought round for the men, hoping Gayla wouldn't show up. Every time she had showed up this past week, he had sent her away, not wanting her cheering up. What was there to be cheerful about, anyway? His neighbors went about mending their lives as if they were nets. Just a stitch here and there and all's good. As if they had already forgotten about the knucker. Life goes on, Alyck kept saying to him with a smile.

Well, maybe it did for most, but not for him. He'd never felt so lonely and miserable in his life. Except of course for the time following Jayden's death. There was no conparison to that. But losing Perthin was nearly as bad—not knowing where he'd wandered off to, whether he was alive or dead, or ever coming back. He'd gotten on with his life all those years back, turned over a new leaf, as they say, and stopped drinking. And raising Perthin had been a balm of sorts, helping erase the pain of former years. But what balm was there for him now?

His friends meant to lift his spirits, but with each day he grew more unhappy. He was tired of their encouraging and hopeful words. "The lad'll be back—just you see." And "Perth's coming home soon. I just know it. Keep hopeful!" The only thing Arnyl could do to keep going was to busy himself with work, helping rebuild his neighbors' lives—since there was nothing he could do to rebuild his own. His life was like a rotted shack reduced to splinters. Nothing useful there to rebuild anything with.

Ever since those fisherman told him they'd seen Perthin at sea, on a ship of ghosts, he had given up hope. How did they expect him to believe such hogwash? And why would they come to him and tell him that? Was it a prank or a mean joke? Or had Gayla put them up to it in the hopes some word—no matter how outrageous—would comfort him? Why'd they have to put in the part about the ghosts anyway? Who in his right mind believed in ghosts?

Arnyl grumbled as he set down the tea and pounded more nails into wood. The mindless occupation of his hands helped numb his heart, but he couldn't seem to turn his thoughts off. They gushed out like water from a hand pump, soaking him with despair. He was resigned to his fortune, now convinced heaven was giving him the punishment he deserved. So be it. Didn't mean he couldn't grumble about it, though.

Now that the docks had mostly been rebuilt, his fishermen friends had been going out to sea each day. And each evening they reported back to Arnyl, saying they'd seen no sign of the mystery ship Perthin had supposedly sailed upon. No surprise there. But not a day passed when Arnyl didn't stand on the dunes near his cottage and stare out to sea, checking the horizon, hoping against hope.

Arnyl lifted his eyes at the sound of children running along the beach. He recognized Bayley's girls—probably bringing food back from market. They were making a racket as they ran toward the house, yelling for their pa.

Bayley came around the cottage from where'd he'd been sawing boards with his one good arm. He put a hand up to his eyes to block out the afternoon glare and called out, "What's the commotion? Didn't your ma teach you anything about being ladylike?"

"Pa, Pa!" the eldest one yelled back, still a ways away and waving her arms. That was Cordella, and Arnyl knew she had some feelings for Perthin—or so Bayley's wife had once said. "Has her eyes on yer lad," was how she'd put it.

The girl, breathless and tripping over her own feet, said, "Pa, a ship! A ship!"

"What? Whose ship?" he asked with a frown.

One of the younger sisters said exuberantly, "A *big* ship, Pa! And they're all dressed up—in fancy clothes. And, Pa! There's a princess!"

Bayley chuckled and mussed up the little girl's hair. "Right, a princess. And what storybook did you get this out of?"

Cordella scowled. "It's true, Pa. Come see! A ship full of people. And they say they're from a place called . . . Palad . . . oh, something like Palady."

Arnyl froze. His blood chilled in the afternoon sun. He looked at Cordella. "*Paladya?*"

A smile broke across her face. "Paladya—that's right!"

Bayley gave Arnyl a puzzled look, but Arnyl closed his eyes in memory. The only time he had encountered the name of that place was when he'd read the note in the trunk fifteen years prior. The note that told where the babe had come from—the name of the kingdom where a king sought the death of his son. His Perthin. How in the world . . . Why would a ship from a grand kingdom like Paladya arrive in their little harbor? Unless . . .

Arnyl dropped his hammer and grabbed his crutch. He nearly didn't need it anymore, but he didn't want to risk twisting an ankle and falling. He wished he could run as fast as the wind, but he had to settle for hobbling his way toward town. Bayley called after him, but Arnyl didn't answer. He'd have to explain why he was excited, and he had no time for that. He had to see if by some miracle Perthin was aboard that ship. Why else would it be here in Tolpuddle if not to bring Perth home?

A large crowd was gathered around the huge sailing ship, and what a beauty she was. The finest, most magnificent ship Arnyl had ever seen. Its triple masts sported pristine white sails that billowed in the breeze, and on deck were dozens of uniformed men—soldiers, from the looks of them, but certainly without hostile intent. They all bore smiles, and called out in greeting to the crowd as crate after crate was hauled down the gangplank to the dock.

"What's going on?" Arnyl asked a woman on the outer edge of the mob. He searched the decks for any sign of Perthin, but only saw the men in their red-and-black garb. It would take some pushing to get through the throng of people to see better.

"They've brought supplies! Food and linens—and ale and timber!"

Arnyl took in the jubilant faces of his neighbors. He spotted Alyck's tall head a few yards away; he was helping clear the way so the large crates could be rolled down the dock. Crate after crate came down the gangplank, and then Arnyl saw a woman standing near the prow—the one Cordella must have been speaking of. She was dressed in a beautiful pale-green gown, and wore a crown on her head. Was she related to that king of Paladya—the one who had hoped to kill Perthin? She couldn't be Perth's mum—she was way too young. In fact, she looked to be the lad's age. Perhaps she was a princess after all.

Suddenly, a hush rustled through the crowd and everyone became quiet. The princess walked over to the top of the gangplank and held up her hand. She spoke loudly for all to hear.

"Villagers of Tolpuddle, we of Paladya have come to help you in your time of need. We ourselves have suffered attack from the great sea monster, but I am here to tell you the beast is no more!"

With those words the crowd erupted in a riotous cheer. Arnyl's jaw dropped. What great news! The girl waited a moment for the cheering to subside, then smiled and spoke again. Her voice carried across the docks in the afternoon breeze. "I have brought you the hero who has killed the fearsome beast, and to celebrate his victory and our deliverance, Paladya has brought the finest foods and drinks, and our best cooks, to prepare a banquet in his honor."

She let her words stir the crowd. A loud murmuring filled the air as the villagers spoke excitedly to one another. Arnyl, however, wished she would hurry up and finish her speech. He had to know if she had seen Perthin or knew who he was. It was too much of a coincidence for this ship to have arrived at their port just to bring them supplies and throw a party. What was Tolpuddle out of all the small seaside villages along the coast? Nothing special, that's what.

Again she waited for the noise to die down. And then, with a grand sweep of her arm, she said, "Here is your deliverer—Perthin Quay, of Tolpuddle!"

Arnyl about fell down as the crutch slipped from his grasp. The crowd went completely silent. He watched his son—or a young man who looked very much like his son but was dressed in regal attire fit for a king—step out of the wheelhouse and come alongside the princess.

"It's the shrimp!" Arnyl heard someone say.

"No! How can it be? Perth the small fry? A hero?" another called out.

Arnyl ignored the puzzlement of his neighbors and pushed through the crowd, nearly knocking them down as he wormed his way through, trying not to hit anyone with his crutch. His heart felt about to burst with joy. His son had returned!

Upon recognizing Arnyl, the villagers moved aside and let him walk up the gangplank. Perthin spotted him and his face lit up.

He ran to Arnyl and wrapped his arms around him, and Arnyl squeezed his eyes shut in a flood of emotion.

Tears spilled onto his cheeks as he muttered over and over, "It's you. It's really you. You're alive!"

After a long embrace, Perthin pulled back and smiled. He had a few of his own tears on his cheeks as well, Arnyl noticed. "Pa, I told you I'd be home. As soon as I fulfilled my vow to heaven."

Arnyl's head swam with a thousand questions. But the crowd rushed up the ramp and encircled them, cheering wildly and making such a ruckus that Arnyl couldn't hear himself think. He looked over at the princess, who wore a big smile on her face. She leaned over to Arnyl and said loudly, so he could hear, "You must be Perth's father. I'm Inaya."

Arnyl could only shake his head as more tears poured out. Perthin slapped him on the back and said over the din, "I can see you have a lot of questions, Pa. And I know you didn't want me to set foot on a ship, but—"

"But heaven had other plans for you, I see that now."

"The stories I have to tell you will take days, but first, we have a celebration to prepare for." He turned to Inaya. "Please have your men escort my pa up to the inn on the promontory." He pointed. "That's where we'll hold our feast."

Arnyl shook his head as more crates rolled down the ramp. "I sure hope someone has warned Gayla that a few people are planning to show up for dinner."

Perthin laughed. "Oh, she knows! Although Grinda has locked herself in her room and won't come out."

Arnyl chuckled thinking of the high-strung innkeeper who fretted over every little thing. "Well, with all the cooks and help and such the princess has brought with her, I'm sure Gayla is thrilled. She likes nothing more than to see to it folks are well fed and happy."

"And wait till I tell you about the trolls!" Perthin said with his eyes dancing.

"Trolls! Don't tell me you brought the likes of them aboard as well!"

Perthin and Inaya burst into laughter. After a minute Perthin caught his breath and wiped more tears from his eyes. "No, Pa. No trolls. I can assure you you've seen the last of them too."

Arnyl put his arm around Perthin's shoulder and hugged him close as the villagers of Tolpuddle ran about helping with the crates and running off to get ready for the big feast. This would be a day that would live in the memories of all for a long time to come, but Arnyl figured no one would cherish this day as much as he would. For the second time in his life, the sea had brought him a son. The first time in a wooden trunk, the second time in a wooden ship. More tears made their way down his cheeks as the words ran through his mind: *"The sea gives and the sea takes."* The sea had taken his son away, but it had faithfully returned him to his arms.

He raised his eyes to heaven and gave thanks for his blessings. Heaven sure did things in a puzzling way—never set your feet on a straight and clear path, but gave you a crazy, winding one that took all kinds of unexpected turns. He looked at Perthin, love pouring from his heart, and said, "You've heard me say this before, but I'll never question it again—accept the way God does things, for who can straighten what he has made crooked?"

Perthin laughed and said, "No one—that's who!"

THIRTY

GAYLA, COME join us," Perth called out across the noisy room. The simple, spacious breakfast room had been turned into a banquet hall, though it was too small to fit the entire village of Tolpuddle within its walls, so most of Perth's neighbors had piled the scrumptious food high on beautiful porcelain plates and found a spot on the bluff upon which to eat. Summer had arrived early, and the evening air was balmy and warm—a perfect night to look out at the sea and count blessings. Perth surely had many, and so did his neighbors. He could probably count all night until he ran out of numbers.

Perth knew Gayla was more than curious to learn about his recent adventures, so when she saw him gesture to follow him and his pa outside, she set down the large punchbowl on the table overflowing with floral bouquets and hurried to meet up with them. Earlier, Danyl and Tanin had walked with him and Inaya up to the inn, and Perth had chuckled the whole way watching the astonishment in their faces as Inaya gave them an enthusiastic telling of Perth's encounters with the *Tse'pha* and the knucker. All they could do was nod with their mouths open and their eyes as wide as suacers. Perth doubted they'd ever call him *shrimp* and *small fry* again.

Perth held both his and his pa's plate as Arnyl managed to squeeze out of the door on his crutch and lead them to the blanket Perth had laid out for their feast. Inaya was already sitting there—now dressed in a comfortable skirt and lace blouse, and sipping a hot drink.

When she jumped up to help him, Arnyl waved her away. "I c'n manage, Your Highness."

"Oh, just call me Inaya, please."

Perth noted his pa seemed a bit flustered, but he could understand why. It wasn't every day that royalty from another land joined you for dinner on a blanket on the grass. He turned and looked back at the entry door and finally saw Gayla coming through. She spotted them and came over, holding her plate of food in hand, but remained standing. Perth wondered about the strange, serious look on her face.

"Gayla, sit," Perth insisted. "I want to tell you about my adventures." He glanced over at his pa, who seemed awfully busy tucking into his food—and he knew why. He wished his pa wouldn't be so self-conscious around Gayla. He just didn't get it that she cared for him—a whole lot. Why couldn't he just tell her how he felt and get it over with?

Perth just shook his head and patted the blanket. "Gayla?"

She tipped her head and said to Inaya, "Your Majesty, you are . . . the king's daughter, yes?"

Inaya gave Perth a puzzled look, then stood and extended her hand to Gayla. "Please, just call me Inaya. I am King Pythius's daughter, yes. But he is dead . . . and that's a story for Perthin to tell."

Perth watched a rush of emotion rise in Gayla's face. "Dead . . . how?" She turned to Perth. "That is a story I would like to hear." She sat down next to Perth, and his pa scooted over to make room for her plate, obviously just as puzzled by Gayla's comment as he was. Inaya sat back down and started in on a buttery roll, nodding for Perth to tell his tale.

Perth didn't know where to begin—there was so much to say. But somehow he managed to tell most of the tale—from the moment the ghost of King Cakrin had appeared on the dunes to the discovery of King Pythius—turned to stone—on the palace parapet. Through the telling Gayla said nothing. His pa kept making little noises of amazement and shaking his head. No doubt the story would hardly have been believed if Inaya hadn't been there nodding her head to confirm the truth of each detail. Perth hadn't yet mentioned the trolls, but he wanted to save that for later. He knew Inaya was impatiently waiting for him to mention what the seer had said, and the claim that Perth was the king's son, but he wasn't sure how to bring it up.

And Gayla's expression perplexed him. He paused in his telling to look at her wan face and asked, "Gayla, are you all right?"

His pa grew concerned. "Are you sick? Maybe you should drink some water. Here." He handed her his water flask.

She shook her head and breathed deeply. "No, thank you, Arnyl, I'm fine." She laid her hand on his, and Perth noticed his pa didn't pull away. A little smile crept up his face at the sight.

"Quite a story, lad. Quite a remarkable story!" his pa said. "And this ghost king . . . and you with the sword and cutting off that evil creature's head. What a tale!" His pa just kept shaking his head between bites of food. He swallowed and added, "I would love to see that sea monster now—his stone head sticking up out of the water. What a sight that must be!"

Inaya smiled and said, "I would be glad to take you back with me to Paladya." She turned to Gayla. "And you too."

Gayla froze. Now Perth knew there was something she wasn't telling them. "Gayla, what is it?"

"Perth, it's not polite to pry," his pa chastised. "She'll speak her mind if it's to her liking."

"It's all right, Arnyl," Gayla said, trying to make light of something Perth could tell was bothering her. Inaya saw it too.

"There is something Perthin didn't mention." Inaya looked at Perth and he nodded to her to talk. He was glad to let her tell the bit about the seer. It was one thing to come back a hero but another altogether to come back a king. Perth still didn't believe it, and he wondered if there would ever be a way to truly know if the seer's words were true. And if they were—what did that matter? He had no interest in ruling Paladya—Inaya would handle the job just fine.

But deep down he really did want to know the truth about his birth. He needed to know if Emelee really was his mother, and more than that—he had to find a way to understand why he felt so drawn to Elysiel. King Cakrin said he had come to him because of his vow to heaven, yet . . . he had been dreaming of the land and yearning for it before the ghost had appeared to him. There were still too many pieces to his life and his past that he must understand. But how?

Perth realized Inaya had been telling his pa and Gayla about the seer. He turned when he heard Gayla gasp, and then, without warning, she fell back onto the blanket in a faint.

"Oh my," Inaya said. She took her napkin and soaked it with water from her glass.

His pa leapt up and cradled Gayla in his arms. He took the cloth from Inaya and patted Gayla's forehead. "Gayla, Gayla, wake up. Oh, what's the matter with her?"

"Maybe she's just exhausted from all the festivities. She was probably working hard in the kitchen all evening, and it gets pretty hot in there," Perth offered. He'd never seen his pa so worried and flustered.

After a moment, Gayla's eyes fluttered, then opened. She stared into Arnyl's eyes and smiled at his concern. "Oh, Arnyl, I'm fine. Really, no need to fuss."

Perth's pa hurried to help her sit upright, clearly embarrassed by the realization he'd had Gayla in his arms. And when she gave him a kiss on his cheek, his pa turned as red as a rutabaga.

"I am sorry," Inaya said to Gayla. "Clearly something I said upset you greatly."

Gayla's eyes shone in warmth at Inaya's words. Perth noticed her hands were trembling as she turned and looked at him in an odd way. Suddenly a great laugh erupted from her mouth and tears spilled down her face.

"What? What is it?" his pa asked.

Gayla turned to Inaya. "You said the seer told you about a prophecy made to King Pythius years ago—how his son would murder him. And how he claimed Perthin was that son."

"Yes . . ." the princess replied. Perth stared at her and held his breath.

"Do you know the story of Queen Calli and how she had learned the king meant to kill the babe, and had run away to keep her child safe?"

Perth frowned. *How in the world would Gayla know this?*

Inaya nodded. "I was told the queen and her child drowned. Her clothes had been found on the beach, and the king searched for years but never found either the queen or the babe."

Gayla turned to Perth and said in a trembling voice, "Perthin, come here."

He gave Inaya a curious look and shrugged. *What was Gayla doing?* His pa just sat there with his mouth open, looking much like a codfish.

Gayla stood and turned Perth so his back faced her. She sucked in a breath and lifted the hair off his neck. Her shaking hands were cold as she gently pushed his head forward. And then he heard her cry out in another burst of tears. "Oh, oh, oh," she said over and over.

Perth was afraid to move. "What is it? What's on my neck?"

She said, "Arnyl, you've known about this birthmark since you found him, haven't you?"

Found him? Perth spun around and faced Gayla, who seemed beyond joyful. Without warning she grabbed him and embraced him, nearly choking the air out of him. "Oh, Perthin! Heaven answered my prayers, but oh! Never would I have imagined God to be so gracious and kind as to reunite me with my lost son in this way!"

His pa jumped up and stared at Gayla. "Wh-what are you saying? That Perth's your son . . . that you . . ." Arnyl dropped to his knees on the grass, and Perth gasped.

"Will someone tell me what is going on?"

Inaya came close to him and took his hand. "Isn't it obvious, Perth? Gayla is your mother." She looked with admiration upon Gayla and said, "Which makes *you* the rightful queen of Paladya."

"What?" Arnyl cried out. "A queen? Gayla?"

"Is that any more unbelievable than Perthin being a prince?" Inaya asked him, then narrowed her eyes. "But, you already knew that about Perthin, didn't you?"

Perth spun around and faced his pa. "You did?"

His pa nodded and cleared his throat. "I found you tangled in my nets. In a trunk." He looked over at Gayla with a puzzled expression.

She continued for him. "I put you in the trunk with a bag of gems, and a note saying you were King Pythius's son, and for whoever found the babe to raise him in love and never tell him who he was or where he came from—in order to ensure his safety." She bit her lip as she stared deeply into his eyes. "I had named you Collin—after my grandfather . . ."

His pa looked at Perth apologetically. "I made a vow that day, Perthin. A vow to heaven I would never tell, and that I would raise you as my own and keep you safe. That's why I never let you go to sea."

Now it was Perth's turn to cry. Tears made their way down his cheeks, but he didn't care or wipe them away.

His pa kept staring at Gayla. "No one in the world knew about the trunk. Or the gems or note."

"And look," Gayla said, lifting her long swath of thick pale hair to expose her neck. She turned so both Perth and his pa could see. Perth saw she had a birthmark that looked like a five-pointed star. He looked at his pa.

"Is that what's on my neck?" His pa nodded. "But . . . isn't that kind of odd—that we'd both have the same birthmark?"

Gayla turned and took both his hands in hers. She just stared at him speechless for a moment as more tears flowed unchecked. Finally she swallowed past a lump in her throat and said, "All the members of my family bear this mark." She added, "It is the way of Elysiel."

Perth gasped and stumbled back. "Elysiel? I don't understand. I thought you were from Paladya. The queen of Paladya."

"My sweet boy, I was living in Paladya when I met Pythius. But I was there taking care of my aunt—the former queen. She had married King Declan to form an alliance between our two king-doms—Paladya . . . and Elysiel."

"You're . . . you're from Elysiel!" Perth said, astonished beyond belief.

"I am. And so are you. King Cakrin was my uncle. So you are not only of King Cakrin's lineage, you are also the only remaining heir to the throne. Perthin, Elysiel is waiting for its rightful king to come and free the land from its curse."

"You know about that?" Perth asked. Too many thoughts were barreling into his mind at once. He was the heir to the throne—in *Elysiel?*

Gayla turned to his pa, who stood speechless and with his mouth still open. "I'm sorry I never told you the truth about my past, Arnyl. I wanted to. But until I knew that Pythius was dead, I couldn't risk him ever learning my whereabouts. He was an evil and relentless man who would have sought me forever, and no doubt he had his men looking for me up until the day he died. He would never have stopped until he found me . . . or my son. That's why the note didn't give you his name." She gave Perth a loving look.

"When I escaped from Paladya, after sending Collin off in the trunk, I wandered for weeks up the coast. My intent was to somehow find a way home in disguise, which took many months of hard journeying. But when I arrived at Elysiel's border, I could not enter. The entire kingdom was under a sheet of ice. I learned from those in the southern hamlets what had happened, and that my father and both my brothers had been killed—in the war with Vitra. So, grieved by this news and having no home, I walked west, toward the sea, until I arrived at the Shivery Coast. There I lived until the storm destroyed my village. The rest you know."

She turned to Inaya and said, "I came here six years ago, no doubt led by heaven in answer to my prayers. For the only thing I wished for—yearned with all my heart for—was to be reunited with my son and to learn he was safe and had been rescued from a terrible fate. The hope that one day I would see him again was the only thing that kept me going day after day. I held such guilt over having sent him out to sea in the trunk. But heaven had provided that trunk. And had sent him here, to you, Arnyl. Because God knew you would be the perfect father to my son. And for that, I am more grateful than words could ever express."

To Perth's surprise, she took Arnyl in her arms and kissed him. He could see his pa's neck turn bright red, but Perth was glad his pa didn't struggle to get out of her embrace. Inaya and Perth exchanged a brief look of amusement.

When Gayla finally release his pa, she said to him, "Arnyl Quay, you must know I've loved you for some time. And I suspect you love me equally. Since you are his true father and I his mother, it makes sense we should marry, doesn't it?"

"M-marry?" Arnyl said. "B-but . . . you're a queen!"

She chuckled. "I'm just Gayla now, although years ago I went by the name of Callandra of Elysiel. But I would ask, if you're not too attached to this wonderful village of Tolpuddle, if you would escort me back to Elysiel and live with me there. For I believe that is where Perthin will be spending the rest of his days—as king and Keeper of Elysiel."

"Keeper?" Perth asked, somehow finding his voice. "Do you mean Keeper of the sacred site?"

Gayla looked at him in surprise. "Why, yes. The Keeper is also the king of the land. He rules with heaven's blessing . . . and with the crystal scepter. Although, I have no idea if the scepter is in the ice cavern, where Cakrin would have last kept it—"

"I have it!" Perth announced. "I have the scepter!"

"You . . . how?" Gayla asked in shock. "Did you find it when you were there? Did King Cakrin's ghost lead you to it?"

Inaya spoke up. "My father had it. I don't know where he got it. It was lying at his feet where we found him turned to stone—on the parapet."

"I was told Pythius was the one responsible for the curse, for Elysiel turning to ice. He must have stolen the scepter from the king years ago," Perth said.

Gayla nodded. "Yes, that must have been what happened. For no other action could have put Elysiel under such a curse. And so the return of the scepter—and Elysiel's king—should undo the curse."

Perth thought of King Cakrin's words—how he had said the true king must return to Elysiel to restore the land to its former glory. He never said he meant *him*, though. Now it made sense that all the kings of Elysiel's past had been with him and aided him to victory. And now he also understood what Cakrin meant when he said "Elysiel is watching over your father; do not worry," when Perth left to kill the *Tse'pha*. He meant *Gayla*. For she was tending to his pa, and *she* was Elysiel! It was all too much to take in!

Inaya interrupted his thoughts. "Perthin, that is why the seer said you're a king twice over. You are heir both to Paladya and to Elysiel. But I think we all know where your heart lies."

Her words clanged in his head. The seer had said that to him—*"Oh King, it is no secret where your heart lies."* Yes, Elysiel was calling him—as it had been doing in his dreams for many months. Calling him home.

Perth looked at Gayla, his mother. He saw himself in her gray eyes and hair the color of eggshell. He had her cheeks and her mouth. All these years she had been like a mother to him, and he had welcomed her affections. What a strange twist of fate! He had gone off to save his village and seek his destiny, but had returned to find a sister and a mother he'd never known he had. His pa was right. Heaven never laid a straight path for a person's feet; the journey always took twists and turns, but somehow you landed in just the place you were meant to be. There was no questioning heaven's ways, but why would he?

Perth's pa pulled his enamored gaze away from Gayla and said to him. "Hey, what about those trolls? You said they were gone for good—"

"Trolls be hanged, Arnyl Quay!" Gayla said playfully, tousling his hair. "You haven't given me your answer yet!"

"Answer?" he asked.

"About whether or not you'll marry me."

His pa fumbled with the words. "Well . . . if you'll have me . . ."

She planted another kiss on his lips, then turned to Perth with love radiating in her face. "In Elysiel, one must ask the blessing of the king to marry. What say you, Perthin Quay? Do we have your blessing for this marriage?"

Perth laughed. "Do you? I've wanted to see you two hitched for years now! Now maybe my pa will stop fretting over me and spend his time making sure *you're* safe and happy."

His pa threw his head back and gave another hearty laugh. Perth had never seen him so happy in all his life. Then his pa leaned close and said, "So your given name is Collin. That's a fine name—a name fit for a king. You always did hate the name *Perthin*. I s'pose you'll want to change it back to what yer mum named you—"

"No," Perth said, never more proud than at that moment to be the son of a simple fisherman. "I'll stick with Perthin. It's who I am—although I'd be glad to have Collin for my middle name."

Inaya poked him in the ribs. "Maybe we can make a banner for you and use the fish for your sigil. Maybe put one of those trolls on the banner too, grabbing at the fish—"

His pa said, "Wait, what about those trolls?"

Perth, chuckling at the idea of trolls on a banner, turned to his pa, who was engulfed in a big embrace from Gayla. "No doubt you'll see them when we arrive in Elysiel. I expect they'll be at my coronation ceremony."

"They'll what? You want trolls at your party? What on earth are you talking about, lad? Have the trolls taken your wits?"

Gayla looked at him with a puzzled expression. He said, "Let's finish our dinner, first, before I tell you about the trolls. I want to go into all the grimy details, and I wouldn't want you to lose your appetite."

Inaya laughed and picked up her fork. Behind them, music began to play—a fiddle, some drums, and a harp. A minstrel started to sing a lively song, and some of those around them got to their feet and danced on the rolling lawn as the moon rose up from the sea, making the water explode into a shimmering blanket of sparkles.

Perth stared out at the water, the sparkles reminding him of the crystals in the cavern where he had stood and looked out over the beautiful land of Elysiel in his vision. As wonder and awe—and deep gratitude to heaven—filled his heart to overflowing, he asked again for the hundredth time: *Why me? Why am I so blessed?*

He heard King Cakrin's words in his head as if he were there, right beside him, standing on that sun-drenched hill draped with acres of fragrant flowers. *"That is the way of Elysiel. It is the way it always has been and always will be."*

THIRTY-ONE

THE CARRIAGE came to a stop. Perth looked at Gayla, who announced with excitement, "We're here."

Perth threw open the door and jumped down from the carriage. They had come to the end of the dirt road they'd been traveling on the whole day. After all these months, they had finally arrived at the border of Elysiel. The late autumn sun was already setting, and a cold wind blew across the wide prairie before him. He pulled his cloak tight around his neck as Gayla helped her Aunt Carryn step down from the coach. His pa followed and walked about, stretching his legs and rolling his neck. Perth wished Inaya was here to share this exciting moment, but he understood her need to stay behind in Paladya and try to restore order and establish her rightful rule over the kingdom.

When they had arrived back in her beautiful harbor to return her to the palace, the head of the giant sea monster welcomed them. His pa couldn't stop remarking on its terrible face, no doubt recalling his encounter with the beast at sea when it had taken bites of out Bayley Tettenhall's ship. But the *Tse'pha*'s evil spawn would harm no one again, and Perth stood proudly at the prow of the ship as all aboard oohed and ahhed at the sight.

Just before they'd headed out on their long journey, a bedraggled and beaten contingent of soldiers had arrived from a battle in the northeast—against a land ruled by a regent named Sherbourne.

Inaya had listened in shock as she was told how her father had fomented this lengthy conflict and how she now had to face negotiations of surrender. Perthin noted how grieved she was upon learning of Pythius's cruel campaign, and she swore to make rich compensation to the suffering people of that land. Perthin did not envy the new queen the enormous task before her, but he did not doubt Inaya could handle it, and handle it well.

Inaya grew teary-eyed at their departure and made a promise to come to Elysiel as soon as she could get away, and Perth knew she intended to keep that promise. He was glad for a renewed, stronger alliance between Paladya and Elysiel—one that Perth knew would endure throughout time. He and the new queen of Paladya had made a vow to see it come to pass and to ensure that peace lasted for as long as the two kingdoms existed—which Perth suspected, with heaven's blessing, would be a very long time indeed.

Perth stood on the prairie and watched the other carriages pull up behind theirs, and their drivers unhitched their teams of horses to let them graze. Throughout most of the journey they'd seen no grass, and very little vegetation other than scrub brush, so the horses were more than eager to tuck into the rich browning grass growing almost knee high around them.

The ride had been a little bumpy despite the elegance and comfort of the carriage's padded seats. It had only taken Perth a few moments to arrive in Elysiel before, using his magic boots. But as he had only one pair and did not indend to go alone, he had to travel the way others did—by riding along the Great Northern Road. They'd taken their time, with six carriages in their entourage, each loaded with food, supplies, and tents. Each night they had slept comfortably out of doors under heaven, and the time had been a blessed one, with Carryn sharing stories of her childhood in Elysiel, and telling of the kings who had ruled the land. Perth had soaked up the history—his history—although with each story, he grew more and more anxious to arrive.

But what was this place? Perth frowned as he scanned the empty landscape. There was nothing here—only a small ice-encrusted brook that bisected the open space. He had envisioned gates or a grand archway—something to mark the entrance to the land.

Gayla came up beside him and handed him the small box containing the scepter. "It's not what you expected, is it?"

Perth shook his head. "Where's the boundary?"

"It's the creek. For centuries Elysiel has been hidden from its enemies, but now that those enemies are no longer a threat, perhaps it will no longer need to hide. But that would be a matter for the king to decide."

"Oh, I see," Perth said thoughtfully. In his haste to enter Elysiel, he hadn't given much thought to his kingship. So much would be expected of him with an entire kingdom to rule. And what did he know about ruling? Absolutely nothing. How would he proceed, and what would he have to do? What if he did something wrong? Would his subjects turn against him? He was only fifteen, still a boy. Yet an entire kingdom would be looking to him. How long would it take him to settle in and feel like he was a true citizen of Elysiel? Sure, it was in his blood, but he'd been raised in a humble village by a fisherman. Would his rough and unlearned ways cause him embarrassment?

Gayla chuckled and took his hand. "I can tell what you are thinking, Perthin. Do not fret. Heaven never makes a mistake; you have been chosen to rule Elysiel. You will make a fine king. Be patient and give it time. All of Elysiel will support you and aid you in this task. You will be a most beloved king. And know this truth: 'The king's heart is in the hand of the Lord. Like the rivers of water, he turns it wherever he wishes.' Heaven will guide you, and so will all the kings of Elysiel's past. It is the way of Elysiel."

"All right," Perth said a little hesitantly. He realized that despite all of Gayla's and Carryn's stories, he really knew so little about Elysiel. How big was it? What were the townships like? What wares did the people produce? Did they have specific customs and holidays and ways of doing things that were different from the way folks did things in Tolpuddle? Suddenly he felt terribly overwhelmed. All this would take years for him to learn.

"So," Perth asked Gayla, "what do we do now?"

"*We* wait. *You* need to step into Elysiel wielding the scepter. The land should awaken upon recognizing your blood and the scepter in your hand. It may take some time, but just . . . go in," she said with a shrug.

Perth opened the case and carefully lifted the scepter out, holding his breath in amazement. The crystal gave off a faint blue light as the heart beat in the handle with a steady, strong rhythm. He stared at it, riveted by its beauty. Gayla had told him about the first king, Lantas, and how heaven had put his heart in the handle because of his faithfulness and sacrifice. And how the kings were then appointed Keepers over the sacred site, and lived long lives. She said the kings were bound to the land and the scepter, but Perth did not know what she meant by that.

He walked down the short, steep embankment and looked at his reflection in the water. The clouds above floated downstream as the water in the little brook rippled over small rocks. He could even make out some silver fish flitting in the reeds near his feet. He took a few steps back uphill and saw his pa, Carryn, and Gayla standing together, watching.

He gave them a little wave and shrugged, wondering if he should take off his boots when he waded through the water. This made no sense. The Elysiel he had seen was truly under ice, but all he could see ahead of him across the brook was another stretch of prairie much like the one behind him.

Not wanting to dally a moment longer, he decided to ford the creek and live with wet feet. But when he stepped into the water, he jolted forward as his boot hit something hard. With care he set his other foot on what seemed to be ice. Odd, that ice hadn't been there before. He took a few more steps, staring at his reflection below him, the clouds billowing and gathering over his image's shoulder. He slid across, one step at a time, and then stopped at the movement near his feet.

Colors began swirling atop the ice, as if someone had spilled paint and was spinning it in a circle. He bent down and studied the greens and blues and browns as they changed shape and began resembling trees and flowers and grass. Perth looked up and around. He was still standing on the surface of the brook, and the landscape looked the same. But the scenery around his feet changed into a beautiful picture of the land he had seen in his vision.

He held the scepter close to the image to see better, but when he straightened back up, a cold, biting wind raked his neck. Bits of ice smacked his cheeks, and the cold air made his hands instantly numb. The banks on both sides of the brook were buried in mounds of snow, and the wind howled mournfully as if grieving.

Perth stood frozen in the middle of the brook, squinting to see across the land in the dim hazy light as snow blew in whorls across the ice-covered prairie before him. A tremendous loneliness and misery seeped into his heart, as if he had sensed it from the land before him, and from all who had lived in Elysiel, past and present. King Cakrin had told him all life remained dormant under the ice, awaiting the king's return. But Perth's emotions brought tears to his eyes—tears that fell frozen with a quiet *clink* as they dropped onto the ice. If he didn't believe what the king had told him—about

Elysiel's restoration—he felt his heart would truly crack and break at the sight of this magnificent land so barren and lifeless.

He took in a long breath that seared his lungs with cold, then walked off the ice and onto the snowy bank. He figured he would just walk and see what happened, although he hoped whatever was going to occur would happen quickly—before he turned into a statue much like King Pythius had.

He didn't have to wait long. Within moments, the chill wind warmed and tickled his neck. A pool of water formed around his boots as the ice melted near his ankles. By the blue light of the scepter, Perth watched the ice recede away from him and grass begin springing up, freed from the confinement of the weight of the ice. A tree a few yards away began to sprout tiny green leaves on its slender naked branches. And then, something extraordinary shook his thoughts and made him stumble and fall to the wet, soggy ground.

In his head, Perth heard voices. Not just the voices of people, but the speech of animals and insects and birds. He held his head and closed his eyes. The sound at first was quiet, but then, with the awakening of all life in the land, grew loud and exuberant. And it was not just sound that came to him, but thoughts and emotions! He thought he would black out from the wonder of it all! What was happening to him? Was he hallucinating, or was Elysiel some-how speaking to him?

In his mind's eye he watched the land shake off its dormancy and come to life. Birds emerged from hollows in the ground, worms crawled through soil, and beetles clambered over rocks as the snow melted and springs began bubbling. Perth could see lakes and streams, waterfalls pouring down the faces of mountains, flow-ers erupting in spectacular color from the formerly hardened earth. He smelled the loamy soil and the spray of water and could nearly taste the air around him.

And then he heard singing. Not just humans singing, but a song composed and performed by every living, breathing thing in the land. It swelled until it became a magnificent choir of prodigious strength, all creation praising the Creator. Perth now saw the entire kingdom and he knew it—knew it as if he'd walked every inch of it over an entire lifetime. He knew every hill, every rock, every tree. He *was* Elysiel! This was what he had felt in his vision in the ice cavern, this awareness and understanding. It was truly a gift from heaven.

He jumped for joy, then ran across the soggy grass as birds flocked in the sky above him, warbling in song. He ran north as herds of horned animals galloped ahead of him and bellowed out in their own deep-throated song. He ran and ran until he came to a rise that gave way to the view he had seen in his dreams—the range of towering jagged mountains, tinted purple and capped with snow. And there, far off in the distance, was the capital city with its thousands of people—his people. His subjects. And they were waiting for him to arrive.

Perth fell to his knees, humbled and awed to the core of his soul. He sat on the top of the hill, letting the sun warm his shoulders and the breeze ruffle his hair. He breathed all of Elysiel in and thanked heaven for such unspeakable joy.

As much as he wanted to run to the city, he knew he couldn't do so without his pa and Gayla at his side. They were waiting for him back at the brook.

He looked at the scepter, which shot out a blazing blue light, its heart beating hard and steady with his own. And as he stared in wonder, the ghost of King Cakrin appeared before him. His beatific smile expressed the joy Perth felt in his heart.

"You are now king, Perthin Quay—king of all Elysiel. You were the king foretold to deliver your land once and for all from the evil that has tormented her for centuries. But the *Tse'pha* is now forever gone, and Elysiel will finally see peace—thanks to you."

"But I couldn't have done it without your help—and the help of the kings! I cannot take any credit for her deliverance at all."

"But you can. You made a vow before heaven, and even though you were asked to do difficult things, you proved faithful. You trusted heaven to guide you, and that is all God expects of anyone—great or small. Whether the matter attended to is small or great, it is of no importance. What matters is the heart. The heart of the matter is a matter of the heart, Perthin Quay—this you now realize to be true. Man judges by the outer appearance, but God sees the heart, and yours is true.

"Guard your heart, oh King," Cakrin said to him with a deep bow, "For it is the wellspring of life. If your heart is true, you cannot fail." He gave a final smile and rose up into the sky.

Perth watched as the ghost shredded into wisps and blew away on the afternoon breeze. Although he knew he would see the king again—for he now understood the kings were there to help him rule with honor and wisdom—he felt sad at his departure.

With the awareness that all Elysiel was awake and alive and thriving, Perth headed back the way he'd come, and as his feet found a well-trodden road, he began humming a song, one that people everywhere in Elysiel were singing. It was a song that spoke of peace and prosperity and joy. It was the song of his heart—the anthem of Elysiel.

THIRTY-TWO

"A TOAST—TO our king!"

A man Perth knew to be King Cakrin's former army commander—Rolan—stood and held up a crystal chalice of wine. The light from the many lit sconces along the walls of the great hall made the amber liquid sparkle, and hundreds of hands raised their glasses in a shout of "Hurrah!"

Perth looked upon Rolan with great affection, for he knew him well, and knew his true and faithful heart. He felt truly at home in this room—not a stranger at all—for each and every citizen of his kingdom was known to him, and he loved one and all. He was not only bound and tied to the land; he was linked to every one of his subjects, and his love for them filled his heart with a keen desire to see them prosper and enjoy the fruit of peace. So many years they had fought their enemies, and had suffered great losses and much grief. Perth knew all their pain and felt it as his own. Their memories were his memories, and although the thoughts and feelings at times were burdensome and suffocating, he was learning how to live with all of Elysiel in his mind and heart and still be himself. Would he ever stop marveling at this indescribable gift from heaven? He doubted it.

As Rolan gave a lengthy speech praising Perth and his heroism, Perth glanced to his side at his pa and Gayla—or Callandra, as he now knew to call her. Although, to him, she would always be

Gayla of Tolpuddle—his mum. How regal and elegant she looked in her gown threaded with pearls, her hair done up in a lacy net of diamonds. And his pa didn't look half bad either in his fancy suit. He'd never seen his pa so dressed up, and he looked, as his new wife had remarked, "quite the man." Perth didn't think he could be happier, and he looked around, setting this moment to memory, knowing this day would replay over and over in his mind for many years to come.

This day marked a new age, a new beginning for Elysiel. This morning, as Perth visited the ice cavern, the morning after his coronation and his vows before the sacred site to be the Keeper of the promise—the *ra'wah ten'uah*—he noticed the ice had begun to melt. The walls of the cavern dripped in steady rivulets that spilled onto the floor of the cavern and streamed out the entrance to trickle down to the meadows below. Soon, Perth knew, all the ice would melt, for heaven no longer needed to hide the sacred site. In time, the crystal slabs would stand majestically in their circle in the open air, with sunlight glinting off them in glorious beauty. All of Elysiel would see them, as would any from distant lands desiring to gaze upon them, for the borders of the kingdom would no longer be entrenched in mystery and hidden away. Perth had commanded Elysiel to open its arms to one and all so that the blessings of heaven could spread far and wide and not be confined to just his people. All in the world needed to know the blessings available to those who sought heaven's favor and grace.

Perth had ridden over to the ice cavern as dawn smeared the sky orange and pink and the sun rose into the world shining with all its might. He had laid his hand upon one of the crystal slabs in the cavern's dim light and waited for a vision, but, to his surprise, none came. Apparently, the future was an unwritten slate, but Perth welcomed the mystery. The crystal had been silent and only reflected his curious face back to him—the face of a small boy who had the heart of a king. That itself was a vision that startled him as he realized how his life had altered so suddenly. Only weeks ago he had been helping his pa sell his fish and looking to prove his bravery by stealing from the trolls, and now . . .

Perth looked down the long table to his many relations, all of the royal lineage—and there were many. Not a few were brave warriors who had been turned to stone on the battlefields by the *Tse'pha,* but upon her death had been restored to life—much to the shock and thrill of their families. Perth had learned they had come in great numbers, stumbling into Elysiel—cold, tired, and hungry—after he had gone to stop the sea monster with Vitra's head. Carryn was seated beside her three nieces a few seats down from him, and Perth finally knew their names: Rabelle, Sybelle, and Danelle. Their transformation was astounding. No more tusks or slime or warts or wiry hair. They truly were princesses, and each one beautiful, and he watched them gracefully hold their glasses of wine aloft as Rolan finished his speech.

As soon as the joyful shouting subsided, an attendant came to Callandra's side and filled her crystal chalice with wine. His pa held a hand over his own glass, refusing the drink. Perth knew his pa had made a vow to heaven all those years ago when Jayden drowned. Not even in Elysiel would he break that vow, and Perth respected him for it. A smile inched up his face as he turned to his mum and held up his own glass for the attendant to fill.

"D'you figure I'm old enough *now* to have a drink?"

She laughed and nodded. "Well, not old enough, but, yes, Perthin, go ahead. But don't let it go to your head."

Perth wondered if she meant the drink or the privilege . . . or both. He lifted the glass to his lips and took a large swallow . . . then about spit the stuff out.

His mum and pa looked at him in surprise, and then chuckled. Perth said, "It's so sour! Is it s'posed to taste like that?"

His mum nodded. "It's an acquired taste—one you develop over time."

"Well," Perth said, pushing the glass away and reaching for his flagon of water, "time's something I have plenty of. I'm in no hurry."

His pa laughed heartily and patted Perth on his back. He nodded at the three princesses, who were digging into the plates of food that had just been set before them. Perth noted they seemed quite enthusiastic over the haunches of meat, and . . . what was that? Ranelle had a bit of drool sliding down the side of her cheek. Perth stifled a chuckle and tucked into his own plate of food.

His pa said in a whisper, "Are those really the trolls—the ones that had been terrorizing our village?"

Between bites of potato Perth said, "Yep, the very ones."

"And you claim there were only the three—no more."

"No more, no less."

His pa shook his head and took a bite of warm buttered brown bread that smelled divine. "Hard to imagine—how someone could turn such lovely ladies into such . . . ugly creatures. They must be so relieved to have their true forms back. Imagine—cavorting in refuse dumps and eating rotted fish and wiggly grubs. Makes my stomach turn to think about."

Callandra nudged his pa. "Arnyl, can we please change the subject? Not the best topic to chat about while we're having this lovely meal."

His pa made a face. "Oh, sorry." He narrowed his eyes as he continued to stare at the princesses. "Oops, I think I caught their attention."

Perth looked down the table and saw the three young women rise and come toward them. They whispered excitedly among themselves, and Perth wondered what they were up to. When they came to his side, they bowed respectfully, and then Ranelle, the one with the thick glasses on her face, said, "Cousin, my sisters and I want to thank you for saving Elysiel and removing the curse. You truly proved to be trustworthy and honorable among men. To show our gratitude, we want to give you this gift. It was our father's, but we feel you should have it . . ." She shrugged, and Perth noticed through her thick lenses that her eyes were a little crossed.

The other two sisters crowded in as Danelle, sporting a lovely lace hat, handed a small silver-inlaid wooden box to Perth. As Perth began to open it, Ranelle nudged him and pointed to the floor. "Do you like my shoes? Look, they fit! Now I can finally wear them all—"

"The minnow doesn't care about your shoes," Sybelle said in a loud whisper. Perth looked up and noticed all at the table were staring at them.

"Shh!" Danelle said, lightly pushing Ranelle aside, "you're making a scene—"

"I am *not*!" Ranelle hissed back. "I just wanted to show him my shoes—"

Perth held up his hand, and the princesses quickly shut their mouths. "My dear cousins, thank you for this gift." He opened the rounded lid and took out a silver chain from which a small star dangled. The star had one arm and one leg a little longer than the others—just like the birthmark on his mum's neck—and no doubt like his own as well.

"Here, let me help you put this on," Sybelle said, reaching for the chain, her own many necklaces hanging down and tickling his ears.

"You and your obsession with necklaces!" Ranelle said with a scowl.

"It's not as bad as your thing about shoes!"

Perth straightened and glanced around the room. Now all the guests in the great hall had set down their glasses and silverware and were staring at the commotion at the table. The princesses, however, did not seem to notice and were not in the least concerned over who was listening. And they seemed to forget they were standing before their king. But Perth only chuckled all the more loudly as they prattled on.

Danelle grabbed the necklace from Sybelle and pushed her sister forcefully out of the way. "It was *my* idea in the first place to give him the necklace—"

"No it wasn't—it was *my* idea!" Danelle protested, trying to grab at the chain. But Sybelle hid it behind her back.

Then, to Perth's surprise, Ranelle leaned in front of Perth and stared at his plate. She turned to him and asked, "Are you done with that mutton leg?"

Before Perth could open his mouth and answer, she snatched the large piece of meat off his plate and stuffed it into her mouth. Drool slid down her chin as she chomped and groaned in delight. "Oh, this is tasty," she mumbled with her mouth full.

Perth pushed his chair back and stepped out of the way of the flying slime to the sound of his mum and pa erupting in laughter.

Perth joined in, and soon everyone in the room was laughing so hard, the princesses' banter was buried by the noise.

Perth's pa stood and held his sides as tears streamed down his face. "Why, trolls be hanged. I never . . ." He shook his head. "Are they always like this?"

Callandra shook her head. "No, they are really three very lovely and well-comported ladies. I imagine the curse put upon them hasn't quite worn off."

His pa kept staring at the princesses as they grabbed food off plates and make unladylike snorting sounds. "Well, I hope they don't stay like this forever."

Perth stood with his mum and pa against the back wall of the hall and watched the goings-on with amusement. The group of musicians picked up their lutes and fiddles and drums and began to play a loud, rousing jig, and the guests forgot about the princesses and spilled out onto the dance floor, merry and eager to dance the night away.

"Here," Perth's mum said, taking hold of his closed fist. Perth had forgotten he was holding the chain with the silver star, and he opened his hand for her.

She took the chain and lifted the hair up from his neck to clasp it shut. "There you are, Your Majesty." Her eyes shone with adoration and pride. In a second, her years of sadness and pain flashed in his mind, the months of grieving she'd done after sending her babe out to sea in that trunk, the years she had lived up in Bluster on the Shivery Coast, and all the times she had stared out across the water and prayed to heaven, wondering if she would ever see her son again.

And then he turned and looked at his pa, who was watching the dancers with a big grin on his face. In his mind, he saw how his pa had knelt on the beach that day after a big storm, on the anniversary of Jayden's death, racked with guilt and wishing he had the nerve to end his own life. Perth watched him pull on his tangled nets and draw out a large watertight trunk. And then he saw the surprise and joy in his pa's eyes as he lifted the lid and found a small babe inside, alive and well and waiting for someone to love and care for him.

A few tears dibbled down his cheeks as he watched his mum take his pa's hand and lead him out to the dance floor. His pa had prayed for heaven mercies, and so had his mum. And heaven had answered both their prayers in just the way they needed answering, although taking a completely unexpected path. But Perth knew—that was the way of heaven. The way it always was and always would be.

THE END

A DISCUSSION OF
THE CRYSTAL SCEPTER

UNLIKE SOME of my fairy tales in The Gates of Heaven series that are inspired by a number of traditional tales, *The Crystal Scepter* is mostly a rendition of a story called "The Terrible Head" from Andrew Lang's *Blue Fairy Book*. I read through dozens of tales, hoping to find one that dealt with some of themes I was interested in exploring in this tale, and also was looking for a land of ice, since I knew I wanted the fifth sacred site to be in a frozen land, and the slabs to be made of ice instead of rock (although I settled on crystal instead, which would be much more lasting in a dramatic climate shift). When I chanced upon "The Terrible Head," I saw a lot of potential for a great story, and did further research into the Greek myth the tale was drawn from—one many people are familiar with: the legend of Perseus and the Gorgon. I love those old movies that show Medusa's ugly snake head and thought she could be turned into a great fairy tale nemesis for my hero. So although *The Crystal Scepter* has a quite different plotline than the Greek legend, there are a lot of similarities to the fairy tale—with the hero having been sent out to sea as a babe in a chest and being raised in a faraway land without knowing his true heritage, and the element of the sea monster, and the use of the terrible head to turn the beast to stone.

I also love the element of a self-fulfilling prophecy and borrowed from *Oedipus Rex* and a beautiful play by seventeenth-century Spanish playwright Pedro Calderón de la Barca entitled *Life is a Dream*. In that play, the King of Poland has kept his son Segismundo secretly imprisoned since birth because an oracle prophesied that the prince would bring disaster to the country. Telling his subjects that the boy died soon after childbirth, he manages to keep his son hidden until he has grown to be a man. Upon learning what his father, the king, had done to him, he sets about destroying him. As in *Oedipus*, the child grows up to fulfill the prophecy of killing his father, although in *Oedipus* the hero is unaware of his culpability and the fulfilling of the prophecy—which was how I wanted the storyline of *The Crystal Scepter* to play out. I also drew a little bit on Shakespeare's penchant for revealing true identities and having wonderful reunions at the end, as in *Twelfth Night* and *The Comedy of Errors*.

Perthin has no idea his valiant effort to rid the world of both the *Tse'pha* (which means "snake" in Hebrew) and the sea monster will result in the death of his real father, but one element is the same in all three stories: a king who, in an attempt to thwart fate, ends up bringing that fate upon his head. I think there is a message in there somewhere of our need to be alert to God's leading in our lives and to fulfill the purposes he planned for us long ago (Ephesians 2:10). We cannot thwart the purposes of God, but of course, he means our good and not our harm. However, the book of Jonah shows how futile it is to try to run away from our "destiny."

As in the other books in The Gates of Heaven series, references to Bible passages are sprinkled throughout this tale. When Pythius asks Calli about taking the scepter, she tells him if anyone does so without heaven's permission, "in that day they will surely die." When he confronts the Lady Vitrella about this matter, she says Pythius has been lied to, that if he takes the scepter, in that day his eyes will be opened and he will acquire great wisdom, know good and bad and "be like a god." I drew from the scene of the serpent talking to Eve in the garden of Eden, for Vitra, having been spawned by the Great Serpent, speaks the same lies. And Pythius's outrage over Calli's fleeing that results in his killing all the male infants of Paladya parallels Herod's scourge in the Holy Land, by which he hoped to kill the promised Messiah. In both instances, heaven provided a safe haven—a trunk in the sea for little Collin, and a warning to Joseph to flee to Egypt in the case of Jesus.

As with all the books in the series, I provide some study questions appropriate for book club groups and homeschoolers. I welcome any thoughts and questions on this book and any of my other fairy tales. You can contact me through my website: www. cslakin.com. I hope you find the stories both entertaining and inspiring.

1) The theme of vows recurs throughout the novel. Perthin says, "Once a vow is made, it must be kept." Calli mentions it is better to vow not than to vow and not pay (Ecclesiastes 5:5). She vowed to care for her aunt, and Perthin vowed to stop the sea monster—whatever the cost. Often the Bible will use the word *swear* to mean a similar thing. A vow usually involves committing to a course of action, whereas swearing by something or to do something means you are promising to do what you say. On occasion, God himself makes an oath or swears to something, to assure his people he is faithful and will do what he says. Take a look at some other Scriptures that talk about vows and consider their import: Ecclesiastes 5:2, 4; Genesis 47:31; Isaiah 54:9; Psalm 110:4; Matthew 5:33–37.

2) One theme woven through the book is tied to Ecclesiastes 7:13: "Accept the way God does things, for who can straighten what he has made crooked"(NLT). Perthin's pa, Arnyl, quotes this

from time to time. What does this "saying" mean to him, and why does he embrace its truth in the end of the story?

3) Arnyl also believes in this saying: "Finishing is better than starting" (Ecclesiastes 7:8 NLT). What does he mean by this, and how can we apply the same philosophy in our lives?

4) The heart is at "the heart" of *The Crystal Scepter*. Clearly, the heart, being the seat of motivation, is the focal point for each character, both literally and figuratively. Pythius seeks the king's heart in the scepter for selfish reasons, but Cakrin tells him if he hardens his own heart, it will shatter and break, which literally happens to the evil king. The Bible says the heart can do many things: it can melt, burn, be divided, store up wrath. You can lose heart, the eyes of your heart can be opened, or you can set your heart upon a task. Arnyl quotes Proverbs 27:19: "A man's heart reveals the man" (NLT). What does this mean, and what does Jesus say about what defiles the heart in Matthew 5:17–20? Jesus said, "Wherever your treasure is, there the desires of your heart will also be" (Matthew 6:21 NLT). As the seer asked Pythius, you might ask yourself, "Where does my heart lie?"

5) Perthin's encounter with Vitra's army in the arena, where Cakrin shows him the heavenly help rallied but invisible to his eyes, is drawn from the account of the prophet Elisha and his servant as they faced the Aramean armies. Read 2 Kings chapter 6 and look at the similarities. How does Elisha's revelation of God's backing give his servant the strength and courage to do what is asked of him? How does this play out in Perthin's situation? What comfort does it give you to know that God's mighty forces are "behind the scenes" watching over and protecting his servants? (See Hebrews 1:13–14.)

6) Pythius longs for eternal life and mourns the futility of gathering wealth that must be left to someone else when he dies (see Ecclesiastes 2:18, 22; 5:11; 6:2). He is plagued by a dream about a man who chides him for storing his wealth and feeling

secure. Read the parable this dream is taken from in Luke 12:15–21. What words of wisdom does Jesus gives about what kind of treasures to store up?

7) The theme of part three is taken from one of the Proverbs: "The king's heart is in the hand of the Lord. Like the rivers of water, he turns it wherever he wishes. Every way of a man is right in his own eyes, but the Lord weighs the heart." (Proverbs 21:1–2 NKJV). Gayla (Queen Calli) tells Perthin, her son, not to worry about ruling Elysiel, and quotes to him this verse. What does this assure Perthin about God's hand in his monarchy, and how is this a comfort to him? Even though we aren't kings, how does this reflect God's spirit acting within us, and how we should respond to its leading? What does it mean that "the Lord weighs the heart"? Obviously, this is not a literal weighing, but discuss how the Bible uses the concept of weighing and weights to imply value at Daniel 5:27, Job 31:6, Psalm 62:9.